ISBN 1-451-51969-9

EAN-13 9781451519693

Manufactured in the United States of America

First edition published 2010

Cover art © 2004 by Cynthia Nilsen

THE WITCH AWAKENING

Karen Nilsen

To my parents, who taught me how to live my dreams.

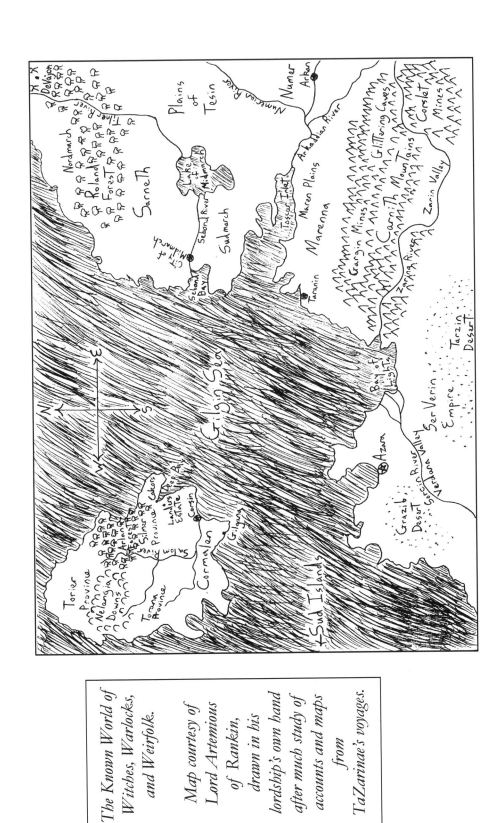

The Known World of Witches, Warlocks, and Weirfolk.

Map courtesy of Lord Artemious of Rankin, drawn in his lordship's own hand after much study of accounts and maps from TaZarinae's voyages.

Chapter One--Safire

The sky had cracks in it. Then the wind rose, and I blinked, startled, as the cracks moved and transformed into the writhing bare branches of the old oak. Shivering, I sat up and pulled my cloak around my shoulders. Dusk had crept across the fields with shadow feet while I lay here, half in a doze as I watched the clouds. I should have been home an hour ago.

I stumbled up and shook the dust from my clothes. The blood stirred in my veins, stinging my numb skin as I began to walk along the rutted wagon track. The moon hung low and huge over the smudged shapes of the trees. "Go away," I told it. "I'm already late enough as it is."

The house wasn't far. The track wound through two fields, stubby with wheat stalks, and then through a tangle of trees before it stopped at the edge of the cobbled courtyard. My breath made fog as I stared at the light spilling from the large front windows on the first story of the house. Father and my sister Dagmar were there now, eating. Grimacing from the cold, I plucked up my skirt and headed for the side door.

As I went across the courtyard, a horse whickered. I glanced toward the stable and froze. My father couldn't have done this to me. I had told him, insisted that he never invite that man again, at least when I was around. But did he listen? No. There stood the evidence, eating out of its feed bag, oblivious: Peregrine of Bara's horse.

Even in this light, no one could mistake that silver gray coat with the black stripe down the back. The biggest scoundrel on the coast had the loveliest horse. Peregrine. If I had known he was here for dinner, I would have stayed out in the field all night. I threw open the front door and slammed it as I tossed my cloak on a bench.

Dagmar hurried through a doorway, her blond hair piled on her head in an explosion of ringlets. She stopped and stared at me. I glanced down at myself, holding out my skirt. I wasn't dressed for dinner--I wore my oldest frock and my slippers were covered with dirt.

"Where have you been?" she demanded. "Dinner started a quarter hour ago, Safire."

"I forgot."

"You forgot! You're always forgetting--and look at you! Get upstairs and put on a decent frock. Father's going to throttle you. And do something about your hair . . ." her words trailed off as I sauntered to the mirror over the hall table.

I had to stand on tiptoe and lean over the table to get a good look at myself. *Someone tall must have hung this mirror.* I poked my tongue in my cheek. There was a long smudge of dirt running down the side of my face, and my freckles stood out worse than usual. My red curls, my best feature, were stringy. I turned and looked at her.

She stood there, hands fluttering limply at her sides. "Safire . . ."

"I like the way I look. It's fitting for our company." I tossed my hair and strode towards the banquet hall.

"Stop it." She reached for me. But I was already through the door.

Father glanced up from his place at the head of the table, a vein standing out under the wisps of fading gingery hair that drifted over his forehead. He usually had a ruddy complexion, but his skin looked positively crimson tonight, his orange aura aflame. I faltered, taking a half step back. Then my gaze drifted to Peregrine. Bold blue eyes met mine in a look that could only be described as a leer. Lustful toad. I had never been able to see his aura, only smell it--he kept it hidden from sight like an ace up his sleeve.

My head high, I slid into my accustomed chair. "My apologies for my lateness. I was unavoidably detained."

"Obviously not by your lady's maid," Father retorted,

stabbing a piece of pheasant with his fork. "You look like you've been digging in the potato patch."

He must be really angry, to let Peregrine see his displeasure. "Father . . ." I began.

"Up to your chamber, Safire."

Biting my lip, I rose as Dagmar crept into the hall and silently took her seat.

"Now, Avernal," Peregrine said, his voice slippery as oiled silk, "Don't tell me I'm to be deprived of your daughter's presence thrice in a fortnight. Last time I called she had a headache, and the time before that she had a fever."

"That's because you make me ill."

Father's face went purple. "Safire, you headstrong . . ." he choked.

I put my hands to my mouth. He was going to have apoplexy right here, just like Dagmar and I had always feared. And it was my fault. I stumbled around the table, reaching for him.

"Father, breathe. Just breathe." My fingers curled around his arm, and I felt the tight ropes of his muscles through his shirt. As I had done many times before, I concentrated on the tension, drawing it away from him and into me. Tonight, it was like swallowing a swarm of hornets. His shoulders jerked with the effort to exhale and inhale, a motion that gradually subsided to an even rhythm. But I backed away only when he raised his palm from the table.

"Enough," he said gruffly. "Sit down, daughter."

~ ~ ~ ~ ~

My hand clutched the charcoal stick, all the tautness inside me draining out on the paper in strong, black lines. It was a storm scene--a raging sea and jagged bolts of lightning and clouds pregnant with darkness. A bird struggled in the midst of the storm as it searched for solid ground. I paused over the last bedraggled feather and closed my eyes as I leaned against the rough boards of the stable wall. Finally, I was empty again, and what I wanted most in the world was my cozy bed with its goose down pillows and heavy quilt. Yawning, I set aside my sketch board and breathed the sweetness of hay and old leather and horse sweat.

The lantern flickered from a sudden draft as the door flew

open. "I knew I'd find you out here in the animal pen," Dagmar exclaimed. "Oh, Safire--you've been messing with that nasty charcoal again. You know Father hates that. It makes you look like a hearth sweep."

I sighed. "Leave me be."

"I won't. Someone needs to take you in hand."

"What do you want, Dagmar?" I hugged my knees.

"I want you to quit worrying Father."

I rolled my eyes. "Do you always have to be the older sister? Leave me out of it for once. Seriously, what do you want? Are you content marrying Selwyn, having his babies?"

"I suppose so." She shrugged. "What else is there?"

"But you don't even like him."

She shrugged again. "It's a great honor, Safire, marrying into the House of Landers. There's not a higher noble House at court. I could be doing worse."

"But . . ."

"And you--you could be doing worse than Peregrine."

"I could be doing better, too."

"Your pride's going to be the ruin of you. Ridiculous."

"I bet you wouldn't think it was so ridiculous if you had that horrid man breathing down your neck, asking to marry you."

"Peregrine of Bara is handsome, well-mannered, and high at court. Not to mention the fact he's dripping with coin."

"Dirty coin."

"That's not true. That was just a nasty rumor, and you know it. You're lucky that some man even wants to marry you, with how you carry on. I can just see you now, an old spinster wandering the hills, muttering to yourself and gathering witches' herbs. That is, if you're lucky. If you're unlucky, a serving wench or some dirty dockhand's mistress."

"To be honest, sister, I'd work as a tavern wench who served more in the beds than at the tables before I'd ever stoop to marry that man." I smiled and grabbed my sketch board under one arm as I got to my feet.

"I bet you would. I bet you would bring shame on the family, just to prove you could. Ruin everything Father's done to build this

House's position at court, just to prove you could. Father should have sent you to the convent." She picked up the lantern and followed me out of the stable, still talking. "You'll regret it, you know. In ten years, you'll regret it. But it will be too late then--no man will want you then."

I stopped in front of Peregrine's mount. He stood in the stable yard, languidly munching on some hay the groom had put out for him. I reached up and scratched the place between his ears. He tossed his head, neighing, and regarded me with dark, suspicious eyes. "Hello, Trident," I whispered. "Don't you remember me? I'm the one who told you to throw Peregrine."

"Safire, honestly . . ." Dagmar gasped.

"What is it?" I glanced around just as Peregrine stepped out of the shadows behind the stable door and strolled towards us, hands in his pockets.

Dagmar muttered something and fled to the house. Damn her--she knew I hated being alone with him. I shrank against the horse as he came closer, his boots echoing on the cobbles. He paused a few yards from where I stood.

"You like my horse?" he asked.

I met his stare with one of my own. "I suppose. He's a fine animal."

"He's yours."

"I already have a horse."

"Sell him then. Buy a new frock. Or better yet, save the coin for your future as a barmaid--you'll likely need it."

"You heard that?"

"Yes, I heard everything."

"Good."

Peregrine shrugged. "It's not anything I haven't heard from you before." He took a step closer, and I shifted my sketch board so it was between us, a feeble shield. "Your Father's practically promised me your hand, you know."

"He wouldn't do that, not without my consent."

"He doesn't need your consent, pet."

"If he wants to keep me as a daughter, he does. The answer is no, Peregrine. How many times do I have to tell you?"

"As many times as it takes for you to say yes."

"Only God can wait that long. I suggest you take your suit elsewhere." I ducked beneath Trident's head, giving him one last pat before I headed for the house.

"There is nowhere else for me to take it, Safire."

I whirled on him. "I hate you. I always will. Now leave. How much plainer can I make myself?"

"How can you hate me? I haven't done anything except bring you presents you don't accept."

"It's not anything you've done," I spat. "It's what you're thinking of doing every time you look at me. It's disgusting."

"If that was all I wanted you for, I wouldn't be offering marriage." His voice lowered to a silky hiss as he leaned closer. "And a true maid wouldn't know what I was thinking when I look at you."

I slapped him, but he only chuckled, grabbing my arm. I wrinkled my nose at the overpowering scent of ambergris, an earthy sweetness that reminded me of the dust from the carved wooden saints in the ancient parish church, the scent of centuries-old driftwood slowly decaying. It was something only I could sense. When I had first met him two years before, I had told Dagmar that he reeked of ambergris cologne. She had given me her best older sister look and said that all she smelled was soap and expensive pipe weed, proper gentleman smells, and that I must have a cold. So I had said no more of it. Usually auras were something I saw, not smelled, but Peregrine was different apparently. Likely if Mother had been alive, she would have sensed the ambergris too and been able to explain why he was different to me, but Mother had been dead for over a year by the time we met Peregrine.

"How dare you--let go of me!"

"Is everything all right, Lady Safire?" Boltan, our head groom, appeared in the stable doorway, holding a carriage whip. Peregrine instantly released my arm.

"Everything's fine, thank you, Boltan. Sir Bara was just leaving." I glared at Peregrine as he mounted Trident.

"Groom," he said curtly as he pointed at the hitching post. Boltan undid the reins and tossed them to Peregrine.

"Anything to speed your departure, sir." Boltan's tone was insolently bland.

"You had best keep a civil tongue in your head," Peregrine snapped before he turned to me. "I'll have a ring for you soon, sweet. Whatever you want."

"Pearls from the moon and gold from the sun and rubies made from the heart you don't possess. Then I might consider it. And how dare you upbraid Boltan?"

"Good night, Safire. You're in my dreams," he finished with a leer.

I was hunting some clever retort when Trident wheeled around and galloped to the road, carrying his master away into the night. Boltan and I stared after him long after he had vanished, the sound of hooves slowly fading.

Boltan shook his silvered head, lowering the whip. "Don't take his ring, my lady. He's a bad one."

I sighed. "Tell my father that." Forcing myself to more cheerful subjects, I said, "Has Strawberry had her carrot yet?" Strawberry was my mare, a fiery little chestnut with a white star on her forehead.

"Now you know she only takes carrots from you."

"You don't break them up in small enough pieces, that's all. Here, let me show you." We headed into the stable.

~ ~ ~ ~ ~

The next day, I pretended a headache and stayed in my chamber all morning, sketching madly. Sometimes in the afternoons, telling the others I was going for a ride to the cliffs near the shore, I would gallop to Calcors and try to sell my drawings at the market there. At first, it had been difficult. Few people besides me liked my storm scenes or my faces wailing in bottles or my studies of dead birds. But when I started drawing flowers and landscapes with cows grazing and other nice, proper things, I actually managed to sell a few, always passing them off as the work of my nonexistent brother. I signed everything S. Marsh--if I had put S. of Long Marsh, everyone would have known I came from a minor noble House, and some would have recognized the name and known it was a minor noble House with no sons.

There came a knock at the door. It was several moments before I glanced up from the sketch of the tomcat chasing mice on the paper before me. I added one last tuft to his ears, then picked up the drawing just as the knock sounded again, louder this time. Likely it was Dagmar, come to nag. "Just a moment," I yelled as I stowed the drawing in the trunk. I thought I caught the cat's tail twitching out of the corner of my eye as the shadow of the descending trunk lid overtook the sketch. I lifted the lid, curious, but the sketch was still, like any other sketch in the full light. Of course it was still. Shadows always made drawings seem alive--for an instant. I shook my head at my own silly fancy and let the lid slam down.

Father opened the door. "Dear God," he muttered. "I come here to reprimand you for one misbehavior and find you committing another. You're hopeless."

I crossed my blackened hands behind me. "I thought you were off to Calcors on business this morning."

"That business has been delayed." He began to pace. "Your behavior last night shames your mother's memory."

"Don't mention her, Father. It's not in good taste to use the dead to shame your children."

"It's also not in good taste to insult a guest at your father's table."

"Even if that guest happens to be a lustful toad?"

"Safire, I wouldn't let a man who was dishonorable court one of my daughters."

"What about a poor man? Would you let a poor man court me?"

He stopped and looked at me. "You're young, so young, and you don't understand. If you had brothers, I wouldn't worry so much. They could take care of you when I'm gone, make certain you married well."

"'Married well'--what does that mean, exactly?" I crossed my arms, not minding the smears of charcoal on my sleeves.

"You know it means money, so don't goad me." His tone grew harsher as he began to pace again. "Money and the security that comes with it. I would be a poor father indeed if I didn't leave my daughters with some provision for the future."

"Father, don't talk like this." My voice trembled. "You have years left."

"Like your mother?"

"Don't," I whispered.

"I'm sorry. I'm just trying to make you understand." He sighed. "You know, I thought you would be the easy one. My bright little Safire, so like your mother. Then she died, and I lost you. I let you grow wild, stubborn, unwomanly. Now you make all those odd sketches, wallow in the animal mess. Then you go lie in fields for hours and brood all the time. It's not natural."

I hated that word--brood--it made me sound like a chicken hatching eggs. I laughed suddenly, having an image of myself with droopy tail feathers and a sign that read *don't disturb--she's brooding* tied around my neck.

"Don't laugh," he snapped. "Not about this. The estate is in debt up to the roof, and there's no humor in that."

"In debt to whom?"

He shifted, realizing he had said too much. "It's not your concern, sweet."

"I know you owe the Landers. Who else?"

"I said it's not your concern."

A sudden, horrible thought came to me, and I blurted out, "Peregrine? Are you in debt to Peregrine?"

He hesitated an instant too long before he answered. "No, of course not."

"Oh no. No, Father. How could you think of selling me to that, that scoundrel to settle a few debts . . ." I sank down on the bed, my breath coming in shallow gasps.

"No, never, Safire. Not like that. I would never force you to marry someone you were so opposed to." He sat down on the bed beside me and put his hand on my shoulder. I shied away. "I just want to see you settled, taken care of. Like Dagmar."

"Not him," I said through clenched teeth. "Never him. I'd go to the convent first."

"You made that clear last night." Father's tone was dry. "I hoped . . . well, never mind what I hoped. If you hate him so, I won't let him see you anymore. All right?" I nodded as he squeezed my shoulders. "Now, listen. I'll not let you go to the convent either. Sweet, how would you like to go to court?"

I swallowed. "Court? But I thought there wasn't enough money for me to go yet, not so soon after Dagmar."

"Shh, don't worry about that. It's just a few new frocks, really. I'll get Boltan to take you, so we won't have to hire a coach. The court treasury pays the rest, and I'll give you an allowance for the small expenses. Though if I find out you've spent it on drawing paper, I'll cut it off."

I smiled secretly to myself. Father was so naive. For months now I'd been selling my sketches and using the money to buy more supplies, and he still had no idea. Some of the coin I had saved up made a nice little stash in the corner of my wardrobe--for what I didn't know. Sometimes I ran the silvers and coppers between my fingers and counted them not because I was mercenary exactly but because they were mine, and I had earned them. I had never been able to say that about anything before in my life except my sketches, and even they had been drawn on paper bought by others until now.

"In fact, if the Sullays pay what they promised for our winter stores, I might be able to send both you and Dagmar to court for the spring at least, if not the summer," Father said.

"Dagmar?" I groaned inwardly, already foreseeing early curfews, lots of sisterly advice, and no fun.

"Dagmar's been to court before. She can watch out for you."

"Father, I'm eighteen now . . ."

"Barely eighteen."

"I can take care of myself."

"Would you rather stay home, marry Peregrine?"

"No."

"Well then." He stood up, his hand sliding off my shoulder. "It's settled. You and Dagmar will go to court together."

Chapter Two--Merius

Two jacks, one ace, a deuce, and an eight. I arranged the cards so the jacks were next to each other. The game had been going on for over an hour, and there seemed no end in sight. Everyone had full coin pouches tonight--a rare occurrence. When Selwyn had asked me if I wanted to go to the inn for a game, I had expected it to be a short affair. We had only four players tonight, less than the usual number, and ale always made someone foolish with his coin. But tonight, all my companions held their cards close, each hand slower than the last. I sighed and glanced toward the other end of the common room, where Imogene was pouring ale for a bunch of loud, fishy sailors.

Imogene wore lots of gypsy bangles up and down her arms, bangles that clinked together when she held a swaying tray of full mugs over her head. I had kissed her the last time I had been here. I had written a poem about those clinking bangles slithering like a snake over my neck when she twined her arms around me, a poem which I had promptly burned before Father found it. Father had forbidden me to write poetry, especially poetry about chasing barmaids. He wanted me to chase the noble courtesans at court if I had to chase something. These courtesans were the sort of women he used as his mistresses. According to him, they were less likely to have the pox than barmaids. They were also less likely to wear bangles, which was why I had ignored him. Unless this game ended sometime soon, I wouldn't be getting close to any bangles tonight, gypsy or otherwise.

"Anyone raising?" Selwyn asked.

I looked around at my companions. Selwyn, my kinsman, Gerard of Casian, a red-faced, blustery sort from a minor noble House, brave and loyal as a champion warhorse, and Peregrine the cheat, who met my gaze as he sipped his brandy. He would never lower himself to drink ale. I grinned with clenched teeth. He had just dealt off the bottom of the deck, but I didn't say a word. The last time I had fought Peregrine for cheating at cards, my father had almost killed me. Peregrine was one of his merchant toadies at court, and I was supposed to be diplomatic to my father's toadies.

I threw a silver piece on the copper pile in the middle of the table. Maybe losing all my money on this hand would get me out of the game.

"Merius, what the hell did you do that for?" Gerard threw down his cards. "I'm out."

Selwyn held up his glass for Imogene to fill. I winked at her, and she smiled before she moved on to the next table. "She's a ripe one," Gerard observed. "I wouldn't mind sniffing under her skirts . . ."

"Ask Merius. He's been doing some sniffing in that direction of late." Selwyn matched my silver piece with one of his own, and Peregrine followed suit.

"So, how does she smell?" Gerard leered.

"'Like gypsy wine, sweet and wild,'" I quoted my favorite Sirach poem.

"What does that mean?"

"None of your damned affair, that's what it means. Go do your own sniffing."

"That's the answer of a man who hasn't been doing enough sniffing to talk about," Selwyn said.

"That's the answer of a man who just won your silver," I retorted, laying my cards down.

"What?" Selwyn grabbed the cards. "Don't sit on your coin, Merius--I'll have it back by the next hand."

"Blame Peregrine. He dealt." I glanced across the table. Peregrine's eyes were narrow as he examined my cards and then his own. Then he looked at me, and I smiled like the diplomat my father wanted me to be. Just because he cheated didn't mean he won. Maybe he would quit using the same marked deck every time, the arrogant blackguard.

Selwyn shuffled the deck, dropping the eight of clubs in his ale. "Saw you on the sea road last night, Peregrine, but you galloped by so fast that I said good evening to your dust."

"I had urgent business in Calcors."

"I understand you had business at the House of Long Marsh as well."

Peregrine settled back in his chair as he lit his pipe. "I wish that witch was business. If she came with a price, I could buy her and be done with it." He exhaled a long swirl of smoke.

"Marry her honestly," Selwyn said, "and she'll buy you. Dagmar comes with half of the Long Marsh holdings as a dowry."

I snorted. "A bag of gold makes a cold bed, cousin."

Cards flew across the table in no particular order as Selwyn dealt. "At least I do my duty instead of mooning after barmaids."

"Duty is the high, lonely road assigned to those who kiss my father's boots. I prefer kissing barmaids."

"You're a fool, Merius . . ."

The ten of diamonds flipped face-up when Selwyn tossed it to Gerard, who swore. "Give me those cards. You can't deal worth a damn."

"Shut up and take the card, or we'll be here all night," I said. "Selwyn wants to do his duty and lose the Long Marsh dowry to us."

"To hell with the dowry. It's the Long Marsh woman I want," Peregrine said.

Gerard and I looked at each other. "Selwyn, with all your blather of honor and duty, I can't believe you're just going to sit here and let him talk about your betrothed that way," I said in a low voice.

Selwyn started. "What, who's talking about Dagmar?"

"Peregrine, you dolt!" Gerard slammed his tankard on the table.

"What he just said? He's not talking about Dagmar. He's talking about Safire. The only thing you lack being a jackass is the ears." Selwyn chuckled.

"Who's Safire?" I asked.

"Dagmar's younger sister."

Peregrine grinned as he picked up his cards. "The Lady Dagmar is a worthy match, but her earnest charms are not for me."

"I can't believe you've never heard of Safire," Selwyn said. "Did you really think Dagmar was an only child? I would get all the Long Marsh holdings as a dowry then, not just half."

"What does this Safire look like?" I asked. "Maybe I've met her and don't remember."

"You'd remember this one." Peregrine added a silver piece to the ante. "A tiny vixen redhead."

"With a tongue as wicked as her hair. It's no wonder you haven't met her. Avernal doesn't let her out much. Afraid she'll use that dagger tongue on the wrong person, I suppose." Selwyn glanced glumly at his cards. "I'm out."

The tavern door flew open, the sudden draft sweeping away half the candle flames. Everyone looked up, even the drunken sailors, as my cousin Whitten stumbled in from the night. His sopping cloak hung limp from his narrow shoulders. Water dripped from his dark hair down his face, glinting like tears in the shadows.

"What's happened?" Selwyn demanded, his cards fluttering to the floor.

"Horse thieves," Whitten panted. "In our stables."

I pushed my chair back and stood up, reaching for my cloak. "Which direction did they go?"

"I don't know." Whitten collapsed on a bench. "They threw me in the water trough. I couldn't see."

"In our stables? How the hell did they breach the courtyard gate?"

"The two grooms you hired last month, the brothers . . . I saw them among the thieves."

I told Selwyn not to hire them--they had the eyes of hungry weasels. "Where were the other grooms, the stable boys? Didn't they help you?"

"Drunk."

"All of them? But when Selwyn and I left two hours ago, everything was quiet."

"I think the knaves put something in the ale. It tasted odd . .

."

"You had some?" Selwyn's tone was sharp.

"Just a taste. I couldn't stomach it, the bitter stuff."

"Damn it, Whitten, never drink with the servants. Lackwit sot . . ."

"That's not important now," I interrupted. "What we need to do is get the horses back."

"Summon the magistrate-" Selwyn began.

"The magistrate! Lemara!" Gerard grimaced. "He's so pickled, he can't tell the difference between a pretty dock whore and his horse most nights, and you expect him to find your horses?"

I threw my cloak over my shoulders.

"Where are you off to?" Selwyn asked.

"To get the horses. We can't let those bastards sell Silver to some flea-ridden horse trader." My favorite mare, Silver had foaled Peregrine's famous gray stallion Trident as well as my horse Shadowfoot.

"Do you think we should go after them?"

I shrugged. "Better than staying here all night."

"That's easy for you to say--you're losing."

"Selwyn, you know Lemara won't find those horses. Do you remember that time someone stole a whole flock of Sullay's sheep? The thief turned around and sold the sheep to Lemara himself when he was in his cups."

Selwyn grinned. "He searched every field this side of Calcors, looking for those damned sheep, and the whole time they were in his own fold."

"How did he ever get to be magistrate?" Gerard asked.

"His nephew Herrod commands the king's guard and got him the post. At least that's what Father said. So, who's with me?"

With a clattering of benches and coin, they trailed me out of the common room. At the door, I clasped Imogene's hand and gave her a silver for the ale. One dark brow arched as she tucked the coin in her bodice. As I headed outside, I glanced through the window in time to see her take a seat on a sailor's lap. I had known better than to think that she wore her bangles and her smiles just for me, but acid still needled my insides. Clenching my sword hilt, I strode into the stable where lanterns swayed and flickered in the breeze.

I saddled Shadowfoot; metal clanged against metal as I tightened the girth. I leapt into the saddle and spurred the horse into a restless canter. The night was so large and fresh after the stable that he galloped around the trampled mud of the inn yard a few times before I tugged him to a stop. He neighed impatiently, prancing as the others joined us.

"We're short a horse," Selwyn remarked.

I glanced down to see Whitten standing without a mount. "I ran here from the Hall. They stole every horse, even lame Ned."

Peregrine whistled. "That's at least twenty horses, with the breadth of the Landers stables. Their greed evidently eclipsed their wits."

"Whitten could ride pillion," Gerard suggested.

Selwyn and I looked at each other. When Whitten's father had died two years before, Whitten had become the official head of the House of Landers. The title meant little, since Whitten could barely rule himself, much less a forty thousand acre estate with hundreds of tenants who produced countless bushels of grain each harvest. While my father was at court, Selwyn and I were in charge of the House. Father would not forgive twenty lost horses, much less drunken servants. If I sent Whitten back, come morning we'd likely find him passed out with one of the scullery maids.

"Someone needs to see to the servants," I said. "Selwyn, give Whitten your horse. Set things right at the Hall."

Nodding, Selwyn dismounted and handed Whitten the reins. "But . . ." Whitten began. "I only have my dagger . . ."

"Is it sharp?"

"Well yes, but . . ."

"Then it's good enough for tonight's work. Come on." I tightened my knees, and Shadowfoot jumped forward into the dark beyond the circle of lanterns.

~ ~ ~ ~ ~

The hollow pounding of hooves on the turf and an occasional clink of metal were the only sounds. Even Gerard's tongue had stilled as we approached the sea road. There shone a pale luminescence from the stars and moon far overhead, coldly silvering

Shadowfoot's ears and mane.

A sudden wind swept away the stillness. I tugged on the reins and paused as the wind passed, leaving a salty tang in the air. As soon as I smelled the salt, I heard the muffled rush of the sea, and I realized that the sound had been there a long time, in the background, but I had not noticed it.

"Merius," Gerard whispered fiercely. "Where are we going? We've been riding for a good two hours, and my rear is sore."

I gestured towards the sea. "The cliffs."

"Why the cliffs?" Peregrine asked.

"It's the only hidden way. They wouldn't dare take the horses to Calcors. It's too close to Landers Hall."

"Why not go west, into the hills?"

"Still too risky. Too many watching eyes. Silver's known throughout the province as a Landers horse. They won't go that way, not if they have any sense. No, I wager we'll find them on the shore under the cliffs, making their way south to the Syren docks and a smuggler's ship. As long as the tide's out, they've got a clear path that can't be seen from the sea road."

Gerard yawned and shifted himself on his saddle. "You play cards like a cheat and think like a horse thief, Landers. You better be right."

For a half hour or more, we plodded along the cliffs, searching for a path. Whitten almost went over the edge when his horse stepped on a loose stone. After that, we dismounted and looked on foot. Finally, Peregrine found a narrow track cut into the side of the cliff, just wide enough for a horse and rider.

When we'd picked our way down to the shore, I silently pointed at the fresh circles of hoof prints in the wet sand, dozens of them. Gerard grunted, and Peregrine nodded, but Whitten just looked cold and miserable. I reached over and lightly punched his wet shoulder, wishing I had a flask of brandy to offer him. He fought well enough when he had a few shots warming his blood, better than Selwyn actually. Sober, he was a bundle of nerves who stabbed at shadows and thought he was bleeding to death at the slightest nick.

"All right," I directed Shadowfoot around and started back up the path to the sea road. "Come on."

"Wait, what are you doing?" Gerard demanded. "We found the tracks. Aren't we going to follow these bastards and get them?"

Peregrine grinned. "Ambush, my friend. Ambush."

"Exactly. We can't ambush them if we're following them, Gerard."

"How are we going to ambush them?" Whitten spoke. "We can't ambush them if they're in front of us."

"No, but they won't be in front of us for long if we take the sea road. We have four horses, a nice, dry road of packed dirt. They have over twenty horses, and they're trying to lead them through the surf in spots. Who do you think is going to travel the fastest? Come on."

Shadowfoot began to gallop as soon as we reached the top of the cliffs, his hooves thundering. There was a full moon, and it lit everything deep blue and silver. My sword jostled at my side, and I felt the hilt of it, running my fingers over the elaborate scrolls of the Landers insignia.

After we rode hard for an hour, I veered sharply to the left, back towards the sea. There was a way down here if we could just find it. After a few minutes of trotting by the cliff edge, I spotted the twisted, ancient cedar that marked the old ones' path to the shore. Thousands of years ago, they had worshipped their gods here, chiseling a wide track in the cliff down to caves where they had offered their firstborn babies to the sea. Why the gods demanded such a sacrifice, no one knew for certain. The old ones had supposedly been a strong race, a few of the texts I read even hinting that they possessed unnatural abilities that made them impervious to disease. Perhaps the sacrifice of their firstborn was a way to curb their numbers and ward off famine. If the wind was just right, one could still hear the wails of the drowning children in the caves. Sometimes when I had come here with Selwyn, Whitten, and Gerard and explored the caves, I had heard the wails and wondered. I was my father's only child. Would he have offered me to the waves or hidden me away? I wanted to think he would have hidden me away, but Father was a stickler for protocol. I spurred Shadowfoot forward on to the sand, clutching my sword hilt so hard the Landers insignia left a scrolled, painful L on my palm.

We paced all around the shore but saw no tracks but ours. "We passed them," Whitten said in wonderment.

We rode back north until we came to an outcropping of rock that jutted towards the sea, leaving only a narrow strip of shore. Not only did the rock hide us from view, but they would have to go around it single file. I dismounted and tossed my reins to Peregrine. I climbed up the rock and looked over the edge. Just cliffs and sand and the endless swish-swash of waves. A tinge of gray silhouetted the horizon where dawn began its long creep across the sky. I motioned to Gerard, who had the sharpest eyes. Swearing, he joined me on the rock. "See anything?"

"No . . . wait." He peered forward. "There's something moving way up there where the coast curves back around."

"Is it them?"

"Give me a moment." He squinted. "I think it is. They're moving this way. There's a lot of dark shapes, a few glints of metal like harness. Or swords. Hell, Merius, what are we in for?"

"You can go back if you want. They're not your horses. Though if you stay, you'll get Silver's next colt."

Gerard waved an impatient hand. "I don't want a colt. Got too many damned horses now to feed. I'm just saying we might be outnumbered."

"Let's wait and see."

"If we wait too long, retreat will no longer exist."

"True. But why would warriors want to retreat?"

Gerard snorted. "You're calling Whitten a warrior?"

"No, but you and I and Peregrine are. And even Whitten's pretty good with a dagger. Remember that fight in the tavern with the sailors?"

Gerard clapped me on the back. "All right, Landers."

We slithered down to the bottom of the rock. I landed on the sand with a soft thump. "They're coming," I told Peregrine and Whitten. "Now, I don't want any killing if we can help it. We want live horses, not dead men."

Gerard spat on a stone. "Before we take prisoners, do we have any rope to tie them?"

I reached in my saddlebag, pulled out a length of hemp, and tossed it to him. "There's some in Selwyn's saddlebags as well. We were using it earlier to round up stray cattle in the north pasture."

"I suppose we're set then. All we can do now is wait."

"I want Silver's next foal for this one, Merius," Peregrine muttered.

I shot him a narrow look, recalling last spring when Gerard and I had saved him from a nasty street brawl. "You'll get it. Hell, I bet she'll be so grateful to be rescued that she'll go into season right here for you, which is more than I can say for most of the girls you've chased."

Gerard guffawed, and even Whitten managed a snicker. Peregrine's gaze was cold, and I cursed myself. My mouth would get me in trouble yet, even after all my father's training.

Whitten held the horses near the path in case we had to mount in a hurry. The rest of us crouched in the shadow of the cliffs, time slowed to a trickle as we waited in silence, our swords and daggers drawn. When the first man rounded the edge of the rock, Gerard grabbed him and put a blade to his neck. He yelled, and the next one around the rock leapt at me, his sword tearing a hole in my sleeve.

I jumped back, and he dove towards me again. I brought my dagger up and blocked his sword. He dodged to the side, anticipating my lunge forward after the parry. I spun around, and our swords rang in a series of fast, deafening blows. He got in one hit, a nasty cut to my shoulder, and I swore, charging forward. He jumped aside, but too slowly, for I struck him on his sword arm, slashing him from elbow to wrist. The tip of my blade caught in the hilt of his, and he let go of his sword. I stepped on the blade before he could pick it up. He ran for the cliffs, clutching his arm, and I started after him.

Suddenly the cold metal of a blade tickled my throat. Someone clutched my shoulder. I plunged my dagger into the man's leg, and he let me go, gasping. I spun around. It was one of the weasel-faced grooms. He leaned against a rock, grasping his upper leg. Blood dripped between his pale fingers. He panted, his breath wheezing. Then he lunged forward. I cut his arm with my sword, and he bellowed, dropping his weapon on the rocks. I grabbed his shoulder and put my knife to his throat.

I dragged the groom over to Whitten. "Tie him!" I yelled. "Tie him now!"

Whitten hesitated, gaping. "Here." I reached for the rope myself, cuffing the groom when he tried to bite me. Finally Whitten moved. He grabbed the rope and bound the man's arms.

I raced away, searching for the man who had cut my shoulder. I paused in the shadow of the cliffs. The roar of the surf in the background dulled any sound he might make to give himself away. There were caves here, pockets of darkness where he could hide and ambush me.

I crept along the edge of the shadows. My eyes roved in every direction, my ears tensed for the slightest noise. There was a ripple in the darkness, the echo of a loose pebble the instant before he jumped out a mere yard in front of me. If I hadn't heard the pebble, his sword would have pierced my side. I sprang back, our blades glancing off each other as he carved a swath in the air.

My shoulder a throbbing reminder, I attacked fiercely this time, forcing him back down to the open beach. His arm injured, he didn't parry fast enough, and my sword tip caught him in the stomach. He fell on the sand with a groan, blood flowing out of him in a black pool that vanished in the surf, only to reappear again when the wave retreated. I swallowed and backed away. Did men bleed faster at night? It seemed so, watching him.

There came the muffled clamp of boots behind me, and I spun around. My sword met the second groom's sword with a clang. We swung at each other for a minute or two, but he had not the skill of his dead comrade. He took a careless cut at my shoulder, and I ducked away, bringing my blade back around in a giant arc that disarmed him. His sword flipped into the air, a dizzying swirl of silver that landed several yards away. I knocked him senseless with my hilt and left him for Whitten to bind.

Peregrine emerged from the shadows suddenly, his sword darting to and fro as he fought with the last of the thieves. The thief was a brute with a thick cutlass, several inches taller than me, and even though he wielded it with a quick skill, Peregrine's rapier seemed an ill match to the sturdier blade. I raised my sword to help him, but he cut me off, trying to disarm the man with a jab to the wrist. "You arrogant ass," I muttered. "You'll never . . ."

At that instant, Gerard leapt on the thief from behind, and he and Peregrine soon had the man disarmed and tied up. "Thank you, but I could have taken care of him myself," Peregrine said.

"Like hell," Gerard sputtered.

"Looks like you killed one, Merius," Peregrine remarked, effectively ignoring Gerard and distracting him at the same time.

I nodded, my stomach tightening. "I didn't mean to, but he came after me."

"Self-defense," Gerard said. "Lemara can't be too upset about that." He jerked his prisoner up and forced him over to the huddled group by the horses. Counting the one I'd killed, there were seven thieves in all. We bound their wounds and our own as best we could, and then we loaded them on to mounts. Whitten and Gerard rounded up the horses for the trip back to Landers Hall. Peregrine and I escorted the prisoners to Lemara and his men in Calcors. Lemara was pleased with our work, probably because it meant less for him. Sometime, much later that day, I fell into bed after a long bath. If I had dreams, they were dark ones.

~ ~ ~ ~ ~

"You were supposed to return to court two nights ago, Merius." My father stood looking out the window, his hands behind his back.

"Would you rather I let a band of thieves make off with our best horses?"

"That's what magistrates are for."

I stood up and began pacing the length of the library rug, measuring my strides so that my feet fit in the pattern of golden scallops. My toes were the perfect width to cover those ridiculous flourishes . . .

"Father, you know Lemara is too drunk most times to find his own horse, much less anyone else's. We never would have retrieved those horses if we'd relied on him."

He turned his head and looked at me. His eyes were the gray of night shadows on snow. "To hell with the horses, Merius. That was a foolhardy thing to do, taking only three men with you to face unknown numbers. Besides, when I tell you to return to court, you return to court."

"But you told me to watch the estate as well. The horses are part of the estate . . ."

"By the time the horses were stolen, you should have been on the road to court. You should have left here at the latest by mid-afternoon, so what were you doing at the tavern at ten that evening?"

"Playing cards."

"Were you short of coin? Did you have to gamble your last copper to buy oats for your horse because he was too weak with hunger to travel?" His sarcasm cut like a whip.

"I had plenty of coin."

"So you disregarded my summons?"

"I forgot."

"You what?"

"I forgot about court."

"You forgot a summons you'd received that very morning?"

"You send a lot of summons, Father."

"I see," he said, his gaze returning to the window. "My unreasonable requests for you to return when I ask and be punctual about it have overwhelmed you. My apologies, Merius--I forgot that you're four and unable to decipher a clock face."

"I didn't get your summons until noon. I was going to leave within the hour. Then some cattle broke out of the north pasture, and Selwyn and I had to help round them up. The bull knocked Lem Rivers off his horse and tried to gore him . . ."

"Why did you have to help the Rivers? The north pasture is theirs as long as they pay their rent, and I assume those loose cattle were theirs as well. Hence, it's their responsibility to round them up, not yours."

"They're tenants, Father. Our tenants."

"Ah, you had no choice but to disrespect your father and charge off on a reckless mission to save a few lost cattle."

"I wasn't disrespecting you. I just forgot . . ."

"Lower your voice. A man who has to shout has already lost the argument. Do you remember nothing from court?"

"Always court, always damned court."

"Stop pacing," he hissed, his eyes never once leaving the window. Only when I stopped, my hands clenched in my pockets, did he turn and face me, his gaze expressionless. "Yesterday morning, the council met with the Marennese ambassador. Do you know what we discussed?"

I pondered this a moment, my eyes skipping to the map of the known world hanging over the fireplace mantel. As always, my gaze first lighted on the lonely green blotch that marked Cormalen, cut off from the main continent by four inches of bright blue sea teeming with the artist's fanciful sea monsters. I had been so disappointed when I had accompanied Father at the age of ten on my first sea voyage and seen no monsters like the ones on the map. Four inches of sea on the map translated to a week long voyage to Sarneth, our mother nation on the mainland--the Landers had been among the first Sarneth adventurers to subdue the old ones and settle Cormalen. Sarneth was a far larger green blotch than Cormalen-- endless verdant plains and forests, presumably. Marenna, a grayish slash of mountains and metal and precious stone mines between Sarneth and the SerVerin Empire, the huge tan-colored desert that consumed the southernmost third of the map. Tiny oases, camels, and dancing girls dotted the desert--I would have enjoyed following this map artist around. He'd had some adventures, with all the sea monsters and dancing girls. I looked between the hard gray of Marenna and the bright green of Cormalen and immediately understood why the Marennese ambassador was in Cormalen instead of his home country. Cormalen didn't have dancing girls but at least we had trees and growing things, unlike Marenna. All they grew there were rocks, apparently . . .

"Merius?" Father's voice sliced into my thoughts. "Did you hear me?"

Oh hell--he hated it when I had one of my trances, as he called them. "You had a council with the Marennese ambassador," I repeated what he had said, stalling for time as I frantically ran though the implications of a discussion with the Marennese ambassador. Cormalen and Marenna were bonded by a royal marriage between our princess and their crown prince but little else.

"The Marennese ambassador offered us half the mines in

Marenna if we would take Prince Segar's harpy sister back," I spoke my first thought aloud, desperate to say something, anything to fill the heavy silence.

"I'm ill of your jests," Father snapped. "If you'd been at the council as you should have, you would have known that he begged for the assistance of our king's guard to quell the SerVerin slave traders on Marenna's southern border."

"What did the king say?"

"He hemmed and hawed and brayed like a royal ass. His Majesty's son Segar and I argued to send a small contingent of our best fighters to let the SerVerin Empire feel the nip of our teeth, and His Majesty bleated about that for a bit."

"What about Herrod?"

"He had the court treasury spent on war ships and swords before the Marennese man even finished his plea."

I smiled. "Always, Herrod itches to go to war. What did the council decide?"

"They didn't. There weren't enough council members there to take a vote. I had to explain afterwards to Prince Segar that my wayward son couldn't be bothered to attend council that day. If you ever disgrace me like that again-"

"Father . . ."

"Remember, I can disinherit you, Merius."

"It was just one council, Father."

He clenched the window sill. "It's never just one council. When are you going to understand that? Details, Merius. Details are the stuff of statecraft. And appearance. Appearance is everything. Snub a prince by missing his council, and a year later, he gives the ambassadorship that could have been yours to someone less heedless. And you're so damn heedless. Heedless and quixotic. A stolen horse, a tenant with a stubbed toe, an ace up some gambler's sleeve, and you're off on a damned quest. You'll never have any career to speak of if I don't rein you in."

"If I had returned to court and let those horses get stolen, you would be lecturing me about mishandling the estate," I said quietly. "What can I do to please you, Father?"

He ignored me. "I should stay here until Friday. Avernal and

I need to decide which parcels of Long Marsh land we receive under the betrothal. I trust you balanced the ledgers while you were here?"

"Yes, sir. Only the Declans still owe us from last year's harvest."

"Good. Then I want you gone within the hour. And attend the court ball tomorrow, all week if you can. You're almost twenty-one. You need to make a suitable match soon." He walked out of the library.

I stood there for a few minutes, my hands braced on the mantel, staring at the ashes in the grate. His words *appearance is everything* hammered into my brain over and over again. I grabbed a glass vase off the mantel and hurled it into the grate. I straightened as it shattered, my headache fading.

Chapter Three--Safire

My hands tightened on the ledge of the coach window as we rocked and bumped on the stone roadway. "Dagmar, look. We're in the city."

"Shush, now. You'll make me lose count." Dagmar's lips were pursed as her fingers moved over yarn loops on her knitting needle. "Just as I thought. I dropped a stitch." Sighing, she began to unravel the row.

"How can you still be doing that?" I demanded. "Just look-- we're passing through a street fair. That man's eating fire. Look!"

"You're like a little child," she grumbled, but she laid aside her knitting and leaned over to join me at the window. I laughed, delighted as a blue-faced man in motley ran up, holding a white rose.

"Copper for a flower," he panted.

I reached into my skirt pocket and slipped him a coin. "Safire!" Dagmar hissed, trying to grab my hand.

His blue mouth widened in a smile as he handed me the flower. "Put it in your hair, love. Two such beautiful things should go together." I laughed again and waved as he disappeared in the crowd. Then I settled back in my seat and tucked the rose behind my ear.

"I can't believe you." Dagmar shook her head. "That copper was to tip the manservant at court."

I shrugged. "I have more coin. Why, do you want the rose?"

"Hardly. You look ridiculous."

I grinned and touched the rose. My fingertips came away smelling of a dew-draped trellis in mid-summer, heady and exotic.

The scene outside the window had changed from the market to houses and shops, mostly built of gray stone. "This city is bigger than Calcors, isn't it?"

"I should say so. Corcin's the largest city in Cormalen. It's the capital, the king's seat, the main port . . ."

I bet I can sell a lot more drawings here than on the Calcors docks. Unbeknownst to Father and Dagmar, I had packed my portfolio and sketchboard in the bottom of my trunk as well as my coin stash, and now I was glad I had. Humming to myself, I looked out the window. The houses were grander now, with colored panes of glass in the mullioned windows and carved pediments over all the doors. Suddenly, the coach made a sharp turn to the right. Dagmar sat up expectantly and put away her knitting. There was a tall wall before us with a double-hung iron gate. We passed through the gate into a huge cobbled courtyard that bustled with coaches much like ours and wagons of foodstuffs and wine casks. Liveried servants rushed everywhere, leading horses, carrying trunks, shouting at each other. As our coach stopped, a group of men wearing green and gold cloaks with swords on their hips marched past. "Who are they?" I asked.

"King's guard," Dagmar said. Boltan opened the door and helped first her and then me down to the ground.

"Boltan, why did you have to stop so near the stables?" Dagmar pinched her nose at the strong, earthy smell of manure. Not minding the odor as much, I stretched--it had been two hours of sitting since we had stopped at an inn for refreshments. Several servants appeared out of nowhere and inquired where they could take our trunks.

"Here, give me some of your coppers. Now wait with Boltan. I'll be back," Dagmar said. I barely had the chance to nod and hand her the coins before she was off with the men and our trunks.

I wandered to the head of the coach, where Boltan was unhitching the horses. "Can I help?" I patted the bay's velvety nose, realizing then how much I was going to miss Strawberry.

Boltan grinned. "That's all right, Lady Safire. You wouldn't want to get dirt and horse sweat on that fine frock."

"It's not that fine." I reached for the harness but he stopped my hand. "Boltan . . ."

He gripped my wrist. "I've been with the House of Long Marsh since before you were born, before your sister was born, so I'm taking the liberty of speaking to you like this for your own good. Listen, sweet, you're not in your father's house anymore."

"What do you mean?"

"You're a grown lady now, and you need to act like it, at least while you're here. You can't help with the horses and then go to dinner with stable smell on your frock. Servants are invisible and mute unless you have an order for them."

"I know that." I jerked my wrist from his hand.

He unbuckled the harness. "Fact is, you can act as unladylike as you wish when you return home."

"I thought you were supposed to be invisible and mute, so why am I still hearing you?"

"Because you don't follow advice very well." His mouth twitched. "Don't worry. I'll give Strawberry carrots every night."

"Remember--keep the pieces small, like I showed you."

"You've spoiled that mare, my lady. She won't be fit for anyone else." He led the horses away toward the stables.

I leaned against the side of the coach and watched two boys battle with wooden swords, a servant trip on a loose cobble, a woman in a black veil walk a long-haired lapdog . . . there were so many auras to sense that I began to feel dizzy and had to look at my feet. There came the clatter of hooves on the cobbles, such a constant sound that I barely noticed it. Then the hooves stopped directly in front of me, and I snapped my head up. "What are you doing here?" I demanded.

Peregrine chuckled as he dismounted Trident. "I might ask the same of you. I thought you were too good for court, Safire."

"Now that you're here, court's not good enough for me. I never had any particular opinion about it before." I crossed my arms and gazed downwards.

"You almost look a lady today. I don't think I like it."

"Then leave."

"Who gave you the rose?" He reached out to touch my hair, and I swatted his hand away.

"It's none of your affair who gave it to me. Now leave."

"You've never taken a flower I've offered you."

"I've never picked up a snake either, lest it bite me." Deciding he wouldn't leave, I made a move to duck around the back of the coach and join Boltan. Instantly, Peregrine's hands were on either side of me, blocking my retreat. My eyes widened and then began to water as I choked for breath. That ambergris odor was all around, so overpowering it stole my air. And only I could sense it. Sinking against the side of the coach, I closed my eyes, dizzy and weak and wanting to retch.

"I'll scream," I heard myself whisper like a vapid heroine in a bad play. "I'll scream. Go away."

"There's nothing to scream about," he spoke reasonably from far away. "I just want to talk to you."

I choked again. What was I thinking, threatening to scream? I could barely breathe. "Father said . . . said I never had to see you again," I croaked.

"Now, why would you never want to see me again, sweet? I'd buy you a dozen white roses made of diamonds, if only you'd accept them. Cruel flirt, to play with my heart like a cat with a mouse when all the while you know you'll say yes."

"I'll never marry you." I glowered at him through bleary eyes.

His smile grew distant. "Do you know your father owes me ten thousand silvers? Gentleman that I am, I've decided to ignore the debt until the next harvest, though men have been put in prison for owing less. However, even gentlemen can be provoked by insult. Think on that, pet, if my wooing doesn't suit you."

And suddenly he was gone, mounting Trident and spurring him towards the gate. I put my hand to my mouth. Ten thousand silvers? Ten thousand? "Oh Father," I said dully.

~ ~ ~ ~ ~

The lights--I couldn't believe the lights. I had been standing on the balcony for a half hour, just staring at the lights. Far below gleamed a mosaic floor, set with thousands of glazed tile bits. Scattered over this floor were fifty or so giant candelabra on elaborate, sinuous legs. Each candelabrum held twenty candles at least, and some of the biggest held fifty. A swarm of servants rushed around during the breaks between dances, trimming wicks and relighting the flames that had died in the drafts from the open terrace doors. Then the music and dancing began again. The women wore jewelry around their necks, in their hair, on their wrists and fingers. Diamonds, sapphires, rubies, emeralds, opals--all grabbed at the light with greedy vanity. From this vantage point, the glimmers of the jewels joined together in a blinding silver fish net that moved over the waves of the crowd. Around the edges of the ballroom stood giant mirrors that tossed back this brilliance, magnifying it a hundred times for each candle flame.

"Do you mind a pipe?" someone asked behind me.

I turned. A tall man stood in the balcony archway, partly obscured by shadows. "I'm sorry. I didn't mean to startle you," he continued.

I pulled my wrap back over my shoulders. "That's all right. I didn't expect anyone else to find the way up here."

"This is my escape balcony." He stepped forward then, moving with the stealth of someone more comfortable hunting in the forest than attending a court ball. The light glinted off the reddish strands in his thick brown hair. Young, about my age, with something vaguely familiar about the deep set of his eyes, his strong jaw line. I racked my memory, puzzled. Surely I would have remembered this one--he had a silver aura. Sparks crackled off him like static. I had seen golden auras, red auras, dark auras, auras of every color. But never a silver one.

I arched a brow, trying not to stare. "Escape balcony? That sounds rather dashing, like a jewel thief or something."

He snorted, stuffing weed in his pipe from a leather pouch. "Hardly. To be honest, my father wants me to find a wife down there, and I'm dreading the prospect."

"What sort of wife?"

"A suitable one." He grabbed a candle from the stand beside me and lit his pipe, puffing. "I think that means one with a giant dowry and a father on the council, though my definition of suitable and his tend to differ," he mumbled around the pipe stem with some skill. Then he caught my intrigued look. He instantly took his pipe out of his mouth. "Oh, I'm sorry. You never said if you minded smoking."

"It's fine."

"Are you sure? You're not just being polite? I hate it when people are just being polite."

I shook my head, smiling. "Really, it's fine. I like the smell."

He still looked suspicious. "Most ladies don't like it. The smell, I mean."

"Who says I'm a lady?"

He grinned, and I liked the way his dark gray eyes sparkled and crinkled at the corners. He was the first person I had met here who smiled with his whole face, not just his mouth, the first I had met who didn't seem to be wearing a mask. "Maybe if I had met you on the floor down there, I wouldn't have left it so quickly. Do you have a name?"

"Yours first."

"Merius of Landers."

"That's it!" I exclaimed, recalling Dagmar's betrothal. Now I knew why he looked familiar. "You're Mordric's son."

He stepped back, his pipe frozen inches from his mouth. "How do you know that?"

"Haven't you ever looked in a mirror? You resemble him." When I noticed his blank expression, I quickly amended, "A little, really. Just around the eyes, the jaw, your voice . . . He's a handsome man . . ." *I'm making a horrible mess of this.*

The pipe had gone out by this point, but he still held it. Clenched it rather. "I avoid mirrors," he said.

"Why?"

"I don't know why, really."

"You don't like your resemblance to your father, do you? That's why you won't look in mirrors. You see him looking back at you."

Oh no, I hadn't meant to say that aloud. Why hadn't my parents cut out my tongue before I could talk? I shook my head as he started, a slight tightening in his jaw. Quickly, he glanced away. I closed my eyes and hid my face in my hand. Mordric had come to the House of Long Marsh to settle the betrothal between Selwyn and Dagmar a few months ago. He had seemed a cold, exacting man, the sort that made me nervous. But this Merius was nothing like that--he had a silver aura and crinkled up at the eyes when he smiled. I peeked at him between my fingers. Now he was watching me intently.

"So, witch-girl, what's your name? Or don't you have one?"

Chapter Four--Merius

She lowered her hand from her eyes, and her lips curled in a mocking smile. "Safire, Safire of Long Marsh."

Peregrine was right. I would have remembered this one. Red-gold hair hung in loose curls down her back like molten copper--I always had been partial to redheads. Large eyes lit her narrow-chinned, angular face, her skin pale as fey moonlight. Arched brows and a splash of freckles across her nose hinted at the pert wryness already apparent in her speech. My gaze traveled downward--she was small, at least a foot shorter than me, but well-proportioned. No angles below the neck. All curves with willowy arms. I stuffed my pipe in my pocket, deciding to forego smoking.

"Your reputation precedes you," I said.

"What, did your father warn you about me?"

Her question threw me, as she had thrown me earlier with that spooky remark about mirrors. She was supposed to have asked "what reputation?" to which I would tell her "your beauty" or some other inanity. That was how conversations with young noblewomen usually went, which was one reason I preferred barmaids.

"No, not a word."

She glanced down at her hands. "I don't think he liked me much."

"Why do you say that?"

Her eyes flew up--they were the exact green of peridots. "When he and my father were negotiating the betrothal between Selwyn and Dagmar, I told him he should consider trading cattle for a living since he seemed so skilled at it. My father made me leave then, so I don't remember how the trade worked out. Dagmar, however, seems satisfied with her share of the Landers livestock."

I grinned. She was more entertaining than any barmaid. "Wicked words, but true. My father measures life by gold, not heart's blood."

Her brows arched. "And how do you measure life, good sir?"

"Call me Merius."

"Merius," she repeated, testing it. I liked how she rolled my name off her tongue, like a poet's name instead of the name of some stodgy ancestor.

"I measure life by the company I keep. At the moment, life has me spellbound."

She flushed, her gaze escaping mine. "You said my reputation preceded me. Where did you first hear my name?"

"In a tavern."

Her eyes widened, and then she let go a startled laugh, covering her mouth with one hand. "I haven't been doing anything that wicked, despite my words," she giggled.

"It's the truth. Your sister was mentioned over the same game of cards."

"Evil man--I should be insulted."

"Then why are you laughing?"

"A tavern? Dagmar!?"

I held up my hand. "I swear." I noticed then that Peregrine was standing on the balcony across from us, leaning on the rail and smoking. "Look, there's one of the men who mentioned you."

Safire turned her head, swallowing when she saw Peregrine. Then she looked back at me.

"Do you want to dance?" she asked abruptly.

"What?"

"Dance, you know . . ." She grabbed my hand. Her fingers were cool and smooth and slipped between mine as easily as water. She dragged me through the arch, and I stumbled.

"What? Aren't I supposed to do the asking?" I exclaimed, my brain finally catching up to my feet.

"Shh," she whispered. "I don't need you for your conversation."

"What do you need me for then?"

She paused a moment at the head of the stairs. "You'll see. Now, hurry up--you're too slow." The flirty, knowing grin she gave me shot straight to my loins, and I swallowed.

It was a short journey down to the ballroom floor, just a quick jaunt through a darkened hall and a few steps down a curving marble staircase. I hardly remembered going down the stairs afterwards, except a few vague impressions of an iron railing and a blue runner. What I did remember was how Safire's hand felt between my fingers. Under her skin, her bones moved light and buoyant as a bird's. A sweet smoky scent trailed after her--she smelled like cedar.

I hesitated at the bottom of the staircase. Before us whirled an ever changing maze of light and sound. Whatever they were dancing, it wasn't a waltz. The couples seemed no more than glittering pinwheels of color. But Safire never paused. She towed me into the fray. We stopped in the middle of a dizzy circle of dancers, facing each other. I slid my hand around her waist, her hair brushing sparks over my skin as I pulled her closer.

"Do you know the steps?" she asked.

"No," I shouted and spun her out into the crowd, drawing her back after several beats. Then I began to steer her around the floor, my hand tight around hers. If I was holding her too close, she didn't protest.

"But you just said you didn't know the steps . . ."

"I'm a quick learner." I spun her again.

"I should say so," she said breathlessly when she returned to my arms. We said no more as I swept her off into the tumult. I twirled her several more times, watching how her hair whipped over her shoulders. She had to know that wearing her hair down was an outrageous gesture. King Arian considered any woman who wore her hair down a wanton harlot. He had even publicly chastised his daughter for doing so, and since then, court fashion dictated no woman dare leave a strand loose. Until tonight. I smiled and whirled Safire around yet again. She threw her head back and laughed as I placed my hand on her waist. The sound rose over the voices, over the violins, over the clinking of glass, rose over everything until her laughter was all I heard. Like the time I had been fifteen and had drunk a whole bottle of wine, I knew then that it was too late to grab a rope or handhold. I was falling, and there was no way back up.

~ ~ ~ ~ ~

I ran my fingertip around the edge of my goblet, intrigued by the way the red glass lit the polished oak of the council table. Someone--Prince Segar, maybe--was talking about something-- SerVerin slave traders, maybe--with an odd droning passion. Every once in a while, he would hit the table with his fist, and the goblet would tremble, sending thousands of scarlet flashes across the table and my scattered notes. I waited for these moments as I thought about that girl at the ball last night and how my fingers had caught in her fiery hair during the last dance. Warm and silky, her hair moved like a live thing in my hand, and instead of stopping myself immediately and muttering some awkward apology as I should have, I had deliberately combed my fingers through the length of it. And instead of backing away and blushing as she should have, Safire had grown still and let me do as I wished, her eyes never leaving mine. Hastily, I shifted in my chair, my arm brushing the goblet. It wobbled and toppled over, a drop of wine running out on the table.

"Merius," Peregrine whispered.

"What?"

"How are you going to vote?"

"On what?"

"Haven't you been listening?"

"Not really--it all sounds the same after a while." I righted the goblet, hoping against reason that Father hadn't noticed. I glanced to the upper end of the table, where he sat with the other provincial ministers. He appeared completely absorbed with Prince Segar's endless monologue, but he always looked that way at council.

"You have to vote. We all do."

I sighed. "All right. Tell me exactly what we're voting on, and maybe I'll tell you how I'm voting on it."

"What to do about the SerVerin slave traders on Marenna's borders--Prince Segar wants . . ." Peregrine stopped as Herrod threw his chair back and lumbered to his feet. The commander of the king's guard, he was a large man with a grizzled black beard and a thick coat of hair covering his hands and exposed arms. He had the expression of a charging bear.

"Am I to understand that Your Highness believes a few well-placed arrows will dissuade these southern dogs?"

Prince Segar remained standing. "If they're truly the dogs you call them, these slave traders should retreat with their tails between their legs at a few well-placed arrows. They're no warriors, Herrod. Your most skilled king's guards as well as a few recruits from this table should be sufficient."

"Too sufficient," a hook-nosed merchant named Sullay muttered.

"What was that, sir?"

"I was just saying, Your Highness, that I don't understand why we need to involve ourselves at all in this border dispute. It's a Marennese problem."

"It's a little more than a border dispute. Innocents are being stolen from their beds at night, taken across the Zarinaa River into the Empire, and sold as slaves."

"But they're not Cormalen innocents. Marenna should defend her own."

"Marenna is fighting a costly war on its eastern border with the Numer rebels. It hasn't the means to defend the south as well."

"Let them have Marenna, I say. It's just a bunch of mountains and jabbering foreigners."

Sullay crossed his arms and wiggled around in his chair as if the seat had a stone in it. I picked up my pen, dipped it in the inkwell, and began to sketch a thumbnail picture of him on the edge of my notes. Except it wasn't him but a vulture with his features, a crooked beak and crown of scraggly feathers on its head to resemble Sullay's long straggles of yellowing hair. Peregrine caught a glimpse of this and snickered, though he probably wouldn't have been as amused if he'd seen the one I'd drawn of him as a snake a couple weeks ago. After Peregrine spied out the one of Sullay, I abandoned it and moved on to Herrod, whom I drew as a big, fierce bear.

" . . . and we need to demonstrate our full power to these SerVerin bastards before they try to make us the last province in their empire," Herrod bellowed. I glanced up, puzzled--I must have missed something. They had been talking about Marenna, not the SerVerin Empire. Hadn't they? I forced myself to put down the pen. God knew how much I had missed. I pushed my notes over the pen and tried to forget it was there. My pen was always getting me into trouble at council. I would start fidgeting or drawing or writing verse and become oblivious to everything else.

"We can't afford a war with the SerVerin Empire, Herrod," Cyril of Somners remarked. He was the head of the council and had been my mother's cousin. Father loathed him.

"Nor can we afford to neglect this situation," Father said quietly.

"What do you mean, Mordric?" Cyril sounded wary.

Father waited a moment before he answered as if daring anyone else to interrupt or hurry him. "We need to send our best warriors, and they need to strike and strike swiftly, in small contingents. If we want to avoid war with the SerVerin Empire, the prince's strategy is the only way."

"But I would think such interference with the SerVerin slave traders would be the most likely way to spark war," argued Sullay.

Father ignored him. "Emperor Tetwar has no interest in Marenna. It's an irritating fly on his borders, easily swatted. As long as he can get cheap gold from its mines without the bother of conquering and governing it--particularly the last--he'll leave it be for the most part. So why the sudden desire for Marennese slaves? They've been a free people for a thousand years, troublesome rebels who make terrible servants. If they escape before they reach the SerVerin deserts, they can find their way north back home unlike his other slaves, who come from Krytos far across the Gilgin Sea. The Marennese seem more trouble than they're worth. As slaves. As pawns, they're invaluable. These raids are an indirect challenge to Cormalen. Why do you think they started after our princess became the Marennese queen? Tetwar knows we don't tolerate slavery among our people, and he wants to see if we'll back our words with force. If we don't respond now, he'll grow more brazen, gather his strength, until we really will find ourselves in the midst of a war." He spoke smoothly, never fumbling his words, the mere sound of his voice commanding everyone's attention--how did he do that? I shook my head, wondering if I could ever match him here.

"I say we're delaying the inevitable," Herrod grumbled after a long silence.

"Yes, we are delaying the inevitable," Cyril said. "We eventually will go to war with the SerVerin Empire, but not now."

"Why the hell not? We could win." Herrod pounded the table.

"We could win now, but at what cost? The SerVerin emperor is strong and flexing his muscles. We need to weaken him, make him doubt his strength, before we go to war with him and his tens of thousands."

"And how do we weaken him without fighting him?"

"We could do something we should have done years ago: cut off trade with the SerVerin Empire." Cyril settled back in his chair as if he had thrown everything out on the table and the council be damned if no one liked it.

Devons, a prominent merchant with a perpetually red face, cleared his throat. "Do you want a black market the size of the seven seas on your hands?"

I propped my elbows on the table. "What about threatening to raise the tariff on our grain?" I asked. Many heads swiveled in my direction, which I hadn't expected. I had expected they wouldn't hear me at all, which generally happened with younger, so-called "apprentice" councilors. "I mean," I faltered. "I mean, the desert lands need our grain. The SerVerin emperor knows that, but I think it's time we reminded him."

Devons shook his head. "You nobles never think in terms of trade. An increased tariff will create a black market almost as readily as cutting off trade completely would."

"I didn't say raise the tariff. I said threaten to raise the tariff. A threat like that, coupled with a few of the prince's well-placed arrows, should be enough to make Tetwar's slave traders retreat for now."

"What if he doesn't believe our threats, and we're forced to follow through on them? It could turn the gold in the king's coffers to copper if the demand for our grain falters or shifts to a black market," Devons said. "And if His Majesty thinks he'll make any coin for his coffers from a tariff, he's sadly mistaken."

I shrugged. "Threatening to put a tariff on our wheat is a risk, but hardly a reckless one. Tetwar's not stupid. He doesn't want hungry slaves and peasants revolting because they can't afford a loaf of bread. His reign is shaky enough after the assassination of his father without a massive slave revolt." *Besides,* I wanted to add, *if all the merchants were as honest as Devons and willing to unite behind Prince Segar and the throne, we wouldn't have to worry about a black market. It's blackguards like Peregrine who would dishonor the title merchant with illegal smuggling.*

I fell quiet and returned to my notes, thankful the ordeal was over. A straightforward fist fight was far preferable to the tortured labyrinth of court intrigue. The son of a high courtier, I had a better idea than most of the unspoken alliances, the constant jockeying for position, and the secret vendettas that seethed in the council chamber like invisible smoke. Still, my tongue stumbled and I found myself speaking in unnatural rhythms whenever I ventured to remark on the proceedings at hand, feeling a fool within the first few sentences.

At some point soon after, Prince Segar called for a vote. I raised my hand with the majority for sending a contingent of the king's guard to the Marennese border while at the same time threatening to impose a wheat tariff on the SerVerin Empire. There was no particular sense of triumph in me that my addition to the proposal had passed the table; that had more to do with being my father's son than anything else. Everyone stood up with a clatter of chairs after the vote and began shuffling out, Sullay and some minor noble loudly debating the finer points of hunting hounds. I remained in my seat, puzzling over the end of a verse I had begun a few weeks ago.

"Merius."

Inwardly, I started like a guilty adolescent, but outwardly, I maintained my cool as I laid the plume of my feather pen over the verses. "Yes, Father?" The last councilor disappeared through the door at that moment, and chamber was empty but for us.

"You did well today, considering your attention was otherwise engaged for three-quarters of the discussion."

I scraped my chair back and stood, only then looking at him.

Early afternoon light broke through the high windows, giving him a halo of glowing dust. Our eyes met, and his were pale, silvered by the sunlight. He had to be blinded, standing there, but he didn't blink, at least not that I noticed. He rarely blinked, rarely fidgeted, rarely smiled, rarely allowed himself the petty weaknesses of other men. It was at times like these that I wondered if I had been sired by something inhuman.

"Father, you said a few days ago appearance is everything. As long as I give the appearance of interest, why do you care where my attention is really engaged?"

"Because it's sheer carelessness, being as distracted as you are. You're bound to make a mistake."

"I didn't make a mistake today."

"No, but it's only a matter of time. Why can't you pay attention? Is it so difficult for you to concentrate?"

"Yes," I flared. "Council's too damned dull. And shallow. The only ones who really believe in anything are Cyril and Devons and Herrod. All the rest do is fawn on the prince or plot against him."

"That's court, Merius. If you had any maturity, you would realize that's life as well. Ideals, causes, beliefs--these things are the province of intemperate youth. They'll get you nowhere in the long run."

"But Cyril--he's head of the council, and he holds strong beliefs about slavery and how we should deal with the SerVerin Empire . . ."

"Cyril doesn't argue against slavery because he believes it's wrong. He argues against it because the king believes it's wrong."

Something dropped inside, and I swallowed. "No. He's not like you."

"He's exactly like me."

"Is that why you hate him so much?"

Father gave me a wintry smile. I would have preferred one of the backhands he used to give me when I was twelve and being smart. "You're young, naive, and you have too much of your mother in you . . ."

He suddenly reached out and ripped away the top page of my

notes. The quill fluttered to the floor as his eyes skimmed over my verses. "You take excellent notes, Merius. 'Out where the sea-hawks soar and cry . . .'" he read before he crushed the paper into a ball and tossed it in the corner. "If you ever do that again at council . . ."

My fingers fisted. "You had no right to take that."

He acted as if he didn't hear me. "If I had to gamble on the success of a young courtier, I'd pick Peregrine over you."

"Peregrine's a son of a bitch . . ."

"You shouldn't have any problem being a son of a bitch as well--your mother saw to that." He turned to leave.

I made a move toward him, but he was already around the table. The door closed silently behind him. The blood thudded in my ears. I went over to the corner and retrieved the crumpled paper. It shook in my hands as I smoothed it out. Mother--Mother would have liked this poem. It told the story of a king's funeral as his people sent him out to sea. Mother had liked story poems. She had recited many to me while she spun with the other women in the long, sunlit room under the eaves at Landers Hall. Her words had fallen around me like feathers, soft and shimmering. I folded the paper and put it in my pocket, my temples aching dully. Next time I was in the Landers graveyard, I would leave it by her stone.

~ ~ ~ ~ ~

I drew back the bowstring and anchored it under my chin, the flax fiber cutting into my fingers. The belly of the bow blurred as I focused on the blood red target, its yellow center. The breeze whistled by my ear, and I adjusted my aim before my muscles tightened. Then, release. A distant thwack as the arrow struck. Bull's eye. I took a deep breath and stepped back, my bow loose in my hand.

Peregrine came up beside me, gazing at the target. "Well over a hundred paces."

"A hundred and twenty," I said shortly, reaching for another arrow.

"May I?" He indicated my quiver, which I had set upright on the ground. I nodded, and he plucked out one of the arrows and ran his finger down the length of it. "Birch?" he asked, pointing it at the target. I nodded again and straddled the shooting line with my feet before I nocked the arrow. Then I brought the bow up and drew the string taut. This time it was off, hitting the edge of the second ring. I sighed.

"I've always thought the arrows as important as the bow, maybe more important," Peregrine said. "Who makes these?"

"One of our tenants. Jared Rivers. He does everything, from finding the wood to fletching them."

"Can I try this one?" He held up the arrow.

"Go ahead."

"If I like it, maybe you could talk to him for me."

"He only makes arrows for Father and me and his sons, but if you pay him nicely, I'm certain he'd spare you a few." I smiled. Then I noticed something at the edge of the field. Not something. Someone. A flash fire of copper hair, a swaying, light-footed gait that delighted me in deep and unspeakable ways. She carried a large, leather bag of some sort--from this distance, it was difficult to see what it was exactly. I stared after her as she struggled with opening one of the side gates that went out to the city. Why was she going out that way? It led down to the docks and the market, not a place for unescorted young ladies. Of course, by her own admission, she wasn't a lady.

Peregrine followed my stare. "I didn't know you knew Safire, Merius."

I shrugged and deliberately looked back at the target. "I danced with her last night. Last time, too. Beautiful, but Selwyn's right about her having a hellish tongue. I prefer the quiet ones myself."

He chuckled as he began to string his bow. "I intend to marry her before the snow flies."

I flicked my eyes in his direction. "Does she know that?"

"She has a pretty good idea," he grunted as he bent the bow and slipped the string upwards on to the nock. I absorbed this without comment as I picked up my quiver and slung it over my shoulder.

"Where are you off to?" Peregrine straightened, shading his eyes from the sun.

"I have to help Father draft a letter to the Marennese

ambassador." The lie dropped off my tongue as easily as quicksilver. "There's a wicked breeze from the northeast, by the way." With that, I headed for the target to retrieve my arrows and then go to my chambers. I had to prepare for a witch hunt.

Chapter Five--Safire

The Corcin market jostled around me, alive with the shouts of hucksters and children and the savory smell of the taverns and bakeries and spice shops. Along the cobbled streets I wandered in a daze, my portfolio forgotten by my side as I gaped at all the wares. Under the bright tents, there were vegetables, perfumes, pots, fruits, fish, bolts of wool and silk and linen, jewelry, books, talking parrots, fruit from the Sud Islands . . . the Sud Islands? I'd never even heard of such a place. This market put the Calcors market to shame, and I felt very small in this great crowd and humble in my carefully mended frock. At that moment, a white-haired priest ran into me carrying an armful of parchments. The parchments and my portfolio went flying.

My self-consciousness vanished under a dark wave of fear. A priest . . . many priests preached my talents were evil, incited witch burnings with their fiery condemnations. I always fidgeted in chapel, worried I would somehow reveal myself, so quiet there most of the nuns and priests thought me mute. I forced myself to breathe and glanced at the priest's aura. Light blue and soft-edged, with no hint of malice--just a kindly old man who happened to wear the black frock, an old man who likely fed pigeons and snuck sweets to children when their mothers' backs were turned. Certainly not a man who could send anyone to the stake. The tension left me, and I bent to retrieve the scattered papers.

"My lady, I'm sorry," the priest said, kneeling beside me as I gathered up the parchments. "Really, don't soil your hands with that."

"It's all right. I was on the verge of buying one of those horrid parrots, and you knocked me out of my madness. I should be thanking you."

"I advise you not to buy a parrot," he said crisply. "They have pretty feathers, but they curse scandalously. They learn it from the sailors. Not at all something an innocent maid should have about." He picked up my portfolio.

I smiled at him. "My sister would agree with you."

One of the drawings had slipped out of the portfolio. The priest glanced at it, pausing to examine it more closely. He held it out to me then. It was one I had done a few weeks ago of the Calcors harbor. "This is wonderful," he said. "If you'll forgive me prying, who did this?"

"My brother." The lie should have come easier with time, but I found myself biting my tongue.

"He's a lucky young man, to have such a talent." He sighed and gave me my portfolio, the drawing still in his hand. "I grew up in Calcors. The ships didn't have so many masts then, but otherwise this is just as I remember it."

"It's for sale," I prompted.

A covetous gleam lit his dark eyes. "How much?"

"How much would you pay for it?"

"Well, aren't you a shameless girl?" He chuckled and looked at the sketch again. "Two silvers."

"I won't rob a priest. One silver and a copper."

"No, I said two silvers, and I meant two. Here, before I regret it." He dug in the folds of his robes and handed me the glinting coins. Tucking his parchments under his arm with the sketch, he tipped his head. "Bless you and your brother," he said over his shoulder.

"Thank you, Father." I pocketed the money and walked to the end of the market, where I found a tiered fountain resting on a granite slab. I set out some of my drawings on the slab, anchoring them with rocks. Many people passed this way to go down to the docks, sailors and brightly-clothed foreigners speaking in jagged tongues and housewives with their market baskets and bustling clerks. Few nobles, though, which suited me just fine. I sold several more drawings over the next half hour, inwardly exalting.

I sat cross-legged, gazing at the entrance to the market and wishing I had my charcoals and a blank sheet of foolscap. Of course, I could hardly sit here and draw while trying to pass my work off as someone else's . . .

"I thought my tutor was the only one who knew the story of the old ones and their path down to the sea," a quiet familiar voice said beside me. It was Merius, and he was holding one of my drawings. I almost fell in the fountain.

"You don't make a lot of noise, do you?" I said.

"I apologize--I seem to keep startling you." Merius stepped back as I hastily got to my feet and faced him.

"Where did you come from?" I demanded.

"I often come to market in the afternoons." His lingering eyes told me that I was a welcome sight. My face grew hot. Finally, he glanced back at the drawing in his hand. It was, as he had correctly identified it, a nighttime rendering of the old one's path down to the sea, the track they had used to bring their firstborn sons to the caves as a sacrifice. In one of my more morbid moods, I had placed several figures in dark robes descending the path, one carrying a baby while the others held torches. I had debated showing others this particular picture. It hardly went with the pastoral country scenes that sold the best, but it wasn't quite as strange as the picture of the faces in the bottle, which I never put out. And now Merius was holding it, his gaze thoughtful. Sad, even.

"It's well done, but eerie," he said then. "Who's the artist?"

"My bro-" I stopped, my heart leaping in my chest, my head light. This wasn't some peasant or sailor or priest. This was someone who was far more familiar with the noble family trees and heraldry than I was, and I had just betrayed myself to him.

He looked at me again, expressionless. "Your brother, you were going to say?" I swallowed and didn't answer. "What's his name again?"

"How dare you?" I snatched the drawing from him, shaking inside as I set it with the others.

He stepped forward, his hand out. "Please, don't be upset. I shouldn't have said it like that--I knew you were the artist the moment I saw the drawings. I was just anxious to talk to you again and stepped on my own tongue in my haste. Forgive my clumsiness."

My shock and anger buckled in the face of his honesty, and I sank down on the slab, my arms clasped tight around my knees. "Father will have apoplexy," I said, hardly aware that I spoke aloud as my eyes darted over the cobblestones, searching out the cracks in them. "It's not just an expression in this case--he really will. He wants me to be good, a lady, and I've disappointed him so many times, and well, this will be the last straw. He hates my drawing," I paused over this, half hearing the flutter of pigeon wings as several landed near my feet. "If he knew I was selling my pictures like a common wench with her wares and enjoying it, enjoying the charcoals and the paper and the coins clinking in my pocket . . . he'd die from yelling, and I'll have killed him, all to do something wicked I should never have thought to do in the first place. If I was good like Dagmar, I'd rip all this up and burn all my paper and give all my coin for alms. But I can't. I just can't-" I choked then, my breath coming in little hitches.

"Listen. Here. Here, don't," Merius said, awkward as he sat down beside me and stretched out his long legs. Then his hand was on my shoulder, and I felt that same odd, tingling heat from the night before, like the sun on my skin after a long dip in a cold river. "Listen, I'm not going to tell anyone. Not your sister, not your father, not anyone."

"You're not?"

"No. Why would I?" He began to knead my back then, and the warmth crept through me, loosening my muscles until I could have fallen asleep against him, there on the cold granite of the fountain.

"I don't know." I sniffled, having a hard time thinking while his hand was on me. "I thought . . . I thought men told each other things like that. Like it's a duty. You're obligated to tell my father I'm disgracing the family name."

"How can you disgrace the family name when you're hiding that you're the artist?"

"Good point."

"Besides, anyone who can draw as well as you can shouldn't be a disgrace to any family."

"Thank you. They're really not that good--I haven't been trained properly. But it's nice of you to say."

His hand grew still on my back. "Are you doubting my taste?"

"I didn't mean it like that."

"Listen, if I say your drawings are good, then they're good. Let me see the rest of them."

"You've seen them. I put them out."

"No. The ones in the portfolio. I see the corner of one sticking out. Give it here."

More than a little reluctant, I handed it over. The drawings I sold, the landscapes and the pretty flowers, I didn't care if anyone saw. The drawings in the portfolio--my storm scenes, my beloved faces in the bottle, my strange birds, my oak with the moon behind it--were the dark secrets the charcoal had released from the attics and cellars of my mind. They were for me, not anyone else. I watched him as he flipped through the pages, jittery inside when he paused over one of the sea cliffs in a squall. What was he thinking? I didn't know him, not really, not enough to read his face. He wasn't smiling, he wasn't frowning, his brow wasn't furrowed. Just a stolid concentration that narrowed his eyes. Oh no, he hated them. Well, if he did, it was his own fault, demanding to see them. Domineering sort. What right did he have, looking at my sketches in that detached way? I should snatch the portfolio away before he invaded any more of my secrets with his stranger's eyes . . . he glanced up then, giving me that intent scrutiny again.

"I like these," he said in a tone that allowed no argument. "They don't look like anything I've ever seen before. They're very original."

All my uncharitable thoughts evaporated. "Really?" I managed, finding it difficult to talk over the glad warmth rising inside.

"Yes. Why don't you put these out?"

"They don't sell. People think they're strange."

"Well, I'd buy them," he said, as if that settled it.

"I don't meet people like you everyday."

"I'll take that as a compliment." He flipped open the portfolio again and examined the topmost sketch. "I don't suppose many appreciate such dark passion." Dark passion? Suddenly I remembered that I was a maid and had no right drawing things with any passion, especially a dark passion, and then showing them to a strange man. Dagmar would say it was positively immodest.

"You're blushing," Merius observed.

"Am I?"

"Yes." Hesitant, he brushed a loose curl from my cheek. I felt the spark of his silver aura prickle my skin, and I shivered. "You blush pretty," he said softly. "You do everything pretty, I suspect."

Trembling inside, I reached up and touched his fingers. Our hands intertwined, palm to palm, and I saw in his eyes that he had never been a stranger.

~ ~ ~ ~ ~

I stood before the mirror, dissatisfied. After a frantic half hour of trying on most of the frocks still packed in my trunk, I had finally settled on a lime green damask with a crisscrossed pattern of dark green velvet ribbon over the skirt. It was a lovely frock. Too lovely, considering the short, freckled me who wore it. Maybe if I put my hair up, I wouldn't look like a twelve-year-old trying on her mother's dress. I grabbed the pearl combs off my washstand and jammed them in my curls, skinning them back like I had seen Dagmar do a hundred times. The combs stayed in place--for almost two seconds. I let out a gusty sigh. The girl in the mirror was not cooperating, probably because I visited her so rarely. Dagmar and I didn't have lady's maids like most of the women at court, and although it wasn't a luxury I missed most of the time, it would be nice to have someone to mould my hair in the fancy shapes and curlicues that were so fashionable now. As I bent down to retrieve the combs, there was a tap on the connecting door between my chamber and Dagmar's.

"Come in," I said.

"Where have you been?" Dagmar demanded as she entered.

"At the market. Do you think ribbons in my hair would look too silly? I can't get these combs to work."

"You went to the market alone?"

"Yes." I found a satin ribbon, but it was too shiny to match the frock. "You don't have a velvet ribbon, do you?"

"Safire, never go unescorted to the market here."

I rolled my eyes at the mirror. "Why not? We go to the Calcors market all the time without an escort."

"This isn't Calcors. How many times do I have to tell you that?" Dagmar said.

She came over and stood beside me, looking critically at my reflection as I tried the combs again. They tangled in my curls this time, snarling the strands.

"Your hair's almost as impossible as you trying to fix it." She dragged the bench from the foot of the bed and set it before the mirror. "Here, sit." For once, I didn't question her.

Her hands magically plucked the combs away. "You know, you have Mother's hair. You should do more with it," she remarked as she began to brush out the snarls.

"It's too damned thick," I complained. "It's hot on my neck when I leave it down, but when I pin it up, it gives me a headache."

"Quit whining. And don't swear either. A lot of women would kill for this hair."

"As long as they don't kill me, they can have it."

Dagmar flashed a rare smile in the mirror. "Come, little sister, don't tell me you have no vanity. Men look at hair like this. A lot."

"Well, there is one man who's looked at it," I conceded.

"Who? Peregrine?"

I hunkered down on the bench, scowling. "No--you know I hate him."

She tugged on my hair none too gently. "Sit up. I thought maybe seeing him in a different setting had made you reconsider."

"An ass is still an ass, even in the king's stable. You know he-" I stopped. I couldn't tell her that Peregrine had threatened me with Father's debts. All she would do was worry and wring her hands, and she already worried enough. It wasn't as though she could do anything about it, anymore than I could. I bit my tongue. That scoundrel.

"Do I know what?" Dagmar's hand paused over the combs.

"Nothing. I hope there's a ball tonight," I continued brightly.

"Not likely. It's the eve of a holy day."

"Damn!"

"Safire!"

"I want to dance."

"You won't get any partners, swearing like that," she said severely. "One would think you'd been raised on the docks."

"Sorry," I muttered, not sounding sorry in the least. It wasn't like I had used one of Father's curse words, which would rival anything those parrots at the market could mimic. *Would Merius mind if I said damn?* I wondered as Dagmar sniffed and slid the combs in my hair. Somehow, I didn't think he would. He had walked me back from the market. It had been nice, the way he held my arm. He had kept his hold loose, his palm barely brushing my sleeve. His touch had been a constant but light presence, just enough to let me know he was there if I needed him.

"There," Dagmar said then. "Look."

My reflection slowly grinned at me. My sister had worked her usual wonder with a pair of combs. She had tamed my curls into a neat cascade from the top of my head, the sides smooth as polished copper. I twisted a curl, and it sprung from my fingers. I turned and impulsively hugged her. "Thank you--it's lovely."

"I told you it would be. No need to get all weepy about it." But she hugged me back. "After all, I can't let you scandalize the king again just because you're hopeless with a hair brush."

Chapter Six--Merius

The air of the hothouse slipped around me like a damp cloak, the green hands of the palms grazing my shoulders as I wandered up and down the rows of plants. I came here in the winter to read and write and escape Father's lectures on politics and swordplay. Located on the southern side of the palace, it was far warmer than the drafty library and had more natural light. Even now, so close to sunset, I could still see well enough to name each plant by its leaves, though my memory would have failed me if I had actually attempted such an exercise. The only thing I remembered from botany was the apothecary at home showing us how to brew poppy seed potion to dull pain. My cousin Eden had mixed up her own potion, which she then gave to Whitten and Selwyn. She had promised it would make them invincible like the king's assassins, but all it really did was make them sick. She had tried to give some to me as well, but I had refused, declaring I wouldn't drink any unless she took a sip first. Eden had yellow eyes like the picture of the demon in my mother's poetry book.

"Can I do something for you, Merius?" the hothouse master asked, startling me out of my memory.

I looked at the old man. "Do you have any orchids?"

His forehead wrinkled. "Orchids? A few. I keep them locked in my private solarium."

"Could I buy one?"

"It'll cost you. Almost as much as a whole mandrake root."

"That's all right." I jingled my coin pouch. "I'm willing to pay."

"Very well then." He turned, his black robe swirling. "Follow me."

His solarium was even more humid than the hothouse. I inhaled the earthy sweetness of growing things as I glanced around. There was a mess of trowels and dirt and pots on the tiled floor, several mossy pails of water along the inner wall, and a pile of books tottering on the corner of one shelf. "Surely you don't keep texts here?" I exclaimed.

"No, of course not, they'd molder. I do quite a bit of my reading here, though--I find the warmth soothing to my old bones." He gave a dry chuckle. "I've seen you reading in the hothouse, though not, I suspect, for the same reason."

"I find it easier to stay awake in the hothouse than in the library, especially when my father gives me a stack of those damned legal treatises to read. Excuse my language, sir."

"Believe me, I've heard worse, and I'm sure you've said worse. Remember, I taught you, Merius."

"I'm sorry."

He chuckled again, leading me past a long shelf of bottles and a marble counter with many different mortars and pestles, all sizes. "You have a quick mind. Too quick. That's what I told Mordric after that incident with the glider on the parapet."

"It flew. Until I crashed it into the river wall and broke my arm."

"You're lucky you didn't break your head. How are you doing on the council?"

I shrugged. "I don't do anything on the council except hold up my hand when my father tells me to."

"Your razor tongue hasn't dulled any, I see." He sighed. "Are you satisfied with the life of a courtier?"

"Not particularly."

"Does Mordric know that?"

"More or less. There's not much to be done about it. I'm his only heir."

"In the end, we must all bow to duty, though it seems a shame . . ." he trailed off. We had come to a wall of shelves, overflowing with greenery. "Now where did I put . . . ah, here they are, behind the SerVerin flowering jade." He clambered up on a stool and slid out a tray with several small clay planters on it. A slender stem, festooned with fat, lined leaves, shot up from each planter. At the ends of the stems were intricate, odd-petaled flowers of various colors. The tray swayed precariously as the master stepped off the stool, and I grabbed for it.

"I think I want the purple one," I said, glancing over the orchids, which nodded at me in apparent agreement when he took the tray from my hands and set it on the counter.

He dusted his hands on his robe. "A gold piece. These devils take a miracle to grow. You have to divide the roots and pray over them every day."

I handed him the coin before I picked up the orchid. A heady scent floated in the air around it, like a woman in a ball gown. "Thank you, sir."

"Unusual for someone to want one of these." His gaze lingered over the purple petals as if he regretted letting me have it.

"She's an unusual girl."

He lifted his brows. "Anyone I know?" It was a simple, three-word question, but at court, the simpler the question, the more careful one had to be answering it. He didn't mean just anyone, but only those of the high noble Houses.

"I don't think so."

"You know, Merius, life is full of walls. Be wary, lest you break more than your arm on the next one," he said.

"Cowardice never won any battles," I retorted. "Thank you again, sir. And good night."

~ ~ ~ ~ ~

Moonlight flooded the library, pouring through the ceiling-high windows along the far wall like silver milk. I paused as the double doors whispered to a close behind me. Abandoned, as I had expected it would be at ten o'clock. Where was Safire? I glanced around at the shadowed recesses of the shelves. She was nowhere in sight. Maybe the steward had forgotten to deliver my message. Maybe he had thrown the note away and taken the orchid for his sweetheart. Maybe he had delivered the note, but my request had insulted her. After all, a young lady did not meet a man after dark in a strange library without a chaperone. Maybe . . .

"Merius?"

My eyes traveled up to the second-story balcony. "There you are."

"Were you worried?" She hurried towards the spiral staircase, trailing one hand on the balcony railing. Her movements rustled, a provocative sound that made me wonder what she wore under her frock.

"I didn't know if you liked orchids." A tickling started near the bottom of my rib cage.

"Is that what the flower is called? I'd never seen one before. It's lovely, just the way I'd imagine purple would smell if it had a scent."

"I'm glad you're here, Safire."

She lowered her chin and covered her mouth with the back of her hand, suddenly shy, and although I couldn't tell for certain in the poor light, I thought she flushed. "Thank you. I-I have something for you as well."

I met her at the bottom of the stairs, my hand sliding over the scaly snake's head carved on the end of the railing, the odd whim of some long dead king. My fingers closed over hers. She grew still for a moment as she had at the market earlier when I had touched her, the shadows of the stair steps above her cutting the moonlight into a blue triangle across her face. Then, slowly, her fingers curled around mine.

In her other hand, she held a book and a scroll. "I hope you like it," she said as she held out the scroll.

"Here, let's go over to the windows so I can look at it properly."

As soon as we sat down on a window seat, so close together our legs touched, I took the scroll from her and unrolled it. It was her spooky sketch of the old one's path to the sea, the one that had attracted my gaze earlier. In the silvery-blue brilliance of the moon, the figures on the path seemed to move, stirring in the confines of their tragic myth. Far off, I heard an infant's wail, and I swallowed. "Thank you," I said finally.

"I saw the way you looked at it before, like it spoke to you."

"It does. Even more so by moonlight, it seems. The figures seem to move, even, it's so real."

"Do you like it?"

"I don't know if like is the right word. Like is a word for things you can forget. I can't forget this." I gave the sketch one last glance before I carefully rolled it up and set it aside.

"You speak like a poet."

I leaned against the window, pretending it was an accident when my hand brushed over her hair. "I write some verse on occasion," I said casually. Scribbling verse was not an acceptable occupation for noblemen, and it was my secret shame that I hadn't broken the habit yet. If I spoke of it at all, I made light of it, as though it was some jest I was playing on myself.

"I want to read it." Although it might have been my hopeful imagination, I could have sworn she moved a hairsbreadth closer.

"I'll show it to you sometime, if I can find it. I haven't written in a while." Liar--I was such a rotten liar. I had reams of the stuff hidden in my wardrobe, not including the one about the king's funeral that I had finished at council today. That one was still folded in my pocket.

She watched me closely, her eyes narrow. "Why are you ashamed of your writing?"

"What?" I demanded.

Now it was her turn to be flustered. "I'm-I'm sorry. I'm always saying things I shouldn't say."

"No. No, it's all right. Just . . . how do you know that?"

"I know a lot of things," she stammered, clutching her book.

"Obviously." I raised my brows, remembering back to last night when she had said that uncanny thing about Father and mirrors. And people hardly ever knew when I was lying. Not even Father. "I think you're a witch."

"Don't call me that."

"Why not? You've cast a wicked spell on me." Hardly aware of the idiotic words coming off my tongue, I leaned forward, my hands suddenly on her shoulders. Her book fell to the floor with a thud as our mouths met. She gave a little sigh, and her lips parted under mine. All my muscles tensed as I tasted her. *So this is what witch wine is like, all frothy and sweetly dark* was my absurd thought before thought became impossible. All I could do was taste her and drink her and inhale her and touch her. *Safire, Safire, Safire* drummed the blood in my ears. Her hands clenched against my back, knotting my shirt. I buried my fingers in her hair, dislodging the combs as I kissed her eyelids, her cheekbones, her neck before I returned to her lips. Safire . . .

She pulled away, her grip painful on my shoulders. "Merius," she gasped. "Merius, stop. Stop. We barely know each other . . ."

I straightened, trying to catch my breath. Finally, I said, my voice hoarse, "Safire, if you insist I woo you according to convention, I'll do it gladly. I'll kiss your hand and nothing more for a year of Sundays, if that's what you want."

"That's not what I want. Not exactly." She primly smoothed her skirts, not looking at me.

"What do you want then? Exactly?"

"You're teasing me now."

I trailed my finger up her cheek, and the corners of her mouth rose with it until she was smiling. She still wouldn't look at me, though. "Let me kiss you again. You're adorable," I said.

"No."

"Later?"

"No, you're too bold." Finally, her eyes darted up to meet mine. And then darted away again as she retrieved the combs and tried to put them back in her hair.

"Leave it down. It's beautiful."

"My sister will ask questions."

"I wager your sister will be long abed by the time you leave here." I plucked the combs from her hand and set them with the sketch.

"Give them back!" She tried to reach past me.

I stayed her hand, lifting it to my mouth. "You'll get them back when you kiss me again," I muttered over her palm.

"Wicked man . . . oh, I like that," she breathed as I nibbled her fingertips, the side of her wrist. "Oh, Merius. Merius, stop. Stop." I dropped her hand with little ceremony. "I didn't mean just stop. Not like that." She crossed her arms, looking severely at me.

I shrugged. "What can I say? I'm a gentleman."

"Ha." She tossed her head. "You kiss like a rogue."

"And what would you know about a rogue's kisses?"

"I've read about them in books."

"What have you been reading, anyway?" I bent to pick up her book.

"A little Lhigat."

"No one ever reads a little Lhigat." I flipped open the book to the page I wanted. "'And so sang the mermaids/of long-lost love, found again/a blue fire in the veins . . .' Your hair looks like blue fire tonight."

"You know Lhigat?" she exclaimed.

"Of course I know him. My mother was in love with the man, or with his bones at any rate, since there probably isn't much else left of him."

"I love Lhigat too," she sighed. "But Sirach's my favorite."

"Sometimes they put on his plays here."

"Really?"

"I'll take you." I tucked a loose strand of hair behind her ear, visions of us alone together in the Landers private balcony at the theater quickening my pulse.

"You're thinking about kissing me again, aren't you?" she whispered, the lace along the low collar of her gown visibly rising and falling.

"Will you let me this time?"

She glanced away toward the window, biting her bottom lip. The moonlight outlined her elfin features, her slightly upturned nose, her long lashes, her narrow chin. "In a little while, maybe. Will you recite some more poetry? I love your voice, like pipe smoke curling to fit the words."

When she looked directly at me again, her eyes luminous, I knew we were going to be there for a long time, perhaps forever. Us and the moon. The listening moon.

Chapter Seven--Mordric

Stupid mistresses. The morning light slanted across the neat stacks of papers, gilding the bindings of the books lined up on my desk top. The inkwell and the red sealing wax lay on the blotting paper where she had left them. I returned them to their proper pigeonholes. Meddlesome woman--I had told her to stay away from my desk. When I had awakened and caught her sitting here last night, she had tittered and said she thought I wouldn't mind if she wrote a letter to her sister. Letter, hell. She was probably one of Cyril's spies, though not much of one. Like all of my mistresses, she wasn't very clever. Best to dismiss her tonight, before I wasted any more jewelry on her. I was bored with her anyway. I was hardly in my dotage, and her puritan small clothes and fluttery manner held no more charms for me. I glanced down at my desk again. Barely ten o'clock, and already I had six letters.

I picked up the first one and started to slit the seal with my dagger. The blade slipped and cut my index finger.

"Damn it," I swore as the wound began to sting. At that moment, my steward Randel entered the chamber, carrying my boots, freshly polished. He drew up short.

"Sir, are you all right?"

"I'm fine." Blood dripped on the letter as I tried to wind a handkerchief around my finger. *Age must be thinning my blood--if it had flowed so fast when I was young, I would have bled to death during the Gilgin War.* "Where's Merius?"

"Asleep, I think."

"Asleep? Still? Has he a fever? If not, I'll take a strap to him. There's no excuse for such laziness."

"I think he had something of a late night. Or early morning, rather."

I glanced up from knotting the handkerchief. "What was it this time? A card game? Another one of those damned poxy barmaids? I really will take a strap to him."

"I don't think so. Warden told me--Warden's another steward, you know . . ."

"Yes?"

"Said that last night Sir Merius paid him to deliver an orchid and a message to a certain young lady here at court."

"What young lady?"

Randel swallowed. "Warden didn't say the name. It wasn't one of the major Houses, I know that."

"My son's a fool," I muttered. "Orchid, hell."

"What's that, sir?"

I shook a small key out of my pocket. It went to the lock in the middle drawer of my desk. I kept several pouches of gold and silver coins there. Also some secret court papers and letters, a few spare baubles for my mistress of the month, and some of Merius's poetry I had confiscated from his chamber a couple weeks ago. I told him that I had burned it. I needed to burn it, as it was probably seditious claptrap, but I usually read it first before committing it to the flames. It wasn't all as seditious as that one about the king's funeral he had been working on at council. What if that had fallen into the wrong hands? Poetry, for God's sake. What possessed him to take up such a pastime? It must be the last trace of his bitch mother's poison working out of his veins. I never should have allowed Arilea to nurse him herself. I wagered that was where all this nonsense had started.

I took out a silver piece for Randel. "Find out this girl's name."

He pocketed the coin. "Yes, sir."

~ ~ ~ ~ ~

When Merius had still not appeared by one, I corked my inkwell, removed my spectacles, and went over to the wardrobe. Randel had brought a tray of bread and sausage earlier, but I needed stiffer sustenance. I reached behind the polished boots and pulled out a silver flask. Inside was the nectar of our fair land, the purest rye spirits distilled in Cormalen. I took a long swig and wiped my mouth as the whiskey iced my veins. Heady stuff--already my legs felt twenty years younger. As a young cavalier, I had jeered at anyone who drank liquor like it was courage in a bottle. I required no help with my fighting. But I wasn't going to fight with Merius. I was going to talk to him.

As I entered the lower hall on the way to Merius's chamber, Eden slunk past me. I grabbed her shoulder. "What are you doing here?"

Her amber eyes glittered, a smirk sliding across her full lips. "I seem to have lost my way, sir."

"I should say so. Your chamber's upstairs."

"Thank you for reminding me. I'd forgotten--it's been several nights since I last visited it."

Gritting my teeth, I pulled her out of the corridor and into the alcove under the stairwell. The daughter of my long dead second cousin Slevin, she was a year older than Merius and almost as much trouble.

"You also seem to have forgotten our little discussion," I hissed. "Although you may not believe it, I can find some fool to marry you. Somewhere there's a liver-spotted country squire who's been lying with the goats so long that he won't mind the stench of used baggage like you." Those cat eyes narrowed, and she opened her mouth.

Before she could speak, I put my finger to her lips. "Listen now, if you want to stay here. I don't mind a courtesan in the family. A clever courtesan can be far more useful at court than a hundred simpering brides as far as the Landers position is concerned. I do, however, mind an indiscriminate slut."

"I haven't been indiscriminate."

"You've been indiscreet, which is almost as bad. No woman in your position leaves a man's chamber at one in the afternoon."

"When should I have left it, pray?"

"When you were finished with him last night. Discretion is the one virtue no courtesan can do without, my dear."

Eden smiled. "Of course." I wondered sometimes if she secretly used pipe weed; her voice had an unusual smoky quality. "Everyone will wake up in the proper beds from this day forward, Mordric. I promise. Oh, and that reminds me . . ." She reached into her bodice and pulled out a letter with a red seal on it.

I took it from her, the parchment faintly scented with the exotic spice of her Marennese perfume. "Is it as I suspected?" I asked her as I stuffed the letter in my pocket, not daring to read it here.

She nodded. "He has the Bishop in his bed, though I doubt he finds His Grace quite as entertaining as me."

"Blackmail?"

"Perhaps. You'll have to read it, see what you make of it. I'm but an indiscreet slut, so I'll leave the difficult work to you."

"Don't sulk, Eden. It doesn't become a lady."

"I thought I was a courtesan, not a lady."

"All the great courtesans have been ladies. Understand that, and you'll have the court at your feet."

"You're certainly free with advice today."

I ignored her cheek--impudence was bad in a wife, but then she wasn't destined to be anyone's wife. "Have you seen Merius?"

"Last I saw of him was the other night. He was dancing with some provincial redhead."

"What redhead?"

She shrugged. "The same one Peregrine's been panting after. I was with him on the balcony when he saw her and Merius. I think he said her name is Safrine, Safire, Satire, something silly like that. It suits her. Myself, I don't see what all the fuss is . . ."

"Redhead, Safire . . . that's Avernal's younger daughter," I said.

"Avernal of Long Marsh?"

"Yes." It had been months since I'd seen the girl. Little sharp-tongued minx, not at all like her decorous older sister. For the younger daughter of an indebted minor nobleman, she had certainly carried herself proudly. Vain of her looks, I supposed. Most of the beautiful ones were, as I had discovered during my marriage.

"Well, she is prettier than Dagmar," Eden sniffed, "though

that's not saying much."

"Sheathe your claws," I said. "I don't want to see you on this hall again. Is that clear?"

"Yes, sir," she muttered.

"Remember you're at court on my whim, Eden."

"I remember, sir."

"Good. As long as we understand each other. Now, off with you." She disappeared up the stairs, her slippers silent on the marble. I walked down the hall, pausing outside Merius's door. After a moment of silence, I knocked.

"Come in," he yelled.

I entered the chamber and closed the door behind me. He sat at his desk, writing what I hoped was a proposal to King Arian about threatening the SerVerin Empire with a tariff on our wheat. Whatever it was, inkblots covered it as well as Merius's hands. If he had filled his pen with ink and then shaken it over his desk, things couldn't have been messier. Of course, the blotting paper, if there was any, was lost under a rough sea of papers. I had made him straighten everything two days ago after he had misplaced his council notes, but training Merius to be orderly was like training a horse to clean its own stall. I put my fingers to my right temple, anticipating the jab of pain.

"You were supposed to be in my chamber at ten, Merius."

"I was?" His expression was carefully blank, a look he likely practiced in front of the mirror. He rose, holding the ink-blotted mess of parchment. "I've been drafting this proposal, Father, and I can't figure it out."

"What can't you figure out?"

He began to pace in a tight circle around his desk chair, even though he knew it drove me mad. Why couldn't he stay still? "How we can threaten the SerVerin Empire with raising the tariff on our wheat and not ruin the entire wheat market. I'm worried Emperor Tetwar will laugh in our ambassador's face and tell his subjects to buy their wheat elsewhere, perhaps from countries that support the slave trade. Devons was right yesterday at council."

"There are no countries that produce wheat like Cormalen does, Merius. You, not Devons, were right yesterday at council--the

SerVerinese would starve without our wheat."

He sighed. "We shouldn't be trading with the SerVerin Empire at all, maybe--it's wrong to trade with a country that deals in human flesh."

"The SerVerin slaves would starve if we didn't ply our wheat to their masters. Our tenants would be in poverty if the demand for the wheat they grow falters. Your blind idealism would cause a famine on both shores of the Gilgin Sea."

His mouth worked, as if he held back several swear words. Finally, he said, his voice clipped, "You never said anything about being in your chamber at ten this morning."

"Of course I did. Yesterday at dinner."

"Dinner?" he repeated.

"It's a holy day today," I said. "Happens once every fortnight. There are no councils on holy days. Hence, what do we always do on holy days?"

"Father, I . . ."

"We review our correspondence, don't we?"

"Just let me . . ."

"And why do we review our correspondence? To be certain we've answered every letter, to be certain we haven't missed anything. And why would we have missed anything? Because your desk is a godforsaken unholy mess." I stopped myself, realizing my voice had risen. And I hadn't meant to bring his desk into this.

He stared at me, both of us motionless for a long moment. Then, with a sudden, violent movement, he swept everything off the desk. Papers and quill pens fluttered in the air as the inkwell hit the stone floor and shattered. Ink splattered on my boots.

"There, Father. My desk is clean."

I paused before I responded. I had struck him a few times when he was younger, but he was too old for that now. Besides, thrashings had never worked well with Merius. Nothing had ever worked well with Merius.

"A stripling boy wouldn't be so immature," I said finally.

He shrugged. "Treat me like a grown man if you want me to act like one."

"A grown man would have been on time this morning."

"On time for your unrelenting criticism? I think not."

"My standards are no higher than what the council will expect of you when you inherit my position."

"I don't see the council in here straightening my desk." He crossed his arms. "Father, if I'm so unfit an heir, then give me leave to join the guard. We're too different for me to be anything but a disappointment to you in the council chamber."

I noticed his toe tracing invisible patterns on the floor--he had never been able to keep still. Never. My brother Gaven had been like that--always restless. Merius had his hair as well, a brown mess that began to curl if he let it grow too long. One time when I had been away for several months when Merius was an infant, Arilea had let Merius's hair grow until it hung in ringlets. Some idiotic old wives' tale about how cutting a baby's hair was bad luck--at least that was what she had said. She had cried and called me a heartless bastard when I had drawn my dagger and chopped off the curls. Merius had babbled and played with his own hair trimmings throughout the whole proceeding, obviously not perturbed. Later, I had found one of the ringlets in a box under Arilea's and my bed when I was searching for my boots. In the same box had been a miniature of Gaven and his letters to her, letters which the cheating bitch had sworn she'd burned after his funeral. The box had been in plain sight near the edge of the bed, like it had been waiting for me. It probably had. Arilea had loved her little games.

"Father?" Merius demanded.

I shook myself and looked at him. So he resembled Gaven in some ways. Children often resembled their uncles. It was nothing. "You're my son, I trained you--we can't be that different. You'll make a fine councilor when you shed your slovenly habits. You're not slovenly when it comes to your sword, your dagger, your horse. This is the same thing."

He took a deep breath. "No, it's not. Mother used to say . . ."

"Merius, your mother lied. Constantly," I said through clenched teeth. "How many times do I have to tell you . . ."

He stood, preparing for battle. "Not this again," he said evenly. "She's dead, for God's sake--leave her in peace. I'm sick of you calling her names. I'm sick of you blaming her for what you do, for what you did. I saw you slap her, all right? I saw you hit her once. I saw you . . ."

"You saw me do worse than that? Spit it out then."

His brows drew together. "What are you talking about?"

"Don't be deliberately dense," I snapped. "You were seven, Merius, old enough to remember, so don't pretend like you've forgotten. You keep needling me with it, so let's air it once and for all and be done with it. She started it--I doubt you remember that, but she did. She liked to start things. If I'd known you were in the chamber, I never would have drawn the knife, but I was drunk and she was being a bitch, as usual. It had nothing to do with you." His mouth was slightly open as he gaped at me. "What? Well, say something, damn it."

"What the hell are you talking about?" he repeated finally.

"You know what I'm talking about. You were reading in the corner. You saw the whole thing. You wouldn't talk for days. Arilea panicked and summoned the Calcors physician. You don't remember all that?"

He sank into the chair. "What did I see?" he said, his voice hoarse.

"Not much, really. An argument, no worse than any of the others we had. This one I just happened to draw my dagger. I wasn't going to use it, hurt her or anything like that--I just wanted to get her attention. She screamed, of course--she was good at screaming. I think that upset you more than anything else."

"The dagger." Merius sounded monotone, like he was talking in his sleep. "I remember now. The silver blur of the blade when you swung it at her. You were trying to kill her."

"No. I never swung it at her. That's what I'm trying to tell you. I was going to shake her to get her to quit screaming so I dropped the dagger. She picked it up and swung the blade at me. When I went to wrest it away from her, the tip left a cut on my arm. I still have the scar. See?" I rolled up my sleeve.

He began to shake his head, his fingers splayed at his temples. "That could be a scar from anything. It didn't happen."

"But you just said you remembered."

"No, no--I'm remembering something else, a tavern fight I saw when I was younger." He swallowed. "No, maybe not that fight, but another fight. I've seen a lot of fights, a lot of blades flashing. I don't know. All I know is you're lying."

"Merius . . ."

"I never would have let you draw your dagger on her."

His incoherence shook me. Merius was often hot-tempered but rarely irrational. Had Arilea talked to him afterwards, made him think that I had swung the dagger, made him think that somehow he should have protected her? She had loved her games.

"You're always doing this to me."

"Me? Your mother's the one who lied to you . . ."

"Leave," he said flatly. "Leave now, Father."

I shrugged and turned to the door. There was no point talking to him when he was like this--he wouldn't listen. Not that he listened to me anyway. He had swallowed his mother's poison for so long that the truth meant nothing to him. My chest tightened, a fire in my lungs. Maybe none of this mattered. Maybe he really was Gaven's get. I looked back as I grasped the door knob. Merius raised his head and glowered, one hand poised on his dagger hilt and his eyes dry, daring me to stay. That hangdog Gaven would have been quivering like a woman by this point. I suddenly wanted to laugh, though it would have been for the benefit of a bitch ten years in the grave. Merius acted like me when he was in a rage. At least she couldn't take that from me.

Chapter Eight--Safire

For the third time in an hour, I tossed down my charcoal
stick and ripped up the drawing, letting the scraps of paper fall to the
floor. Then I leaned against the window frame and chewed my lip as
I examined the blank expanse of my sketch board. Nothing seemed
to be working today. Like every day since I had come here, I sat on
my window seat and sketched whatever interested me in the
courtyard below. Horses and their riders, servants unhitching
coaches, the queen and her entourage in their flowing silk gowns, the
king's guard at practice--all of these had been captured in my
portfolio. Today, however, I was like a butterfly collector, pinning
the lifeless image of the thing to paper while its soul escaped me.
Maybe I was tired. But I didn't feel tired, despite the fact that I'd
been up most of the night. I felt jittery. I set aside my sketch board
and rose, stretching. It was almost time to get ready for Merius.

At the thought of him, a flush tingled over my skin, and I
grinned. His name was Merius. He was the only son of Mordric of
Landers, provincial minister at court. His mother had been Arilea of
Somners, who died when he was only ten. He was two months shy
of his twenty-first birthday, and he had graduated from the court
academy three years ago, first in his class. None of this he told me. I
had found it written in the register of high nobility this morning, all
the while glancing over my shoulder to make certain no one was
watching. One would have thought I was looking at naughty pictures
instead of a respectably dusty register of Houses. Maybe I was afraid
some former, more sensible version of me would come around the
corner and find this new, silly Safire pouring over those few tidbits of

his life like a fifteen-year-old with heart flutters.

I tarried over my hair too long, and the church bells caught me lacing up the front of my brocade gown. Six o'clock--I was supposed to be meeting Merius right now in the stairwell. Hastily, I tied the bodice strings and pushed my feet into satin dancing slippers. The hallway was cold as the door clicked shut behind me. I shivered a little and hurried to the stairs. Twilight darkened the sky outside the hall windows, gray clouds so low I could have brushed them with my fingers. "Please don't rain," I prayed as I started down the steps. Merius wanted to take me somewhere outside, a surprise. And I had forgotten my cloak. I paused, looking back up the shadowy stairs. It was too late to go back and get it. Swearing under my breath, I continued on my way. Maybe Merius would kiss me again--that would keep me warm.

I stopped on the second floor down from mine. No Merius. I glanced down the empty corridor, my feet on the threshold. This was the single men's hall. Proper girls didn't go on this hall. We had agreed to meet here, hadn't we? Maybe it was the floor above--I thought that was where the Landers had their rooms. After all, it had been four in the morning when we had made our plans, so I probably hadn't heard him right. No, I was certain he'd said the second floor down. I waited for a moment or two on the landing, too nervous inside to stand still for long. Finally, unable to wait any longer, I tentatively put my foot on the flagstones of the hallway floor. It didn't feel any different from the other floors. Dagmar said only wicked women came here, so I was wicked now. Stifling a giggle, I began walking past the doors, wondering which was his and if I dared knock on it. One door, two doors, three . . . I stopped. I heard the sliding of a bolt and then the knob of the door next to me turned.

Merius opened the door, then froze when he noticed me in the hall. We stared at each other. Suddenly, boots thumped below, and male voices echoed up the stairs. Merius grabbed my hand and pulled me into the chamber, shutting the door behind us. We waited in the darkness until the men had passed, laughing, down the corridor.

"Safire," he whispered. "You're not supposed to be on this hall."

"I know that. What, do you want me to leave?"

"No, of course not. I'm sorry I wasn't in the stairwell. I was on my way, but then the steward delivered another damned letter."

"That's all right."

I heard him move away to the other side of the chamber, where a few coals still glowed in the fireplace. There was a scrape of metal, and a minute later, a wavering light leapt on the walls as he lit a candle from the embers and set it on the mantel.

"There," he said, turning to me. "At least I can see you now."

I glanced around the chamber. Books and papers everywhere, as I had expected. My eyes came to rest on him. He leaned against the mantel, unblinking as he watched me. I quickly looked away, wondering if I had done something wrong. His aura glowed dully tonight, a somber pewter instead of its usual crackling silver. Maybe he was tired.

"Last night . . ." I stammered finally. "You must know every word of the Celandine speech from Sirach."

"God knows I've read it enough times to know it by now."

"Who's your favorite? Sirach or Lhigat?"

"Sirach. Lhigat was my mother's favorite, but I've always thought Lhigat was too perfect to be anyone's favorite. Lhigat is almost too perfect to read, in fact. I can only take so much of his poetry. But Sirach--I could read Sirach for days and days." He sighed and kicked at the embers in the grate. "How is it your father let you read all those poems and plays? Most fathers won't let their daughters read Sirach--he's a trifle too . . ."

I arched one brow. "Erotic?" I hoped the shadows hid my fierce blush.

Merius grinned, the candle flame catching in his eyes. "Yes, erotic," he repeated softly. "Too erotic for proper young ladies." An invisible petticoat called chastity slid to the floor, and I swallowed.

"My father doesn't like to read, so he's never read any Sirach. If he had, he would have censored his poems long ago."

"My father reads only practical things, so he's never read Sirach either. He thinks poetry a waste of time." Merius touched his temples then, rubbing them a little.

"Do you have a headache?"

"Sort of."

"Here." I swept the clothes off the trunk at the foot of the bed. "Sit down."

"What are you going to do?" he asked.

"Just have a seat. You'll see."

"Bossy wench," he said, but he sat. I ran my fingers through his hair, letting them come to rest on his temples. "This is a promising start," he murmured. "Do you know you smell of cedar smoke? It's strangely--dare I say it--erotic."

"Shh."

"Oh, no. You're blushing again. You'll be permanently scarlet if this keeps up."

I furrowed my brow as I massaged his temples. "Behave."

"I don't know how."

"Do you want this headache gone or not?"

"Kiss me--that'll cure it."

"You had enough kisses last night." I squinted my eyes, concentrating. The tension wrapped around his head like a tight rope, and I was having difficulty finding the knot. "So tense," I whispered. "Why?"

"You're touching me, and you ask why I'm tense?"

"Are you saying I gave you this horrendous headache?"

He snorted. "No."

"Then what did?"

"I had a fight with Father earlier, but . . ."

"Ahaa . . . there we go." In my mind, the knot loosened under my fingers, and the rope came free, falling away into oblivion.

"There we go what . . . oh, it's gone," he exclaimed, reaching for his temples. "Completely gone." He looked at me. "How did you do that?"

I fell back, uncomfortable under his piercing gaze. "It's an old remedy. Touching the temples like that--it releases the bad humors and . . ."

"I've massaged my temples a hundred times and never had a headache vanish like that."

"It's having someone else do it--that's the secret."

"No, I think the secret is that you're magical. You know

things you shouldn't know, heal with your touch."

I shook my head. "No."

"I think," he continued, "that you're a witch."

"Stop it." I stumbled over some boots, trying to find my way around the bed. "I have to leave."

With the lightning reflexes of a swordsman, he was up and around the footboard and grasping my sleeve before I could reach the door. "Sweetheart, don't. It was a jest."

I struggled against his grip. "Witches burn in the market square of this city all the time, and you call it a jest?"

"I didn't mean it like that--I'm sorry. Come here."

Reluctantly, I let him take me in his arms and then was glad I had. He smelled of pipe smoke and leather, and his woolen vest was warm and scratchy against my cheek. His aura, bright again, was all around us like a silver cloud, shielding me. "Shh, you're not a witch," he said, his breath ruffling my hair.

"But I am a witch. I see and hear things I shouldn't. Feel things I shouldn't . . ."

"There's nothing wrong with you, Safire."

"There was nothing wrong with those women in the square, either, and they burned them."

"No one's going to burn you. You're too beautiful."

"You haven't really looked at me, if you think that. And red hair is a sign of the devil," I sniffed.

"Now you're being silly." He loosened his hold, keeping his hands on my shoulders as his eyes met mine. "And I'll never let them burn you." He paused. "I love you."

I gasped and stepped back. "But, but, Merius . . ."

"You're blushing again," he said, but he wasn't smiling this time. His face was intent, watching, waiting for my reaction.

My tongue cleaved to the roof of my mouth, and I began to pace, my hands clasped behind my back. His chamber had many obstacles to pacing--piles of books, boots, a quiver of arrows, a couple of leather bound chests. I found myself stepping around these items and over them, noting them with the detached interest of one in complete shock.

"No one's ever said that to me before. Not like that," I

managed finally. What did I mean, not like that? How stupid of me . . .

"Sweet, stop pacing. It seems I've thrown you into a tumult."

I stopped by the mantel and turned on him. "You are a tumult."

He followed me around the bed. "Too tumultuous for dinner?"

"Why, are you hungry?"

"I don't know--I'm asking you." He stepped on to the hearthstones and slid his hand over mine on the mantel. I was trembling, and I thought he was trembling a little too. Something jabbed my stomach with a thousand icy needles, all silver and tickling.

"No, no dinner," I heard myself say, my voice floating up to the ceiling. "I want to stay here. Stay here . . . oh no." I lunged towards the washstand. Merius swore and grabbed my hand. Somewhere in the middle of my lunging and his grabbing, we ended up in each others' arms. A confusion of hands and arms and heads ensued, a confusion that ceased as soon as our mouths met.

His lips were warm and firm, and he knew how to use them. His tongue was light and teasing across mine. No other man in my limited, furtively gained experience had kissed like this. Either they had choked me with their tongues, or their lips had been cold, like a fish. One had even tasted like fish. But Merius tasted clean and sharp, a searing liquor. Merius had the subtle, practiced touch of an artist. An artist of kisses.

I eased away, just to see what he would do. He groaned, low in his throat, his hand tightening on my waist, the fingers of his other hand clenching in my hair, and I knew then he wanted me. Power--I had power over him, and the girl-woman inside had no idea what to do with it. My mother's voice warned that men didn't marry girls they kissed like this. But the woman argued with the mother--the woman wanted to put her hands all over him. And the girl was screaming, absolutely terrified. I pulled away, gasping for breath.

We stared at each other, and his grip loosened on my waist. "Safire," he said. "Safire, maybe you should leave."

"Why?"

"Your father would kill me."

"He's leagues away, Merius."

"Still . . ." He held one of my curls then and sniffed it, closing his eyes. "Why does your hair have to smell so good?"

"Because I wash it."

He chuckled. "You have puckish eyebrows, and your nose turns up. Saucy freckles and a propensity for wicked grins--I bet you fight with your family all the time." I nodded, and he raised one brow. "I knew it. I knew you were an impossible knot the first time I saw you. I want to untie you. And then I want to tie you back up just so I can untie you all over again and again and again . . . forever, Safire."

"How do you do that?"

"Stay and you'll find out."

"I thought you didn't want me to stay," I said as he swept my hair back.

"I never said that. I just said that you shouldn't stay," he whispered, his lips brushing over my ear lobe.

I raised my hand and loosened his collar. The girl was still screeching somewhere, but I could ignore her. She wouldn't exist much longer. My hand slid under the shirt and over his chest. His breath caught. "Safire . . ."

"I can't let you do all the seducing." The girl finally fell silent. I had seen men's chests before, but never this close. All that crinkly hair and sinewy muscle. And what did they need nipples for? Though I knew better than to voice such a question, I couldn't resist pinching one just to see what would happen.

"Good God. Vixen," he said. He grabbed my wandering hand and brought it to his mouth. He kissed every finger, every knuckle, working his way down my palm until he had inside of my wrist between his teeth. I watched his hand, the blunt edges of his square fingernails. He wouldn't need gloves when he went riding--his hands were tough and strong for a nobleman's hands . . . then I noticed one of those hands crept over my bodice laces, deftly pulling them apart. He paused when he felt my stare. Then I raised my hands to his and helped him, both of us fumbling with the rest of my laces. A rosebud of sweet fear unfurled in my pounding heart.

He eased my dress off my shoulders and over my arms. It

dropped to the floor with a sighing crumple of satin brocade. The petticoats and shift floated away soon after, and I was naked. I stood there, wearing nothing but my slippers, my eyes shut tight. I didn't dare open them. Eve had opened her eyes and lost Eden. So I stood there, staring at the inside of my eyelids, and listened. The drip of water on the stones outside as it started raining. My breathing, fast and shallow. The shuffle of his feet as he walked around me. And then I heard his breathing, and it was ragged, ragged like a man with a fever.

"My God," he muttered hoarsely. "My God, you're lovely. I shouldn't touch you . . ."

"Shouldn't?" I repeated, my words shrill and shaking. "The last time you said shouldn't, you told me I shouldn't stay, and now you've taken away all my clothes so I can't leave. You don't take shouldn't very seriously, do you?"

"Are you mocking me, Safire?"

"Yes."

"Witch. Lovely, lovely witch." His voice was closer, a whisper behind me. His warm breath snaked through my hair, and I knew his mouth was only inches from my ear.

"Touch me, Merius."

A finger trailed lightly up the middle of my back. I quivered inside as that evil finger traced over my shoulder blade and down my shoulder. Agonizingly slow now, it slid down, down my chest to my left breast. It stopped on my nipple, stroking the taut peak with the edge of a fingernail. All my breath came out with a gasp, and my eyes flew open. Eden was lost now, lost forever, and I didn't give a damn. I glanced down, staring at his hand on me, on a place where no man's hand had ever been before, and I began to shake.

"Sweetheart," he said, his teeth nibbling my ear, "you're trembling. If you have any doubts, if you want to leave . . ."

I spun around and answered him with a fierce kiss, my fingers twining in his hair. The woman inside was demanding to be untied by the hands of a poet.

Chapter Nine--Merius

When I awoke, the rain had stopped. The dark of a moonless night pressed against my eyes, and I shut them again, turning on my side and pulling the covers over my head. That was when I found Safire. She lay curled against me like a cat, her hair tickling my arm. When I moved, she huddled closer. My eyes closed, I ran my hand over her shoulder, stroked the arc of her collarbone. My geometry master once described heaven as a place where all angles and shapes met in exquisite harmony so that nothing struck the eye amiss, the unattainable goal of every temple and cathedral builder. Tonight I discovered my perfect temple in Safire's body, and from now on, I would worship there with the stubborn ardor of a true zealot. I had said my prayers once already, and in a while, if she woke and was amenable, I would say them again.

I shifted her shoulders off my arm and tucked the blanket around her. Then I rose and lit a candle. It took me a few minutes to locate some trousers and a shirt. I left the shirt loose and grabbed the first footwear that came to hand: my riding boots. I had some shoes for roaming through the palace in the middle of the night, but they had been lost under the bed months ago, and I was in too much of a hurry to retrieve them.

Picking up the candle, I glanced back at Safire. A slight shape under the blanket, a few stray curls on the pillow, a gentle sigh of breath. A virgin until tonight. If anyone hurt her, I'd kill him. The abrupt, sensational violence of this gut instinct made me pause as my eyes lingered over her again, my hand on the door knob. I examined the thought, imagined the sword in my hand, another man's blood on my conscience. Yes, I would gladly kill for her. It was that easy. The certainty intoxicated me. Finally, I knew exactly how I felt about something, someone. No doubts. No second reckonings. No confusion. No Father.

As soon as I was out in the hall, I locked the door behind me and pocketed the key. It was unlikely Safire would awaken before I returned. Father had taught me long ago never to leave the chamber without securing the door, at least when I was at court. There were many spies here, and the Landers had too many secret royal papers entrusted to us to be careless.

At the end of the hall, one of the stewards slept in a chair, the same man I had paid to deliver Safire's orchid the other night. He straightened as soon as I passed him.

"Warden at your service, sir."

"Yes." I grimaced. The heels of my riding boots made too much noise; I should have worn the leather-soled shoes.

"Anything I can do for you, sir?"

"No, not tonight, Warden. Just going out for some air." I continued down the back stairs, wall-mounted torches lighting my way to the kitchens and stables at the end of the main courtyard. Usually only servants went this way, but at midnight, the unspoken boundaries that governed the palace during the day mattered little.

When I reached the kitchens, I lifted my candle high and navigated the shadowy maze of chopping blocks, wash tubs, and snoring scullions. The banked embers of the three huge fireplaces across the far end of the first kitchen lit everything with a lurid glow as I picked my way to the larder. It smelled of meat drippings from the grease lamps the servants used. I searched the shelves, finally deciding on a loaf of wheat bread, a half-used molding of butter, a chunk of soft white cheese, and several fat pears and mangoes the ambassador from the Sud Islands had likely brought as a gift. Fresh fruit was a rarity this time of year in Cormalen, and the diplomats from the southern climates always exploited this lack by tempting us with exotic offerings. The head butler would have locked the cellars and gone to bed by now, but I found an acceptable bottle of red wine on the back of the middle pantry shelf. I added it to the basket I had pilfered for my haul.

Warden was still awake when I came up the stairs and entered the hall. "Hungry, sir?" he asked.

"A little," I said shortly. I often was up in the dead of night wandering around. This was the first time there had been a steward guarding this doorway, and it irritated me, particularly when he felt compelled to comment on my doings.

Safire was awake when I entered the chamber. She turned from the window, the blanket wrapped around her body. She had rekindled the fire in the grate, and a warm glow lit her skin and hair. "I missed you," she said.

I shut the door behind me and put the candle down before I set fire to something. "I thought you might be hungry," I said, balancing the basket on the bed. "Let's see--there's bread, cheese, some fruit . . ." She came around the corner of the bed, her arms crossed over the edges of blanket. "Damn, I forgot glasses for the wine."

"I don't mind drinking out of the bottle."

I uncorked the bottle with my teeth and handed it to her. "Here, sweetheart." Our fingers grazed as she took the wine, and we both jumped a little, invisible sparks between us.

Safire took a gulp from the bottle. Instantly, she choked, somehow managing not to spew wine everywhere as her face turned red. "I'm sorry," she croaked.

"Are you all right?"

"Embarrassed, that's all. That wine is so strong . . ."

"Here, sit down." I cleared a spot on the bed. The edge of her blanket slipped as she held out her arm, revealing all. She tried to retrieve it, especially when she noticed my stare.

"Are you cold?" I asked, my eyes lingering.

"Yes. A little." She gulped down more wine, her knuckles white as she clutched the blanket to her breasts.

I watched her for a moment. Then I shoved the basket aside, sat beside her, and kicked off my boots. Her eyes cut in my direction before she glanced at the floor, swallowing.

I spoke first. "I'm sorry it hurt."

She started and finally looked me full in the face, her grasp loosening on the bottle neck. "What?"

Gently, I took the wine from her. "Safire, I don't go around deflowering virgins."

She arched one brow. "Even if they're panting to be deflowered? Merius, if that was pain, then I'll take my punishment gladly. And often."

"How often? Really, sweet, if that's how you feel, why are you still hiding under that damned blanket?"

She shrugged. "You're not naked. Why should I be?"

It was I who choked over the wine this time. "Vixen."

"The fact is, I'm still a little scared . . ."

"But love, there's no reason to be."

She put her hand on my arm. "Not scared of you. Scared of myself. When you look at me, your eyes tell me I'm a woman. But Father and Dagmar still see me as an unruly girl who needs someone to hold her hand, and that girl is the one who keeps tugging up the blanket--she doesn't realize yet that she no longer exists. The woman's been here inside a long time, waiting for you, for this night."

I ran my hand through my hair and quaffed the wine. "I should have courted you for a year before I even asked for the honor to kiss your hand. I feel like a seducer."

She tossed her head. "Maybe I seduced you."

I chuckled and set the wine bottle on the floor before I seized her, only to find her seizing me.

Later, as we lay in the sweat-sheened bliss of each others' arms, she whispered, "How many times can we do that in one night?"

"I don't know. Do we really need sleep?"

She swatted my shoulder. "We're being wicked, and Dagmar's going to know in the morning that I wasn't in my bed, and then she's going to find me. Then she's going to see my face, and she's going to know, because all wicked women have the look."

"What look, sweet?" I muttered into her neck.

"Stop it. And I don't know how to describe the look exactly. It involves face paint."

"But you're not wearing any face paint."

"You go on thinking that, and we'll get along just fine."

"Safire, all I noticed was a little kohl around your eyes, and all women wear that at court. Even Dagmar."

"But after tonight, it'll be powder. And then rouge. And then God knows what."

"Don't." My voice sounded muffled as my mouth moved from her neck to her shoulder. "I like you now."

"I won't be able to help myself because I'm wicked. Wicked women have face paint just like skunks have stripes."

"You're not wicked. You're demented with hunger." I reached for the basket. "Here, do you like pears?"

She grasped the pear and bit into it. "Thank you. Did you happen to get a napkin . . ." In answer, I lapped up the juice dribbling down her chin as I idly traced the curve of her right breast. "Stop it--that tickles. Stop . . ." She giggled. "I thought you were hungry . . ."

"Sweetheart, what kind of ring would you like?"

She took another bite of pear. "The last man who asked me that was Peregrine."

"You contrary flirt. What answer did you give him?"

"Pearls from the moon and gold from the sun and rubies from the heart he doesn't possess. But even if he could get a ring like that, I'd still never wear it. I don't much care for rubies. But I do like pearls. And gold and silver, just not together. You have a silver aura, you know."

"Silver what?"

"Aura. It's this light around you, something only a witch would see." She twined her arms around my neck and kissed me. Her lips tasted of pear and wine and salt from the tears she had cried earlier as I'd taken her maidenhead. Her tears burned like the sea on my tongue.

I eased back on my elbow after a long moment, one arm still locked around her waist. "So, what else did Peregrine promise you?" I asked.

Her brow furrowed. "Why do you ask?"

"He said he intended to marry you before the snow flies, and he's not the sort to make vain boasts."

She tensed against my arm. "That scoundrel. How do you know him?"

"I've known him since I was thirteen. We were at the

academy together, and I think he's a no-good bastard."

"Why would he tell you that he wants to marry me? That seems like a rather private confidence to be sharing with someone who thinks you're a no-good bastard." She yanked up the blanket.

I groaned inwardly. "Safire, have you ever heard the saying keep your friends close and your enemies closer?"

"Yes, I have, and I had no idea you were so cynical."

"Love, you have to be at court. And I wouldn't call it cynicism exactly. I'd call it strategy. You don't defeat men like Peregrine by making your intentions clear. All that does is give them an edge."

"So what you're saying is that you have to pretend to like someone you don't and do things you don't want to do just so he doesn't get an edge? If I'd acted that way, I would be married to Peregrine by now."

"How many times has he asked you to marry him?"

"I don't know. Lots."

"I bet you've answered him with a loud no every time, probably with some choice insults thrown in for good measure."

"Of course I've told him no. I'll never marry that toad."

"So, if bald candor works so well in defeating a lying knave like Peregrine, then why does he seem to think you'll be his by this year's harvest?"

Safire grew still. Then she began to shake her head, one hand cupped over her mouth. "Never. I never thought of--of it like that. Oh, Merius, I don't know what to do."

My arms tightened around her. "Shh, I didn't mean to upset you. I was just trying to make a point."

"It's not you. It's Peregrine."

"What about Peregrine?"

"He said . . . he said that Father owed him ten thousand silvers and that he could have him thrown in debtor's prison for far less and . . ."

"Peregrine said this to you?"

"He said he'd do it if his wooing didn't suit me."

"He's blackmailing you, the whoreson."

"I know what it's called." She sighed, lightly running her

hand back and forth across my chest. "I never knew there were so many muscles. Like ropes . . . you must train with your sword and bow everyday."

"Practically. I've wanted to join the king's guard since I was thirteen." I stared up at the ribbed underside of the bed tester, the blue fabric between the slats turned black in the shadows. "If he speaks to you again, you tell me."

Her hand tightened on my shoulder. "I shouldn't have told you about that. It's nothing, really . . . he was likely only bluffing."

"Don't count on it."

"Besides, Father can easily get ten thousand silvers," she added brightly.

I bit my tongue. She had to know of her father's debts, but a daughter's lie to protect her father's reputation was understandable. What was incomprehensible to me was that same father letting a scoundrel like Peregrine court his daughter. I hated my father, but at least he had never tried to sell me.

"Peregrine won't bother you again."

"What are you going to do?"

"Don't worry about it, sweetheart." I tore some bread off the loaf.

"What if he hurts you? I'll warrant he doesn't fight like a gentleman."

I chuckled. "Neither do I. Safire, I've been in several fights with that son of a bitch and won my share of them. I doubt it will come to fighting anyway."

"What will it come to, then?"

"Maybe nothing. You'll be a Landers lady soon, my love, and he'll have no claim on you or your father's silver." I swallowed the last of the bread. Who was I jesting, being so cocky? The truth was, I didn't want to think of Peregrine, of anything beyond Safire and me and the small, safe world of this bed. If only getting married was as easy as us exchanging kisses in the dark. If only we could wake in the morning and find ourselves wed, no worries about contracts or dowries or our families. I sighed and hoped she didn't notice. Father would never approve of me marrying a sparrow noblewoman, not after he'd made unofficial plans for me to wed the king's niece--he'd likely disinherit me for defying him. And her father--he'd not want her to marry a disinherited nobleman, a nobleman who'd seduced her before any proper betrothal. Especially when she could have had Peregrine and his bags of gold. I tightened my grip on her, pressed my lips to her temple. However our families thought or acted, she was mine now, and that was all that mattered. Father could disinherit me all he liked--I didn't want his coin and offices anyway. He might as well have willed me a golden ball and chain. He'd always used the threat of disinheritance to control me, and it would be good to be rid of the chafing weight of his influence. As for her father, I'd prove to him what an honorable man I was, if it took the rest of my life.

"You're my lady now, sweet."

"I haven't said yes yet, you know. I'm waiting to see what the ring looks like." Her voice was the whicker of a mischievous filly bucking her first harness. Or her hundredth--although she made out that her father and sister often ordered her around, I seriously doubted any of those orders had been followed. It was good she was so bold--she would need to be strong to defy our families when the time came for us to elope.

"Who am I jesting? I'd take a glass ring from you before I'd take another man's diamond," she said as she settled back on my arm, her head on my chest. "Recite one of your poems for me, Merius."

I cleared my throat. "Which one?"

"I don't know. The last one you wrote."

I began, my voice low. "Out where the sea-hawks soar and cry/Above the waves that leap and die/upon the shifting sands/Shimmering in the golden rays/of a thousand suns and a thousand days . . ."

She looked at me. "That's not the end, surely?"

"No, not exactly. You likely don't want to hear the rest."

"Yes, I do. I thought that bit was lovely. Tell me the rest."

"It's not written."

"But you just said . . ."

"I mean written in its final form. It's roughed out, not finished."

"Merius, please--I just want to hear it."

"Let's not talk about it anymore."

She rolled over, her chin resting on her crossed arms as she gave me a quizzical stare. "Did I do something wrong?"

"No, sweetheart, it's not you."

"Then why won't you finish the poem for me?"

I shrugged. Mother was ten years in the grave, but it still felt like she was listening sometimes, betrayed that I was sharing my poetry with someone else. "The dead make wonderful critics," I remarked under my breath. "Safire, do you believe in ghosts?"

She was silent for so long that I wondered if she had heard me. "I've seen them before," she said softly, as if confessing a shameful secret.

My hand moved in the silken nest of her hair. "Where?"

"I've sensed several since I came here. They're all around, really, most of them too preoccupied with their own doings to notice the living."

"What are they, exactly?"

"I suppose they're spirits who wouldn't cross over for one reason or another. When I was younger, I tried talking to them, but Mother told me to stop before someone heard me and thought me addled or possessed."

"I sometimes . . ." I hesitated, chilled suddenly. "Sometimes I think my mother's still around."

"Really?"

"It's likely only my imagination." I pulled Safire closer.

"Not necessarily. When do you feel her the most?"

"When I'm at Landers Hall."

"Maybe she's watching over you."

"Maybe." The part of me that hesitated sharing my verse with Safire fell quiet. Slowly, I began to recite:

Out where the sea-hawks soar and cry
above the waves that leap and die
upon the shifting sands
Shimmering in the golden rays
of a thousand suns and a thousand days
Here we send you to a final sleep

In the sapphire haze
of the eternal deep

A shining ship, sails unfurled
will take you to the edge of this world
And what beyond? Who can say?
For what is mortal must pass away

So, we come by light of day
to give you to the endless waters
Silver and gold we bring
To honor you, our tall king
Before the wind-whipped sails
White ship wings
carry you away
out past the day
Beyond the waves that leap and die
Below the sea-hawks that soar and cry.

All was silent for several minutes after I finished. Then Safire leaned over and kissed me, the salt of the sea again on her lips. "Thank you, dear heart," she whispered.

"Why are you crying?"

"Because it's beautiful."

"You're beautiful. I could write a poem about you right now."

She bit her bottom lip and hid her face against my shoulder. She said something, her voice so muffled I could barely hear her.

I slipped my hand under her chin and forced her to look at me. "What did you say, Safire?"

She swallowed. "I love you." Then she hid her face again.

I smiled. "You hold my heart in your hands. Do you know that?"

She lifted her head. "Then I'll hold it as gently as I would hold a dove."

"I know you will. I want you for my wife, Safire."

"I know."

"I'll have a ring for you soon."

She nodded. We fell silent for a long while, neither of us able to sleep. The rain had started again, and I listened to it, very aware of her presence in my arms. It felt like she had always been there, that we had been lying here together listening to rain forever, that everything else but the flicker of the candle and the pitter-patter of drops on the window and her warmth beside me was my imagination. I sighed and touched my lips to the crown of her head, a lover's blessing.

Finally she reached out and snuffed the candle between her fingers. "Love, you have a witch in your bed. Don't you want to find out what makes me fly?"

Her laugh was low and throaty in the dark as I grabbed her to me and kissed her hard, a drowning man.

Chapter Ten--Mordric

The manservant escorted me into Prince Segar's private receiving chamber, a long, paneled room down the hall from Merius's chamber. "His Highness will join you presently, sir," he said. "Is there anything you require?"

I waved him away and pulled my pipe out of my pocket as I went over to the side table with its line of tobacco jars and decanters. Stuffing the pipe bowl with weed from the prince's fine selection, I plucked a candle from the mantel and drew a quick breath as the flame took. Then I sank into the leather cushion of the settle, inhaling the warm smoke until I could inhale no more. The door creaked open. I glanced up--it was Cyril of Somners, my dead wife Arilea's first cousin.

"Mordric." Cyril's nod was stiff as he sat on the chair across from me. A gaunt sort with a bilious temper, he was red-faced today under his neatly trimmed gray beard and moustache. That was what came of too much honesty--lifelong indigestion.

"Cyril." I nodded in return and blew smoke in his direction.

"Has Merius drafted the proposal to raise the tariff on the shipments of our wheat to the SerVerin Empire? Both Prince Segar and King Arian asked about it this morning."

"He's roughed it out, more or less--he lacks the conviction for it that he had at council, and he doubts himself too much to finish it properly."

"Why? It's a good proposal." Cyril sounded almost indignant.

"Why? Because of you and your idealism. He's listened to

your harangues about cutting off all trade with the SerVerin Empire so long that he thinks we single-handedly caused the SerVerin slave trade when we sold a loaf of bread to Emperor Tetwar."

"Our merchants' willingness to trade with those southern slave mongers sends an unspoken message we support trafficking in human flesh."

"Get off your high horse, Cyril. Our merchants' willingness to trade earns Cormalen coffers of coin--and nothing else. Those slaves you're so concerned about would starve without Cormalen wheat. Your own tenants would suffer without a strong wheat market."

"The merchants' trade of the wheat from our and other nobles' estates doesn't earn Cormalen any coin--it earns the merchants more coin. You want to see knaves like Peregrine prosper off the backs of our tenants?"

"Not all the merchants are like Peregrine. You only think so because you've alienated the entire merchant contingent at court with your impolitic posturing." I crossed my arms, watching him through a haze of smoke. "Some of the merchants are honest, like Devons, but whether they're honest or dishonest, they all have a great deal of coin, which means they have a great deal of power. If we nobles expect to maintain supremacy at court and in our provinces, we'd best be more subtle. Your idiocy makes no enemies except among your allies. Threatening the merchants' precious SerVerin market for our wheat with an embargo? I could have jammed my spurs down your principled throat. If Merius hadn't distracted Devons with the wheat tariff and you had persisted, we might have lost the council to the merchants then and there."

"The merchants are still several votes shy."

"Don't count on it. Some of the lesser nobles are so indebted to men like Peregrine they'll piss in the king's cup if the merchants tell them to," I said.

"Sometimes it's wise to use your blunt edge in a duel--it saves the sharp side for when you need it."

"It sounds like you need a new blade, Cyril. I won't let Merius act as your second again. Next time could be lethal to his career."

"That irritates you, doesn't it? The fact that he refuses to be your mouthpiece irritates you. Of course," and here he shrugged, "I suppose all fathers have the same arrogance."

"At least Merius hasn't forgotten his duties at council and defected to the king's guard." Cyril's only son was a captain in the king's guard.

"Give him time, Mordric. Anyone with scruples couldn't last long as your son. Or your wife."

I took a long draw on my pipe. "Strange. The honorable House of Somners didn't seem so concerned with scruples when your father rushed to betroth his niece Arilea to me, a wealthy, influential Landers. I don't remember you making any objections yourself. Hypocrisy never hurt your career, did it?"

"Fork-tongued snake . . ." Cyril began to rise, his face red.

At that instant, the manservant opened the door. "His Highness, Prince Segar," he announced.

Cyril and I looked at each other. "We already fought one duel," he said quietly. "Neither of us can afford to make it two."

It would not do for the prince to see us on the verge of throttling each other. As the two highest ranking nobles at court, Cyril and I had to present a unified front to the rest of the council if the nobility was to keep control. Divided, we accomplished nothing and gave the merchants the power to topple us. The whole court knew of our duel. However, as long as we smiled with gritted teeth and pretended agreement on council matters, no upstart merchant would likely challenge our positions.

"Your Highness." I rose, removing the pipe from my mouth.

He sniffed. "Your pipe--Sarneth long leaf?"

"Yes. From your own collection, actually."

"Do you find it has a richer taste than the short leaf?"

"That depends how it's cured. I find the best place for it is the shop by the river."

"The shop with the thatched roof?" When I nodded, he continued, "That's the only shop I'll let my steward buy from. Good man--he knows his trade." He cleared his throat and perched on the edge of an armchair, his jeweled sword at an awkward angle as he braced his elbows on his knees.

Cyril and I sat as well, settling back in our seats. It sometimes took Segar awhile to find his point, which explained why councils had become so long in the last few years.

"Mordric, Cyril," he began finally. "As my most trusted advisors . . ." Blathering dolt--he wasn't even skilled at flattery. Or spying. The letter Eden had pilfered from his chamber the other day had revealed his ineptitude with court intrigue. Bribing the bishop for secrets of the confessional? A prince should have more subtlety, having been reared in the shadow of the throne. Of course, his father King Arian's throne didn't cast that long of a shadow and neither had his grandfather's. The only reason the royal House of Ewing was still in power was everyone's desire to avoid the disruption of civil war. One bad harvest or too many ships lost in a tempest or an overly ambitious noble, and the royal family would be royal no more. I crossed my arms, wondering about Merius's claim to the throne. It could be a solid claim--both the Landers and the Somners had ancient kings in their bloodlines.

"So," the prince was saying, "Before we threaten to raise the wheat tariff, we should determine what the SerVerin reaction will be. Explosive if mishandled."

"But of course, Your Highness." Cyril sounded surprised, as if he wondered at the fact the prince might have considered otherwise. He had never been adept at keeping a poker face, one of his few useful weaknesses.

"That should be simple enough," I said. "Just don't have our ambassador flush out the SerVerinese. Find someone else for the job."

"But our ambassador to the SerVerin Empire is the obvious choice to approach Emperor Tetwar . . ." Cyril began.

"Exactly. That's why we don't want to use our ambassador. He's obvious. Tetwar will know something's up if our ambassador mentions the tariff. We want to dumbfound Tetwar, not give him advance warning of our plans."

"Maybe a merchant then? A merchant would have reason to mention the tariff." Cyril was a trifle sarcastic. "Of course, what merchant gets audience with the SerVerin emperor?"

"I can think of one."

"Peregrine?"

"Why not? Tetwar trusts him, considers him one of their smugglers."

"That's because he is. There's been rumors of him smuggling cannon powder to the Empire since he took over the House of Bara from his father," Cyril sputtered. "If I had the proof, he'd be off the council."

"Why not use him instead? He's in an advantageous position."

Cyril shook his head. "How would you control the man? He's completely untrustworthy."

"Leave that to me."

Prince Segar watched us through this entire exchange, eyes wide. He rarely consulted us both at the same time, and I wondered if he was regretting it. "Cyril, you're right. Peregrine has the capacity to betray us."

"That's what you want for this sort of work. If he didn't have the capacity to betray us, he wouldn't have the emperor's ear."

"But how do you propose to handle him, Mordric? This is a delicate matter. One step wrong, and we lose the advantage of the tariff and possibly the entire SerVerin market."

"Simple blackmail can work miracles, even with a scoundrel." I smiled grimly at their sudden silence. I had used the forbidden words--blackmail and bribery were a fact of court life, but few were so ill-bred to mention this fact aloud. I really was getting old.

~ ~ ~ ~ ~

When I opened my chamber door, a stack of letters blocked it. I kicked them aside with a muttered oath as I went over to the window seat. There I unlaced my shoes, removing them and lining them up with the other pairs under the wardrobe. The boots Randel had polished yesterday stood beside it like sentinels awaiting orders. I grabbed them and braced myself against the bedpost as I tugged them on.

"Come in," I grunted at the knock at the door.

"Going riding, sir?" Randel asked as he entered the room.

"Yes. Is Merius about?" I straightened, testing the boots. It seemed the cobbler had made them a shade too tight. Of course, they were new enough to creak when I walked, so maybe the leather would stretch with time.

"I saw him this morning." Randel's tone was stiff.

I gave him a sharp glance. "And?"

"You won't be pleased, sir."

"Spit it out, man--I haven't all day."

"The girl I mentioned yesterday--she's Safire of Long Marsh, the Lady Dagmar's younger sister. Warden said she spent the night in Sir Merius's chamber."

Somehow, my feet took me to the window. I stared out at the courtyard below, at the mud from last night's rain baking in the noonday sun. "Thrice-damned fool," I growled, fingernails digging into palms. The barmaids had been bad enough. If he had just tumbled them, that would have been one thing. I had tumbled wenches in my day. But Merius didn't just tumble them. He wrote poems about them, picked flowers for them, got into fights over them. He had almost eloped with one a few years ago. At least, however, an elopement with a barmaid could be annulled. Taking the maidenhead of a nobleman's virgin daughter was something else altogether. There were highbred courtesans like Eden, but the Long Marsh minx, despite her sharp tongue and unwomanly ways, was definitely not a courtesan. The first man who plucked this particular plum had better marry her, or he would lose all semblance of honor. This particular plum, with her twice-mended dresses, her pitiful dowry, her lack of connections. Hell, her father hadn't even sired a son--the House of Long Marsh died with him. A Long Marsh match with Dagmar was fine for Selwyn, who would have no career at court. But Merius . . .

Randel cleared his throat. "There's more, sir."

"What?" I took a deep breath.

"Merius went into the city this morning. Remembering your orders, I followed him. He's bought her a ring."

"Damn him. And I could have gotten him the king's niece." Pain shot through my temples. "Damn him." Randel started to pick up the letters, setting them on the desk. "Leave it," I told him. "I'll answer them later."

~ ~ ~ ~ ~

The sword still fit my hand as if it had been forged yesterday. I slashed the sunlit air of the salon a few times, dust motes scattering in all directions. It had been a fortnight since I had even drawn it from the scabbard, a sorry lapse for a former wartime commander. Randel kept it oiled and ready, but it seemed time for practice came less and less these days. Merius, of course, was down here almost everyday. Everyday that he wasn't busy seducing daughters of the sparrow nobility. I charged at the practice dummy, raining blows on its padded gray shoulders.

"Waste of a fine blade," Herrod the king's guard commander remarked behind me.

"Would you rather I waste it on you?"

Chuckling, he selected a blunt-edged practice sword from the master-at-arm's table. "Does an old dog still know any tricks worth learning?"

"Does an insolent whelp have the mettle to find out?" I sheathed my rapier and picked up a sword from the table, testing the weight. There were wooden swords for regular drills, but neither Herrod nor I used them. They never seemed to have the proper balance. Metal practice swords, even with their blunted points and edges, were more dangerous than wooden ones, but by the same token were more likely to inspire the proper respect for a real blade. I had not allowed Merius to use a wooden sword after he was twelve for that very reason.

We moved to the center of the room and saluted each other. Then, with a sudden flash of silver as his blade caught the afternoon sun, he lunged. I moved too slowly, my sword edge catching the full force of the blow. Bracing myself, I immediately shifted and aimed the point at his shoulder. It made contact, and he retreated, side-stepped, and then lunged with an oath. This time I was ready and leapt backwards, blocking him. The blades hit with the harsh ring of steel. I pretended another thrust to his shoulder, and he parried instantly, leaving his lower torso open. I got in my second hit.

"If this was a battle, the old dogs would be feasting with the carrion fowl," I said.

Herrod laughed. "Ah--the battle may be yours, graybeard, but the war will be mine."

We circled each other, sudden, staccato clashes followed by taut silences. The way the sunlight slanted over the stone floor, the salty tingle of sweat, the hiss of the metal on metal, the terse repartee, the intricate maneuvers, the practice swords--all haunted me. Herrod had never been my pupil, but it seemed suddenly as if he had. And then I remembered. Merius--this was like teaching Merius the finer points of swordplay in the long front room at Landers Hall. It was the summer after he turned thirteen, before he began his education at court, and I hadn't trusted anyone but myself to train him properly. He was always too headstrong and clever for his tutors at Landers Hall, readily getting out of his lessons to ride or hunt or build one of his innumerable projects.

The projects had brought me home from court more than once--his dam flooded the bottom half of the Rivers' fields, his bear snare caught his friend Gerard of Casian, his experimental oil lamp exploded, burning the roof off an abandoned outbuilding. This last was the main reason he had started a year early at the court academy where I could keep an eye on him and teach him some discipline, not an easy lesson for Merius. Not like the sword. Of all the things I had tried to teach him, he learned the sword most eagerly, perhaps because it was the one time he could strike me and not get killed for it.

No, there was no way my brother Gaven had sired him--Gaven had been merely an adequate swordsman, but Merius could be a master. I stepped forward then and met Herrod's descending sword with a solid parry. Before he could retreat, I instantly flicked my blade out. It hit the center of his chest hard, harder than I had intended. He fell back.

"I surrender," he gasped, throwing down his sword as he reached for the buttons of his jerkin.

"I apologize. I'm used to dueling with masters."

His eyes were narrow under bristling black brows. "There's a rumor that you piss vinegar. God, what a mean son of a bitch." He unlaced his shirt and examined the damage.

"Didn't crack a rib, did I?"

"Don't sound so hopeful. You're too old to hit that hard," he said cheerfully, lacing his shirt back up. "Just a bruise. A few bruises in practice makes for lives saved in battle."

"Your father used to say that." I straightened the practice swords so that they lined up in perfect parallels on the cloth surface of the table.

"My father also said you were a faithless cur for not renewing your commission after the war, that you were too skilled a fighter to sit on council and send others to battle."

"I had a duty to fill the Landers council seat and offices." *A duty my hangdog brother refused to fit himself for.*

"Is Merius as devoted to duty as you?"

"Why do you ask?"

Herrod looked at his feet. "The prince has tied my hands on this Marennese affair. I can only take a thousand men, not nearly enough."

"It's only a campaign against a few slave traders, Herrod, not a war."

"If we don't want it to become a war, we need archers and swordsmen. Merius is both."

I began to shake my head. "He's my only son. He's needed here."

"He wouldn't have to join the king's guard, just be a recruit for the length of the campaign."

"But . . ." I began, a sudden thought occurring to me. "Tell me honestly, Herrod," I continued finally. "How long will this campaign take?"

He shrugged. "With passage there and back, four or five months. His Majesty wants us to daunt the slave traders, not conquer the whole SerVerin force."

Five months. A lot could happen in five months. In five months, a young man might lose his hunger for a wanton witch after tasting the bitter fruit of war. In five months, that same wanton witch, bored with waiting, might marry another. The one thing I was sure of is that I couldn't let on to Merius that I'd found out about Safire; he knew I'd be displeased and likely marry her on the spot just to spite me. Now, after Merius left on the campaign, I could reason with Safire. A girl opportunistic enough to risk her reputation and seduce a higher-ranking man into marriage could likely be persuaded to relinquish her hold on him. It just required the right kind of persuasion.

The only two problems I could foresee with this plan were if Merius refused Herrod's offer or married the hussy before he left. The first of these did not worry me, not with Merius's zeal for constantly challenging his own mettle. As for the second, Merius was reckless but honor-bound. To keep his honor, he had to have a career separate from mine before he could marry without my blessing. Therefore, he would not marry the Long Marsh wench until he had joined the king's guard or made some other bid for independence from me and his inheritance. Such as going off on a campaign without asking my leave.

I turned back to Herrod. "You have my permission to recruit him. The true test of a warrior is in battle, and Merius deserves that test. I have only one request: don't tell him that you spoke with me."

"Why?"

"I don't want him to think that his father is interfering in his affairs. Twenty is a proud age."

Herrod chuckled. "I remember twenty. I strutted around like a fighting cock, tensed to punch the first man who hinted that I had gotten my commission because my father was the commander and not because I'd earned it. You will not be mentioned, sir, not unless Merius mentions you himself."

I shook the hand he offered. "Thank you."

~ ~ ~ ~ ~

The door to Eden's chamber was slightly ajar. I knocked perfunctorily and pushed it open. She stood in front of her looking glass, smearing rouge on her face. Her eyes shifted in my direction briefly before she returned to her reflection.

I shut the door and leaned against it, my arms crossed. "You have the cheeks of a consumptive dock whore. Wipe it off, for God's sake."

She smiled, her gaze never leaving the mirror. "The king forbade us to wear our hair down, but he didn't say a thing about face paint."

"That's because he assumed women of breeding would have better sense."

"Prince Segar seems to like it."

"Royalty oft has a peculiar taste for the common. Just don't keep up the habit after you're through with him."

She gave an impatient shrug, putting the lid back on the rouge pot with a clatter. "Or he's through with me. You seem to forget that princes discard their mistresses, not the other way around."

"You're hardly his mistress, Eden, and thank God for it."

She looked at me oddly. "But I thought that's what you wanted--a royal mistress in the House of Landers. The influence the Landers could have through me . . ."

"Is exactly the kind of influence we don't want," I interrupted. "Having a royal mistress in the House is like having the most bountiful harvest in a fallow year. Everyone's jealous gaze would be fixed on the Landers, and some would try to seed our fields with salt. We never want to be the most favored at court--the most favored are the ones most likely to lose their heads when the winds of fortune shift. If he starts giving you jewels and having his minstrels write songs about you, I'll send you away to the Sarneth court. Do you understand?"

Eden nodded as she picked up a perfume bottle. "I suppose."

"I'd rather you'd never attracted his eye in the first place, but since you have, we might as well make use of it." I stepped forward and pulled out the letter she had given me yesterday. "Here, that reminds me. Put this back where you found it."

"Is it what I thought?"

"Yes, and worse. Our prince is bribing the poor Bishop for the secrets told him in confession."

Eden laughed. "I have no doubt he's learning much--about cheating for coppers and overindulging on watered wine. Who confesses to the Bishop but virtuous fools like Cyril?" She pulled the stopper out of the bottle and began to dab perfume on her bare shoulders and between her breasts.

The faint scent of roses filled the air. Rose water. I choked on the smell, remembering how Arilea would get up naked from our bed and go directly to the washstand where she kept a bottle of the stuff. She'd splash it all over her body before she put on her chemise. She had never worn any other scent. Every morning, I'd smell rose water first thing, even before my coffee. It had been all over my clothes, my skin, the sheets every time we lay together. Even now, years after I'd smashed the bottle and cursed her, my traitor body knew the fragrance and hardened to it, a mindless predator picking up the scent of his prey. I gagged and gripped the back of a chair. Arilea might as well have bathed in the stuff, the bitch. I had no doubt that her burial shroud still smelled of roses, her bones even . . . My hand over my mouth, I reached for the door knob.

Eden turned and stared. "What is it?"

"Only whores wear that scent," I managed as I dragged open the door. It slammed behind me. The sound reverberated down the corridor, followed by the faint, mocking echo of a woman's laughter.

Chapter Eleven--Safire

As the pale light of morning drifted through the room, I became aware that I was wonderfully warm, the first morning I had been warm in this drafty stone palace. I wiggled my toes, content. It felt like there were a hundred purring cats in bed with me. I stretched. Something scratchy rubbed against my side, a rough wool blanket perhaps. It reminded me of the blanket Dagmar had knitted for me when she was five and I was two, a knobby scrap of knotted yarn that I had insisted on sleeping with every night before it finally unraveled. Smiling at the memory, I nestled against the blanket, and it tightened its arms around me . . . my eyes flew open. Blankets didn't have arms.

I glanced down, realizing that I wore no clothes. A sinewy forearm, too large and hairy to be my own, lay across my middle. Merius . . . last night . . . what had we done?

Already, I could hear Dagmar's shrill voice. *Wanton, wicked girl, wanton, wicked girl*, it chanted over and over again gleefully. Father would disown me, perhaps try to force me into a convent. I'd be like that servant girl he'd sent away last year, the one whose belly had grown too large under her skirts, the one who had cried and screamed when Boltan had closed the gate behind her. I'd begged Father to let her come back, but all he would say, tight-lipped as Dagmar, was that I was too young to understand, that some sins could not be tolerated under the roof of a virtuous House.

Merius murmured something unintelligible, pulling me closer. Dreaming, I supposed. His hand moved over my nakedness, and I felt my skin flush. Even asleep, he knew how to touch me. Father and Dagmar would say he had seduced me, dishonored me. But it didn't feel like dishonor when he touched me. I brought his wandering hand to my mouth and kissed it. His skin was callused and warm, with the acid taste of ink from the faded stain on the outside of his palm. I had given him what I would never be able to give another man again, all for the feel of his hands on me. And I would do it again without a thought, despite Dagmar's voice in my head, Father's angry reproach. The waiting woman inside stirred, and suddenly everything but him seemed far away. Ring or no ring, honor or dishonor, I would let him have whatever he wanted of me.

"Safire," he said then, awake.

"Hmm?"

In answer, his mouth traveled up my neck and across my jaw, stopping only when he reached my lips.

"Merius . . ."

"Yes, sweetheart?" he murmured into the hollow of my shoulder, nipping playfully as he moved downwards.

My breath caught in my throat, and I gasped, "But what about breakfast?"

He chuckled. "My love, this is breakfast."

"We can't--it's light out. It's morning." *Late morning* I added silently, noticing how the sunlight reached halfway across the clothes-strewn floor.

"It's morning?" Merius propped himself up on his elbow and glanced around blearily, his hair sticking out in all directions.

I slid to the edge of the bed and put my feet on the cold stones. "Ughh," I shivered, pulling a blanket from the tangle of bedclothes and wrapping it around me.

He sat up. "I'm thinking that I could join the king's guard," he said suddenly. "Herrod promised me a commander's post in a year if I joined. We could marry in four months, when my training is over and I'm free to live where I want as long as I report for duty . . ."

"Marry?" I clenched my arms together, my eyes traveling over the heap of our entangled clothes, abandoned so hastily the night before and not thought of since. "You know, Father let all the good fields go with Dagmar's dowry. All that's left for my betrothal are the woods and fallow pastures. And our House couldn't get a council seat if Father stood on his head for a year. Your father will hardly see me as fit for your bedmate, much less your wife."

He toyed with the edge of the blanket halfway down my back, and I started at his touch. "Shh," he whispered. His finger traced my spine all the way up my neck to the base of my hairline, where it stopped. Then he buried his hand in my hair. I arched my neck and closed my eyes, dowries forgotten. He stroked my scalp until I was limp against him, and his arms went around me. I sighed, resting my head on his chest.

"It wouldn't be what you're used to, I know--what either of us is used to, actually," he began, his voice rumbling in my ear. "I would be sacrificing my offices and lands, and the rewards are small, at least the first several years until I've proven my loyalty. We'd have to take rooms in the city at first, maybe hire one servant for the cooking and mending . . ."

"I can cook," I said.

"I doubt it'll come to that, sweetheart, but we'll have to mind our coin, at least until I get a commander's post."

"I can mend too. But Merius, I won't hold you to last night."

He grew still. "You don't want to marry me?" he said softly.

"Of course I do. But not if it means you give up everything. Your position . . . You can't sacrifice that for me . . ."

"Sacrifice what? An inheritance I've never wanted? A dull life writing endless treatises and letters and playing toady to the king? The constant headaches of managing an estate? Safire, I don't want to become like my father--do you know he was a decorated commander in the king's guard? He could have led men into battle, yet here he is, withering away in a councilor's position."

"What happened?"

Merius shrugged. "I don't know. Something with his brother Gaven who died before I was born. The point is, I wouldn't be sacrificing anything. You'll be the one who's giving up the life you were born to. But I swear that it won't always be rented rooms and salted fish five days a week."

"Merius, I've never even had a lady's maid--I'm used to doing for myself." Then I covered my mouth with my hand, realizing what

I had just said. Of course, I had betrayed far worse last night with that comment about Peregrine and the ten thousand silvers. Dagmar and I had promised each other we would never discuss Father's debts with anyone, especially at court, and here I had let slip more to this man than to my confessor. "I shouldn't have said that . . ."

"Why not? If it's the truth . . ."

"It seems that being in your arms loosens my tongue."

"And other things," he said, lazily trailing his fingers over my breasts.

I tried to ignore him, though my cheeks grew hot. "I could sell my drawings for extra coin."

"Does that mean you accept?"

"Accept what?"

He chuckled. "My proposal, love."

"I gave you my maidenhead. What do you think?"

He leaned over and kissed my forehead. Then he kissed my lips, coaxing them apart only when my fingers tightened in his hair. "Such an innocent," he muttered finally. "How can you love me, Safire?"

"How can I not?" I retorted, swallowing. "And I'm not an innocent, Merius. No one is."

He looked down at me, his eyes dark. "You shouldn't marry me--I've had poor teachers. I'll be good to you, but I'll likely not be good for you."

"Things that are good for one are usually tiresome," I giggled. "Now, let me up--I need my clothes."

I eased out of his arms and sat up, wincing at the cold floor. It was only after I'd padded around the foot of the bed that I remembered I was naked. My dress and undergarments lay in front of the hearth, sunlight gleaming over the satin. I sensed his eyes on me and could feel the blush already warming my skin. No wonder he thought I was such an innocent. I deliberately took a long time to find my shift, turning this way and that as I pulled it over my shoulders and laced up the front. Then I raised my head and met his gaze. The skin stretched tight across the bones of his face, his mouth drawn into a narrow line. His eyes glittered, unblinking as we stared at each other. Slowly, I began to play with the laces, tugging at the ends. He leaned forward on the bed as I teased out the knot. The laces slithered through their holes, and the bodice of the shift fell open. I smiled, making sure he got the full view as I bent down and shook the wrinkled shadows out of my dress.

"You little vixen," he said hoarsely as he settled back on the bed.

"Do you still think me an innocent?" I laughed as I tightened the laces again and bit into one of the pears he had brought last night.

He didn't answer, standing up and stretching before he came around the bed. "Here, toss me a mango, sweet. I'm starved."

I obliged readily, pretending not to watch him as he leaned against the wardrobe, pulled a dagger seemingly from nowhere, and began to pare slices from the mango, all the while not wearing a stitch. He had trained as a swordsman and hunter since he was a boy, a lean, dangerous weapon of a man, sharp as a blade with that silver aura gleaming all around him. And those hands . . . He glanced up then and took a bite of mango.

"Caught you looking," he said, grinning.

I swallowed the last of the pear. "Ass."

"Nothing wrong with looking. There's no need to blush, sweet."

"But . . ."

"Shh." He popped a mango slice in my mouth, silencing me. "Do you know what I'd like to do?"

"What?"

"I'd like to spend all day in bed with you, showing you just how innocent you are."

"Do you know what I'd like to do?"

"What?"

"I'd like to draw your hands."

He glanced at them, spreading out his long fingers. "Why?" he asked finally.

I thought a moment and then smiled. "Because your hands can hold a sword or a pen or a woman with equal skill. There are men who can do one or maybe two, but all three? You're a rare catch indeed, my love."

~ ~ ~ ~ ~

I hummed a half-forgotten ballad as I walked along the hall from my chamber to the staircase, filling in the parts I couldn't remember with a made-up tune of my own. My humming echoed off the stones of the walls and floor and the vaulted ceiling and came back as a separate sound from me, not my commonplace, sometimes flat singing voice, but a far richer, more mysterious sound, a fey elf-maid summoning her love in a faraway woods perhaps. I gave a little skip and laughed at my own silliness. Everything seemed so different this morning. Even the flagstone floors, dull last night, gleamed in the sunlight as if someone had strewn minute diamonds over the surface.

"She waited for him in the wood bower/Clad in a gown of vines, leaves, and flowers," I sang as I started down the staircase, making up my own words to fit the visions in my head. I'd have to draw this scene later with my charcoals, the fair elf maid and her verdant gown. "The light and shadows glowed green around her/She sang with the birds . . ." I trailed off, hearing heavy footfalls several landings below me. A man in boots, probably. The footfalls grew louder as he ascended, and a vague darkness dulled my joy like dust settling on glass. I almost turned around, then stopped myself. *Ninny--why should you turn around? You don't even know who it is.* So I continued down the steps, resuming my song with a loud defiance. Even though I had told myself I didn't know who it was, I felt no surprise when Peregrine rounded the corner of the landing directly below me.

We both stopped, looked at each other for a moment before I averted my gaze from him and started down the steps again. My hum grew louder in my ears the harder I concentrated on ignoring him. He wouldn't dare stop me here, not on this stairway that everyone used. He didn't have the nerve. The ambergris scent of his aura reached out to me, barely noticeable under his cologne. I kept humming. As far as I was concerned, the swine wasn't there. He wasn't worth my notice.

He made no move to block my passage, but instead waited until I was almost past him before he reached out and grabbed my arm with lightning speed. *He has a swordsman's reflexes, like Merius* was my first thought.

"I missed you at dinner last night, pet," he said.

I opened my mouth to yell for help, but before I could utter a sound, he clapped his hand over my lips. "Shh, I just want to talk to you." I shook my head violently and tried to wrench myself away, but his grip only tightened. Why had I been such a stubborn fool? I should have fled the instant I saw him. "Now, I'm going to take my hand from your mouth, and if you scream, so be it. Since the last thing I want to do is harm you, you'll look like a hysterical woman and give the gossips plenty to wag their heads about. Safire, you don't need more attention drawn to you--there are already whispers here of your peculiar habits, your father's debts."

I swallowed. No, I wouldn't scream--I was too desperate to breathe. His hand over my mouth forced me to inhale through my nose, breathe in his cologne. When he finally took his hand away, I gasped for air and glared at him. "The only rumors of me here are the ones you've started, you foul swine."

He grinned with perfect teeth, his amusement rendering my rage impotent. "Now why would I spread rumors about my future wife?"

"Because you're a scoundrel. Your attempts to coerce me into your bed would be comical if they weren't so pathetic."

His amusement tightened, his grip painful on my arm. "Force my hand, sweet, and you'll regret your pride tenfold. I'm not an easy man when thwarted," he said.

"And I'm not an easy woman when forced."

"Safire, what kind of man do you take me for? I would never force myself on a woman. All I've done is woo you the way you wanted . . ."

"This is what you call wooing? Accosting me in the stairwell? Threatening me with my father's debts to you?"

He flicked his tongue over his teeth, staring down at me like a snake sizing up its prey. "I'd woo you properly, if that's what you wanted. You've made it obvious, though, that proper behavior would get me nowhere with you."

"That's because I know proper behavior from you would be a lie."

He grinned again. "You think you know me so well, but I

don't know how you can, when you run from me every chance you get. I saw how you grabbed Merius at the dance the other night, just to get out of my sight."

I opened my mouth, hot words trembling on my tongue about Merius, that Peregrine had had nothing to do with me dancing with Merius, that I would have grabbed Merius and pulled him into the dance just because he was Merius and I loved him, not because I wanted to escape Peregrine. But then I realized what I was about to say. The last thing I wanted was for Peregrine to find out about Merius. They would duel, and if Merius got hurt . . . I swallowed. "You've been watching me?" I managed finally.

"Of course. I look out for you, Safire. I watch you far more than you realize. One day, pet, we'll meet each other far away from here, away from your father's House, away from so-called civilized society. Then you'll see what kind of man I really am." A couple landings below, a door creaked open, and someone started up the steps. Peregrine immediately dropped my arm, his lips branding my temple in a kiss so quick I didn't realize what he was doing before it was over. I raised my hand to slap him, but he was already several steps up from me as if nothing had happened. I shuddered and hugged myself, then hurried the rest of the way to the baths, faint ambergris still clinging to my skin and hair.

~ ~ ~ ~ ~

Steam swirled around me as the maid added more water to the bath, and I leaned against the edge of the marble pool, inhaling deeply. I took advantage of this luxury every day that I was at court, staying in the hot water and scented bubbles until my fingers puckered. We had baths at home, but the water cooled too fast in the battered copper tub, the grainy ash soap stung the skin, and I never had the chance to soak as long as I wanted.

I closed my eyes, hearing the swish of the oilcloth curtain as the maid left my bath stall. There was a common pool on the women's side of the palace baths, but King Arian had forbidden its use, seeing it as an incentive to fornication and other fleshly sins. *Silly king* I thought drowsily. My mind wandered in a state half-asleep. Odd word, fornication. Odd and ugly-sounding. I supposed that was what Merius and I had done, though it had felt the most natural thing in the world when he had whispered my name and taken me to his bed. Shouldn't sin have felt unnatural?

The curtain snapped open with a clatter of metal rings. "There you are," Dagmar exclaimed.

My eyes flew open. "Oh no." When I had returned to our chambers over an hour ago, she had been out, and I had left as quickly as I could, not wishing to be there for her return.

"Where have you been?" she whispered fiercely, closing the curtain and standing before it, her arms crossed.

"I'm sorry. I know I worried you . . ."

"I know you weren't in your bed last night. Don't even think of lying to me, telling me you came in late and left early," she continued when I tried to speak again. "I looked this morning before the maids came. The bed was as neat as the night before, not even a wrinkle in the pillow. I know you couldn't have made it up so well, even if you wanted to."

"I wasn't going to lie to you," I said, indignant myself now. "How dare you assume what I'm going to do before I've even the chance to do it?"

"Because you lie to Father all the time."

"What?" I gasped.

"Don't you think I know you've been selling those wicked drawings of yours like some common wench? When you go on your afternoon ride with full saddlebags and return with clinking pockets?"

I shrank in the bath water, embarrassed that I had revealed myself. And here I thought I had been so clever. "Why haven't you told him?"

"Because it would kill him."

"You're right, but we need the coin, Dagmar. I've been tipping the servants with it because Father didn't give us enough."

"That's not true! He gave us plenty. He may be in debt, but . . . how dare you . . ."

"You only think that because you've been using my share as well as yours."

"Don't justify your wickedness with our misfortunes," she sniffed. "Just because we're sparrow nobility doesn't mean you should besmirch the family name with common trade."

"If Peregrine had given me that coin instead of me selling my drawings for it, you wouldn't mind. Somehow it's more honorable to be a rich merchant's whore than to earn an honest living like those women in the market square?"

"Safire!"

"Father was going to sell me to Peregrine, to that lustful toad, all to settle a debt. I'm sorry I lied, but I'm not sorry I sold those drawings. And I'm not sorry about last night, either, except for the fact that I worried you. I shouldn't have done that." I stood up, the suddenly cold water running off my body, took my robe from the hook on the wall beside the pool, and pulled the warm flannel around my shoulders.

"Where were you anyway?"

I looked straight at her, unblinking. "With a man. Does that sound like a lie?"

At that moment the maid returned with more water. Dagmar snatched the curtain from her and closed it in her face. I grabbed the curtain from Dagmar long enough to hand the startled girl a silver coin from my robe pocket. "That'll be all, thank you." Then I snapped the curtain shut again and turned to face Dagmar.

"Did you give her a whole silver . . ."

"Oh shut up--it's my coin. I'll do what I like with it."

"And how can you jest me like that? A man . . ."

"It's not a jest, sister."

She sank against the marble edge of the pool, staring at me. "Oh no, Safire. Safire, no. But how?"

Discomfited that she didn't immediately start yelling, I began to pace. "The usual way, I suppose. Or maybe not the usual way, I don't know. Mother never told us it was like this. She told us it was a sin, and maybe it is. I don't know anymore. All I know is that I love him, and that he loves me. He wants to marry me, Dagmar."

"That's what they all say."

"How do you know what they all say? Have you ever been seduced?"

"How can you be flippant?" she countered. "This could ruin everything for you, for us, and you . . . Who is he, anyway?"

I took a deep breath. "Merius of Landers."

"A highborn man did this to you? He should have more honor . . ."

"We did it together. It's no more his sin than it is mine."

"I heard he was wild, but I had no idea he'd be so dishonorable to seduce an innocent girl," she continued, not seeming to hear me. "This is my fault--I should have kept a better eye on you. Oh, Safire, how could you be so wicked?"

I thought of Merius's hands, the smells of leather and pipe smoke and fresh air that hung around him, the velvet depth of his voice reciting poetry, his crackling silver aura, the laugh crinkles around his eyes, the easy way he carried a sword at his hip, his gently inexorable conquest over all my good intentions.

I tried to hide my grin. "Wickedness comes far more sweetly than you can imagine."

"And Father! How could you do this to him?"

"Father would have sacrificed my virtue for Bara's gold," I said shortly. "It's gone to a worthier cause."

"Fornication is a worthier cause?" she snorted. "At least Bara would have married you first."

I leaned down and splashed her with water from the bath. It hit her straight in the face, and she sputtered. "Safire . . . I'm writing to Father. This afternoon."

I lifted my chin. "You do what you have to do." Then, without another word, I turned on my heel and left the baths. Merius and I were meeting in an hour, and I didn't want to be late.

Chapter Twelve--Merius

Council finally ended with the crackling of fine parchment. The king's scribe sprinkled sand on the official offer of aid to Marenna and blotted up the excess ink before handing it to Prince Segar. He perused the sheet and affixed the royal seal to the bottom as Father, Cyril, and the other provincial ministers lined up around the table to sign it. Stuffing my notes together in an untidy heap, I bolted from my seat. *If I turn in my commission this afternoon, this will be the last council I'll ever have to attend.*

"Merius," someone called behind me as I left the chamber.

I turned around, swearing under my breath. Safire was waiting for me up on the parapet with lunch. "Yes, sir?" I said aloud as Herrod trudged up. It had always amazed me, his skill with a blade--he seemed too heavy on his feet to maneuver quickly. Of course, as Father had tried to teach me, speed wasn't everything, and haste could kill.

"Do you have a moment?"

Still swearing under my breath, I followed him to a quiet alcove just off the hall, a place where court cohorts often met before or after council to plot. "Merius," he began gruffly, scratching his head, "I've an offer for you."

"What sort of offer, sir?"

"Well, you've been at the councils, so you know I have to round up a thousand men for this little Marennese expedition. Too risky to take only king's guard--it wouldn't leave enough men here if His Majesty needs them suddenly. But all the same, I need good men, trained men to send--this is no lark for summer warriors. The terrain's rough there, rocks and mountains and canyons. Men are going to be spread thin, and they'll have to be both good archers and swordsmen. Now, your father trained you at arms, which means you're already fit for a commander's post."

"Commander's post?" I repeated, bemused.

He nodded. "I've watched you in practice. Of course, practice doesn't always show a man's true mettle, but I've heard things as well."

"What things?"

"Well, those horse thieves a few weeks ago, for one. Magistrate Lemara's my uncle, you know. He told me how you brought them in. A tidy job, that. You have Mordric's mettle, just what we need."

~ ~ ~ ~ ~

The wind tore at my cloak as the parapet door slammed shut behind me. I blinked, blinded for a moment in the bright sun. The light had a hard glitter to it up here, particularly in the winter and early spring. I inhaled as another gust swept up from the river far below, carrying the smell of brine from the harbor.

Safire sat on the riverside wall, her feet dangling over the narrow walkway. Clouds raced across the sky behind her. When she saw me, she smiled and brushed the edge of her cloak hood behind her ear. A few tendrils of her hair escaped the confines of the hood, dancing in the wind. The ring I had bought for her yesterday burned in my pocket. I had meant to present it to her last night, but her sister had found us in the library and given us a tongue lashing before I'd had the chance.

Safire jumped off the wall, landing with a billowing of skirts. "You're too late for a kiss."

"You'll kiss me soon enough. Hear my news." I loosened her cloak and pushed the hood back to free her hair. It whipped in the wind, a fiery flag. "There," I said, satisfied. "Ah, leave it loose for me."

"It'll be all snarls," she protested as she gathered it back under the cloak hood. "Now, what's your news?"

I told her of Herrod's offer. "And he says when I return, he'll have a commander's post for me," I finished.

"And how long will this campaign take?"

"Five months. At the most," I quickly amended at her expression.

"Five months?" she repeated faintly. "Oh, Merius."

"Our fighting there could help end the slave trade, sweet. And it's a great honor, Herrod asking me personally like that. And offering me a commander's post. I've never even trained with the king's guard, Safire, just my father . . ."

"I know, dear heart." She put her hands on my shoulders. "Father's always said Herrod was tough as steel and expected no less from his men, and for him to ask you . . . But five months?"

"It's asking a lot of you to wait."

She drew away. "It's hard to meet you and to lose you so soon afterwards . . . the waiting is nothing. It's the worrying. Everyday I'll wonder if you've been hurt or killed or met some fetching Marennese miner's daughter."

"None of them have red hair. I don't think you need to worry." I pushed back her hood again and buried my face in her curls.

"Can I come with you? I could do laundry and cook and bandage. What?" she continued when I chuckled. "Don't camps need washerwomen?"

"They usually do more than the laundry. They're known for keeping things starched."

Her face grew hot against my neck. "You're a rogue. I'd just do your laundry, no one else's."

"Oh, sweet, even if you could come, it'd be too dangerous. If it was a full-fledged war, we might have camp followers. But we'll be moving too fast for that. We won't have fresh food, much less fresh laundry. Or starch."

"Stop it. I really won't kiss you now."

I grabbed her and pressed my mouth to hers before she could dodge it. "Now, where's lunch?"

She pointed at a small basket near the door. We settled on the wall, the basket between us. There was cold pheasant, yellow cheese, bread, and some more of those damned pears, going soft now but still fine to eat. She pulled a bottle of spiced cider from her cloak pocket, and we passed it back and forth, the cinnamon warm on my tongue. When I'd finished, I drew my feet up on the wall, watching idly as she tossed her crusts to the river below, where the gulls swooped down and fought over them with harsh cries.

"I jumped off this parapet once," I said.

"Really?" Safire looked at the water roiling and churning against the rocks at the base of the wall. "How did you manage not to break your neck?"

"The water's deeper than it looks. And I did break my arm, but that was from hitting the wall."

"You hit the wall? It looks like a straight fall to the water."

"Well, I'd built this glider, you see, and I wanted to test it."

"A glider?"

"I got the idea from watching the wings of the hawks when we were out hunting." I tried to throw a loose stone over the opposite wall, but it glanced off the edge and disappeared in the river. "There's always a wind on this river--I thought if I hit the right air current, I could glide all the way to the harbor. So I went down to the docks and bought some old sail canvas and some wood and put it together. I had to hide the pieces under my bed so Father wouldn't confiscate it. Selwyn and Gerard came up here with me the day I tried to fly it. Well, I shouldn't say try to fly--it did fly. I just angled my dive a bit wrong, and next I knew, I'd crashed into the wall. My right arm gave this snap, and down I went. Of course, it was spring, and the river was freezing from the snow melt. It actually made my arm feel better for a bit, that cold water--numbed it, you know."

"I suppose." Safire shivered. "I'm surprised you didn't drown."

"The river widens out past the palace walls--I fetched up on a bit of shore and passed out. Next thing I remember is Father cursing. The court physician had told him my one arm might be shorter than the other, with how fast I was growing and where the break was."

She tipped her head sideways. "It doesn't look any shorter."

I held out my hands. "If it is, I can't tell. Hurt like hell--still does sometimes when it rains. But I wouldn't change it. Those few moments I was in the air were worth it, swooping down over the water just like a bird. The only other times I've felt anything close to that is when I've raced Shadowfoot down a straight stretch of road. My stomach dropped, and I lost all sense of physical limits. It's like your soul escapes your body, if just for an instant--you feel in the presence of God and free of sin, but not the way the priests talk about it. You know," I paused, stammering, "you know, it may sound odd, but it's the same way I've felt the last few days when we've been together. Free."

She grinned, coyly teasing. "So touching me is like praying for you? You'd make an odd sort of monk."

"You can mock me if you wish, but I'm serious, witch. You bring me outside of myself somehow, free me if only for that instant. Some of the great mystics have written that meditation and prayer can accomplish the same state, though it's taken them years of solitude on their knees to reach it. I wouldn't know, though, since I've never been much at praying."

"Me neither." Safire kicked her feet against the wall. "They used to rap me on the head in chapel for falling asleep. So, why didn't you build another glider?"

I shrugged. "Father and the court academy kept me too busy after that to experiment with it anymore. Besides, that was the spring I started noticing girls." My eyes ran over her--her black velvet cloak was too large, which only made her look smaller and paler and even more fey than usual.

"I would have noticed you," I said hoarsely.

"I doubt it. I was short and skinny and freckled. 'Course I still am, and you seem to be noticing me now." She shot me a quick glance under lowered lashes, not shy but questioning. I answered the question by knocking away the basket between us. It rolled on the walkway, its contents scattering.

The rocks were hard, the wind was cold, and it was broad daylight, but neither of us cared. At some point after her cloak fell in the river, we found ourselves on the walkway between the parapet walls, protected from the wind and prying eyes. This was only a brief observation on my part before I returned to the far more interesting business at hand, namely navigating the intricate fastenings and stubborn knots of her undergarments. Her shift ripped as passion overcame patience.

"It's all right," she gasped, one hand clenching against my bare shoulder, the other tugging at my belt. "Just rip it, Merius."

I guided her fingers over my belt buckle. "Unfortunately, you can't rip leather and brass. Here."

Her giggle deepened to a chortle as I kissed a path down her neck and into the hollow at the base of her throat. I ran my hands under the loose edges of her frock and cupped the undersides of her breasts, her flesh sweet-smelling and smooth as a flower petal warmed in the sunlight. She chortled again as my thumbs found the buds of her nipples. The chortling started deep in her throat, the gathered sound of her entire body trembling at my touch, the blood rushing in answer to the quickened rhythm of her heart, the vibration in her bones as she arched into the curve of my hand. Her very skin hummed under my lips. She was a bird caught in my hands, soft and warm and frail and alive, alive, alive . . . life herself, caught in my hands, her wings ready to spread, ready to fly out over the river.

"Safire, take me with you," I muttered, my mouth moving over her breasts as my hands slipped lower, not even pretending patience with laces anymore.

"Merius." Her voice sounded like she'd been crying and couldn't catch her breath. "Hold on to me, love."

I gripped her, trapped her wildness in the cage of my arms, and hoped to God she never flew away from me, for how could I follow the wind? Her chortle became a moan, and I could feel her tremor with my whole body now that we lay so close together. Then I began to move, slowly at first. She rose to meet me, matching me in a dance so ancient it had no name. *Dance, love, dance, love, dance, winged, woman, winged, Safire, love, Safire, Safire, love Safire* the words drummed in my head.

We both cried out at the end, and I collapsed on the stone, my breath coming in rattling gasps as I clutched her. "Safire, Safire." I kissed her jaw, her cheek, anywhere I could reach.

"Look at the sky," she whispered. "It's so blue I can hardly look at it. Little dots start swimming in my eyes every time I try to focus."

I grinned. "The bishop would say you were going blind from

too much carnal pleasure."

She turned her head sharply. "Is that what this is?"

"What do you mean?" I twisted one red curl around my finger.

"I mean," she stammered. "I know there were other girls--you must have wanted them, I-loved them, to do what we just did. Was it the same with them?"

"You mean the way it is between us?" I asked. She nodded and hid her face against my chest. "No, sweet--how can you think that?"

"I don't know. I've never had any other man, and there's . . . well, there's still a lot I don't know."

I slid my hand under her chin and raised her head, forcing her to meet my gaze. "Do you want another man?"

"No, that's not what I meant." She jerked her chin out of my grasp. Her eyes flared. "I just said that . . ."

"Good, because then I'd have to go after him."

"You ass. I didn't even mean that." She sat up and dragged my cloak around her body, her back to me. Then, after a long moment, she glanced over her shoulder, her brows drawn together. "You'd go after him? Really?"

"No. Though the thought of you with someone else makes me ill, so I might punch him once or twice to appease myself. Then I'd let you go gracefully and die of a broken heart."

She snorted. "A broken heart? You? Half the ladies-in-waiting follow you around--you'd have someone else in a week. I'd be the one who would pine."

"God didn't make you for pining, no more than he made you to stay a virgin."

"Merius!"

I grabbed her and pressed my mouth down on hers. It only took an instant for her lips to go pliant under mine and her hand to start creeping around my neck. "See what I mean?" I said with difficulty some moments later. "God made you to kiss me."

"Just kissing?" she teased as my hands began to stray.

"You witch." I straightened, reaching for my shirt. "You know those other girls?"

"What about them?" She fiddled with a knot in her bodice laces, not looking at me.

"They were just practice, sweetheart."

Her eyes flicked up, then dropped down again. "Then I say you've been doing a lot of practicing, sir." She jerked out the knot.

"No amount of practice could have prepared me for you. Impossible wench. Here." I tossed her the small silken pouch from my trousers pocket, catching both her and myself off guard.

She caught the pouch, turning it in her hand before she met my gaze.

"Go on. Open it. I was going to give it to you last night, but ..." The words stuck in my dry throat, and all I could do was watch her as she pulled the drawstrings of the pouch, and the ring fell out on her palm. Although I had already asked her and she had already accepted, they were but words spoken in the warmth of my bed, where there was just the two of us and the rest of the world seemed far away. Now, we were up here in the cold wind, the whole palace and city and sky spread out before us, and my offer to her, so perfect a few days ago, dwindled to the naive wooing of a man with more passion than sense. Without my inheritance or offices, what did I have to offer her? When she could have the likes of Bara and endless bags of coin at her disposal? My gut clenched, a giant fist. She just kept staring at the ring, not saying anything.

"I should have gotten a ruby," I said finally, "but I never see you wear them, and I didn't think you'd want the traditional linked circles. You said you liked pearls, so I started with that in mind. You'd not believe it, but it took me half a day to find that ..."

"I'd believe it. It's unusual." She turned the ring in her fingers, holding it up to the sun. "What's this stone, this green one?"

"That's a peridot. They're hard to find here, more common in Sarneth or Marenna." I paused. "When I first met you, I thought your eyes were the exact green of peridots."

"The way the gold swirls--it's like a river, the pearls floating in it. It's beautiful."

"Aren't you going to put it on?"

She held out her hand, and her eyes met mine shyly. "You put it on me, my love. That way it'll never come off."

Both of us trembled as I slid the ring on her finger. Taking her hand, I brought it to my lips. "It's yours. For as long as you want it."

She threw her arms around me, her head coming to rest on my chest. "Your heart's pounding like you ran a long way."

"It's your fault. It seemed like you stared at that ring for hours--I was almost certain you were going to say no." I draped my cloak around her. "You're shivering. I'll buy you another cloak tomorrow."

"I would have said yes right away, but my tongue seized up. I was beginning to wonder if I'd ever be able to talk again."

I held her close, remembered how I'd fancied she had wings earlier when we lay together. Yes, I'd tumbled girls, and it shamed me suddenly to admit to her that I had. Men weren't supposed to feel ashamed of tumbling, but I felt shame now, a dark, inky weight in my gut like I'd betrayed her before I even knew her. "If I had known what it would be like with you, I . . ." I trailed off, stammering. What was I trying to say? I couldn't express it in words, an unusual thing for me, and I wondered if I should try to say it at all. Likely it was one of those mysterious things best left unsaid. I had the uncomfortable feeling that Father could see me, that he would call me a fool. Certainly he had never been ashamed of tumbling women. Maybe he should have been. Maybe he should have taught me differently. Maybe then I would have wooed Safire properly instead of stumbling blindly into love.

"What is it, Merius?"

"It could be six months before I return," I whispered into her hair. "Promise me you'll wait for me."

"Merius, I just took your ring and said yes. I just promised to wait for you far longer than six months."

"I know, but-"

"But what?"

I exhaled, the sour air burning me inside. "There are so many things that could happen between now and then. What if your father finds out what I've done?"

"What we've done, you mean."

"Safire, I never should have thought to touch you, an

innocent maid . . . well, I mean, I couldn't help thinking about it. I'm always thinking about it. But I shouldn't have acted on those thoughts. Your father might deny us permission to marry when he finds out."

"We don't need his permission."

"I've been a dishonorable fool . . ."

Her hands curled into fists on my chest. "Just stop it. As far as I'm concerned, we married the other night in your chamber, no matter what our fathers say or the church says or anyone else says. You haven't dishonored me or yourself--I've never felt more loved than I have these last few days with you, in your arms. How can that be a dishonor?"

"I know that, but others won't understand it that way."

"So what?"

"So what? I'm leaving you for months. God, I hate to think of it. What if your father casts you out on the streets? My father would, if you were his daughter. You'd be with no coin, no recourse . . ."

She turned on me. "You don't think I can take care of myself, if that happens?"

"I didn't say that. It's just that . . ." I looked her over, head to toe. Even her own cloak had been too roomy for her--mine trailed behind her like a train, draping off her narrow shoulders in long folds of gray wool. Her wild hair, finally loose, frizzed around her flushed face like an unkempt halo. She had the smallest hands of any woman I knew--my ring looked huge on her finger.

"I can't bear to think of you on the docks by yourself. Hell, I can hardly bear to think of you here with just your sister to help you. In fact, don't go out alone anywhere--take Boltan. There's a lot of Peregrines in the world, Safire, and several months is a long time to leave someone who's honest as the sky . . ."

"What?"

"It's just a phrase. It's from an old poem my mother used to read to me. When the sky's cloudy, it rains. When the sky is clear, the sun shines. There's no difference between its mood and the face it shows the world. You're like that, innocent in your honesty . . . there's just no guile in you. You need someone . . ." I trailed off as she sighed and turned back to face the riverside wall, gazing down at her clasped hands.

"To watch over me--is that what you were going to say? You're just like my father, my sister. All of you will trip and fall, watching me instead of watching where you're going." Her tartness left as suddenly as it had come, and she sighed again. "Who's going to watch over you, Merius, while you're so far away fighting?"

I cradled her shoulders in my hands. "As long as I know you're safe, I'll be fine." I kissed the top of her head. "I know you can take care of yourself, sweet. I just don't want you to go through any hardship over this."

She bit her lip. "Aside from pining for you, I'll be fine. Now kiss me again, you wicked seducer. I'd much rather wallow in your kisses than in your guilt."

~ ~ ~ ~ ~

The salon rang with the sounds of the king's guard in practice. The baize-lined door whispered shut behind me, and I paused, watching the masked men lunge at each other in ever tightening circles. Most had their House's insignia sewn on their dueling doublets. Demitri of Somners had a fine form but little precision, Sir Jerall of Falance had a fondness for a lower feints that would get him into trouble, Ragner of Sullay often let anger cloud his senses . . . Father's voice went on and on in my head. I usually managed to ignore this invasive echo, but the practice salon was one of the few places I had gained his grudging approval.

Ragner suddenly swore loudly and charged at his opponent. The man met him with a solid parry. Ragner's sword hit the floor with a clatter as the man disarmed him with a dizzying spin of silver that reminded me of Father. It was a move he had taught me, a lunge and a quick swing of the wrist after a parry. The man lifted off his screened mask then, and I realized why he had known my father's disarming lunge so well.

"Gerard?"

His red face broke into a grin. "Merius?"

"What are you doing at court?"

"I've joined the king's guard." He saluted his fellow guardsmen with a flourish of his blade before he turned from them.

They resumed practice, their weapons clattering, Ragner falling in opposite of Sir Jerall. Gerard wiped his sleeve over his sweaty forehead and set his sword on the master-at-arm's table.

"I see you still remember my lessons with the sticks."

He chuckled. "Yes, they've stood me well the last ten years."

"For learning with a birch switch, you did fair enough by my father's move."

"Fairer than some." He nodded in Ragner's direction.

"Most could do fairer than that."

His brows lowered. "Why don't you take a few turns on the practice floor, Landers?"

"I don't want to tax anyone. They need their strength for Marenna."

He punched my arm. "Ass. I hear you're off on that little expedition."

"They need someone with cunning and skill in the party."

"That's why Herrod picked me."

"Good God, you too?" I clapped him on the shoulder. "When do you sail?"

"In a few days, on the *Stalwart*."

"We'll be sailing together then."

"I'll be bound--that means we'll be fighting together." He lowered his voice. "I'm bringing my cards, some coin. I know gambling's forbidden by the guard and king, but . . ."

"Half of the guard tip their wages with loaded dice on the sly, and the other half use five-ace decks."

"Will they take Cormalen gold in a Marennese tavern? Do they even have taverns there?"

"Miners drink, same as we do."

"What about wenches?"

"They get more Marennese from somewhere."

Gerard was whispering by this point. "I hear they mine them."

"What, the women?"

"I hear there's this cave where they carve the women out of marble, and when they kiss the stone, the women turn to flesh. They have rubies for eyes, rocks for tits, and they can turn back to stone when you're tumbling them. They've found men dead, stuck in stone women."

"Then I suggest you take a hammer and chisel."

He guffawed. "It's a strange land, to be sure, but I don't suppose that bit's true. It's probably some lie they invented to keep foreigners away from their women."

"So, when did you join?" I gestured towards the dueling pairs. "Couldn't have been more than a week or two ago, whenever it was we tracked those horse thieves."

"Well, you know Herrod mentioned the king's guard to me a few years ago, when we left the academy. Casian's but a minor House, and for a younger son like me, the king's guard is one of the few places I can distinguish myself."

"There's always the priesthood."

"Now, Landers, I'm no more fit to pray than you are. Listen, I should get back to practice--the old windbag looks on the verge of bursting." The old windbag referred to Sir Jerall, whose arms training involved many lectures about the golden age of Cormalen warriors, a period some thirty years hence when Jerall had been a young king's guard. Grim looks and sharp words often accompanied these lectures as Jerall surveyed his students, whom he obviously considered unfit heirs for their fathers' swords. He was eyeing Gerard now with quivering jowls, sweat pouring down his round face as he blocked Ragner's blade perfunctorily.

"He wants a break."

"He needs a break, you mean." Gerard picked up his sword. "He can only fight for five minutes at a time before he drops like a stone." He bounded back to practice and gave Sir Jerall a brusque salute before he took the older man's place.

I continued to the alcoves at the far end of the salon, where there were shelves of waxes and oils and polishing rags as well as whetstones of various sizes. I selected the finest grained of these. My sword and dagger needed little sharpening, and a coarse grain could knick the edge. The blade slid over the stone, the metallic whisper of approaching battle. When the sword sliced a piece of parchment neatly in two, I laid aside the stone and found a soft cloth. The smells of warm oil and steel filled the air, a pleasant combination. I rubbed the blade in a slow circular motion, enjoying the thin yet solid feel of the sword in my hands, the easy, natural way I held it. Then Father stepped into my light, and I started, almost upsetting the bottle of oil.

"You rushed out of council. One would have thought there were fleas in your boots," he said, his hands behind his back.

I corked the oil and stood as I sheathed my sword. "I had an engagement."

"With Herrod? I saw him stop you."

"You could say that." I drew my dagger and picked up the whetstone.

"What could he want with you?"

I began to sharpen the dagger, staring at the way the silver gleamed icily against the black stone. "He asked me to volunteer for the Marennese campaign."

"Tinker's whoreson," he muttered.

I tested the blade. I didn't feel the edge until several drops of blood welled up from my thumb tip. "I accepted, Father."

He didn't move. He looked, his eyes measuring me in a close, calculating way that he usually reserved for his most difficult opponents. "You know what this means, Merius."

"Yes, sir."

"Your inheritance, my offices--gone."

"Good."

"Ingrate," he spat. "You'll regret it."

I shrugged, running the dagger over the whetstone again even though it was sharp enough. "Like you regretted leaving the king's guard?"

He froze again, and I knew I had hit a nerve. "My only regret is siring a headstrong fool," he said finally. "If only your mother hadn't miscarried my other heirs--she did it to spite me."

The bile rose inside--I could either punch him or retch or both. My hand coiled into a fist around the dagger hilt. "She miscarried because you were such a heartless blackguard. What kind of man threatens his wife when she's with child?"

His gaze narrowed. "Did she tell you that?"

"She didn't have to tell me. I know you, Father. You never

restrained your cruelty where she was concerned."

"Cruelty is the only way a sane man can respond when faced with a scheming harpy. She likely birthed dead children because her blood was pure acid."

"I lived, you bastard." I shoved the dagger in its scabbard.

"Well, you've a thick skull, as you so aptly demonstrated when you accepted Herrod. He's only using you to get back at me. He's wanted to damage the Landers position for years now, and he just broke the weakest link."

"I'd rather be his fool than yours."

Some indefinable emotion sparked in his eyes. "I reared you, trained you, made you what you are . . ."

"Which according to you isn't much, so you must have done a poor job." I turned from him and put the whetstone back on the shelf.

"No, Merius." His voice lowered, his tone less hard, almost conspiratorial. Familiar with his methods, I steeled myself--if he couldn't bully, he moved to subtler forms of coercion. "Listen, you're far from stupid, so stop being such a hothead and think about this. If I had wanted a different heir, after your mother died I would have remarried and sired other sons. I wouldn't have worked so hard at advancing the Landers position, only to leave it in the hands of a dolt or a toady or a milksop."

I gripped the top shelf just over my head and leaned into it, my feet braced solidly on the flagstones. "If I was still twelve and believed you, that might sway me. As it is, you can save your breath. I'm going on the campaign, Father."

"Go ahead. Go on the campaign. It may be good for you to have some fighting experience. It's helped me in my career."

I laughed, a brittle sound. "This isn't some adolescent rebellion. I'm not doing this to spite you. If you think that somehow your sudden approval will make the prospect less appealing to me and maybe I won't go, then you've overestimated your influence. I don't hate you that much." I reached in my pocket and pulled out my seal ring. "Here, take this."

He hesitated before he reached out and took the ring. There followed several moments of silence while I looked at my boots, waiting for him to leave. There was no one else in the practice salon--the king's guard had left a good fifteen minutes before, and the quiet stretched out, a dark presence between us. Not able to bear it much longer, I opened my mouth to say something, what I didn't know, when he suddenly spoke.

"It won't be like practice, all orchestrated and planned, where you can see your opponent's moves coming. They'll come at you from all sides, at any time, and some of them will know what they're doing. I say that because you've fought before, even killed a few, so you may think you know what you're getting into. You don't. I didn't. That highwayman you killed when you were eighteen--he didn't know what he was doing, anymore than that horse thief did a few weeks ago. They were untrained brigands, thieving because they thought they could subdue with a flash of metal and a few clumsy slashes. Some of the ones you meet the next few months will be like that, easy to kill. Some will be like you, trained since they could pick up a sword but not tested. And some will be battle-seasoned warriors. Those are the ones to watch. You've a way with a blade beyond mere training, but you're not a master. Live through the next few months, and you will be."

He turned then and left the salon. I watched him from under my arm, saw the way the slanted afternoon sunlight gleamed on the side buckles of his boots, the jeweled hilt of his rapier. His back taut, his footfalls quiet, he still walked like he was going to war, even though it had been a good twenty-five years since he'd been near a battlefield. A while ago, some fool had hired an assassin to kill him. The man had leapt out of an alley near the market, dead on Father's sword before he'd even hit the ground. There had been no more assassination attempts.

He was a fighter. A warrior who had never been able to put up his sword, a commander who had never ceased plotting strategy, a haunted soldier who had never stopped seeing the face of his enemy, even when that enemy was long dead and he was looking at his wife and child. Our battle of twenty years, the battle that had taken my mother, had just ended in a truce, and now I didn't know where to go next. I sank against the shelves, my head throbbing, and wished for Safire and her witch hands.

Chapter Thirteen--Mordric

I handed the reins to the Bara groom and dismounted as if I wore a rusty suit of armor. Ten years ago, I had ridden between court and Calcors, a day's ride, with few ill effects. Now even my teeth ached. My horse Hunter whickered and nudged my elbow, and I scratched his withers before the groom led him away. At one time black as soot, he was starting to look a little grizzled around the edges himself.

The door off the stable courtyard was almost as grand as the front door, with its shiny brass fittings and carved foreign wood. The last time I had been here, when Peregrine's father had still been alive, it had been like any other side door, made of stout, unadorned oak. Peregrine's black trade smuggling must be going well. He was still young, only a few summers older than Merius, and something of an arrogant dandy besides.

The liveried manservant who opened the door ushered me through a shadowy series of halls with whispered comments about the new paneling, the paintings, the sculptures, most of which could barely be seen in their sepulchral recesses.

"Does your master pay you to talk?" I asked the man finally when he paused for several moments to elaborate on the finer points of a silver fruit bowl.

His brow furrowed. "Well, not exactly, sir."

"Then please desist. I've had a long ride, and I'm more interested in your master's accounts than his fruit bowls."

We proceeded in silence up to the second floor and into Peregrine's study. The servant threw open a door beside the fireplace which led to a small room with a steaming pitcher, a basin, and several towels on a marble-topped table.

"Mistress Chenoa wishes you to refresh yourself," he said stiffly. "The master will be along presently." Peregrine's mother Chenoa was a generous, fine woman, a rarity of her sex.

I made good use of the hot water, splashing off the road dust. I found a comb under one of the towels and slicked back my hair. The door creaked, and I turned from the mirror. Chenoa of Bara stood there, her hands folded together decorously in front of her. Her graying tresses were pulled into a heavy knot at the nape of her slender neck, the way women had worn their hair when I was a cavalier. It had taken a true connoisseur of the weaker sex to undo one of those knots. One had to know just which pin to pull.

"Do you want any refreshment, Mordric?" she asked. "I'm afraid our doorkeeper has been remiss not to offer you anything." Her voice was low and mellow, her tone cool and cultured, like the voices of the best nurses when one had just been run through with an enemy sword. The perfect court wife, I had often thought--attractive without being seductive, intelligent without being opinionated, polite without being fawning. Merius might still have a mother if I had married a woman like this.

"Thank you for the pitcher and basin." I toweled the last drops of water off my face. "How do you fare, Chenoa?"

"Fine. And you? I heard," she hesitated. "I heard Merius joined the king's guard."

"Just for the length of the Marennese campaign." I loudly slapped the towel through the air before I hung it over the edge of the basin.

"You're good to spare him."

"He's good to spare himself, you mean."

She smiled. "It's hard when you only have one son, especially when he's strong-minded. Levan despaired of Peregrine many times, but he always redeemed himself in the end."

I bet so--the Bara inheritance would make redemption easy, even for a scoundrel like Peregrine. Of course, Merius's inheritance was more extensive than Peregrine's, once I counted the worth of my holdings, and Merius had refused it all in favor of adventure and some witch's fickle love. His seal ring was still in my pocket, an irksome weight. Irksome youth, with its frivolous passions, its conceit, its utter pig-headedness. Why couldn't heirs be born middle-aged and responsible? He'd return in six months, begging back the inheritance he'd so casually thrown away, and he'd manage it because he was young. If I shifted my position like that in the council chamber, I'd be accused of prevarication. I should make him marry as soon as possible when he returned from Marenna--that would settle him down. A suitable marriage could be a condition of getting back his inheritance.

"What of your daughters?" I asked Chenoa.

"Betrothed, all. Selena will wed midsummer."

That was out then. Probably a good thing--Peregrine had coin aplenty, but he could be denounced by the council if Cyril ever got his hands on one dirty ledger. No point in allying the Landers name with potential scandal. We had enough of our own.

"It'll be a lovely wedding," Chenoa continued. "In the Calcors cathedral, with plenty of roses and a velvet altar cloth embroidered in gold. We're having SerVerinese silk and pearls from the Sud Islands imported for the gown. I only hope my other girls' nuptials will be so fine."

"Hmm, well, they're of an age for marriage." It was an asinine remark, but what else could one say when women started talking about their daughters' weddings?

"Peregrine too. It's a shame the Landers haven't any daughters for him." She delicately refrained from mentioning Eden.

"If I had a daughter, he would be my first choice for her." Empty gallantry, that. If I had a daughter, I'd lock her away in a convent if Peregrine wanted to marry her.

"I keep telling him he could marry into a high noble House, but young men never listen to their mothers. He's been wooing a most unsuitable girl. Good, old family, a little poor, but there's no dishonor in that. It's the girl herself. An absolute hoyden, that one. She came here to dinner with her older sister and father a couple years ago. Her hair was uncombed, she knocked over her wine-- twice--and then she suggested that our library wasn't complete because we didn't have some poet. Sirach, I think. What business has a young girl reading that improper Sirach, anyway? And the older sister was so quiet and polite--knew just what to say to the servants, to everyone. If Peregrine had to pick some sparrow noblewoman, why couldn't he have picked the elder sister?"

"Because Selwyn did."

She recoiled. "Oh, I forgot about that. I apologize, Mordric--I never engage in idle gossip, but I could have sworn I didn't say their names . . ."

"You didn't say their names. Your description was apt enough."

"I shouldn't have been so uncharitable with Safire. Really, you should have stopped me. She lacks a mother's influence to calm her high spirits, poor thing."

"I'd say she lacks more than that." I wondered suddenly if Safire was a plot of her father's to bring down all the head Houses. The little vixen had almost brought down Merius, at any rate, and now she was starting on Peregrine.

"It's just that I can't let Peregrine make such a mistake. The wrong marriage can break a House, and Levan worked so hard building this one. Would you talk to him for me?"

"Who, Peregrine?"

She nodded. "He may listen to an older man, especially you. He respects your remarks at council, and I know you're prudent in these matters."

I was saved from comment by the sound of the study door. Peregrine appeared at the entrance of the side room. He acknowledged Chenoa with an incline of his head.

"Good evening, sir," he said.

"Good evening."

"I was just asking Mordric if he would stay to dinner," Chenoa supplied quickly. "Would you?"

"Thank you, but no. Our business here shouldn't take long."

We moved into the main room. Peregrine stood at the side of his desk until I sat in the leather-cushioned chair before it. Then he took his seat, pushing a ledger aside so he could prop his elbows on the desk.

"If you won't take dinner, would you accept any other

refreshment? Brandy perhaps?"

"No brandy, but if you have any whiskey, I'd be partial to that."

She brought a cut glass decanter from a side table with a tumbler to match and set them before me with a heavy clinking.

"Many thanks." I leaned forward and poured the liquor. "Anything else?"

"I'll call Geoff if we need anything else. Thank you, Mother." He dismissed her as he would a high-ranking servant.

Her skirts rustling, she left the room without a word, pulling the door quietly closed behind her. The mild scent of lavender lingered after her, and I almost wished I was staying to dinner. Peregrine sat for a moment or two in silence, his hands loosely joined in a triangle over his mouth as he watched me. I picked up the tumbler and sniffed the whiskey once before I quaffed it in a long swallow. It was fine, but not fine enough to warrant a king's office at court. Peregrine's ambitions were higher than his tastes.

"Has Merius sailed yet?" he asked finally.

"This morning."

"He's wise to go now. If my father were still here to run the House, I'd go on campaign."

"Ah, yes, duty excuses much."

He stiffened almost imperceptibly, an alert cur catching the faint scent of insult. "My duty to the name my father left me is my first priority."

"I only wish Merius's sense of duty was so strong, that he would smuggle and treat with robber princes to uphold the name of Landers."

"I beg your pardon?" His hands were clenched together under his mouth now, a double fist. Calmer than Merius when threatened, but still one of the angry ones. Good--I hated snivelers. I always worried about snivelers when I blackmailed them. If they broke down at a few carefully uttered words, then how could they manage to carry out my orders properly?

"Your father ran seven fleets of merchant ships and always had coin to spare, but he never brought a gold watch to council finer than the king's. Nor did he wear fresh linen on every hunt. You should be subtler, Peregrine."

He shrugged, though his hands were still clenched. "I've had an excellent season--no pirates, only one ship lost in a hurricane. If some are jealous of such fortune, let them be. But that hardly gives them the right to make unfounded accusations."

"I wouldn't say some are jealous--I would say many are jealous. And suspicious. All it would take is one turncoat cohort, one badly balanced ledger, and you could lose not only your duty bound name but your head as well."

"There are no cohorts and there are no ledgers. Why would there be? I've done nothing wrong. You speak of impossibilities."

He abruptly stood and went over to the side table, where he poured himself a tumbler of some amber liquor, likely sherry. He splashed it around in his glass, watching it swirl before he threw his head back and gulped it down.

"The gold watch, the fresh linen, Trident . . . see, I know how much you paid for Trident. I set the price myself, never expecting anyone but the king would be able to pay it. That was your first mistake--that horse was meant for the royal stables, yet I come home one day to find that Whitten had sold him to the son of a middling merchant. Don't misunderstand me--your father was a canny courtier, but he was too much of a gentleman for the dirty competition of shrewd trade. You, on the other hand, have a gambler's sensibility. Cannon powder in wine casks is a common enough ruse, so common the king's agents know to shake every cask to make certain it sloshes. If the casks slosh, they never open them for fear of ruining the wine, so they never find the false bottoms, the watertight compartments underneath stuffed with powder on the outbound voyages, jewels and ivory on the inbound ones. You started long before your father's death, didn't you? No one pulls off such clever simplicity without practice."

He set down the tumbler with a clank. "What hangdog whoreson has been talking?"

"That's my affair. All you need know is that it was difficult. You were careful enough, you see. You likely bought the powder for a generous amount, so generous an amount that your supplier wouldn't dream of betraying such a good customer, which he couldn't anyway since you use proxies. You haven't flooded the jewel or ivory markets. Just a sale here and there, with enough middlemen in between to make it almost impossible to trace it back to you. Your only mistake was boasting of your new-found wealth by buying and investing too much too quickly."

"Again, fodder for suspicion, nothing more. You can't prove any of this." He leaned against the side table, his arms crossed as he watched me.

"I don't want to prove it. Cyril does, and you're a fool if you think he'll stop where I did, once he's picked up on your trail."

"Why did you stop?"

I smiled. "You're in a highly useful position, Peregrine."

"So it's to be blackmail."

"Of a fashion, though you'll benefit more than you'll pay."

He raised his brows. "What are you getting at, sir?"

"If the council's to gamble with the SerVerin market, raise the wheat tariff and such, it would be a good idea to have an insider at Tetwar's court. Someone who could report back to the prince and not raise suspicion. Who but a black market merchant who maintains the mask of his family's legitimate House and name?"

"And how would this benefit me? I have a highly profitable connection with Tetwar that I don't want to jeopardize. They don't care for spies in the SerVerin court--the last one hung by his ankles in the palace courtyard until the vultures picked at his corpse."

"He was a fool, a mere diplomat in over his head. Selling secrets to the pirate Razere, who is a SerVerin slaver on the sly-- naturally he got caught. Of no use to Tetwar, except for his limited knowledge of clandestine treaties. You, on the other hand, know the ins and outs of trade between all the major principalities, who's in the black market, who's not, who can be bribed. All that in addition to the fact you've been a source of Tetwar's precious cannon powder. Even if he suspects you a spy, he'll likely leave you be for now."

Peregrine set his glass down. "In exchange for this little assignment, I expect full protection on the council. Make sure Cyril calls off his hounds, all of that. I assume that was the benefit you mentioned earlier."

"Naturally. We can hardly expect you to stay in Tetwar's

good graces without a pristine record on the council and the Cormalen market."

"What do you mean by we?"

"Prince Segar, of course. He's been rather interested in your activities. If not for my intervention, he might have listened to Cyril's suspicions and cast you off the council."

He turned and poured himself another measure of sherry, all his movements carefully constrained as if what I had just said had left him indifferent. "And why would you have intervened for me?"

"I know an opportunity when I see one. We can hardly expect Cormalen to prosper without a black market, without a few men willing to operate outside the bounds of the law. A saint's land soon becomes someone else's land."

"You could be describing yourself. At least I've never blackmailed anyone." He sat down again, watching me.

I shrugged. "I've never shirked from doing what I had to do to advance my House and my country. That said, you'll never find anyone who'll admit I've blackmailed or bribed them. Evidently, you're not so lucky in your comrades. Your trail was difficult to trace, Peregrine, not impossible. You can only use the same marked cards or weighted dice in so many games before someone else notices. I can only offer you protection as long as you comply."

He thought for a moment, drumming his tumbler on the desk. "Understood," he said finally.

I took a little more whiskey. When my throat felt pleasantly afire, I began to speak. "There is another matter."

"There is?"

I fingered the whiskey bottle again but pushed it away before I could pour anymore. It was ludicrous, offering paternal advice to a man I had just blackmailed. Why had Chenoa asked me? "Your mother is concerned about you making a suitable marriage."

"My mother worries too much." Peregrine propped his boots on the desk crosspiece and stared at the ceiling, bored. "I run this House, I can find a suitable wife. Did she ask you to talk to me?"

"The Long Marsh chit is far from suitable for a man in your position."

His boots abruptly hit the floor. "I beg your pardon? Selwyn is betrothed to Safire's sister Dagmar, is he not?"

"That's different. Selwyn isn't aiming for a career at court. Besides, I snagged all the decent Long Marsh lands in that betrothal agreement. There's nothing left but swamp and fallow fields for Safire's dowry."

"She doesn't need one."

"After a year of marriage and your firstborn son, that dowry and her name will be all that you value, and she has neither."

He shuffled a few papers around. "I appreciate the advice, sir, but it's really none of your affair."

"Of course. I only spoke of it because your mother asked me to." So he really was set on the wench, so set he had dismissed her pitiful dowry without a thought. Interesting. I expected such reckless behavior from Merius, but not from Peregrine. He had always struck me as the coldly practical sort, the sort who would choose a wife based on her name and dowry. It was a bit of information that might prove useful later, should I suddenly find that wench on my hands.

~ ~ ~ ~ ~

It was later that evening, and I was at the table in my study at Landers Hall, going over Selwyn's ledger for the last month. His notations were neat and orderly, his figures generally correct, but some of his abbreviations were confusing. What did "2 bush. red ap." mean? Two bushels of red apples, perhaps? But what did we need apples for? There should still be several bushels worth wrapped in rags in the cellar from last harvest. And if he had meant apples, what was a household item doing in our ledger of tenants' rents? In lieu of coin, tenants could pay with livestock, maybe grain, but not apples. I tugged on the bell pull. One of the house footmen, Baldwin by name, appeared a few moments later, his breath heavy and his livery askew. I shook my head. Selwyn's mother Talia had taken over hiring the household servants after Arilea's death, and the difference was jarring. Arilea may have been a battle axe, but at least she had known how to choose and handle her inferiors.

"Find Selwyn and tell him I want to see him," I said, "and be quick about it. Also, bring me some bread and cheese."

"Yes, sir." With a rude bob of his head that fell far short of the traditional bow, he was out the door before I could reprimand him.

I returned to the ledger, counting down the row of figures under my breath. *That doesn't add up* . . . Selwyn entered the chamber with a quiet knock.

"You summoned me, sir?"

"Yes, could you explain this notation?" I pointed at the line.

He took a glance at it. "I think, ah, yes, I believe that's two bushels of red apples."

"It isn't a question of belief. It's your own writing. Is it apples or isn't it?" I lowered my spectacles.

He stepped away hastily. "It is, most certainly. Two bushels of red apples, sir."

"Why would you note apples on this ledger? That's a household account."

"Because the Declans rounded off their rent with apples, sir. Those were the last two bushels."

"We don't accept payments of apples."

He put his hands behind his back. "Ah, Whitten accepted it, sir. I merely made the notation."

"Ahh." I took off my spectacles. "And did you question him about it?"

"It was such a small amount . . . well, I didn't feel it was necessary."

"It is a small amount but not a small mistake. Accept two bushels of the Declans' apples this year, and next year, they'll bring us twenty. It's a bad precedent. We deal only in coin, grain and livestock in a pinch, but no apples. Keep an eye on Whitten and don't let it happen again."

"Yes, sir."

Baldwin reappeared at that moment carrying a tray with bread and cheese and a knife. "A gentleman to see you, sir," he announced.

"This late? Who is it?"

"Sir Avernal of Long Marsh."

I groaned inwardly. "Already?"

"What, sir?"

"Show him up." I cut a hunk of cheese, tore off some bread,

and jammed it all in my mouth.

"What does he want?" Selwyn said.

Couldn't the fool see I had just taken a bite? "Damned silly ass," I mumbled.

"What was that, sir? Is it something to do with Dagmar?"

I gulped, fighting for air. "None of your affair," I snapped finally. "Now, balance this last page again before you go to bed. Some of the figures are off."

"But I . . ."

I thrust the ledger at him. "Here. Leave. Now."

"Yes, sir. Good night."

When Avernal entered the chamber a few minutes later, his usual bluster had been replaced by a wan anxiety. He answered to my invitation to sit down with a quiet no and remained upright, shifting from one foot to the other. His clothes hung on his portly frame, and it seemed that what muscles he had left from an active youth hunting with the king had all turned to flab overnight.

"If you won't sit down, will you at least have some bread? A little brandy, maybe?" I said finally, more to break the silence than anything else.

"No, thank you. I apologize for disturbing you so late, but it really couldn't wait another minute."

"What is it? Something with the betrothal?"

"No, that's fine," he said absently. "It's nothing to do with Dagmar or Selwyn. It's my other daughter, Safire. It seems," he cleared his throat. "It seems your son Merius seduced her."

I crossed my arms and leaned back in the chair, watching him. "That's a heavy charge to lay on a young man. What proof have you of this, Avernal?"

"Dagmar wrote me a letter from court, and Safire admitted it this afternoon. I confiscated a letter Merius sent her, if you want proof beyond my word."

I continued to watch him, not saying anything until he finally broke down, clasping the edge of the table and leaning towards me, his face drawn. "You have to know I would do nothing to upset Dagmar's and Selwyn's betrothal, Mordric. Believe me, I wouldn't come to you if I didn't think it was true."

"No, I believe you." I stood, went over to the window, and examined my reflection against the dark glass. "Young ladies rarely admit to being compromised--the risk to their reputations is too great. Young men, on the other hand, are all too ready to compromise them." If I could convince Avernal that Merius was a rake who seduced young ladies often, then he wouldn't want Merius for his son-in-law despite Merius's considerable inheritance. As the father of a debauched daughter, Avernal was in a position to demand Merius marry Safire, a position I wanted him to forget as soon as possible.

"I'm certain Merius didn't mean for it . . ."

"Oh, he meant for it. I know my son." I turned from the window, my arms still crossed.

"But Mordric, one lapse is not indicative of man's entire character. I mean, as long as he marries her, there's no real harm done."

"That's true, but considering he left yesterday for Marenna for five months, a marriage may be difficult to arrange."

"He could marry her when he returns . . ."

"What if she's with child?"

Avernal blanched. "I don't know."

"Exactly. We can't know for another few months or so, and then everyone else knows too. It could be disastrous for both our Houses if this gets out."

"What do you think I should do?"

"Is there anyone else interested in marrying her?"

He nodded. "Yes, there's been interest. But she's so damned stubborn . . ."

"She's not in a position to be stubborn at the moment, Avernal."

"I know, but she's of a strong mind. Always has been."

"Impress on her the fact she's ruined herself . . ."

"Believe me, I have."

"Well, keep doing it. By law, she has to marry whomever you tell her to marry."

"But who'll take her, like this?" He sank into an armchair, running his hands through his sparse hair.

"She's a comely girl, what little I've seen of her. Surely some man will have her."

"Some man, certainly," he scoffed. "A dock rat, maybe, when I'd hoped she would marry Bara."

"Peregrine?"

He nodded. "He's been buzzing after her for a couple of years now, but she'll have none of him, the minx. To be honest, I don't know why he's still coming, she's insulted him so many times."

"He doesn't give up easily. He may still have her."

"Who, him? He's too proud to take another man's leavings."

"Why does he need to know?"

His mouth opened as if he was about to speak and stayed that way for several seconds. "But, Mordric, he'll know . . . he's young, but he's no fool. Besides, Safire will likely inform him herself to spite me."

"I suppose, though he may be more amenable than you think."

"But what if he's not, and she is with child? What then?"

I shrugged. I had hoped not to play this card, but there seemed little choice. Damn Merius. "She could always marry Whitten, if it comes to that."

Avernal's shoulders sagged in obvious relief. "Thank you. She's a good girl, really, just heedless. Marriage will calm her spirits, I'm certain of it."

"Bring her here the day after tomorrow, and we'll discuss it further. Now, if you'll excuse me, I've had a long evening, and I have a long day before me. Good night."

~ ~ ~ ~ ~

The mustiness of my long-abandoned chamber had begun to retreat from the maids' hastily kindled fire when I entered it a half-hour later. It had been a damp spring, and the faint odor of mildew still hung in the air with the chill of long vacancy. I prepared for bed, my thoughts ordering themselves for tomorrow. In the morning, I had to finish going over Selwyn's ledger. Then I had to examine the stables and meet with Ebner, the stable master--we were gaining a reputation for fine horses. If Silver could foal another Trident for the king and start a fashion for Landers horses at court, that reputation would be set. Unless Whitten had anything to do with it.

I pulled off my left boot with unnecessary force and lobbed it at the wardrobe. That sotted dolt. Every time he got in his cups (and that occurred more and more these days), he lost what little sense he possessed and made mistakes, some disastrous. Like selling Trident to Peregrine when I had promised Silver's new colt to His Majesty. That could have been a grave political mishap--Houses had fallen for less. Merius had saved the situation by assuring the king that although Trident would have met his expectations, the next colt would be even finer, a steed more befitting the royal bum. The old fool had believed him, too. I snorted. If Merius was impetuous, at least he was as quick-thinking as he was quick-acting. Battle would take some of the impetuosity out of him. Too bad I couldn't send Whitten to war to grow brains.

I unfastened the frogs on my doublet and hung it in the wardrobe. It was chilly without it, and I rubbed my arms as I glanced over at the fire. I had put more wood on the embers when I had entered the chamber, and now the flames roared in the grate, leaving long, black streaks down the back of the fireplace. It should have been warmer, with the size of the fire--it had felt warmer earlier. Likely one of the maids had left a window open, and now the wind was drafting in. None of the drapes stirred, however, and when I checked the window latches, every one was locked and secure.

I threw another chunk of wood on the fire. The flames sputtered and flared with a rain of popping sparks, yet the closer I stood, the colder I felt. I rubbed my hands together, and they were numb, the skin taut with the chill. This was ridiculous--old men huddled by the fireside and shivered. I retreated to the bed and crawled under the covers.

I closed my eyes, watching the patterns of light on the back of my eyelids. Odd thoughts flitted in and out of my mind as I fell into a deeper doze, my awareness narrowed to a sense of darkness and exhaustion. Then I heard the click of the chamber door. I blinked as a cloaked woman tiptoed in, pulling the door to behind her.

"What the hell?" I muttered and tried to sit up. However, I found I couldn't move--my body was numb with cold.

The woman had gone over to the wardrobe and opened it. She leaned over, the cloak sliding off her hair. A mass of blond waves cascaded down her back, the fire light catching strands ranging from rich gold to the pale hue of pine shavings. I knew then. I had run my hands over that hair enough to know.

She rifled through the bottom drawer of the wardrobe, where I kept spare coin, my razor, a wooden box containing old letters, my spurs from the king's guard, and a few other mementoes. She pulled out a flimsy piece of silk I had stuffed in the drawer and forgotten long ago. Clutching the silk in one thin, white hand, she shrugged the cloak from her shoulders. It slipped to the floor and disappeared in the shadows. I lay frozen on the bed as she turned to face me.

She wore nothing, her pale skin shining like moonlight, though the curtains were drawn shut and there was no moon. She had been thirty-two when she died, still untouched by the ravages of age, damn her. My eyes ran up that coldly perfect body. Only one faint scar marred the surface of her skin, just over her right hip. She had snatched my dagger and cut herself there when I told her of my women at court. It had been a ploy to get attention, nothing more-- she had been skilled at those. I hesitated at the neck, and then, cursing myself, I finally looked at her face. Her full lips, dark blue, curved in a mocking smile, and her eyes glinted, sharp as blades.

"You dead bitch. Get out of here."

Her smile widened, and she shook out the bit of silk. It was a summer shift, the material so fine I could still see the outline of her body after she lifted her arms and slithered into it like a serpent reclaiming its skin.

"I told you to get out of here. Your bed is in the graveyard with that hangdog Gaven."

She laughed and ran her hands over her chest and down her sides, pulling the silk tight against her flesh. Her laughter sliced through my brain. I swore and tried to leap from the bed, but my limbs were still paralyzed with cold. She began to walk around the bed. "Don't tell me I frighten you, Mordric."

"Stop it. I can't move, damn you."

"You are frightened."

"I'd strangle you if I could move. It's just so cold--why is it so goddamned cold?" I coughed.

"You've never felt it before, when I've been near. You must be getting soft in your dotage."

"You bitch."

She sighed. "Your insults lack imagination, love. Now, Merius . . . Merius has sensed me many times, though he didn't usually know it . . ."

"Leave him alone, Arilea."

She arched her neck and laughed, her hair shimmering. "Oh, you are amusing," she choked finally. "Here I am, dead, and there you are, petrified with fear in my presence, and you still think you can order me around."

"It's this hellish cold. I'm not afraid of you, demon."

"Let's see about that." She sat down on the bed beside me. The closer she moved, the colder the air became. My breath turned white. I coughed again, my lungs burning. Her fingers touched my face, and I jerked away. Her skin was so cold it seared.

"Shh," she whispered. "This is the one place we never denied each other."

"There's little you denied any man."

She slapped me, and I drew breath sharply, for it felt like a hundred wasps stinging my jaw. I had had frostbite before, but this was absurd.

"How dare you call me a whore, you and your dozen mistresses?"

"I never took a mistress, not until long after you tumbled my brother."

Her hand moved down my neck. "You still believe that?"

"Why wouldn't I? You told me yourself Merius might be his."

She smiled. "Not might be his. Merius is his."

"Lying viper. There's no way that sniveling ass Gaven sired him . . ."

Her laughter pealed. "I only wanted to test you, and I've found you as testy as ever. If you'd only believed me when I told you the truth, you wouldn't be torturing yourself right now."

"And what is the truth? You've told me Merius was mine,

then you've told me in the same breath he was Gaven's. I don't think you know yourself."

"I told you the truth long ago, my love, but you weren't listening. That's unfortunate for you, isn't it?"

"I don't need the truth of a heartless bitch."

"Now we're back to bitch again. Don't you know any other words?"

"Not for you, I don't. And get your icy claws off me."

Her hand had slipped under the blanket, over my chest, and the chill from it spread down to my legs. I could barely breathe. "Succubus," I spat. "There's another word for you."

"You wish I was a succubus--those women at court don't know how to handle you." She lay down beside me, her hand still on my chest and her blue lips beside my ear. "Listen to me," she whispered.

"Go to hell. It might warm you up."

"Stubborn man. You can't go anywhere, you haven't anything better to do than talk to your dead wife, so listen.

"Well, spit it out."

The hairs rose on my arms as her voice lowered to a hiss. "Don't let Merius near that witch again. Ever."

"Witch?"

"The little redhead clairvoyant who's sunk her claws in him. If she comes in this house . . ."

"Clairvoyant--what nonsense are you blathering about now? Arilea?"

I awoke with a start. The fire had burned down to a dull glow of embers. Still half asleep, I flung my arm out, for an instant touching silk-fine strands of hair on the pillow beside mine. Then the feeling was gone, and all there was under my fingers was cool linen. I turned over on my side, my eyes closed again. It had been a dream. I always dreamed about her when I was in this bed, the bed we had shared and where she had borne our last dead child and then promptly died herself. The priest and the servants thought I should have burned the bed frame, but I never had been one to traffic in stupid superstition. It was a perfectly good bed.

I turned again, trying to find a decent position. My hand

landed on silk, not linen. A brief chill shuddered through me, and my muscles locked for a moment. Then I slowly began to move again, feeling the thin cloth beneath my fingertips. It was definitely silk. I gathered the stuff in my hand and brought it my face. The scent of roses filled the air to the point of intoxication as I ran the silk from hand to hand, drawing it tight and twisting it into a rope. Too bad I didn't have her here--I could have slipped it around her slender snake neck and strangled the treacherous life out of her. That beautiful hellbound bitch.

Chapter Fourteen--Safire

Strawberry snuffled into my palm, searching for the last bit of apple. "There is no more, silly," I said, giggling. "That tickles, stop."

She lifted her head and looked at me. She had the most lovely eyes for a horse, long-lashed and bright. "I'm sorry." I reached into my empty pocket. "See, there is no more. You've had enough anyway. You'll be fat as Buckets soon." Buckets was Dagmar's and my old pony, an ancient creature who stood in the same place in the pasture all day chewing oats and biting flies and dreaming of his glory days when he wore a red saddle and pranced around the fields with us on his back.

Strawberry tossed her mane to show me what she thought of Buckets and my lack of apples. Then she turned to her trough, her rump to me. I scratched her back. "We'll go riding tomorrow, I promise. It rained this afternoon, or I would have taken you."

"You talk more to that horse than you do to most people." Boltan came from the paddock, a length of rope twined around his elbow.

"I expect that's because she listens." I propped my arms on the stall gate. The muffled crunch and grumble of Strawberry eating hay filled the silence. It was a sound I could listen to for hours, like the cooing of sleepy pigeons. Like Merius's breathing in the bed beside me. I twisted the ring on my finger as if it could somehow magically summon him. I'd make him take me with him this time, even if I had to play his washerwoman. I'd do far worse things than dirty laundry just to see him again.

"You got another letter today."

"What?"

"A messenger brought it a few minutes ago." Boltan's eyes, dark gleams in wrinkled pockets of leathery skin, were too shrewd for my liking. I glanced away and picked up a piece of straw.

"Maybe it's from Dagmar."

"It isn't from court."

I bent the straw in the middle. "Where is it from then?"

"Gilgana."

Gilgana was a fishing village on the coast, the launching place of Herrod's ships. Merius had left for there five days ago, and already it felt like a year. If I had a letter from him, that meant he had already sailed, which meant that he wouldn't get any more letters from me. They were going to be moving around too much to receive any messages except commands from Herrod. The straw broke, and I threw the pieces down and sighed. How was I going to stand five months of this?

"You've gotten a letter a day since you returned home."

"I made some new acquaintances at court."

"Is that why your father summoned you home?"

I gave him a sidelong glance. "You ask too many questions for a servant."

Boltan grinned. "At least you learned one ladylike propriety while you were away."

"So, where is this letter?"

"On the bench in the front hall."

I hopped down and walked beside Boltan into the courtyard. "How long do you think it takes to sail to Marenna from here?"

He shielded his eyes with his hand and squinted across the fields. "It would take awhile to pull a ship across all that grass, my lady."

I swatted his arm. "Fool, I didn't mean from this house. I meant Cormalen."

"Cormalen's a big country to be sailing anywhere."

"Stop it right now. I'm not going to ask you anything anymore. Either you give me presumptuous advice or mock me."

"You make yourself an easy target, miss. Now, it would take a ship maybe a week and a half to sail from Gilgana to the northern coast of Marenna, given good winds and no storms. Does that answer your question?"

"I never said anything about Gilgana." I lifted my chin.

He stopped and looked at me. "Your father had best marry you off soon. Either that, or keep a better eye on you."

"I don't know what you're talking about."

"I hope not, though I think you're lying. You've looked the last few days like you did when you were five and went swimming in the river and came home covered with mud. You were laughing and jumping in puddles right up to the moment your father switched you. I've never seen a little girl who was so happy being naughty as you, and it doesn't seem you've changed much."

"At least I'm happy, unlike nose in the air Dagmar."

"You'd do better, adopting some of Lady Dagmar's ways."

"What, like tattling?" I left him then and went into the house. The front door slammed behind me, and I strode across the hall to the bench, where Merius's letter waited. The seal tore under my impatient fingers. I shook open the letter with a rustling of parchment and sank down on the bench, my lips moving soundlessly as I began to read.

Dearest Safire,

I'm writing this from the Weaver Thrush Inn in Gilgana. Of course, there's not a thrush for miles. They should call it the Screeching Seagull--there's hundreds of those. One attacked Gerard today. He was eating some smoked salmon when the gull swooped down and grabbed the fish right out of his hand. He was so surprised that he slipped and fell off the dock--not a hard thing to do, as the wood is slimy. When he didn't come up, Roland and I jumped in after him. His foot was caught on the rough edge of a piling, and we had a devil of a time getting him loose.

Sorry about the red spots--some of the candle wax dripped on the edge. I should go downstairs and get more parchment, but I don't want to run into anyone. It's ten at night, and this is likely the most privacy I'm going to get. Everyone else is downstairs, drinking and playing cards and, judging from all the thuds and yells, beating each other with benches.

It's bad your father is so upset. I'd rather he'd not gotten the news in a letter from your sister, but we can't help that now. Perhaps he'll relent when he realizes that I'll marry you the day I return. I can't blame him for being suspicious of my intentions, but I had hoped the troth ring would have assuaged at least some of his doubts. Having suffered from my father's dishonesty, I don't make promises lightly, particularly a promise to you, sweetheart. I'm sorry to have caused this rift between you and your family, but it'll be all put right when I return and we marry. If it would help, I would write to your father myself, but from your last letter, it sounded like that would make things worse at this point. Is there any other assurance I can send him? I hate to think of you upset or hurt. You've given me the sweetest moments a man can hope for in this mortal life, and there will be many more. We've only tasted the joy we can bring each other.

God help me, I miss you. Every time I wake up, the first few moments are bliss, because I think you're here. I wouldn't have thought before I met you that I could become so accustomed to sleeping in the same bed with someone in so short a time. I don't know what to do with my arms now that I don't have you to hold.

I'll write you as soon as we reach Marenna. After that, letters may be a bit difficult to manage, but I'll write as often as I can. The scouts will take my letters to send back to Cormalen, but they won't be able to deliver any letters to me--once we're in the mountains, the scouts never know which troops they'll meet on the paths because travel time in the mountains is so difficult to judge, particularly when you're leading a troop of a hundred men, and our maps are sometimes misleading. So save your letters for me, and I'll read them when I return.

I think about you all the time, you witch, and find myself reaching for the lock of hair you gave me constantly. You've put such a spell on me that my friends hardly know what to make of my new reformed behavior.

I hear Gerard on the stairs. I can always tell it's him by the spurs. We've been ribbing him about being Ronceval Devons's protege--that old pirate even wears spurs in the council chamber, and no one's ever seen him near a horse. I better end this before Gerard comes in. Blow me a kiss and a prayer on the morrow and every day afterwards until I return to you, dearest.

All my love,
Merius

I swallowed and read over it again, holding every word in my mind until I had it memorized. Then I folded it, pressed it to my lips, and put it in my skirt pocket.

The front door flew open with a bang. Father tramped in and tossed his muddy cloak on the floor, sparing me a brief, baleful glance.

"We're going to Landers Hall tonight," he muttered.

"Why?"

"Don't you question me. We're going, so be presentable. That's all you need to know."

"Presentable for whom?" I crossed my arms.

He leaned his hand against the dining hall door jamb, his back to me as he shook his head. "Boltan told me you got another letter."

"Yes?"

"Give it here, Safire."

"I burned it."

He turned his head, half looking at me. "Give it here. Right now."

"No, I told you I burned it. I knew you'd ask for it, so I burned it." I stood up and began to pace, the letter heavy in my pocket.

He seemed to accept this, turning his head away again. There was a long moment of silence before he cleared his throat and spoke. "It's not that I don't think Merius intends to marry you. He likely does. It's just that intentions are different from actions."

"Not for him."

"I can't wait around five or six months to prove my lovesick daughter wrong. Can't you see? Didn't your mother and I at least raise you to have some sense? Honorable men don't seduce young girls. You're ruined, Safire. He ruined you. And I can tell you this-- if he respected you the way a husband should respect his wife, he wouldn't even have thought to touch you."

"I'd hate to be so respected that my husband wouldn't dream of touching me. That would be a dull marriage."

He sighed. "God, I'd whip you if it would do any good. I'll be lucky if some fool man will even have you."

"I'm sorry, Father--I know I've disappointed you. But Merius will have me. He made a solemn vow."

Father turned, his throat working as if he were trying to keep from saying something. "Let me ask you a question," he managed finally, "and just think for a moment before you answer. If Merius is so eager to have you, what is he doing in another country? And why didn't he come see me first, ask for your hand properly?"

"You said a question, not questions."

His hand tightened into a fist. "If you act pert again, miss, I'll find you a husband on the docks. Answer me, Safire. Why didn't he see me first?"

"Because there was no time. Between Herrod asking him to leave and him leaving, we only had three days."

"A day to ride here, a day to meet with me, and a day to ride back." Father ticked the days off on his fingers. "He could have managed it."

I swallowed. "He wanted to be with me those three days. I reckon he trusted my promise to wait for him more than you trust his promise to me, even though he honored it with a troth ring."

"And dishonored you in the bargain. I have no faith in his promises. Many men give their mistresses rings, but do they marry them?"

"How dare you," I choked.

"I dare because I care about your reputation, this family's reputation. Did you even consider that? And where is your supposed betrothed, the man who couldn't even face me to ask for my daughter's hand?" He slammed his fist against the door frame, his face red. "He's in Marenna for God knows how long. What the hell is he doing there, may I ask? When he should be here, making amends for . . ."

"Stop it, just stop it," I yelled. "You don't understand. You always think you understand, but you never do. He had to go. He had to abandon his inheritance, his father's influence, before he could marry me. The only way he could do that is join with Herrod and the king's guard. He's given up everything, risked his life in battle, for me. How dare you stand here and doubt his word?"

"Because Mordric, two days ago, raised no objections to a marriage between you and Merius. So, according to his own father, the reasons Merius gave you for his sudden departure were false."
Triumph flickered in Father's eyes, and even though he thought he

had his reasons to be cruel in order to get through to me, I would never forgive him for that brief dark flicker. It felt like he had brought his boot heel down on my heart.

I sank against the wall and slipped to the floor, my head in my arms as I began to sob. "No. No, Mordric's lying. Merius loves me. He'll be back for me."

"What reason would Mordric have to lie? He admitted his only son was a rake--why would he do that if it wasn't the truth?"

"He's lying." Tears trickled down under my chin, and I wiped my sleeve across my face. "He wants Merius to be just like him at court, and Merius doesn't want that," I babbled. "They fight all the time. Merius has these horrible headaches from it--I must have taken away three or four of them with my hands . . ."

"That's enough, Safire." Father's tone was gruff. He didn't like to hear about how I could take away pain with my hands, even though I had done it several times for him when he seemed on the verge of apoplexy. "Now, get yourself together, wash your face. We need to set out soon if we're to reach there before nightfall."

~ ~ ~ ~ ~

Dusk had almost deepened to night by the time our coach wheels rattled on the cobbles of the Landers courtyard. I had spent the hour long trip staring out the window at the trees shifting from green to gray and finally to black as the sky darkened overhead. I had feared Father would continue his lecture in the coach, but evidently even he had tired of it for he spoke not a word the entire ride. At first, I relished the silence, but about halfway to Landers Hall, it began to weigh down the air to the point that each breath was an effort. A couple years ago, when a spring flood had carried off half the wheat seed in our lower field, there had been the same brooding quiet throughout the house for a week. After Father's considerable rage and bluster were spent, he went into a silent, sullen melancholy which Dagmar and I dreaded, for it brought back memories of the miserable months after Mother's death when he wouldn't speak at meals. The silence felt like a punishment to my guilty spirit, one which I supposed I deserved. However, I couldn't help the one cynical thought amidst my guilt: that he wasn't as upset over my sin as he was over the damage I had done to my already questionable value on the marriage market.

After the coach had stopped, Boltan came around, opened the door, and helped me to the ground. The swaying lanterns at the edges of the courtyard lit a path to the front door but showed little else of the house, a huge, hulking shadow across the starry sky. The only other light came from the far end of the house, a warm, orange light that streamed through an open door and against the side of the stables. There was the sound of someone playing a fiddle and women's laughter--the kitchens and servants' quarters, I warranted. I looked longingly after that light as Father pushed me towards the front door, wishing for a moment that I was just a simple scullery maid. It would be drudgery, but at least I would be free to bestow my favors in a haystack if I so chose. I was wicked for even thinking such a thing. I squared my shoulders and marched up the steps. Whatever happened, at least I had Merius's ring on my finger.

It was cold inside. When the footman tried to take my cloak, I shook my head and crushed the velvet against my arms, shivering as I looked around. All stone and oak beams and tapestries, far older than the House of Long Marsh, even older than the oldest section of court. The Landers were descended from the first shipload of Sarneth adventurers whose blood had mingled with the ancients, a true founding family of Cormalen. The footman ushered Father and me up the stairs. Selwyn came through a door and out on the landing, stopping when he noticed us.

"Good evening, sir," he said to Father. His pale gray eyes paused for several moments on me as if I were an account he couldn't quite puzzle out. I gazed back, unblinking, and he finally looked away. A long face and jaw with features to match and already thinning brown hair. For some reason, Dagmar seemed happy with him, though why I would never understand.

"Good evening," Father replied.

"Is Dagmar well?"

"Oh yes, she's fine."

"One never knows, this time of year. A fever can strike at any time," Selwyn said, his gaze returning to me. I glanced up at the ceiling and bit my tongue.

"Yes, spring plagues are the worst. I've told her to leave the city if one strikes," Father said.

"Dagmar would be just fine but for a plague of the mouth," I muttered.

Father's back stiffened, and Selwyn said, "What was that, Lady Safire?"

I flashed him a smile. "I was just remarking that Dagmar's fine now, but that Corcin has a plague every month."

"Ah, yes. A most unhealthy place. Forgive me, but I thought you were there with her."

"I was, but I . . ."

"Safire's lately come home," Father interrupted hastily. "I wasn't feeling well last week, and she returned to attend me."

"I'm sorry to hear you were ill, sir."

"It was nothing serious. Merely rheumatism of the back--to be expected in this damp weather."

"Merely rheumatism!" I exclaimed. "You were in bed two days, Father. I had to feed you because you couldn't bend your neck. In fact, you look a trifle stiff right now. You really shouldn't be standing like this--it might flare up again."

"Thank you, daughter," he said through his teeth as he shot me a lethal look, "but I'm fine."

"If you'd like, sir, you can sit on this bench," Selwyn offered. I bit my lip to keep from laughing and looked down at my clasped hands.

"No, that's quite all right," Father said, gripping my arm. "Thank you, but we really must see Mordric." He began to tug me off the landing.

"Allow me to escort you. Baldwin, go bolt the door." Selwyn dismissed the footman with a quick nod. "Forgive me," he continued as we went down a long passage. "I didn't realize you were here to see Mordric. He doesn't usually meet with anyone this late."

Father glanced back at me and shook his head just enough to let me know that if I said anything more in front of Selwyn, he would lash me forty times with the coach whip. I rolled my eyes as soon as his back was turned but trotted along silently in his shadow, as a properly chastened daughter ought. I didn't want to say anything more, anyway--Selwyn's attempts to worm out information about our business at the Hall had ceased being amusing.

After several other passages and a short stair, by which point I was thoroughly lost in this drafty warren of a house, we stopped before a paneled door. Selwyn knocked once and only opened the door after a sharp summons came from within.

Mordric rose as we entered. He tipped a pair of spectacles halfway down his nose and watched us narrowly over the rims as Father pulled out a chair for me. I stared at him, not so much out of rudeness or boldness but out of shock. Since meeting Merius, I had forgotten how much he resembled his father. Same lean swordsman's build, same square jaw, same deep-set gray eyes, same hawk-like nose (Mordric must have broken his at one point for there was a slight ridge in the middle.) Merius was likely taller, but only by an inch or two. Both wore a bit of stubble, though Mordric's was iron gray like the hair on his head. There wasn't a strand of color left. He seemed too young to be so grizzled. Father was the same age, and his hair was still reddish-blond. Of course, the gray suited Mordric. I looked away, unable to stand it. Here was Merius after thirty hard years, his silver aura tarnished and hardened to a brittle dark gray, shot through with taut black lines of tension and red patches the color of old blood. I glanced around the chamber at the decorative, twisted legs on the furniture, the vaulted ceiling, the blue and gold tapestry of a lion, not really seeing any of it as I tried to avoid looking at him again.

"Good evening," he said as he reclaimed his seat. I shuddered at the smooth quiet depth of his voice. It was Merius's voice without the warmth.

"Sir," Selwyn began. "I finished . . ."

Mordric raised his hand, his gaze on the papers before him. "Leave us. I'll look at it later."

"Yes, sir." As the door closed behind Selwyn, Mordric lifted his head and removed the spectacles, examining us again. This time I didn't look away, even though his resemblance to Merius still unnerved me. I just had to keep reminding myself that Merius could never come to this. Never. After all, Merius loved me. This man could never have loved anyone.

"You do have lovely daughters, Avernal," he remarked finally.

"It's a shame my blackguard son had to pluck this one."

"I am not a flower to be plucked, sir, and your son is not a blackguard."

For the first time, he looked directly at me, his gaze as piercing as the winter wind through a thin cloak. "This rose has a thorn for a tongue, I fear."

"That's not my only thorn."

A ghost of Merius's smile crossed his lips as he reached for the servants' bell. "Would either of you care for any refreshment? Our cook has put up a fine apple brandy."

"No, thank you, Mordric," Father said quickly. "Now, if we could . . ."

"Excuse me," I interrupted. "This thorny rose would like some brandy, please."

Father turned to me, his face the color of brick. "Mind yourself," he hissed.

"No." I swallowed. "You've held the threat of your rages over me and Dagmar long enough. I won't have it anymore, Father. I'm a grown woman now, and you can't drag me off in the coach at night and herd me into a strange house without bothering to tell me why we're here."

"We're here to save what little reputation you have left and marry you off."

"I won't be married off. My betrothed is in Marenna."

Father lowered his forehead down on his palm, shaking. "It's hopeless. You're hopeless. Thank God your mother's not here to see what you've come to."

The footman who had opened the front door appeared then and took Mordric's order for apple brandy and cheese. "Now," Mordric said when the boy had left, "Avernal, calm yourself. Remember, there's always the convent." He looked at me, a frankly appraising glance that left me chilled. "Though I doubt we'll have to resort to that."

"But she's ruined, completely ruined . . ."

"Good God, man, pull yourself together," Mordric snapped. "There are several prominent court wives who weren't virgins when they married. It's just not talked about--no husband wants to admit he was a cuckold even before the ceremony. All we require is a little discretion from Safire, and we should have her well married in a week or two and none the wiser."

"I'll marry no one but Merius, so expect no discretion from me."

Father shook his head and muttered something under his breath.

Mordric ignored him. "Well, I would make Merius marry you, sweet, if he were here. But he won't be here for several months, so you'd best . . ."

"No, you wouldn't. You wouldn't let him marry the younger daughter of a sparrow nobleman if you could prevent it. You have royal aims for him, blackguard though you call him."

"Safire!" Father started to rise. "Apologize immediately."

Mordric raised his hand, his narrow gaze never leaving mine. "Sit down, Avernal. It's all right. The girl's upset, and I've had worse insults."

"I'm not so upset that I can't tell a lie when I hear it."

Father rose again, this time grabbing for my arm. "You headstrong . . ."

"Avernal, why don't you go next door to the library and let me speak to Safire alone for a minute or two? There are a few things I think she doesn't understand."

Father's hands slipped off my arm. "Alone? But why? I'm her father . . . I have to be here."

"These are things it may be easier for her to hear from an acquaintance than from her father, things it may be easier for me to say than for you. Blood is often too thick to see through."

"Maybe you're right." Father shook his head, his shoulders hunched, and I wanted nothing so much then as to erase everything that had happened since before Mother's death and embrace him. Boltan was right--I had always been a wicked girl. But there had been a time in my life when I knew how to make up for my mistakes so that everything ended up all right in the end. Either the mistakes had gotten bigger or I had gotten more wicked, but I knew nothing would be the same between Father and me after today. And that made me want to cry. Why was it that when we gained one thing, we so often lost another?

As Father was leaving, the footman returned with the brandy. Mordric poured a tumbler for me and then one for himself. "Thank you," I said, taking a sip. The brandy left a pleasant warmth down my throat, particularly welcome since the chamber seemed even colder than it had when we had entered. I pulled the cloak tighter around my elbows and glanced at the fire dying in the grate.

He drained his tumbler and poured another before he spoke. "You lack manners, miss, which makes you unfit to be a lady. However, that's not the catastrophe your father seems to think it is. There is a certain crude charm about you, common in the extreme considering your rank, but Merius has never had a taste for the finer things, particularly when it comes to women. Most men don't, so you should have no problem attracting another husband despite your ruined state."

"I don't care what you say about me, you and your forked tongue." I bridled. "Everything you say is a smokescreen anyway, you've been at court so long. I bet you knew about Merius and me before he even left--I bet you planned to send him away, because you knew he would marry me over any objection you could make. I thought there was something too well-timed about Herrod's request."

"The request was genuine. There is such a thing as too much intuition, my dear." He leaned back in his chair, but I detected a slight tautness about his movements, a faint tightening in the black lines constraining his aura. "Now, you seem a clever girl. You have to know that regardless of whether Merius means to marry you or not, such a marriage is an impossibility. He has responsibilities that he can only ignore for so long in pursuit of a love affair. I'm certain he meant it when he told you that he would relinquish his inheritance for you. I'm certain he meant it when he put that ring on your finger. He meant it with the others as well."

I laughed. The brandy was starting to go all fuzzy and warm in my head. "You'll need to try a lot harder than that. I'm every bit as stubborn as my father says."

He shrugged. "You know, I can make things very unpleasant for you."

"You can try. Listen, I love your son, and I will leave my

family, leave everything, and go work on the docks just so I can see him again. If he doesn't want me when he returns, so be it. I won't marry another, and I won't go to a convent."

I shivered and hunkered down in my cloak then. A sudden draft had swept through the room as I spoke, and the already cold air went positively frigid. How did these people stand it?

"You know, Safire, I wasn't going to mention this, but please remember there's more between your family and mine than an indiscretion on your part. Your father's debts to me have been forgiven, and your sister's betrothal has been contracted, but unpaid debts can be reinstated, and contracts can be broken. Do you want to be the reason that your father loses all his lands and title and your sister ends in a convent?"

"You're bluffing." I coughed, and the cold stabbed like icicles in my lungs.

"Oh, my dear, I wish I was." He smiled. "Now, I have influence, and I can make a good match for you, a match any other girl in your position would envy. You should consider it--I won't offer it to you again. I only tolerate foolish obstinacy so long."

"And what are you going to tell Merius when he returns and finds you coerced me into marrying another?"

Chapter Fifteen--Mordric

The witch sat back in her chair, one thin hand curled around her tumbler of brandy, as if what she had just said settled it.

"I suppose I'll tell him the truth, that you're a scheming hussy who's only after his position and inheritance."

She straightened, the tumbler going down on the chair arm with a clank. "If that's the case, why am I still wanting to marry him, even after he's forsaken his sainted inheritance and position?"

"Because you're hopeful. It's a rare father who follows through on threats to disinherit his only son and heir because of an unwise marriage."

"It's also a rare father who tries to ruin his son's life. You, sir, are such a rarity," she retorted. Impossible little minx. If I could have gotten away with it, I would have locked her in the cellar until Merius was safely married to a nice, quiet girl from one of the first Houses, the sort whose only needles were in her sewing basket.

Maybe I could set her up for some crime and have her arrested--there were already rumors of witchery swirling around her at court. She took long walks unchaperoned, read strange books, and drew peculiar sketches which someone had seen her selling down on the Calcors docks. No, that wouldn't work. If she ended up in prison, Merius would hatch some hare-brained plot to rescue her and get in trouble. She had to be married to someone else by the time he returned. It shouldn't be difficult to find a man for her. There were plenty of fools willing to take a hoyden if she was beautiful enough. And she did have a certain spooky way about her, an oddly perceptive incivility that made me wonder just how much Merius had revealed to her. I had to keep better track of him--if he blabbed to all his bedmates, he would be an easy mark for every dishonest courtesan.

But for the present there was this crisis who sat across the table from me with flaming hair and creamy skin and a faint golden dust of freckles across her cheekbones and far too sharp eyes. A crisis who refused to cooperate, even after I had threatened her with more than I threatened most men with before they buckled. I sighed inwardly, exhausted suddenly. I had been so certain my attempt to coerce her by threatening her father and sister would work, but she had seen it for the bluff it was. The Landers needed that land that came with Dagmar's dowry--there was a stretch by the sea with a perfect natural harbor, land Avernal hadn't the means to use properly but we did. With the way tariffs kept increasing and the black market kept flourishing, a harbor outside the bounds of any port could be highly useful possession. Damn her.

I propped my elbows on the table. "Merius stands to inherit not only thousands of acres worth of income, but all my offices as well: provincial minister, a head seat on the council, king's advisor. He's more than ready to assume all those duties. As you said before, I have royal aims for him, but I wouldn't have those aims if they weren't justified. It would be a crime for him to waste his considerable skills in the king's guard, following others' orders for the rest of his life."

"He wants to be in the king's guard."

"Only because of you. Do you want to be the reason he falls on his sword?" I asked gently. "You're a likely wench, with a quick way about you. I can see why you tempted him. But it can never go anywhere, Safire, not without binding him unfairly."

Her gaze locked with mine. "Like you've bound him with your own ambitions, never considering what he might want? He's wanted to be a guard since he was thirteen--that was years before he met me, sir. I just gave him the reason he needed to leave your poisonous influence."

I blinked, swearing under my breath. Her father would be returning soon, and I had been able to do nothing with her. I poured yet another measure of brandy, not caring anymore. If we lost the harbor, so be it. "Since you refuse to cooperate, there's only one course of action open to me. I have here the contract of betrothal between Dagmar and Selwyn. Let me ask you one more time: shall I break it? We can call your father in now. No use in delaying it."

Safire shivered suddenly, clutching her arms together as she glanced around my shoulder at the fireplace. "Do you have a window open or something?"

"No. What are you talking about?"

"There's a nasty draft in here."

I sighed. All women resorted to the same ploy in the end: female weakness. "You can't avoid this forever, my dear. Are you going to cooperate or not?"

"No. I can't think," she choked. "It's too cold. Stop it."

Some dim image on the edge of memory, a dream half remembered, Arilea's mocking voice whispering in my ear, a bone shattering cold . . . I shook my head to clear it. It wasn't cold in here. She was putting on to avoid giving me an answer. "Safire, this is ridiculous. Now your father's returning in a minute, and we're no closer to an agreement then when we started. Do you want to force my hand? I won't hesitate to . . ."

She pulled her cloak around her as tightly as she could, shuddering so violently her teeth chattered. "No, no, stop," she moaned. "No, please."

I rose then. "Listen, are you all right?" Maybe she had been struck with a sudden fever.

She shook her head and jumped to her feet. The chair slammed against the floor as she knocked it over in her haste to get to the door. "Let me out!" She rattled the door knob frantically. "Let me out, please let me out! Why won't it open? For God's sake, open, please . . . Father . . ."

I came around the table. "What is it?"

She ignored me, throwing her shoulder against the door. "Open, oh God please. Father, help me," she babbled.

I grabbed her arm. The instant my fingers brushed against her, she screamed. "What the hell?" I shook her a little to get her attention, and she glanced back at me with the wild eyes of a caged animal. "Now, listen here, there's no need for this. Calm down."

"Let me out of here!"

"What's the matter with you? Are you ill?" I shook her again. "Well, answer me."

She twisted out of my grip and began beating on the door with her fists. "Let me out! Let me out right now!"

I pulled her away from the door, and she screamed again, beads of blood welling up from tiny cuts on her hands. "Papa! Papa, help!" She kicked and scratched, at one point punching me.

"Vixen," I panted, finally forcing her into a chair. "Stop it right now."

She screamed a third time, and I slapped her, the only effective cure I knew of for hysteria. She kicked my knee and dodged past me towards the door.

"Damn you," I swore, limping after her as she began tugging on the knob again. It must be stuck. Certainly it wasn't locked--I had the only key.

"Open, please open," she pleaded hoarsely. "It's cold. Mama, help me, don't let her get me . . . she's so cold, it's hurts . . ." Her hands slid from the knob, and she sank to the floor, buried her head in her arms as she began to sob.

"Safire?" I crouched beside her, my knee still throbbing. I would have grabbed her and hauled her back to the chair, but I didn't know if my other knee could stand it. Let her father handle her, the damned wildcat. "Look at me, Safire."

She peeked at me between her fingers and then hid her face again like a small child. "Go away."

"Damn you, look at me. I should warn you, I have little patience for female hysterics or playacting." I wrenched her hands from her face.

Her skin was white. Her breath came in shallow pants, and she trembled uncontrollably. Every few sobs, a violent shudder ran through her. Her forehead was clammy to the touch. A sudden fever, then, and not hysterics. Good. I hated hysterical women.

I straightened and reached for the brandy bottle. "Here, have a bit more of this. It'll warm you until Baldwin can take you to a spare room."

"I don't want it." She coughed.

I poured a measure of brandy into the tumbler. "Here."

Still shivering, she peered at the liquor and then gave me a suspicious look. "I thought you were the villain here, sir."

"Meaning?"

"This likely has poison or some such in it. Why else would you be offering it to me?"

"So you don't start raving again."

Safire shrugged, took the tumbler. "I'd almost rather have poison than have her come at me again, anyway," she muttered.

"Her?"

Her eyes shot up, that quick, sharp glance that seemed to see more than it should. "Never mind," she said finally, looking back at the liquor. "I was speaking to myself."

"A sign of delirium."

"Also a sign that there's no one else fit to talk to."

"You seem recovered. Recovered of your tongue, at any rate." I found her cloak on the floor where it had fallen and tossed it to her.

A slight smile creased her still chalky lips. "You're not as cruel as you pretend."

I paused, my hand on the servants' bell pull. The words *little redhead clairvoyant* suddenly entered my mind. Arilea's voice. I shook myself and let go of the bell before I could ring it. "That's a dangerous assumption," I said aloud. "I meant what I said about your sister's betrothal, your father's debts . . ."

"You're bluffing. The Landers need that betrothal, Dagmar's dowry, for some reason, or you never would have lent Father money to begin with . . ."

I cut her off. "You're feverish--you're not thinking about what you're saying. You and your father can rest here tonight, and we'll see how you fare in the morning."

Her eyes widened, and she clutched the cloak to her shoulders. "I'm not sleeping under this roof. Not with her anywhere about."

"Who? One of the servant women?"

She gave another half smile. "No, sir. You have ghosts."

"Ghosts?"

"Now you really think I'm delirious."

"That's because you are. Now, come sit in this chair, and I'll call your father." I offered her my hand.

She refused my help, gripping the door knob as she pulled herself to her feet. "If you'd be so kind to let me out, I think I can find him myself."

"No, you're not well enough. Get in the chair."

Her eyes flared. "I'll not stay in this House one more minute with you or her. Let me out."

"A lady does not make demands of her elders."

"I'm not a lady. Now let me out of this chamber."

I shrugged. "The door's not locked. Let yourself out." She rattled the knob and pushed the door, but to no avail. I shook my head. "Here." I grabbed the knob and twisted it, giving the door a hard shove. It didn't open. "What the hell?" I tried it again, but it still wouldn't budge.

Safire snorted, but by the time I glanced back at her, she had covered her mouth with her hand. "I'd ask you to keep a civil tongue," I said.

"I didn't say anything."

I leaned down and peered at the key hole. "It's a good thing for your backside that I didn't rear you. Insolent women are the devil's work."

"You're quite eloquent, you know. I can see where Merius gets his talent for writing verse," she said airily.

"You'd best hold your tongue if you want to keep it. I'll not bandy words with the raving daughter of a secondhand noble House." I stuck the key in the hole, just in case the door had somehow locked. The key turned easily, and the inner workings clicked, but the door still held firmly shut. "This is absurd," I muttered finally. "It's not locked."

"Then why won't it open?"

"Sit down and be quiet."

Safire swayed a little on her feet as she gazed at the door. "She locked it," she said quietly. "She wants me trapped in this room."

I gritted my teeth. "You don't know what you're talking

about. Will you sit down?"

Gingerly she began to pick her way around the chamber, her hand trembling as she grasped various pieces of furniture. Swearing, I seized her arm and led her to a chair.

She struggled against my grip. "I need to get to the window-- let me go!"

"You're delirious." I pushed her into the chair, and she immediately tried to stand. I pushed her down again, keeping my hands firmly on her shoulders this time. She screamed, her muscles taut and unyielding. Her frantic eyes stared past my shoulder so intently that I glanced behind me. There was nothing there.

A rush of cold air brushed my neck. Safire went limp, slumping in a sudden faint. Her skin was so pale it had the bluish tinge of someone dead. Her head dangled over the back of the chair, and I quickly reached behind her neck and straightened it so she could breathe easily. If she still was breathing.

"Hell flames," I muttered, still holding her neck. My gaze darted around the chamber, searching every shadow as if I expected an assassin to leap out. Of course, there was no assassin. There was nothing. She had a fever, that was all. A delirious fever. I looked down at her. The froths of lace around the collar of her gown rose and fell with slight breaths. The witch was still alive then. I lowered her head so that it rolled against her shoulder and backed away.

My hand found the brandy bottle, and I took a long swig, watching her warily as if I thought she would awaken and start screaming again. Ridiculous, really. Irksome wench. How had she had known about Dagmar's dowry? Merius couldn't have told her-- he didn't know which lands came with the betrothal agreement. No one did, except Avernal and I. Besides, why would Merius and Safire even have discussed such a thing? Youthful infatuations did not welcome pragmatic concerns like dowries. Maybe she had eavesdropped on her father and me, though she didn't seem the eavesdropping kind. She seemed the impractical kind, just what Merius didn't need. He was already impractical enough on his own without an unearthly witch for a wife. Ghosts, indeed. Even if she had been from one of the first families, I still wouldn't have let Merius marry her. He needed a wife who would anchor him, not float away with him.

The girl moaned, and I looked at her again. Still unconscious. Good--that meant her mouth would stay shut a while longer. I could kill Merius for getting me into this mess. Of course, it would be more useful to kill her. I gave her a speculative glance and then shook my head. I had never had anyone assassinated, and I didn't want to start with a young, albeit troublesome, girl. It should be easy enough to marry her off if we kept her gagged. Peregrine wanted her, and he knew what a wicked tongue she had. Some men enjoyed such sparring. She was a clever little thing, too quick for her own good when she wasn't screeching about spirits.

There came a knock at the door. Before I could yell that it was stuck, Avernal entered, easily opening it and closing it behind him. I started, giving the door a sharp glance.

"How is-" he began, trailing off when he caught sight of Safire. He stopped, staring blankly at her. "What? Safire . . ." He quickly went to the chair and touched her arm and then her cheek. "What?" He turned to give me the same blank stare.

"She just fainted. I think she has a fever." I took a step closer.

"But . . ." He picked up her hand and began chafing her wrist frantically. "She doesn't feel feverish."

"She acted strange, delirious after you left--I thought maybe . . ."

He continued to stare at me. "What did you say to her?"

"I told her that Merius had promised to marry other girls, had given them rings and never followed through on it, that she would do best by herself and her House to marry as quickly and quietly as possible to a suitable man who wouldn't ask too many questions."

He turned back to Safire. "She has no color, white and cold as snow. Just like her mother looked . . ." he murmured to himself. "Safire!" He suddenly grabbed her shoulders and shook her. "Safire!"

I stepped closer, my hand out. "Avernal, I really don't think that will help. I'll call Baldwin, and we can find her a chamber, the apothecary . . ."

He continued to shake her as if he hadn't heard me. When I

reached for his arm, he pushed me away with surprising force. "Safire, open your eyes. Stop this. Stop it right now." His face had turned almost as ashen as hers, and beads of sweat stood out on his forehead.

I rang the servants' bell. When Baldwin opened the door, I gestured to him. He rambled over to me, watching Safire and Avernal with an unabashed, slack-jawed curiosity. Damned fool--one would have thought Talia had hired him from a docks tavern instead of another noble household. I snapped my fingers at him, and he started.

"Yes, sir?"

"Do you think you can close your mouth long enough to carry the lady to one of the spare chambers and summon the apothecary?"

He glanced at Safire. "What's the matter with her?"

"That's none of your affair. Just do as I say."

Baldwin nodded and went over to Safire. When he tried to lift her, Avernal hit him. Baldwin stumbled back, holding his nose. I immediately strode past Baldwin and grabbed Avernal's shoulder. "What are you doing? You hit my servant."

His bloodshot eyes bulged. "He's not touching my daughter!"

"He's taking her to find the apothecary . . ."

"I'm not letting any apothecary touch her either with his damned leeches. That's what killed her mother."

I took a deep breath. "No apothecaries, then. At least let us take her to a chamber where she can rest."

"I'll take her myself!"

"Avernal, you're not in a fit state . . ."

"I'm in a perfectly fine state," he roared. "It's Safire who's fainted--what did you do to her?"

"I didn't do a damn thing to her, and I don't appreciate the insult."

"Well, something happened to her, and you were the only one who was here."

"She caught a sudden fever--it happens that way sometimes. Now, I don't like what you're implying, sir, so either be quiet and let us care for her or get out."

"You've cared for her enough," he sputtered. "You and your rake of a son." He hefted Safire up in his arms. Dark red patches appeared on his forehead and round jowls, the rest of his skin a sickly white.

Safire blinked then. "Papa?" she murmured.

"It's all right, sweet. I'm taking you back home."

"Where are we?"

"Nowhere important." He strained for breath.

"No, papa, you're sick . . ."

"Just be still now. I'll get you home." He turned with her and started for the hall slowly, his steps shuffling. He made it to the doorway before he uttered one low groan and collapsed.

~ ~ ~ ~ ~

"Apoplexy," the apothecary said, his ear to Avernal's chest. "A severe apoplectic fit, at that."

I lowered the candle. Avernal's rigid stare gleamed in the light. Absently, the apothecary reached up and closed his eyelids as if he were already dead. "What's to be done?"

The apothecary stepped back, shrugged his narrow shoulders. "Not much we can do. Keep him comfortable. I doubt he'll move or speak again."

"What of the girl?"

"I'm not certain. I'd like to have another look at her."

After I summoned a maid to watch Avernal, the apothecary and I moved next door. Safire sat in a chair in front of the large mullioned window, a single candle burning beside her as she gazed out at the night. She didn't stir when we entered.

The apothecary went over and picked up her wrist. She still didn't move. When he let go of her arm, it fell limply back to her side. "Shock, I'll warrant. Most likely when she saw her father collapse, she . . ."

"But she was acting odd before, delirious like she had a fever."

He scratched behind his ear. "No sign of a fever now. At least not that I can see." He hefted himself up on the window sill and looked intently into Safire's face for a moment. "No, I still say shock." He nimbly hopped down, dusting his hands on his trousers. "Pretty girl--it's a pity, though she'll likely come out of it. She needs a priest to bless her--that'll bring her out of it quicker than anything I can give her."

After he finished with Safire, we headed to the main door, where I paid him with a single gold piece. It was a more generous sum than his time warranted, but honest apothecaries were rare as chaste barmaids.

"Thank you, sir," he said, pocketing the coin before he picked up his medicine chest with a rattle of glass. "I'll return in a few days." He gave a slight bow and headed down the front steps into the night. I shut the door behind him and started up the stairs to my chamber. My bones ached with exhaustion. It had been a long evening.

"Sir?" Selwyn came hurrying from the back hall. "Sir?"

I paused on the landing, taking a moment to swear under my breath before I turned around. "What now?" He didn't even have the courtesy to look abashed. "Sir, I was wondering if I should summon Dagmar in the morning . . ."

"No. I think we should let her return home to find her father at death's door and her sister stuck dumb with shock."

"Really? Don't you think . . ."

I closed my eyes and put my fingers to my throbbing forehead, reminding myself that even complete literal-minded idiocy had its uses. "No, fool. It was in jest."

"So I should summon her?"

"Yes. As soon as possible."

~ ~ ~ ~ ~

Dagmar arrived three days later in the early afternoon. When Baldwin came to tell me of her arrival, she had already been escorted to her father. I found her emerging from his chamber, wiping her eyes with a handkerchief. I waited while she composed herself before I spoke. "I welcome you to the hall, although I'm sorry your visit has to be under such unfortunate circumstances."

"Thank you, sir." She sniffed into the handkerchief. "Safire and I always feared something like this would happen to Father."

"I also apologize for Selwyn's absence. If he had known you would be so early, he would have stayed, but there was some pressing estate business in Calcors . . ."

"That's quite all right. I understand--I'll see him this evening." She put away her handkerchief. "Where's Safire?"

Pretty in a pale, angular way, she was no beauty like her witch sister, but she had a sensible manner, something any wise man would value far more than looks. I took her elbow and led her a short distance down the hall. The peasant maid Elsa, a pleasantly plump dimpled girl with sleek brown hair that reminded me of corn-fed quail, opened the door at my knock. "Yes, sir?"

"Lady Safire's sister is here to see her."

"Yes, sir." She moved aside and let us into the chamber.

Dagmar crossed over to the window where Safire sat on the broad sill, her head angled so she could see the orchard walls and the tops of the blossoming apple trees. Dagmar grasped her arm. "I'm here," she said, a sudden briskness in her voice.

Safire slowly turned and gazed at her for a long moment before she turned back to the window.

"Safire, it's me, Dagmar, your sister," she said impatiently. "Come on now."

But Safire continued to stare out the window. "This is childish," Dagmar snapped. "Our father's dying, and you . . . I can't believe you." She shook Safire's arm, but Safire's only response was to shrug her hand away.

"Safire, stop this. Please. Just say one word, I don't care what." Her voice trailed off, and all was silent for several moments. She turned to me then, her face drawn, the sharp bones prominent as blades. "What's wrong with her?"

"The apothecary says shock."

"Shock," she repeated, glancing at her sister. "Shock." Her fingers worried at the ends of Safire's hair. "Do you have a comb, a brush?" she asked suddenly.

Elsa pulled an ivory vanity set from beside the wash basin. Dagmar took the brush and began to run it through Safire's hair. When the bristles hit a tangle, she gently worked it out, holding the length of hair near the roots so as not to pull too hard. "Such beautiful hair," she murmured. "She was such a wild thing when she was little, out in the woods all day, doing God knows what--she used to come home with burrs and twigs in it. It would take Mother an hour to brush out the snarls." Dagmar looked up then. "Has she spoken at all?"

I shook my head, glancing at Elsa, who cleared her throat. "Only in her sleep. She speaks in her sleep often, my lady."

"What does she say?"

"I don't know, really. Nonsense mostly. Something about a woman in the ice. And cold--she speaks of cold and shivers, even though she's well covered with our best wool blankets. Seems some sort of nightmare."

Dagmar coiled one red curl around her finger again and again, her face thoughtful. "She talks in her sleep all the time. Always has. It seems odd she won't talk when she's awake, if she can still talk in her sleep. Are you certain she hasn't said anything when she's awake?"

"No, my lady. I've been with her almost the entire time, and she's not spoke one word in three days. The second day, we tried to get her to write something on a bit of paper but all she did was draw a songbird in a cage on it. Most life-like it was too. Does she have a bird at home?" "No--she wanted a bird, but the feathers make Father sneeze." Dagmar sighed, clutching the curl in her hand. "Safire, what are we to do with you? It doesn't seem natural, neither you nor Father talking. Usually I'm telling you to be quiet." She choked and bit her bottom lip. Then she dropped the brush as she began to sob.

~ ~ ~ ~ ~

"The apothecary thinks she'll recover eventually," I said, leaning forward in my chair.

"What does eventually mean? A month? Two months? A year? Never?" Dagmar's tone was biting.

"It means he doesn't know, my lady."

"I'm sorry." Her hand tightened around a handkerchief. "Father's apoplexy is a hard blow, of course, but Safire . . . I mean, she's never been sick. A fever here and there, that's all. I've always been the one who caught chills and colds and such, but not her . . ."

I waited while she wound down, not hearing her tirade against ill fortune as I thought about what to do next. I had already delayed my return to court by several days to pick apart the mare's-

nest of the Long Marsh affair. Without Merius to write drafts of
letters and official documents and attend council, my work had likely
collected in several large stacks by now. And Cyril--Cyril would
certainly have lost an important vote on the council by the time I
returned. The fool couldn't be left alone for long, or he'd scare away
our allies among the merchants. I rubbed the back of my neck,
which had ached for two days now. I must have slept on it wrong.
And here was this sharp-faced blond with red streaks down her face
blathering on about one thing or another . . . I stared at her for a
moment, trying to remember who she was and why she was so
important. Oh yes, she was Dagmar, the last remaining Long Marsh
who could talk.

"And I don't understand," she was saying, wiping her eyes
with the handkerchief, "I just don't understand why she can't speak
or write but can still draw. Of course, she's been drawing practically
since before she could talk, but still . . ." I raised my hand, and she
trailed off. At least she was respectful.

"Yes, sir?"

"It seems," I said, "that we have a decision before us."

"A decision?"

"I hate to be blunt, but your sister's reputation is at stake. As
you know, my son seduced her before he left for Marenna. If he
were here, the affair could be easily remedied with a marriage, but he
won't return for at least several months."

Dagmar flushed. "Sir, I'm not my father, and I'd rather not
discuss the matter. It's most indelicate. In Safire's defense, she's
rather young and has always been reckless, especially since Mother . .
."

"I don't care about that," I interrupted, my patience
exhausted. "I apologize for the indelicacy of the situation, but
unfortunately your father can no longer act as Safire's guardian, so
the responsibility falls to you."

She began to weep again, and I cursed myself. I had to
remember she was a young lady and a virgin, her most difficult
decision likely what frock she put on in the morning. Of course,
since I was shut up with her, she had to be a loud crier. Her sniffles,
sobs, and wails reverberated off the ceiling, while I clenched my jaw

until it felt like I'd cracked a tooth. These Long Marsh people would be the ruin of us, with their crying and apoplexies and inexplicable fits and witchery and utter stubbornness. "My lady," I finally said through my teeth. "My lady, please . . ."

She looked up, her eyes so puffy it appeared she was squinting. "I'm sorry. Please forgive me. I just can't . . ."

"That's quite all right, but I do need you to turn your attention to the matter at hand. Now, your sister should marry. As soon and as quietly as possible."

Dagmar straightened, clutching the arms of her chair. "But she's in no state to marry."

"She's in no state to remain unmarried," I retorted. "She could be with child for all we know."

Dagmar sniffled again, and I braced myself for another deluge. Somehow, though, she managed to dam it this time. "But what man will have her like this? She can't even speak the proper vows . . . forgive me, sir, but it would be cruel, both to her and the man she marries. She's not in her right mind."

"All the more reason she needs a legally bound protector. I'm not saying it has to be a true marriage, at least not for the present. But it should be legal, in the happenstance that there is a child."

"But what man will have her?" she repeated.

"Leave me to handle that."

"He must be kind, patient . . ."

"Just leave it to me. All I ask is for your acquiescence and discretion."

"I'll only agree if I remain her primary guardian, and she stays with me until she's herself again. I do fear she's," she faltered, "she's with child. The stigma of that would ruin her life far more than a marriage in name only."

"You're a sensible girl, and your terms are acceptable. Do you agree then?"

After a minute or two, she nodded, daintily blowing her nose into the handkerchief. I took a deep breath, my first deep breath in four days. The Long Marsh harbor and Dagmar's dowry were ours, and Merius and his inheritance were safe from scheming witches. Finally, this absurdity would be at an end.

Chapter Sixteen--Safire

It was warm here. I floated through the fluid darkness, brushing against vague shapes. Every once in a while, a shaft of light pierced the waters from far above, blinding me. When I blinked, the light retreated. I often tried to follow it, the tiny star racing away far above, becoming so small that it seemed at times to be imaginary. As I kicked upwards toward the star, the water grew colder and colder until I could not feel my body anymore and I was forced to stop struggling and float back down to the warmth and the darkness.

When I slept at the bottom of the lake, I had strange dreams. In these dreams, I was in a bed chamber with whitewashed stone walls, richly carved oaken furniture, and a window through which I could see a walled orchard and wooded hills rolling away in the distance. When the window was open, I could hear the roar of the sea far off. Sometimes I was alone in this dream, but often there was a brown-haired girl with a round pleasant face and rosy cheeks. She helped me wash at the stone basin and ewer. One time she handed me a scrap of paper and a pen; I drew a pretty canary in a cage for her since she sang with the birds chirping outside the window. She spoke to me often, telling me of her widowed mother and her brothers and sisters, who all lived in a tiny thatched cottage beyond the hills and raised gray geese for market. I never spoke in these dreams, but my lack of response never seemed to bother the brown girl, as I came to think of her. Colors swirled around her like autumn leaves caught in an updraft, golds and oranges and reds and browns, solid, comforting hues that left the smell of cinnamon in the air.

Other people came in the chamber sometimes. A thin, sharp-featured blonde with nervous hands who called me sister and cried when I didn't answer. I embraced her and drew her pictures because I felt sorry for her. Poor thing. An aged apothecary appeared one day in a battered black hat and tattered cloak, his wooden chest rattling with many bottles and packets of herbs. He examined me carefully, his eyes resting on my face so long that I finally looked away. If it hadn't been a dream, I would have told him he shouldn't stare at people like that, as if they were no more comprehending of his presence than a sick animal. He was kindly enough though, and I drank the concoction he gave me. Dream medicines couldn't hurt, after all.

In the dream after the apothecary, two other men came. The taller one I had seen before, and I shrank against the window at the feel of his gray chill, wondering if this was to be a nightmare. The other was young, with limp brown hair and an uncertain step. He seemed to need the elder to tell him what to do. After they consulted for several minutes, the younger moved toward me and picked up my hand. I let him, watching his eyes. They were wide and blue-gray and fearful as he lifted a cool band to my finger. There was already another, far lovelier ring on that finger, a swirl of gold and pearls with one green stone set in the middle. When he tried to take this ring off in order to make a space for his band, I snatched my hand away. He turned to the tall, gray man.

"What should I do, sir?" he asked.

"How do you think it's done? Put the ring on her finger."

"But she won't let me. There's another ring already there-- she won't let me take it off."

The gray man stepped nearer, and the younger moved quickly aside, as if he was afraid to be too close to him. Before I could draw away, the gray man grabbed my hand in his, his grip surprisingly warm. When I tried to escape, his fingers tightened, and I gasped.

"Be still now, wench," he warned gruffly. I glared at him, but he pretended not to notice. A flicker of something--sadness, though I couldn't imagine this man being sad for another--passed across his face as he examined the ring on my finger. "Merius, you damned fool," he muttered. He dropped my hand without touching the ring.

"What was that, sir?"

"Nothing." Sparing me one last glance, the gray man turned away.

"But what should I do with this ring?" The younger man held out the band.

"Put it on her other hand."

"But, but, sir, it's supposed to go on that finger. Tradition . . ."

The gray man chuckled, a mirthless sound. "You sound like a woman. That's an old wives' saying, what finger the ring goes on. It'll do the same job on another finger, Whitten."

I clenched the fingers of my left hand together tightly and hid it and the gold and pearl ring in the folds of my skirt, just in case they decided to take it after all. It meant everything to me, though I couldn't remember why. It was like a flower from a long ago summer picnic pressed between the pages of a book and not found again until winter when all had been forgotten. My inexplicable joy when I touched the ring was almost as faded and fragile as that long dead flower, but it was the only memory I had, and I clung to it. In the confusing swirl of days and nights that followed, I touched the ring whenever I felt unsteady. It was the most solid thing here in my dreams.

Long after, perhaps weeks, I floated back to the dark and warmth and awakened. I touched the ring again, feeling the ridges and smooth curves of the pearls and the sharp edges of the peridot. Peridot--who had told me about the peridot? I hadn't known it was a peridot in the dream, so someone must have told me. But there was no one else here. And if the ring had been in my dream, how could it be here too? The ring was real . . .

The sudden flash was terrible and wonderful in its swiftness. A high, stony place, the blue sky all around, and my love standing before me, nervous and awkward, his hands stuffed in his pockets as I turned the ring between my fingers. "That's a peridot," he said in a voice like pipe smoke, smooth and dark and low. "They're hard to find here, more common in Sarneth or Marenna." He shuffled a little, glanced down at his boots before he looked up again, his gaze locking with mine. "When I first met you, I thought your eyes were the exact green of peridots."

"Merius," I whispered. "Merius." I tried to breathe so I could say his name again and again and again until I saw him, but then I remembered I wasn't breathing. I couldn't breathe here. I was under water.

I began to choke, for the first time noticing that I was drowning, had been drowning for God knew how long. Kicking, flailing my arms, I pulled myself up, fighting for the surface. The water grew frigid as I rose, soon burning my skin with the cold fire of ice. She was here.

I froze and instantly began to sink back to the depths. For a moment, I let myself go. It would be so easy to retreat to the dark warmth and forget, not fight her anymore. But that would mean forgetting Merius again and likely never remembering him.

I struggled against the weight of the water over me; my muscles burned with the cold. The water was almost ice up here, cold enough to make my heart stop if I quit moving.

She was above me, pushing me back down. I punched her, shoved her away as I fought for air. We were so close to the surface that the water was clear, and I could see her hair waving in long golden snakes, her pale, beautiful face contorted in an open-mouthed fury. Her long fingers closed around my neck. I clutched my hands together in a double fist and drove them between her arms, forcing her to release me. She scratched my leg in an attempt to grab me as I escaped her. Only a fathom more . . .

I hit the surface, my knuckles cracking and bleeding against it. Solid ice. In shock, I wasted a precious moment drifting, the air in my lungs so stale it seared. I longed to exhale; the burning was so intense I could think of nothing else. I began to pummel the ice, the thought of the fresh air just inches away consuming me. That was how she found me again. She laughed, grabbed my foot, began to pull me towards her, her grip even colder than the frigid water around us. I did a somersault, kicking at her in my madness to escape. She terrified me even more than drowning. My foot hit the ice, and it cracked. I kicked it again, and it broke. I whirled around, digging at her face with my heel. She screamed and let go of my foot as I broke the surface, my ribs expanding as I took that first painful breath, a rebirth.

I opened my eyes, coughing. A painted wooden ceiling loomed above, three circles of light chasing each other over and around the broad beams. Candle flames dancing in a draft--that was what made the circles of light. There was a feather tick under me, a silken squared quilt over me. I stretched and yawned. The ceiling was quite pretty; a deep red with golden flowers and green vines painted around the crevices of the beams. We had only one painted ceiling at home, and it was an ugly thing; it was supposed to look like marble, but whoever had done it had stopped halfway through, leaving it a hideous chalky blue. I had always wanted one painted as the night sky, with a midnight blue background and a crescent moon and a scattering of silver stars. Perhaps when Merius and I had our own house, I could paint the ceilings.

Where was he? I turned my head. The pillow beside mine was flattened in the middle, like someone had been there not too long ago. Maybe he had gone for food. I had the vague feeling I'd been dreaming about him, some nightmare with a snake-haired woman and drowning, but I couldn't seem to remember anything before that. Where were we, anyway? An inn, perhaps? Gilgana? He had said he would be docking in Gilgana when he returned, so maybe I had met him here. But why couldn't I remember? I giggled nervously--it was one of those things we would be laughing about in a few minutes when he came back to the chamber, how I'd woken so disoriented that I couldn't recall where we were.

I pulled myself up, paused as a slight wave of dizziness hit me, then swung my feet off the bed and on to the floor. There was a washstand in the corner, and I went over to it, wincing at the cold boards under my heels. Maybe if I splashed some water on my face, I would feel myself. It was that damned nightmare--it had been so awful that I couldn't remember anything before it. More and more images flashed through my mind as I filled the basin from the pitcher. That evil woman, with her blond snake hair and her grasping hands, the icy water burning my lungs, the mad struggle to reach the surface before she drowned me--it had been so real. I set down the pitcher and put my palms to my face, my knees suddenly weak. She would have killed me. She wanted to kill me.

"Merius," I whimpered. "Merius . . ." I sank against the wall, telling myself over and over again that it was just a nightmare, that Merius would be back soon, that everything would be fine.

I lowered my hands, wiping away tears and feeling a fool. Crying over a nightmare like a child--what was wrong with me? I clasped my arms around my knees and shivered a little from the cold floor, wishing Merius would return soon. At least he would know where we were. What grown woman became so flustered by a nightmare that she forgot where she was?

I shook my head and rubbed my hands together to warm them. The rings on my fingers clacked against each other. Rings? I held out my hands. There was Merius's ring on my left third finger, where it was supposed to be. But on my right hand there were two golden rings I had never seen before. One was a twisted band, a traditional betrothal ring. The other was a seal ring, a large flourished L with vines twined around it. The Landers insignia. I slid it off my finger and examined it more closely. It was a perfect fit like it had been made specially for my finger, so it couldn't be Merius's ring. Besides, he had given his seal ring to his father before he left for Marenna. He had told me that the last time he had come to me with a headache, that he had just spoken to his father about the campaign and had given up his ring. I had kissed him then and we had fallen back on the bed and talked about how we would make our own House together, how the seal ring would have a pear on it since that was what we had survived on the last week, stealing pears from the kitchens between our trysts. Then Merius had laughed and grabbed me and said that his headache was gone just from talking to me and that he wanted to get started making the House right that moment.

I smiled and then sighed, even more impatient for his return. I glanced around the chamber, rubbing my bare arms. Surely he would be back in a minute or two. He wouldn't have left for long without telling me where he was going. Of course, I couldn't remember anything before waking up here, so maybe he had told me where he was going and I just had no memory of it. Gulping over the lump in my throat, I clutched my knees to my chest. This might not be Gilgana at all. This could be anywhere, for all I knew. I closed my eyes and hid my face against my knees, shivering. My mind desperately pawed over the contents of my memory. Bidding

Merius farewell in the court stables, sobbing in the coach on the way home, yelling at Father as he burned Merius's first letter, Strawberry nosing my palm for more sugar lumps, Boltan teasing me, Landers Hall at night, Mordric . . .

I paused at the thought of Mordric, mulled over our conversation. He had threatened me with Father's debts and Dagmar's betrothal, I remembered that much. The chamber had been cold, I had made some remark about a window being open, and then . . . then *she* had come. I had sensed spirits many times--there had been several at court, in fact, one of them a little girl who had died of a fever in my chamber forty years ago and had awakened me once with her cries for water. That one had disturbed me more than the others because she had been so young and pitiful. Mostly, though, I could ignore them--Mother had told me long ago that they wouldn't hurt me and that I couldn't help them, that they were just moving portraits of those who had died that only she and I could see. They became part of the scenery after that, no more remarkable than the paneling or the drapes of the chambers they haunted. Until that night in Mordric's study.

The attack had started with her laughter, stabbing like an icicle in my ear. There had been a sudden, splitting pain in my head, cold, sharp-nailed fingers at my neck, and oddly enough, the smell of roses everywhere. I choked even now, remembering that smell. It had been so sweet and pervasive that I had almost vomited--there had been no air left to breathe, just the roses. That she had wanted to hurt me and could hurt me had been clear, and I had realized then that there were things Mother either hadn't known or hadn't told me about our hidden talents, a fact that terrified me as much as the malevolent thing attacking my mind. She had dug her claws into my brain, whispering that I had pretty hair, so pretty that she would like to rip it out.

The tears came unbidden, streaming down my cheeks as I remembered. She had said other things, terrible things, about how I was a lowborn witch whore who wasn't fit to have Merius walk on my grave and that I was a halfwit if I thought Mordric or she would ever let their only son marry a wicked chit who should have burned at the stake years ago. All the while her icy fingers kneaded my brain like bread dough, the cold tingling through my entire body, a frostbite that seared all the way inward to my heart.

That was my last clear memory, hearing her laughter and cringing from the chill. After that, there were a few jumbled images and feelings--Father carrying me like I was a child again, the familiar terror that he was on the edge of apoplexy, a brown-haired, brown-eyed servant girl I had never seen before, drawing a canary in a cage on a scrap of paper, and the nightmare that had awakened me in this strange place. I looked around again, trying to place something, anything in my memory, but the only thing familiar about this chamber was my trunk at the foot of the bed. My hand on my collarbone, I took several deep, shuddering breaths in an attempt to calm myself. Wherever I was, a panic was not going to solve anything. After all, Merius might return at any minute--he could help me figure out what was wrong. Keeping this hopeful thought firmly in mind, I reached behind me and grasped the edge of the washstand as I stood.

As if in answer, footfalls echoed outside the door, and a key rattled in the lock. I shut my eyes for the briefest moment and muttered a prayer of thanks as the door opened. But the man who entered the chamber was not Merius.

My scream startled me as much as it startled the strange man. He took a step back, almost dropping his candle as he blundered into the door frame. I pressed myself against the wall and stared at him as he stared back. Lank-haired and pale, he had the sloped shoulders and slender frame of a scholar, his slightly bulging eyes bloodshot as if he'd been reading close text for too long. His aura was barely present, a thin line of blackish-blue around his body--the color, what little I could sense of it, put me in mind of a nasty bruise. I had the vague impression I'd seen him before, like someone I'd dreamed about but couldn't quite remember the next morning. "Who are you?" I managed finally, my voice faint.

He started again, looking at me as he might look at a pet dog that suddenly spoke to him. "You talk? They didn't tell me you could talk . . ."

"Get out--get out right now."

"They told me you were mute . . ." he went on.

"Get out of here! This isn't your chamber, sir." I crossed my arms over my breasts and hunkered down in the corner--all I wore was a shift, and the hem went only to my knees.

He continued to stare at me. "But . . ."

"My husband will be back any minute."

"But, sweet . . . sweet, I am your husband."

The exact moment I heard him say he was my husband, a buzzing started in my ears. Out of the corner of my eye, I noticed the white pitcher on the washstand had a pattern of blue flowers painted on it; as I looked, the colors reversed, and the pitcher turned blue, the flowers white. Before I could ponder this oddity, the world went dark.

~ ~ ~ ~ ~

"What did you say to her, Whitten?" Dagmar asked. Her voice sounded indistinct, as if I were hearing her on the other side of a wall.

Whitten mumbled something in reply, and although I couldn't make out his words, I did recognize his voice. The man who had come into the chamber and said he was my husband now had a name. Whitten. The official head of the House of Landers, Merius's cousin. Merius had mentioned him once or twice. Whitten--heavy drinker, prone to melancholy, feckless, often caught the brunt of Mordric's cold rages. I had had the impression Merius pitied him.

"She seems to be coming around," Dagmar said. "Safire!" Someone shook my shoulders.

With a great effort, I opened my eyes. Faces swam in a haze of candlelight before me--a pale and drawn-looking Dagmar, the brown-haired servant girl I remembered but couldn't put a name to, and at the foot of the bed, Selwyn and Whitten hovered in and out of focus. Everyone wore nightclothes, Dagmar in a dressing gown of sumptuous cranberry satin that I couldn't recall ever seeing her wear. I tried to sit up, but Dagmar held me down. "Don't try to sit up yet-- you might faint again."

"Where are we?" I said hoarsely.

Dagmar started much as Whitten had when I had spoken to him the first time. "Safire, you just spoke."

I raised my eyebrows. "Yes? So, where are we?"

She threw her arms around me, an impulsiveness that she only showed at times of great distress. "Oh, it's so good to hear your voice, hear you talking again. It's been so long . . ."

The walls of the chamber, which had been coming slowly into focus, suddenly went hazy again. "What do you mean?" I asked, my voice trembling. "How long?"

"Two months." Her arms tightened, and I felt the damp heat of her tears on my shoulder. "And Safire, Safire, Father's not . . ."

"My lady," the maid exclaimed. "She's just woken up. Maybe . . ."

Dagmar pulled away, wiping her eyes. "You're right, Elsa."

"What about Father?" I asked.

Dagmar shook her head. "Not now--you need to rest."

I struggled out from under the confining covers, pausing when I felt light-headed. "No, I can't rest now. What is it? Apoplexy?"

Selwyn cleared his throat, glancing at Dagmar before he answered. "Yes."

"Is it serious?"

"He's bedridden. Can't move or speak."

I closed my eyes and fell back on the pillows. "No," I said, shaking my head. "No, no, Father. Papa . . ." My heart pounding my ears, I curled into a ball, clutching my arms around my knees as I began to sob.

The feather tick sank in the middle as Elsa sat down beside me. "There, there, it's all right, my lady," she said, rubbing my back.

"No, it's not all right. It'll never be all right again."

~ ~ ~ ~ ~

The next day after I had risen and washed and forced myself to eat a little, Dagmar and I visited Father together. The dark chamber stank of sickroom smells and apothecary herbs, and Dagmar went over to the window and flung the casements open. The fresh light and air of a warm May morning flooded the dank stone corners, but it only brought relief to Dagmar, Elsa, and me. Father was beyond such comforts.

He lay on the bed, half propped up with pillows and cushions. His mouth hung open; every once in a while, Elsa would tip a little water or broth down his throat and wipe the drool from his chin. When I moved closer and took his hand in mine, I realized even his skin had changed. It had become so smooth and thin that it had a dull, brittle glow to it--it was the skin of a profoundly ill person. "I'm almost afraid to touch him, lest I bruise him," I murmured.

"He has bed sores on his backside," Elsa remarked. "The apothecary said there's little to do but put the salve on them and turn him every hour."

"Oh, Father." I squeezed his hand, but I might as well have been squeezing wax. "Are his eyes always shut?" I asked, desperate for some sound besides the faint rattle of his breath.

"Yes--he can't seem to open or close them."

"That's horrid, to be trapped in your body and not even be able to see." I knelt beside the bed, still holding his hand, and put my head next to his. "I love you, papa," I whispered. Dagmar came up behind me, and I glanced at her. "It's my fault he's like this. If I hadn't . . ."

"Nonsense, Safire," she snapped. "You could just as easily say it was my fault."

"But I'm the one who always provoked him. I should have behaved better, like you . . ."

"He wouldn't have loved you as much then."

"Dagmar!"

"It's true--you're his favorite. You know it too, so don't look so taken aback." She crossed her arms, paced the length of the chamber. "It doesn't matter now anyway. The fact is, we knew this was coming. He's always had a temper, the court physician told him to control it, lest it burst a vein, and he didn't. There's nothing we could have done about it."

I straightened. "There's nothing we could have done about it," I repeated, gazing down at him. "But there is something I can do about it now." I leaned over the bed and circled Father's head with my hands as I had done many times before, for him, for Merius, for Dagmar. The only time my hands had failed me was when Mother had died.

Dagmar glanced at me sharply. Then she saw my hands, the way they were positioned, and her eyes widened. She began to shake her head, pointing at Elsa. I shook my head back at her. Elsa wouldn't say anything. Elsa's grandmother had had the second sight, and she had learned not to fear such things. I looked at the servant girl, who was bent over her knitting, and wondered how I knew about her grandmother. It seemed she had told me, one of those little bits from the last two months that suddenly had popped to the surface of my murky memory. Since waking this morning, I had remembered other little bits, mostly about Elsa and the kindly apothecary.

I looked down at Father again, concentrated my attention on him before I closed my eyes with a clear picture of him. The rest of the chamber, Dagmar's pacing, Elsa's knitting, the birds fighting over the seeds scattered on the window sill, the green smell of spring slowly freshening the air--all these things faded into the background. Father's labored breathing filled my ears, and I gradually matched my breaths to his, so that we exhaled and inhaled as one. After several minutes of this, I reached into the darkness that was now his mind.

He could still hear, though not the same as before. Because it was the only sense left to him, his hearing had sharpened to the extent that each bird had its own voice, though he could not comprehend that he was sensing this. Fighting back tears, I reached further. Most of his knowledge, his memories had fallen into a black, depthless well, and it would be impossible to draw them back out again. The essence of him still lingered here, but only for a short while longer. I had come too late.

Silent tears streaming down my face, I motioned to Dagmar and Elsa. "Help me turn him."

"My lady, we just turned him a quarter hour ago."

"I suppose, but there may be something I can do for his bedsores." I wiped the tears with the edge of my sleeve.

The burning skin on his back oozed with dozens of sores, especially around his shoulder blades. Closing my eyes again, I placed my hands on his shoulders. The heat of the infection was easily sensed and drawn away from him and into me. As soon as his skin was cool and the sores closed, I went over to the washstand and plunged my hands in the basin, letting the water take the heat and sickness away as I scrubbed my fingers clean.

Elsa stared at Father's back. "The sores are gone. How did you . . ."

Dagmar swiftly crossed to the bed and pulled the sheet over Father. "The apothecary's salve must be working," she said briskly, giving me a narrow look.

"But . . ." Elsa gazed at me, and a sudden comprehension lit her face. "I knew there was something about you. A healer . . ."

"Like your grandmother."

"You remember me telling you that?"

I nodded. "I am remembering a few things."

"Let the next thing you remember be some discretion, sister," Dagmar said as she jerked the bed curtains straight. "Elsa, you're a good girl with good sense--don't repeat any of this. Not everyone understands such things."

"Oh no, my lady--I won't say a word. I usually never talk about grandmother, either, except Lady Safire seemed to enjoy my chatter when she was mute, and I didn't see the harm in it."

"I still enjoy your chatter. Chatter some to Father, if you think of it. Dagmar and I should come in and talk to him everyday."

"Do you think he'll understand us?"

"Probably not, but he'll recognize our voices. It may comfort him." I motioned to Elsa, and she helped turned him over on his back. I patted his cheek, smoothed his sparse hair down. Then I kissed his forehead. "I'll be back soon, papa."

As Dagmar and I left the chamber, Whitten came around the corner of the hall. He stopped when he saw us, and I quickly turned to the right, going in the opposite direction from him. "Safire, wait . . ." he began.

"Don't be so familiar with my name, sir." A shaking started inside, and I clutched my arms tightly as if to hold myself together.

He followed me. "Wait, please."

Unfortunately, the hall came to a dead end, so I was forced to comply with his request. "Leave me be," I spat, whirling on him.

He backed away several steps, almost knocking over Dagmar, who had followed both of us. "Listen, I just want to talk to you."

"We have nothing to say each other."

"Sweet, you don't have to shiver so--I'm not going to hurt

you."

"You were in my bed last night, before I came out of whatever fit I was in the last two months. You were in my bed, and you were," I choked, "were intending to come back to it. Don't you dare come anywhere near me or speak to me again."

"Wait, you touched her?" Dagmar's voice rose unsteadily. "You touched her?!"

Whitten's aura took on a sickly grayish hue, and he swallowed once, very rapidly, before he spoke. "I thought . . . I thought she was just mute. One night, when I'd come back from the tavern, she was in the hall. It was like she was waiting for me. She looked so pretty, and I couldn't help but kiss her and she never stopped me or nothing, and I thought . . . after all, she is my wife."

"No, I'm not. I never consented to it."

"You were never supposed to touch her." Dagmar's face was as red as Father's when he was in one of his rages, and I realized I wasn't the only one who had inherited his temper. "Mordric sat down with both of us and explained it. A marriage in name only in case she was with child, a marriage in name only to protect her, her dowry and title from men who might make claims that Father had betrothed her to them before he fell ill. You agreed to that, Whitten--I heard you."

"I know what I said," he exploded, startling both of us. "But I'd had a bit much ale, and she never stopped me."

I shut my eyes, wanting to retch. "Merius is going to kill you," I whispered.

"Merius?"

"My betrothed."

"Is Merius the one who put that ring on your finger?"

"Yes. He means to marry me when he returns."

"For God's sake," Whitten groaned. He turned to Dagmar. "You never told me about Merius."

"I assumed you knew, that Mordric had told you. Besides, what difference does it make to the fact you touched her, you disgusting swine?"

I put my hands over my ears and sank to my knees, hiding my face against the wall. I couldn't take anymore--two months gone,

Father dying by inches, and now this. Why had I ever woken from that fit? Merius--because I wanted to see Merius again. But Merius wasn't here. Merius was an ocean away, fighting, perhaps dying himself. I didn't realize my mouth was open and I was screaming until Dagmar wretched my palm from my ear and put her arm around me. "Safire, shh, shh, he won't touch you again. It's all right, sweet."

"I want Merius," I blubbered inanely.

"Merius isn't here." She paused, hesitating before she continued gently, "You shouldn't want him anyway even if he were here. He's false--he left you, Safire."

"Left me so he could gain his independence and we could marry. I hardly call that being false."

"Mordric said he's done it to girls before, just none as highborn as you. But it's all right. It'll be all right. We'll get your marriage annulled, find you an honorable husband."

"What lies are you telling her?" Whitten demanded. "Merius has never done that to a girl, seduced her and left her like that. Not that I know of, anyway, and I've known him since he was born. He's honorable."

"Maybe you were in a drunken stupor when he did it," Dagmar retorted. "His own father told me, and I hardly think he would lie about it. Now, go away--you've done enough."

Whitten glanced about to make certain we were alone before he bent down, cupped his hand around his mouth, and whispered, "You'd best learn this now. Mordric lies, my dears. All the time, for all sorts of reasons known only to himself. Just ask your Selwyn, Dagmar. He'll tell you the same, though you'll have to drag it out of him." Then he straightened and continued on in his normal voice, "There--I bet I'll regret I told you that, but you can't go on living in this House and believing everything you hear."

Dagmar glared up at him. "You think I believe you? The ale speaks for you."

Whitten shrugged. "Believe whoever you want to believe. You'll find out soon enough."

"He's right, Dagmar," I said softly.

Her arm tightened around my shoulders. "Just ignore him."

"No, he's right. Mordric's an awful old liar. He lied to me about Merius. I don't care what anyone says, even you. Merius loves me, he's coming back for me, and nothing . . ." I stopped, my breath fogging before my eyes. The air in the hall had suddenly turned frigid.

"Safire, what is it?"

I scrambled to my feet and looked around wildly. Already, I could smell the roses. The snake-haired woman's distant laugh echoed down the stone corridors, and the cold reached long, slender fingers into my lungs, choking me. "I can't stay here," I gasped, lurching headlong down the hall in the direction of my chamber.

"Wait, stop . . ." Dagmar's voice faded behind me as I raced into my chamber and slammed the door. As if that would keep the chill out. It followed me, circling my ankles and creeping upwards as I threw open the lid of my trunk and rifled through the contents. Nothing at the bottom had been disturbed since I had last looked through it at court. Evidently Dagmar had brought it straight from home and only taken out the clothes, leaving my drawing things, journals, and coin safe and hidden. My hands shaking, I grabbed my coin purse and portfolio as Dagmar began knocking at the door.

"Safire?" she called. "Safire, open this door--you're scaring me."

"I'm not the one you should be scared of," I muttered. I opened the door so suddenly that she almost stumbled across the threshold, her hands braced on the door jamb. Whitten stood behind her, and for an instant, I faltered. Then the hairs on the back of my neck rose as I heard that high, spooky laugh again, closer this time. That settled me--I ducked under Dagmar's arm and ran blindly for the stairs. I had to get out of this House.

Chapter Seventeen -- Merius

"Have you seen Sirus?" Gerard asked.

I glanced up from my water skin. Gerard was a silhouette against the bright morning sun. I shielded my eyes with my hand, cursing the terrain for the hundredth time. Pale-eyes weren't made for a land of no sunsets and no sunrises. There were no gradations to the light here in the Marennese mountains; either the sun shone bright as midday or there was no sun. Night fell like a rock without twilight to soften it, its sudden shadow frightening in its very swiftness.

"Last I saw of Sirus was last night, when he went off to piss," I said.

"You didn't see him come back?"

"No--I must've fallen asleep."

"Damn it, no one's seen him." Gerard sounded sharp around the edges.

I glanced back down at my water skin. I had been attempting to fill it with the trickle of water the Marennese called a stream. At least it was cold, a spring straight out of the heart of the stony mountain behind us.

"Maybe he walked off the side of the path in the dark--that one drop-off yesterday had to be a good fifteen hundred feet."

"That's grim, Landers."

I shrugged. "That's the kind of place we're in. Grim."

I glanced around. I had never seen such high mountains. When we had landed on the northern plains of Marenna and I had gotten my first glimpse of the far off Carnith Mountains, they were barely discernible dark blue shapes against the lighter blue of the sky. As we had traveled across the plain, they had become more distinct, rough-edged giants with caps of snow. Once we'd fought our way into the foothills, they towered around us, dark and full of echoes. I made Gerard remove his spurs because the ringing echo of them was enough to cause an avalanche.

"I think he got stuck in a rock woman," Gerard said.

"You and your rock succubus." I chuckled and clambered to my feet. Behind us, I heard the sounds of the men breaking camp. It had been difficult to find a hollow large enough for all of us to camp together, six noble captains and a hundred foot soldiers. Of course, there weren't a hundred foot soldiers left anymore. Roland and I had counted eighty-five last night after two of the men had vanished in the dark. And now, if Sirus was truly gone, we'd have five captains instead of six. I swallowed, the enormity of his absence sinking in. Sirus and I had practiced together some at home, enough for me to know he was a good swordsman and even better archer. He had a quiet, capable manner, a steadying presence on his men, and he was one of the best card players I knew, able to bluff with naught but a pair of deuces.

"Landers." Gerard's voice dropped to a hiss.

"What?"

"You don't think the slavers took him?"

"We better hope they did--there's a good chance then he's alive. They don't get any coin when they kill their captives."

"But that'd mean they're close." Gerard glanced around as if he expected sinister forms to pop out from behind every rock.

"Good. That's why we're here, Gerard--to flush the slaving bastards out and teach them a lesson." I clapped him on the shoulder with an enthusiasm I didn't feel.

"Don't be so damn pompous, Landers, not now."

"I was being sarcastic. I want to be home just as much as you do." I touched the braided lock of Safire's hair I carried in my shirt pocket, swallowing. I dared not think of her now, I dared not, or I'd run down the path the way we'd come and stow away on a ship home. Quickly, I looked toward the men breaking camp, my comrades and my duty. Merdcai, a small, dark-haired sort who jumped five feet in the air at every pebble clattering to the path. His father was a fisherman in Calcors. Karl Silar, the blacksmith's apprentice turned soldier, with the broadest shoulders and biggest muscles I'd ever seen. We'd had to find special chain mail for him. Wright Lorin, who sneezed whenever I asked him a question or gave him an order, as if I had the same effect as hay dust on him. Darle, the prankster of the group--he'd somehow slipped Marennese church incense into our pipe weed one night. Roland and I had each given him three lashes for that--it could have been a dangerous prank if we'd been ambushed in the middle of our incense-induced stupor. Late at night, though, I couldn't help but chuckle at the memory of Gerard, befuddled by incense, caressing a mossy rock because Roland told him it was Princess Esme's breast.

Merdcai, Karl, Wright, and Darle were but four of the seventeen men under my direct command as a minor captain. Roland, the oldest and most experienced fighter at age twenty-six, was the major captain to whom all the men, including the five minor captains, reported. I quickly sought out my men amongst the milling crowd, reassuring myself that all seventeen were there. If Sirus was indeed gone, we'd have to split his men up amongst us remaining commanders.

"What have you got in your pocket? You keep reaching in there like you're carrying the queen's pearls." Gerard made a grab for my shirt pocket, and before I could stop him, he'd pulled out the lock of Safire's hair. Even after all these weeks of hard travel, it glowed copper in the harsh light, a boon of unbearably sweet memory in this desolate place. She'd been so serious when she gave it to me, as if I asked for her little finger or a vial of blood. She had knelt naked in the rumpled bedclothes as she plaited her hair. Then she'd leaned forward and let me cut the lock with my dagger--with the morning sun on us, it looked like I was cutting fire, a flame of her I could carry with me to the darkest ends of the earth.

"So, Landers," Gerard leered, shoving me rudely back into my current reality. "Who's the wench?" He held up the lock of hair. "I bet she's a right tasty barmaid, with hair this color. I've always wanted to try a redhead to see if they're as wicked as all the legends say."

I snatched back the hair and hid it in my pocket. "Damn it, Gerard, she's not a barmaid. The next time you pull a stunt like that, you'll be picking your fingers off the ground."

"All right, settle down. I didn't mean to insult your wench. I am curious though, something I've always wondered about redheads--is her nether hair the same color as the hair on her head?"

I smiled. "Wouldn't you like to know?" I patted my pocket one last time to make certain her lock of hair was safe, then donned my gambeson and chain mail with a loud clinking that rattled in my ears and echoed off the rocky sides of the hollow around us. I only took off my mail once a day--to wash as best I could in whatever spring we camped near. It could be a foolish indulgence if we happened to get ambushed, but I seriously doubted anyone would try to ambush us in the morning when we were most alert.

"You've been acting strange since we left Cormalen, but I'd no idea it was a wench."

"Quit calling her a wench, Gerard."

He grinned and subsided. We had to get ourselves and our men ready to march further into the mountains, and his ribbing would have to wait. I knew, though, he would bring it up again, likely around the fire tonight so all the others could get in on the fun.

We walked together back to the camp, moving through the men until we found Roland. He crouched on the ground, attempting to shave with the edge of his dagger. Blood dotted his jaw, and he swore under his breath, leaning closer to the pocked surface of the shield he used for a mirror.

"That's the most asinine thing I've ever seen." Gerard could always be counted upon. "You don't even have anything to shave, Roland. Your chin's smooth as a boy's."

"Gerard, I'm your captain here. I could have you lashed till you don't have a chin to shave, so shut up," Roland said. "What do you want?"

"Orders would be nice, sir," I said. "You know, I have a magic razor in my pack for shaving invisible hair."

Gerard guffawed and elbowed me. Our running banter had grown more outrageous the further we climbed into the mountains, our way of whistling in the dark. Roland generally jested back, his easy confidence in his position as commander unspoken but present all the same. Gerard and I had met Roland our first year at the court academy, when he had been eighteen and in his last year at the academy. I had been a gangly thirteen-year-old at the time and remembered being dazzled by Roland's graceful moves in the practice salon--he had garnered more oohs and ahhs from the ladies than any other fighter his year. I had never expected to become friends with such a paragon, but when Roland turned up to assist with training us in arms our second year, the paragon quickly became the older brother I had always wanted, a man and fighter I could respect but still jest with.

Roland smiled at his shield and straightened. "Watch it, or I'll make you pack-donkeys carry my gear today. Any sign of Sirus yet?"

"No," Gerard said, the mood suddenly turning somber.

Roland scanned the perimeter, shielding his eyes with his hand as if he expected to see Sirus come around the edge of a rock. "If we could, I'd scour these mountains till we found him and the other two, but we've already spent half the morning, and Herrod's orders were clear: 'No searching for lost men in the mountains--you'll only lose more in the attempt.'"

"What do you think happened to him?"

Roland shrugged, tried to look nonchalant, though I could see the lines tighten around his mouth and across his forehead. "Probably the slavers. I think that's what happened to the two common soldiers who disappeared last night as well. A bit odd that all three of them should go missing at once, unless the slavers took them."

"What should we do?"

"Keep heading into the mountains--we've only had a few skirmishes so far. No sense in returning until we've driven back the slavers as far as we can. The best chance of finding the slavers who took Sirus and the other two is for us to continue further into the mountains, towards the SerVerin Empire. Herrod ordered me to lead you men around the Gargin Mines, all the way to the Zarina River."

I nodded outwardly, though my heart sank under the weight

of all the days it would take to march to the Zarina River. What had I gotten myself in for? By the time I returned, Safire would be tired of waiting. I would be tired of waiting for me, after all of this. Some other man would have claimed her, and then I'd have to fight him. Or what if something happened to her while I was gone? What if her father forced her to marry? Fathers had a way of doing that with their daughters. Damn it, why had I left her?

"This isn't the place to be in one of your trances, Merius. Stay alert," Roland said.

"He's thinking of his redheaded wench." Gerard guffawed again, and I threw him a dagger look.

"What wench?" Roland demanded.

"We need to go everywhere in pairs from now on," I said quickly, trying to change the subject. "There's eyes all around--can't you feel it?" The other two fell silent for a moment as the dark mountains brooded around us.

"That's grim, Merius--you're as saturnine as your father underneath your cloak of jests," Roland said finally. "Now, who's this wench? Maybe she'll cheer you."

"Don't call her a wench."

Roland and Gerard grinned at each other in a way that did not bode well for my future peace of mind. I'd have to watch my back now every time I wrote Safire a letter, lest I wanted it read to the whole camp before I had a chance to give it to one of the scouts who relayed messages between troops and Herrod's main camp by the sea.

"The only red-haired woman I know who's not a wench is my mother's housekeeper Wrennie. She's almost fifty, with the muscles of a warhorse and a bosom that could sink ships. I should have brought her to command our troops--she has the voice for it." Roland shrugged with a chuckle.

"Shouldn't we be readying to leave instead of jabbering?" I said.

"So, Merius, this ship-sinking bosom sounds a bit formidable. How do you handle something like that?" Gerard was in high form today, so high I longed to shoot him down.

"Shut up." I cuffed Gerard's shoulder, none too gently, and

he cuffed me back.

"Quit, or I'll lash you both for fighting," Roland said, suddenly all business as he cleaned his dagger. "Ready your men--we leave in a quarter hour."

"What about Sirus's men?"

Roland considered for the barest instant before he ordered, "Merius, you take half of Sirus's men. Gerard, you take the other half."

"Yes, sir," we said in unison. Gerard added, "Since I'm first today, which path do we take? I should get my men lined up before the others . . ."

"You're not going first today." Roland sheathed his dagger, then busied himself with tightening his pack fastenings, not looking at us.

"But it's my turn," Gerard insisted. In some places, the mountain paths were so narrow that we could only walk single file, and so all us noble captains took turns going first. There were wider roads that carried merchant caravans over the passes, but there we would have been sitting game for the slavers, so we stuck to the lesser known paths.

"We're not taking turns anymore. I'm the commander here, and I plan to lead us on this path till we reach the river," Roland said.

Gerard and I glanced at each other--I wondered if he felt the same tightening inside that I did, as if my ribs were caught in a vise. "Roland, at least let us draw lots," I said after a long, tense moment. "It's only fair we divide up the responsibility of who goes first."

"I'm well aware of that, Merius." Roland looked at me, his gaze narrow. "Are you questioning my authority?"

"No, I just . . ."

"Good--now you and Gerard best get your men ready. We have a long march ahead of us today."

Gerard and I stalked back through the camp. "What's he thinking?" Gerard muttered. "I was supposed to lead today."

"Losing Sirus rattled him."

"So he goes first because he's scared?"

"No, he goes first because he's a leader. Our leader. Think about it--would you order any of your men to go ahead of you into danger?"

Gerard kicked a stone. It flew over the ground and into a fissure in the side of the mountain, likely the entrance to a cave or abandoned mine. I was going to congratulate him on his aim, but the rattling echo the stone made as it bounced into the impenetrable darkness of the fissure made me feel so lonely suddenly that all I could do was swallow. To this ancient place, so far from any lasting human activity, we were but gadflies flitting over its harsh surface, our existence too brief for it to acknowledge. These mountains would be here, unchanged, long after we died, even if we survived this campaign and lived a hundred years. I shivered, my skin prickling, and hoped Gerard didn't notice.

~ ~ ~ ~ ~

We had been hiking hard for an hour. The path we took climbed steadily up toward the Gargin Pass, or at least what looked like the Gargin Pass on our maps. We had argued last night over those damned maps and which way we should go, finally resorting to a vote amongst the captains--the paths on the maps were little better than squiggly lines through darker squiggly lines denoting rivers that had long since dried up and other land marks we couldn't identify. I longed to wipe my sweaty brow, itching under my helmet, and silently cursed the weight of my mail, weapons, and pack. I had taken Sirus's pack as well as mine and now wondered if I could convince Gerard to take it when we stopped. What was Sirus carrying? Rocks? It hadn't felt heavy at all when I had first hefted it, but now the weight of the strap bore into my shoulder through my mail, and I cursed out loud this time.

"Everything all right, sir?" Darle asked behind me.

"Everything's . . ." my voice trailed off, my gaze caught by a dark outline of something moving down the side of the mountain to the left of the path ahead. I squinted. It resembled the shadow of a small cloud moving over the side of the mountain, but there were no clouds today. "Look out!" I shouted into the wind.

Roland kept moving--likely he couldn't hear me. He was first in line, followed by Gerard and his men, and then me, which meant there were about twenty-five men between me and Roland. He reached the top of the path at that instant, a tall figure against the distant sky.

"Look out!" I shouted again, louder this time, and Gerard turned and looked around wildly. But Roland continued over the crest of the path. He took a few steps down the other side, the top half of his body still visible. A black gleam sliced the air beside him-- the sunlight glancing off the glassy black stone of a SerVerinese arrowhead. The arrow hit its mark, the narrow band of exposed flesh between Roland's helmet and mail, the force of its flight burying its cruel point deep in his neck. He reached halfway up, his hand fumbling for the shaft, the blood already a crimson wash on his skin and mail. He bled so much so quickly, each heartbeat a fatal one. His hand suddenly stopped moving, and he stood for an instant, a man frozen in his last mortal moment. Then he crumpled out of sight, beyond the crest of the path.

Someone yelled unintelligible curses, so loud I wanted to cuff him for bursting my eardrums. Then I realized the someone yelling was me. Those bastards. They'd just killed Roland. I dropped my pack, Sirus's pack, dropped everything except my sword and bow and arrow quiver.

"Go back!" Gerard shouted. "Everyone, go back!" He hurried back down the hill, urging his startled men to turn and retreat.

"Go back!" I yelled at my own men. "Darle, get them back to the plateau where we camped, now." The other two captains and their troops behind us started doing the same, turning around and retreating as fast as they could. I made certain all the men started back to safety before I scrambled up the side of the mountain, loose rocks slipping under my feet. All I could see was Roland, falling like a deer. Bile rose from my gut, and I gagged, feeling the impact of the arrow in my own neck, the cold black point slicing through my throat. The bastard would regret his aim, whoever he was.

The rocks cut my hands as I climbed in the steep spots, drops of blood the scarlet tears of the rage that consumed me. The wind blew even more violently up here than it did on the path, its keening wail echoing in every crevice. I welcomed its cool slap prickling away the sweat on my neck. The air thinned the further up I clambered, forcing me to pause to catch my breath. I glanced back, surprised at how far away the path appeared, the men a black line of upright ants. Then I swore, for I heard a distant spill of loose stones and saw the glint of a helmet bobbing over the edges of the rocks I had just climbed. Someone was following me.

"Gerard, you ass," I muttered, just knowing it was him from the determined progress of the helmet. "Stay with your men, damn you--no sense in both of us risking our necks."

I started to climb again, wishing I hadn't looked behind me. Seeing the men and path so distant reminded me of just how high I had come--and how far I would fall if I lost my footing. Or how far Gerard would fall if he lost his footing. Why was he following me? We had an unspoken vow to watch each others' backs, but this was strictly my enraged folly to pursue. Knowing Gerard followed, taking the same risks I took, made me consider turning around, and I didn't want to turn around. I wanted to find the whoreson who had shot Roland so I could slaughter him.

I slipped then, the stone under my foot loosening and then clattering down the side of the mountain. "Damn it!" I gripped the edge of the rock overhead and pulled myself up with a grunt, my knees finding purchase and then my feet. I dragged myself over the rock on my belly, discovering that I had breached the ridge top in this final attempt. I now could see over the other side and all around, everything blue and cold in the distance. If this was the mouth of the world, the world was a wolf--peaks like jagged teeth everywhere I looked, sharp enough they cut into the sky and made it bleed. Some SerVerin bastard had shot Roland with an arrow, but these mountains would devour his bones, and I hated them as much as his killer.

I descended the other side cautiously, conscious that any noise I made could alert Roland's assassin to my presence. The realization came to me suddenly that I might find a whole band of men, not just one man. I swallowed at the thought and froze for a moment before I pushed myself onward. I had to avenge Roland, lest this fiery rage in my gut consume me.

After slithering backwards for several minutes, I landed with a soft thump on the blessedly flat surface of a small plateau, much like the place we had camped last night. Dusting my hands, I glanced around. Huge rocks dotted the ground, obscuring my view--there could be men concealed dozens of places, and I likely wouldn't know it until they attacked.

A rain of stones hit the ground, and I jumped, sword already in hand. Gerard landed behind me, the zealously polished gleam of his distinctive helmet pike unmistakable, and I relaxed.

"That was a hell of a climb," he said.

"You shouldn't have followed me then."

"What was I supposed to do?"

"You should have stayed with your men."

"You should have stayed with your men. Merius, what the hell are you doing?"

"Avenging Roland."

"You're a clever ass, but you don't have any damned sense sometimes. Good God, what if all of us had decided to avenge him? Damn it, you didn't see me breaking ranks to go charging up the mountain God knows where. That is, until I saw you doing it. You're going to get us both killed . . ."

"Shh." I touched his arm--a falling rock bounced somewhere close by. We both listened for a tense moment, then heard the scuffle of movement over rough terrain. Echoes confused the sound, and I couldn't tell from which direction it came. Gerard and I glanced at each other, then, without speaking, we both hunkered in the shadow of the mountain, our backs flush with the stone. The scuffling became distinct footfalls, and then I heard the staccato mutter of someone trying to talk softly in SerVerinese. It was a sharp-edged, harsh language which did not lend itself well to whispering, and the speaker's words reverberated off the stone walls.

At that instant, two men in the black and silver uniform of the SerVerinese army rounded the edge of the nearest rock, not twenty yards from us, glinting scimitars drawn. My stomach dropped like a sandbag, the mountains looming too close for a moment and then receding rapidly, so rapidly I felt dizzy and slightly unreal. The men were too close to reach for our bows, so I reached for my sword instead, Gerard following suit.

They looked like assassins, with their sleek uniforms of battered black leather and silver fastenings. They even wore black masks like assassins, masks that hid all but the gleams of eyes and teeth. Father suddenly said *Lift your blade, Merius, and quit gaping. Your whole right side is open, damn it* . . . even here, a sea away, in the midst of battle, I heard him. Was he inescapable? Gritting my teeth, I charged forward, mindless action the quickest way to silence him for the moment.

Gerard yelled something, probably calling me a reckless ass, but at that instant, the taller SerVerinese lunged, his scimitar meeting my sword in a deafening clang that drowned all other sound. With the echoes, it reverberated like a hundred blades ringing against each other, an invisible army fighting around us. A ghost army, with echoes for weapons.

A madness seized me at the sound, the anger that had propelled me over the mountain bubbling to the surface and flaring to flames that blistered my skin. My rage would burn me alive, but not before I killed this slaving bastard. No matter who he was, the man I faced was SerVerinese, and a SerVerinese had slain Roland. Therefore, this man must die.

I tried to stab the man, and he leapt back, nimble despite the uneven ground. I swore and lunged at him. He made a quick, sharp swing at me, his blade coming within inches of my chest. I swallowed, my heart pounding so fast and loud in my ears that I couldn't hear single beats anymore. Instead of moving forward to engage while I was stunned, he retreated again. Why did he do that? Suddenly, out of the corner of my eye, I saw the other SerVerinese turn and run off, Gerard in pursuit. They vanished around the edge of a large rock, and I tried not to be distracted by the distant clangs of their swords. So I moved towards my opponent, this time holding my sword low, at a wide angle to block the blow I knew was coming. He chuckled and swung his scimitar with such force that he almost knocked the sword hilt from my grip. Then he gracefully jumped away, in retreat yet again. He was baiting me, the son of a bitch. Father had used a similar technique several times when he was in the training salon with me. *You're a hothead, Merius. You're always too eager to attack, and someday an opponent will use that to wear you out or draw you into an indefensible position.*

Cursing, I ran at the man, blade extended, Father's voice still tormenting me. *You idiot--he'll slaughter you. All he needs to do now is step aside and catch you with a draw cut to the back.* The instant before my sword tip made contact with my opponent's midsection, he did indeed step aside to my right, just as the shadow father in my mind said he would. *I'll show you, damn it.* I lunged to my left, just in time to miss his scimitar slicing my back. As it was, the curved tip of his blade caught me in the side, pushing my chain mail through my gambeson and shirt and into the tender flesh between my ribcage and my hip. There was no pain in the first shocked moment, then a dull throbbing that time would whet to sharp burning. Blood flowed warm and sticky on my skin, but I dared not look down, lest I lose my nerve at the sight. Instead, sensing the SerVerinese drawing in for the kill, I spun around, blade fully extended. My sense was correct. My opponent was a mere couple yards from me, preparing to stab me in the back. My sword hit his scimitar with as much force as I could muster, and he grunted, stumbling backwards, his midsection exposed as he threw his arms out to catch himself. I vaulted over the ground and jammed my sword so far in his stomach that the point hit bone. I faltered then, sickened by the enraged force of my blow. Through my sword hilt, I had felt the steel of the blade vibrate when it scraped his skeleton. Gagging, I tore off my helmet and threw it down before I propped my hands on my knees. The ground swayed in front of me.

"Barbarian filth," the dying man spat in SerVerinese, then choked.

A gut wound, a particularly nasty way to go. He could lay here for hours on the hard rocks before he died. Roland, on the other hand, probably hadn't even known what hit him. Roland, who would never laugh, tumble a girl, hunt, or fight again. Roland, who had crouched by his shield, trying to shave with his dagger just scant hours ago. Roland, who Gerard and I had jested with so many times. Wait, Gerard--where was Gerard? I glanced around. Nowhere in sight. I listened for any sound of fighting, but all I heard was the wind, and then the metallic scrape of a sword against the rock, much the same sound I imagined my sword would have made when it scraped against the SerVerinese soldier's bone . . . sourness rose in my throat, and I gagged again, desperate not to retch, even here where there was no one else to see me. Father had never retched in the midst of battle, I was sure of it.

Too late, I wondered what had made the metallic sound. Then I saw the flash of the dying man's scimitar as he raised himself on his elbow, panting, and swung at my legs. I jumped aside, tripping on my own feet, clumsy with surprise. Blinding white sparks exploded before my eyes as I fell, blinding white pain soon following, radiating from the back of my neck and skull before everything went mercifully black.

~ ~ ~ ~ ~

Someone nudged my side, hard. "All right, all right, Father," I muttered. "I'll get up in a minute." Then I rolled over, expecting the softness of my pillow against my cheek. Instead, I choked on a mouthful of foul-tasting sand and pebbles. "What the hell?"

"Up, barbarian," someone said in crude Corcin. "Up, so I kill you like man, not beast."

I opened my eyes, then swore. The hard light of the sun pierced my eyeballs. I groaned. My head throbbed. It hurt to think. Evidently, I'd fallen and knocked my head on a rock. Why had I taken my helmet off? What an idiot thing to do.

A SerVerinese soldier stood before me, a dark shape against the light. His uniform blinded me in spots. It appeared to have more silver on it than the uniforms of the man I had killed and Gerard's opponent, which likely meant he was the commander. So where were Gerard and his opponent? Dead . . . if Gerard died . . . oh hell . . .

"Up, damn you," the SerVerinese commander said then, prodding me with his foot. "Or I kill you as you lay."

I grabbed for my sword, only to grasp an empty scabbard. The SerVerinese chuckled grimly. "After I kill you, I bury your blade with my brother. You kill him, I kill you, barbarian, and leave your bones for vultures."

"Who are you? If you're killing me, I want to know." Maybe I could distract him long enough to retrieve my sword.

"No matter who I am. My name too good for Cormalen filth to hear."

"You're a fine example of your people's diplomacy--with a

manner like that, you'll soon be an ambassador for Emperor Tetwar." I pushed myself off the ground till I knelt on the stone. The world spun around me, my head so light it could float away. If I had drunk a whole bottle of my father's whiskey in one sitting, I wouldn't have felt this ill. Blood still oozed from the cut in my side, and the sight of it made me want to retch. I almost wished this nameless SerVerinese would kill me and put an end to it.

"No mocking me." He kicked my ribs right above my cut, and I groaned, almost falling back to the ground.

"If you want me standing, you'd best let me do it," I hissed, inhaling sharply at the pain in my side. I glanced around, frantic for my sword. It was tucked in the SerVerinese's belt. Then something cold prickled against my neck, and I swallowed. He had the edge of his scimitar around my throat. The blade bit into my skin.

"You die now," he said.

I shut my eyes, shaking. What would come next? Unbearable pain, gasping for breath, and then utter darkness? Would that be the end? How could that be the end? I cursed myself for letting my mind wander in chapel so much. I tried to remember a prayer but none came. Instead, I remembered Safire, the burned cedar scent of her hair, her wicked chortle of a laugh, her witch touch, her impossibly long-fingered hands tight against my back and neck when I kissed her. "Safire," I whispered, and her name sounded more like a prayer to me than anything I'd ever learned in chapel. "Safire," I repeated, my voice stronger.

There came a dull thwack, the sound of an arrow hitting a target, and the SerVerin soldier toppled against me. I fell to the ground, his scimitar landing with a clatter beside us. The fall knocked the wind from me, and I lay motionless for a moment, stunned that I still lived. Then I felt a liquid warmth soaking the sleeve of my gambeson--SerVerinese blood. I swore and rolled over, grabbing my sword from the dead man's belt. I was as unsteady as a toddling babe getting to my feet.

Gerard slung his bow over his shoulder and jumped down from his perch on a rock, some twenty yards distant. We looked at each other; his face was in shadow under his helmet, and I suddenly felt unreal, as if he had turned into a stranger that I'd have to get reacquainted with. I glanced down at my sword, and it took me a moment to remember that it was an ancestral blade, my great-grandfather's sword, and that my great-grandfather had been a Landers, as I was. Landers--yes, my name was Merius of Landers, son of Mordric and Arilea. I held out my hands, squeezed my nails into my palms until I felt pain. The pain was real enough, but distant somehow, as if some other Merius were feeling it. I took a deep breath. Was this what almost dying felt like, this abrupt return to a world that should be familiar but now seemed like something seen through poorly made glass?

Gerard approached slowly, almost warily, as if he didn't quite know what to make of me either, his boots crunching on the loose stones and pebbles. He paused near one rock and bent down to pick up my helmet. I retrieved my sword and sheathed it, my hands trembling.

"Good shot, Gerard," I said as loud as I dared. "You saved my life. Thank you."

He handed me my helmet before he clapped my shoulder. I clapped his shoulder back. In lesser circumstances, we might have given each other a bear hug, but in dire straits such as these it was best to be stoic, lest we be weakened by a show of emotions.

He cleared his throat finally. "The man I fought drew me off a good ways before I finally killed him. As I was making my way back, I heard some sounds like there were other men around, so I climbed up on that rock to get a decent view. That's when I saw you and that bastard. Sorry it took me so long to shoot--I couldn't get a clean shot till he moved. Anyway, I think if we head over to the edge there," he said, pointing to right side of the plateau, "we can find the path. That's where they shot Roland from, the edge of the plateau. The path must come out under it somewhere."

I nodded. "We need to get back to the men." I paused, not knowing what to say next. "I'm sorry I broke ranks. I was angry when you started following me, but I'm sure glad you did now."

He met my gaze, his eyes as old as our fathers. "I'm glad too, Merius. I couldn't make it here if both you and Roland were gone. This is a hellish place to be without comrades."

"I know what you mean. Let's get back to the men, while

there's still light enough to find a place to camp and do what we can to honor Roland."

He nodded, and I clapped his shoulder again before we started to pick our way over the rocks, back to the path and our fellow warriors.

Chapter Eighteen--Mordric

Dinner was still on the table when I returned home shortly after sunset, so I made my way to the banquet hall without even removing my boots. Selwyn, Whitten, Talia, and Dagmar all glanced up at the sound of my heels on the floorboards, the two men rising before I waved them to sit down again. Usually I liked to hold to the formalities, but not when I was half starved after a day of riding.

I slung my cloak across the back of the chair at the head of the long table and sat, two maids instantly at my elbows pouring water and wine and filling my plate. I drained the water tumbler before I attacked the food. Roasted suckling pig, bits of buttered yam, new peas, crusty rolls to soak up the drippings.

"How was your journey, Mordric?" Talia asked. Selwyn had inherited her bothersome, fussy manners, which included asking pointless questions at the most inopportune times, all under the guise of politeness.

I wiped my mouth with the napkin, looked up, grunted an unintelligible response, and returned to the food.

Only a fool would be encouraged by this, but Talia was a fool. "Oh, that's too bad. The roads have been all mud this spring, almost impassable. We went to Calcors the other day in the coach, and it was scandalous, the amount of mud the horses kicked up. And after Ebner's fine paint job, too--the coach was ruined. It looked a disgrace, I tell you. Like some peasant's cart. I was embarrassed to ride in it. I don't see why they can't cobble the shore road . . ."

"Mother, the expense . . ."

"I don't see why. It's just a few rocks. The whole of Calcors is cobbled, every little dirty alley and peddler's street, yet they can't--"

"The merchants pay for that, and there's plenty of cheap labor for street crews in the city. We'd have to sacrifice our tenants several weeks a year if we wanted cobbled roads. Better to buy a new coach."

"But cobbled roads would look so much nicer." She pouted, an obnoxious gesture for a woman her age, for a woman of any age as far as I was concerned.

"I don't know what you're talking about," I said then. "The roads were dry and hard today. Not a speck of mud except in the low spots." I shoved a forkful of pork in my mouth.

"But you just said it was muddy."

I shook my head, chewing furiously. I had never said anything about it being muddy, hadn't said anything at all in fact, but she could manufacture an entire statement out of a neutral grunt. Damned harpy--best to ignore her.

"Sir?" Selwyn asked after several moments.

This time, I didn't bother looking up. "What now?"

"I wasn't going to mention this at dinner, but it's rather serious and likely requires your attention. We were actually thinking of sending you a message at court, but as you were returning anyway . . ."

"Your forethought is almost as remarkable as your circumlocution."

"Thank you, sir."

I raised my eyes, my fork halfway to my mouth, and looked at him. He appeared slightly pleased, in a pompous sort of way. Poor devil--he had been a plodding scholar, neither good nor bad. He usually understood Merius's sarcasm, but not mine. I let it go.

"So, what were you going to tell me? Spit it out."

"Dagmar's sister . . ."

"Safire," Dagmar prompted.

"Yes, I remember," I said impatiently. As if I could forget. "What about her? Has she recovered?"

"Well, yes, sir, but--"

"But what?"

"Well, she's left, sir."

"What do you mean, she's left?"

"She ran right out the front door and disappeared down the main road yesterday. Most unladylike display I've ever seen, skirts flying everywhere. She almost knocked me down in the hall," Talia sniffed.

"She wasn't feeling herself," Dagmar said. "She'd recovered her voice and her wits, but she was in shock from Father's illness and Whitten's," here her eyes narrowed as she glanced over at Whitten, who was staring at his empty plate, "Whitten's wickedness."

"Now, sweet," Selwyn said, "he didn't mean any harm. He thought . . ."

"I don't care what he thought. It was wicked what he did, drunk or not, husband or not. He agreed . . . well, never mind what he agreed. It's not fit for the dinner table. You know what you've done. But let me tell you this now, if anything happens to Safire before we find her, I'm blaming you."

Whitten swallowed but didn't say anything, still staring at his plate. I put down my knife and fork, finally giving up any hope of eating in peace. I had a pretty good idea what Dagmar was talking about, but there was time to throttle Whitten later. I should have known--the feckless drunk had never been able to keep his paws off the serving wenches, much less some comely girl who wasn't in her right mind to say no. I rubbed my eye with my palm and sighed. Another long night, after two long months at court without Merius to assist me at council. And I wanted to walk the property tomorrow, maybe hunt a stag. Damn it.

"Now, what's all this blather about finding Safire? When did she come out of her fit?"

"The other night, she came out of it. She didn't remember the last two months, just bits and pieces. Yesterday morning, she and I and Whitten had a discussion, and she got so upset she ran. I let her go--I thought she needed time alone to think about things, like she did on those long walks she used to take. But she always returned from her walks. She never returned last night."

"Could she be lost in the forest?"

"I don't think so. Even upset, she would have sense enough not to wander in strange woods. Besides, we searched today, and everyone who saw her says they saw her on the road, heading towards Calcors."

"What could she want there?"

"I don't know."

"She had money with her," Talia remarked. "A good-sized purse--I heard the jingle of coin. And some sort of leather bundle under her arm."

"Money? Where did she get money?"

Dagmar bit her lip. "I don't know where it came from."

"You're lying, my lady. What, did she steal it?"

Her eyes blazed. "No, Safire's not a thief. And I don't appreciate you insinuating that she is, sir."

"What else am I to think when you lie to me?"

She took a deep breath. "True enough. All right, then. Safire likes to sketch--she's actually quite good. She used to go to the market with her drawings. She may have made the coin that way."

"You mean, she sold the drawings?" Talia demanded. "She was engaged in common trade--a gentleman's daughter?"

"The little hussy," Selwyn said, but I detected a hint of admiration in his tone. Money impressed Selwyn, whoever had it, wherever it came from. He was the one who kept asking Peregrine to join the card games down at the tavern, long after Merius had made his reservations known by punching Peregrine in the jaw.

"It wasn't right, her selling those sketches," Dagmar said, "but at least she wasn't selling herself. Don't call her a hussy."

"It's not your fault, dear," Talia said through her upturned nose. "Certainly, we wouldn't impugn you for your sister's behavior--you're a good girl."

"So speaks the pillar of virtue. Too bad it's made of salt," I muttered.

"What was that, Mordric?" Talia turned her magpie eyes in my direction.

"I was just asking if any attempt had been made to find the girl in Calcors."

"Whitten and Baldwin and I looked some on the docks this afternoon, but not a sign of her," Selwyn said.

"First of all, if she has any sense, she won't be on the docks.

Did you look around the market at all?"

"We didn't have time, sir."

I bit into a yam, thinking. "If she is in Calcors," I said to myself. "All right," I said aloud. "After dinner, I'll look for her."

"But sir, we didn't expect you to--"

"What did you expect? You didn't find her," I snapped. Damn fools, damn girl, damn Merius for getting himself entangled with her in the first place. I continued to eat, not tasting anything. A report had come to the council a few weeks ago--Merius's band had split off from the rest and gone deeper into the Marennese mountains overlooking the Zarina River, a hard, dangerous country full of tight spots and daily opportunities for ambush, far beyond the reach of Herrod's messengers. I stabbed at the last of the pork. Herrod and I had gone into those mountains some twenty-eight years ago after a bunch of renegade miners had taken the old king's cousin hostage; we had been the only two of our party to emerge alive several months later. Herrod should have known better than to send any of the men so far inland. Merius was well-trained, a good fighter in all respects despite his inexperience, but I didn't know about the other men. At least Gerard was one. He and Merius would watch each others' backs; they had since they were boys, practicing with sticks. I pushed away my plate, not wanting any more food but still feeling a gnawing emptiness in my gut.

~ ~ ~ ~ ~

After dinner, I ordered the coach readied for our trip to Calcors. I was sick of the sight of my saddle, and if we did find the girl, I certainly didn't want her riding pillion with me. I chose Selwyn and Ebner the horse master to help me search. Selwyn was thorough at least and would follow my orders to the letter. Ebner was our most trustworthy servant and had a great deal of common sense. With the three of us searching the inns around the square, I doubted it would take us long to find her. Bothersome little witch.

We rode in silence for some time in the coach until Selwyn cleared his throat. "Excuse me, sir?"

"Yes?"

"Why are we searching tonight? Whitten and I thought it would be easier to spot her in the daytime."

"That's where you're wrong. She's likely staying in a inn, right?"

"I suppose."

"Then if she's there at all, she'd be there at night, wouldn't she?"

"Well, yes."

"And there are only so many inns in Calcors, just a handful around the square itself. All we have to do is ask the innkeepers if she's at their inn. A young noblewoman with hair that color all alone--she's not likely to blend in with the other guests, now is she?"

"Not her, no sir." Several moments passed before he again interrupted the silence. "But sir, what if she's not in Calcors?"

I shrugged. "We should at least have a look--it's the most likely place she'd be."

"Oh."

We left the coach at one of the stables near the square. I tossed a silver to the boy on duty as we walked out to the street. "We'll only be a few hours, if that," I told him.

"That's fine, sir. There'll be someone here, whenever you're ready."

When we reached the well in the middle of the square, I stopped. I took a long drink of water from the common bucket--it was brackish. They never should have dug a well this near to the sea.

"Now," I said, spitting out the last of the water. "We'll split up. Selwyn, take that far side of the square, the one closest to the town wall. Ebner, you take the foreigners' market and Aislers Corner. I'll search the area closest to the docks where all the alley inns are. When we're finished, we'll meet back here."

They both nodded, and we went off in our separate directions. The so-called alley inns had their main entrances on side streets rather than on the square itself, so my search took me through several patches where there were no lanterns. I found myself stepping in all manners of refuse, bumping into shadowy figures on missions of their own, and in general swearing under my breath. My boot heel caught between two cobbles at one point, and I had a devil of a time getting it loose. I should have sent Selwyn this way.

The first inn I stopped at was the Red Door, a fairly

respectable establishment with good dark ale. I remembered it from years ago--drinking a mug of that ale was as filling as a meal almost, it was so rich. While I waited for the inn-keeper, I ordered a tankard of the stuff and drained it before the barmaid's wide-eyed gaze. It washed away the brackish taste from the well water and left my legs with a wonderfully solid heaviness. For once, something good had stayed the same. When the inn-keeper came out, wiping his plump hands on a towel, I set down the tankard and paid the maid. The keeper's pale moon face looked familiar, and I realized he was the son of the man who used to run this inn when I frequented it.

"Good ale," I told him. "It's the same brew your father used to make."

"Yes, sir--we've kept the same casks and everything. Now, Sally said you were looking for someone?"

"Yes. A small, red-headed girl, about eighteen." I cut a swath with my hand through the smoky air to show him how tall she was. "Rather pretty. A noblewoman, all alone. Have you seen her?"

He thought for a moment. "Bright copper hair, all in ringlets halfway down her back?"

"Yes."

"She's not staying here, but she was in our common room last night. Sally pointed her out to me--some sailors were giving her a time of it, and I made them leave. We don't put up with such here."

"You said she's not staying here--do you know what time she might have left last night?"

"Around seven. She was a nice girl, thanked me for getting rid of the sailors. She drew a right fine picture of my nephew--he's the one over there." He pointed at a tall, bony youth of about sixteen summers who was filling pitchers from a barrel and handing them to the barmaid. "Never seen a woman draw like that. She would have stayed, I think, but we were full last night. You say she's noble?"

I nodded but didn't volunteer any more information. He had told me enough. I thanked him for the ale again and headed out the door. I went through four other inns and boarding houses over the course of the next hour, following what I thought Safire's probable path would have been. No one had seen anymore of her since the Red Door, and I was about to give up on this side of the square before I noticed yet another swinging sign and lantern down an unfamiliar alley.

This inn was smaller and darker than the Red Door, the sort of place that looked like it might be concealing a few rats in the shadowy corners. A sallow girl of fifteen or so with grubby hands answered my knock. "Full up," she said before I even had the chance to say anything. "Sir," she added sullenly, eyeing my cloak with its silver fastenings.

"I'm not interested in a room."

"What d'you want then?"

"I'm looking for a girl a few years older than you. Small, redheaded . . ."

"What's it worth, if she's here?"

"I'm the head minister of this province. If you don't answer my questions and do it in a polite manner, I can have you arrested. So I think it's worth quite a bit more to you than me, my dear."

She drew up, her eyes narrowing as if she was considering slamming the door in my face. Then her gaze moved over the silver fastenings of my cloak again, and she paused. "Well," she said finally. "Putting it that way . . . like to come in, sir?"

"Not unless the girl's here."

"She's not now. Ten minutes ago she was."

"Damn it," I said softly. "Do you know where she went?"

"Left with a man." She hesitated then, as if she'd said too much.

"A man? Can you describe him?" Despite my earlier comment, I held up a copper. Shiny coin never hurt when one was dealing with rat mongers.

A sailor pushed past her then, staggering over the threshold and into the street. "Have a good night, my sweet-sweet," he cackled as he stumbled into the gutter.

The girl, thinking I had been distracted by the drunkard, tried to snatch the coin, but I held it away from her. "No, my dear. The description first. I might turn it silver, if you make your description especially detailed. A name, perhaps?"

She bit her lip, her voice so low when she finally spoke that I had to strain to hear her. "Peregrine--that's what the men call him."

"What men?"

Her eyes darted towards the dim interior and then back to me. "Can't say--they meet here sometimes. Well, this Peregrine came here looking for them, but they wasn't here, you see. Came in anyway to talk to my father. That's when he seen that girl. She didn't seem none too pleased to see him, but that didn't bother him none. Grabbed her arm, then, he did, and took her. Had a fine sword and dagger strapped to his belt. I think I seen the dagger blade. I told Father, but we're real busy, and he didn't . . ."

"I understand." Her father was likely one of Peregrine's underworld comrades and wouldn't care if the man hauled twenty girls at knife point out of his common room. "Thank you. You've been most helpful." I handed her the promised silver.

She grabbed the coin and hid it in her apron pocket. "My father . . . he's not in trouble, is he?"

"Is there a reason he should be?"

"No, course not."

"That's what I thought. Good evening." I turned then and swiftly left the alley, going towards the left when I reached the square. This way would lead me down to the docks. I debated briefly finding Selwyn and Ebner to go with me, but by then, the trail would likely be a half-hour colder.

The main thoroughfare down to the docks was better lit than the alleys and more heavily traveled. I pulled my cloak hood over my head--no sense in being seen and recognized when I didn't have to be. I paused at the street that led to the Bara house. Would Peregrine have taken her there, with his mother and sisters and all the servants in attendance? His warehouse on the wharf seemed a far likelier possibility--it was abandoned this time of night except for a couple of watchmen who were their master's toadies and wouldn't dare question him. Of course, I was thinking of what a cunning man would do in his situation, not necessarily what he would do. He was an arrogant blackguard, and he wanted that girl for more than a tumble. He had staked ten thousand silvers on her, offered her marriage more than once.

Peregrine had acted disappointed when that ten thousand silvers had been paid off in accordance with my orders to settle

Avernal's estate and debts. He had asked after Safire several times during the exchange and offered a generous amount to pay her apothecary. Most peculiar. I wagered he would take her to his house, claiming to his mother and anyone else who might ask that he had found her wandering dazed and lost in the square.

On this hunch, I turned down Bara's street. It took me into the merchant's realm, away from the shoddy dives and cheap boarding houses that marked the beginning of the docks. The smell improved considerably, and all the houses and shops were built of fine stone, not half-rotted wood. More lanterns hung beside the doorways here as well, casting far reaching pools of light. I hurried along, seeing only a few other fellow travelers. Most of the people who lived here would be safe in their beds, bolted in against the night. I wouldn't mind being in my bed right now. My muscles still ached from the day's ride, and this little jaunt was not improving matters. I could throttle that witch the instant I found her. I had half a mind to leave her to her fate. The only thing that stopped me was the thought of Merius coming back and turning knight errant when he learned that Peregrine had her. I had gotten him too far to lose him in a duel over a silly girl.

Little broke the night silence here save an occasional distant yell from the city watchmen and the cathedral bell tolling the quarter hours. So when I heard raised voices, I slowed and began looking around more closely. An open window, perhaps? No, the sound seemed to be coming from outside on the ground level, though it was hard to tell from where for certain because there was an echo. I glanced down several of the small paved streets and alleys shooting off the street before I found them.

Peregrine had Safire cornered in an alley. She evidently had attempted to escape, and now he was trying to coax her back. I considered intervening immediately, but it was never wise to act too quickly when swords might get involved. Besides, I wanted to see what he would do. "Now, sweet," he was saying as I silently stopped behind him in the shadows. "Don't you think you're being a bit foolish?"

"No." Her voice trembled like she'd been crying.

"Safire," he said softly. "Safire, listen to me. There's a good meal, a bath, a warm bed if you come with me. You don't want to stay out on the streets, do you? I don't like to think of you out here all alone. You're lucky I found you when I did. There are nasty sorts out at night, and . . ."

"Nasty sorts? What, like you?"

"You don't want me to come in there after you, do you, sweet?"

She moved forward and bent down, her red hair catching the light shining from a nearby lantern. When she straightened, she held a large rock, so large that her fingers strained to grip it. Her eyes gleamed like a wild animal's.

He chuckled. "You can barely lift that, you little fool. What makes you think you can throw it?"

"I can throw it. Maybe not as well as you, but I can throw it so it'll hurt."

"You can't hurt me with that."

"Come closer, and I reckon we'll find out who's right."

"Stop this foolishness, Safire. I mean it." I noticed his hand flit over his dagger hilt.

I stepped out of the shadows. "I see you've found our runaway, Peregrine."

There was a gasp from the alley as Safire struggled to keep hold of her weapon. Peregrine maintained his customary cool, though he had the set poise of a swordsman on the verge of an unexpected duel as he half turned towards me. For an instant, it seemed that the barely registered thought flickered across his mind to pull his blade and challenge me, though an instant later, it was as gone as if the urge had never existed. He was not a stupid man, but my interruption had obviously more than irritated him.

"Good evening, Mordric," he said through his teeth.

"Good evening." I kept my hand surreptitiously near the hilt of my sword. "Where did you find her?"

"In a dive. She would have been robbed or worse if I hadn't taken her." He wiped the cuff of his sleeve over his mouth, staring at Safire. "I was going to summon you in the morning to fetch her, but for tonight I thought she could stay in one of our spare chambers."

"Thank you, and I'm sorry for the inconvenience. She's not

been right since her father's illness," I said.

Peregrine eyed me closely, no doubt wondering how much I had heard of his and Safire's exchange. "It's no bother, sir. There was a time I was quite taken with her--it's a shame to see her like this."

Safire's eyes flared, and she seemed to be struggling to hold her tongue. I motioned to her. "Put down the rock and come here."

She shot Peregrine a look before she cast the stone aside and dusted her hands on her skirt. As soon as she was close enough, I gripped her arm and steered her behind me, away from Bara. He noticed this, his gaze sharp as he looked me up and down one more time. I kept my expression bland.

"I trust you'll have a good night, Peregrine. Again, thank you. I'd best be getting her back to the Hall."

"Yes, I suppose. It does seem a shame . . ." he trailed off.

"What was that?"

He cleared his throat. "I was just saying it seems a shame that Whitten should be tied to her and she to him if she's not in her right mind."

"Yes, well, we all have different burdens."

"It does seem grounds for annulment, though. After all, he needs an heir if the Landers are to have a legitimate leader."

Safire choked behind me, and I tightened my grip on her arm and hoped she got the message to stay quiet. "And she needs a husband to protect her from those who would abuse her title or her lands."

"I would protect her."

"Any man of honor would. And how long before you sail for the SerVerin Empire?" It was a bald hint, but I wasn't in the mood for subtlety.

His stance became more guarded as he shoved his clenched hands in his pockets. "A week."

"Excellent." I smiled, noting his discomfort. He hadn't forgotten our discussion then about him going to the SerVerin court and worming information out of the Emperor in exchange for me keeping his dirty ledgers out of the council's hands. Sometimes young men became so convinced of their invincibility that they didn't take blackmail seriously and needed occasional reminders.

"You'll make a fine ambassador, I'm certain," I said. "All the good ones have been known for their ability to tell only the truths the listener wants to hear. It's a rare talent." Safire snorted.

"Thank you, sir," he muttered, thankful as a muzzled dog.

"Have a good journey, then. Merius had a rough passage from what I understand, but he made it. The sea only punishes those who can take it." I ended with the old sailors' adage.

"That's what I've heard." He kicked viciously at a paving stone.

"Good night, then."

"Good night, sir. Safire." He nodded a brief acknowledgment, his eyes never leaving her. Most unhealthy, such fierce lust for a woman who hated him. That was what I wanted to tell him, but I was not in the habit of giving paternal advice, particularly to a man whom I found more and more reprehensible each time I encountered him.

I led Safire away; when I looked around briefly at the corner, I saw him still standing there, watching us. "Wait," Safire said then as she suddenly stooped to pluck something up from the pavement.

"What's that?" I demanded.

"My portfolio." She clutched it to her chest. "I dropped it when I got away from him."

"What about the coin? Your sister said you had some coin."

"He took it, the thieving toad."

"He took it?" I glanced back again, but Peregrine had vanished around the bend.

"I reckon he thought it would keep me from escaping, not having any coin of my own."

"I suppose. Well, if he hadn't taken it, I would have."

Her eyes flew up, examined me for a moment. "Yes, I suppose you would. You and he are just alike, using others as your chess pieces."

"Be still, you ungrateful wench. It's ridiculous, a woman with coin. You're lucky some thief didn't leave you dead in the street."

"Ungrateful?" she scoffed. "And what have I to be grateful for where you're concerned? You arranged to have Merius sent away on a dangerous mission, you tried to coerce me with threats to my father and sister, you married me off to a drunkard when I was incapable . . . I wouldn't even have been in that dive for Peregrine to find tonight, but for you and your manipulations. No, sir, I agree with you. I am a most decidedly ungrateful wench."

I shook her arm. "I told you to be still, lest I cut out your tongue. I didn't abandon my dinner and warm bed to listen to your chatter. You were better mute."

"If my company's so distressing to you, you can always leave me here, you know." She tried to wrench her arm from my grasp then and make a dash for it, but I was ready for her. I whirled her around until she was dizzy and pushed her against the nearest wall, both my hands on her shoulders.

"Don't try that again," I rasped.

She tried to hit me in the chest with the portfolio, but I moved my hands down her arms so all she could do was flail about.

"Let me go!"

"No."

"Why not?" She paused a moment in her struggles. "I'm no more use to you."

"My dear, you never were any use to me. At your best, you were a mere nuisance. Now you've become a misfortune, and soon you'll likely be a catastrophe."

"Good. You deserve a catastrophe. What do I have to do to become one?"

"When Merius dies in the Marennese mountains because that fool Herrod made a strategic error, you'll be a catastrophe. Now, come with me."

She swallowed and shook her head. "I'm not going back to that House."

"You'll do what I tell you."

She lifted her white face and looked directly at me. "It's your fault he's there, you know."

"You little bitch."

"So leave me here. How hard is that?"

"No, you're coming with me. You're a member of my House now, and you'll not be wandering the streets, sullying the Landers name in the muck. If by some miracle, Merius returns, you'll not be free to dig your claws in him again." I began to tow her after me, taking such long strides that she almost had to run to keep up.

"He'll kill you," she panted. "He'll kill you for this and go to the gallows and . . . Is that what you want? To be killed by your own son?"

I drew up short. "Get this straight in your scheming head right now . . ."

"I'm not scheming," she screamed, catching me off guard as she hit my arm with her portfolio. More surprised than hurt, I lost my grip on her, and she made a run for it. After twenty yards or so, she tripped on the curb and fell to her knees. I stumbled after her. She attempted to get up again but collapsed after I grasped her shoulder.

She clutched her hands around her legs and curled her head down so that someone might have mistaken her for a tightly wrapped bundle of clothes left on the street if she hadn't been wailing like a banshee. I tried to wrench her to her feet again, but all that did was make her wail louder. "Leave me alone!"

I glanced up and down the street. Empty, though I couldn't imagine it would stay that way for long. She must have woken up half of Calcors with that scream. "Shut up," I hissed. "I mean it."

She shook her head, her shoulders heaving. "How could," she hiccupped, "could Mer-Merius come from you? You and that cold thing at the Hall?"

"Stop blathering presumptions. What can you know about my son from sharing his bed a few nights?"

She looked up at me, her eyes red-rimmed and accusing. "I know he's like you in many ways, so many ways that it hurts to look at you because I'm afraid that you are what he's to become. But he's kind, almost to a fault, and warm, and I don't see a bit of kindness or warmth in you. I did at first, and earlier tonight, when you pushed me behind you, away from Peregrine, but now you're just cruel." She began to sob again, of course, deep, racking sobs that rattled her frail ribcage.

I crossed my arms. "Get up, Safire." She didn't move. "Get up now, unless you want me to drag you."

"I don't care what you do."

"Stubborn," I muttered, walking away before I yielded to the strong urge to reach down and shake her. She had dropped her portfolio near a puddle, and I picked it up. I flipped through it. The light from a nearby lamp flickered across the sketches, and from what I could see of them, they weren't bad. I knew little about drawing, considering it a waste of time, but I supposed it had its uses. At least she had made some coin selling her work, which was better than Merius with his poetry.

"What are you doing?" She glanced up, wiping her eyes with her sleeve. "What are you doing? You can't look at those--they're mine." She leapt to her feet and snatched the portfolio from me. Several of the sketches scattered across the cobbles. She raced about, frantically gathering them up before they blew away.

As soon as I could reach her, I grabbed her arm. I picked up the last sketch and tucked it in my cloak pocket with one hand, keeping a firm grip on her with the other. Without a word, I started striding up the street, and she was forced to follow.

Chapter Nineteen--Safire

I half ran behind Mordric, my legs no longer mine but two foreign limbs that moved on another's volition as if I were part marionette. In my mind, I fought this, but my body was exhausted and didn't care anymore as long as it found a soft bed tonight. My feet had no more feeling than blocks of wood as they thudded over the paving stones--I had trodden in a puddle earlier, and the cold water had soaked my slippers.

At some point, Mordric either grew tired himself or realized that he was half dragging me, for he slowed down, his grip loosening slightly on my wrist. That arm was all over bruises by now, what with Peregrine yanking it and then Mordric grabbing it. My stomach growled, and I realized one more reason why I was miserable at the moment. Peregrine had taken me from the tavern before I'd had the chance to eat. The barmaid had been going to bring me some stew, and it had smelled so nice from where I'd been sitting, with carrots and potatoes and beef broth, and I hadn't eaten all day because I'd been too busy selling drawings in the square . . . I had made such a lovely pile of coin today, and now it was all gone to a man who had kidnapped me and planned to do far worse things to me. I told myself sternly I should be grateful that I was still alive and mostly unmolested, but all I could think about was that delicious stew and my hard-earned coin, both gone forever. To my dismay, tears began to swell under my already swollen eyelids, and soon I was sobbing again.

Mordric drew up short and shook me. "For God's sake, be quiet before you wake the square. What the hell is it now?"

The last thing I wanted to do was talk to him, but I found the words flowing out of me, as unbidden as the tears. "He took my coin. I earned it, damn it, and he took it. And I want-wanted to save it. Save it for Mer-Merius and me, for when he returns. Like a dowry, since all Father left for mine was the swamp and fallow fields . . . I wanted us to have something, and now it's gone to that toad. He took it all at the point of his da-dagger . . ."

"He would have taken far more from you at the point of his dagger if he'd had the chance," Mordric said. "Ponder that, my dear-- perhaps it will make you more grateful in the future, though I doubt it. Your sort never learns."

We reached the well in the square. Feeling his hand relax on my arm, I tried to escape one last time by lunging away from him. However, my legs buckled under me, and I fell against the side of the well, the rocks tearing my sleeve.

"Damned witch," Mordric exclaimed. "I'll throw you down this well if you don't stand still. Now get up."

I attempted to stand but fell back again. The damp edges of the cobbles in the square caught the lantern light in thin lines, and these lines began to spiral together in dizzying patterns before my eyes. I blinked, but the cobbles still swirled. Mordric jerked me up then, and I toppled forward. He swore and grabbed me before I hit the ground. "What's wrong with you? Oh, hell, you're bleeding."

"I am?" Then I felt the trickling sensation on my elbow, glanced down, and noticed that I had a long cut running down the length of my upper arm. "It doesn't hurt," I said stupidly. "Why doesn't it hurt?" Then I slipped away in a dead faint, my new talent.

I came to as someone tipped my head back and poured liquor down my throat. I coughed and sputtered over the fiery taste, opening my eyes. Mordric released my neck, straightened, and corked a silver hip flask before he pocketed it. "When did you last eat?"

I shook my head and tried to speak--it took a couple of attempts before I managed, "I don't remember."

Selwyn had appeared from somewhere while I was unconscious, hovering around the edge of my vision. He shifted from foot to foot and started to speak several times, each time catching Mordric's expressionless look and subsiding. Oddly enough, I found his presence comforting. A familiar figure, he was a bit of unavoidable reality. His aura, usually a clear brown with steady dark blue lines laced around it, was muddy with confusion tonight, the lines stretched with the effort of holding in all the questions he dared not ask for fear of Mordric's wrath, I supposed. I focused on him--as long as I could see him, I couldn't faint again.

"Selwyn," Mordric barked.

"Yes, sir?"

"Do you have coin?"

"Yes, sir."

"Go to the nearest tavern and get her some bread."

"No," I protested. "I'll faint again."

They both looked at me. "Is she drunk?" I heard Selwyn whisper.

Mordric shook his head. "Just get the bread. Ebner's bringing the coach, so meet us back here. And be quick about it. I'd like to see my bed sometime tonight."

I watched Selwyn until he disappeared on a side street. The tears began again as soon as he was out of sight. My one anchor to reality, gone. I wailed, my face hot, my head aching, my eyes on fire, but still I couldn't stop. I should have run dry by now; there could only be so many tears in one body. It was so stupid, really. Why couldn't I stop? I sniffled and closed my eyes and blew my nose in my ruined handkerchief, but all to no avail. If anything, the tears flowed faster. Perhaps this was how the seas were made--one lost woman crying for all eternity.

There was a rattling on the cobbles, and a red coach and four pulled up. The horses, the great wheels towered over me, and I recalled briefly what it was like to be a small child again and feel the fascinated terror of a world designed for giants. Then Mordric lifted me into the coach and deposited me on one of the seats like a sack of potatoes. He tossed my portfolio on the seat beside me, and I clutched for it.

"Thank you," I sobbed.

He paused, looked at me sharply a moment, one corner of his mouth twitching in the light of the coach lanterns. He reached in his pocket and pulled out a perfectly folded handkerchief. "Here." He handed it to me, and I gaped. All the edges met without a wrinkle-- never had I seen such a neat job. I was afraid to use it. However, necessity demanded I use something, so I succumbed, still marveling at its precise folds. My father had balled his handkerchiefs up into wrinkled messes, and I had assumed all men were the same. Merius always seemed to have just lost his handkerchief whenever it was needed, and in the few days I was in his chamber, he had mislaid several other personal items in the masses of papers and books that surrounded him. I thought suddenly how this absent-mindedness must have grated on Mordric, who obviously took order seriously.

I blew my nose again as delicately as possible. "Do you have any water?"

"Will you stop bawling like a barn cat?"

"I'll try."

He brought me a large dipper from the well. I grasped it and gulped down every last drop of water, only then realizing how thirsty I was. He filled the dipper again and took it away after I'd drained it a second time. Then he climbed into the coach and sat across from me. His eyes were intent gleams in the shadows, and I grew uncomfortable under that unblinking gaze. "Elsa can see to your arm when we return," he said suddenly.

I glanced down at the bloodied edges of my ripped sleeve, the beaded dark line of the cut against my pale skin. "It doesn't hurt."

"It should. It looks deep."

"I'm fine." Although I had never been able to heal myself for some reason, I could sometimes separate myself from minor pain. At this moment, my wet feet were bothering me far more than the bruises and cut on my arm. I suddenly thought of Father and was ashamed of my small complaints.

"Has there been any change in Father's condition?" I asked, knowing the answer but hoping for a miracle anyway.

"No."

I sighed and stared down at my hands twisting Mordric's handkerchief into knots. Selwyn returned then and clambered into the coach. He sat beside me, and I grabbed my portfolio before it slid to the floor. He carried a long, narrow loaf of bread, the good sort that was hard and crusty on the outside but soft on the inside and stayed fresh for days. Mordric leaned out the window and said something to the driver. With a jerk, the coach started to move.

Selwyn held out the loaf as Mordric settled back in his seat. "Here, sir."

"What do I want it for? Her, Selwyn--it's for her."

"Oh, right. Sorry." Selwyn pulled a dagger from somewhere, the blade edge glinting as he sawed the bread into generous hunks. "Here."

I took the first hunk and tore off a piece, only then realizing how hungry I was. Even without butter, the bread was delicious, the best thing I'd ever eaten. I gnawed at the crust, wishing for some more water to wash it down. Soon it was all gone, and I brushed the crumbs from my lap and glanced outside. We were moving through the country around Calcors now, stars and bits of blue-black sky shining through the dark lace of the leaves and branches. The sea cliffs would soon come into view, with the long expanse of the ocean glowing faintly even on this moonless night.

The warm weather still jarred me, even now several days after I'd awoken from my fit. It had been a blustery March when I could last remember, and suddenly it was late May. The evening, although cool, had the damp, sweet smell of early summer, with all the flowers in bloom and gentle rains. Time had folded for me, bringing two disparate edges together and tucking the mysterious middle away in a deep crease. In my mind, Father had been well up until a few days ago, and the fact that he had lain silent and still in that sickbed for two months had yet to impress its reality on my shock-numbed sensibilities. It only seemed a week or so ago since I'd last seen Merius, and I couldn't rid myself of the feeling that he would suddenly reappear, laugh away all this madness, and carry me off. I sighed then and turned from the window. Mordric had said Merius was deep in the Marennese mountains, that he could die there. Neither Merius nor I had mentioned the possibility that he could die--it hadn't seemed like a real possibility when he was right there, alive and warm and breathing beside me. Now it seemed real, terribly real. Mordric had been right to call me a little bitch for saying what I said. It was his fault Merius was in Marenna, but it was also my fault--

Merius wouldn't have risked himself if it hadn't been for me and his need to prove his father wrong. I bit my lip so hard I tasted blood.

I glanced at Mordric, who was only a vague, silent shadow. If I could have seen him or Selwyn, I might not have been so bold, but I was desperate to know. "Has Merius sent me any more letters?" I blurted out finally.

Mordric was silent for so long that I wondered if he was either asleep or hadn't heard me. I was on the verge of repeating the question when he said, his voice low, "Yes."

"How many?"

The shadow shrugged, shifted position. "A dozen or so, I suppose. There may be more--your father's manservant brings them with the other messages from the House of Long Marsh when he can."

"I had no idea you knew Merius, Safire," Selwyn exclaimed.

"We met at court," I said curtly. "Where are the letters, sir?"

"I burned them."

My fingers grew so taut around my portfolio that the stitching along the side pressed into my palm. "How could you? They weren't addressed to you."

"It's not for you to question me."

"They were my letters."

"They were Safire of Long Marsh's letters. You, my dear, are Safire of Landers now."

Bile rose in my throat, and I let loose a wordless cry of rage, punching the seat beside me. Selwyn shrank against the far wall. "You cold-blooded . . . he's your own son, for God's sake."

"That is precisely why I burned them. I've never seen such a collection of indiscretions. If any of those letters had fallen in the wrong hands, if anyone at court found out Merius had written so frankly to a married woman, he would at best be branded a fool and at worst be accused of adultery and thrown off the council."

"Wait, indiscretions . . . frankly . . . you read them? You read them?!" I sank against the seat, my head swimming.

"Of course I read them, what little I could stand."

"How could you . . . whatever he wrote, it was to me and me only, not for anyone else to see. You reading those letters--it's even worse than you burning them. It's, it's--" I broke off, not able to finish. I crossed my arms tightly over my portfolio, as if I could somehow shield myself from further invasion.

There was a long silence. I felt sick inside, as violated as if someone had spied on Merius and me in the privacy of his chamber. It was an uncomfortable feeling, especially paired with the silence, and I desperately searched for distraction. I became conscious of the rattling of the wheels, the horses' hooves, the roar of the surf at the bottom of the cliffs, the small sounds one usually never noticed. Selwyn must have a cold, I thought--his breathing was loud and whistling, and he cleared his throat every few moments.

Mordric sat unmoving until we left the sea cliffs and entered the woods again. Then he shifted, the leather of his boots creaking, and sighed. It was so unexpected--him sighing--that I jumped a little. "You don't understand," he said then, his voice heavy, toneless. "I didn't read the private bits, at least not anything past a sentence or two before I realized what they were. I certainly wasn't interested in them. I just wanted some idea of what he was doing, where they were, if he'd been in any skirmishes, if he had trustworthy men around him. He wrote quite a bit about that."

"In a letter to a sweetheart, to a wife, the whole letter is private, not just bits of it."

"I know that. It's just that he won't write to me, and I do want to know how . . . how he's faring." Mordric said this last as if it pained him, breaking his terse monotone. I started and stared at the shadows where he sat. It was the same shock I would have felt upon observing a stone statue suddenly begin to weep. This man I would have called hard-hearted, cruel, conniving, ruthless--this man loved his son.

"So, how is he faring?" I asked, not knowing what to say exactly but needing to say something to cover the awkwardness.

"Well enough, I suppose. Of course, all those letters were written before that hangdog Herrod sent him into the mountains, so God knows how he fares now."

"Why are the mountains so dangerous?"

"There are only a few passes through them, and it's easy to get cornered and ambushed, especially if you're not as familiar with the territory as your enemy is. Camped along the passes, there are bands of brigands that wait for merchant caravans, horses, weapons, anything that they can sell in the lowlands. Many of them are in league with the SerVerin slave traders and seize unwary travelers to be sold south of the Zarinaa river, so they have plenty of reason to fight our men." Mordric paused. "Herrod's sometimes a hothead fool when he gets in the thick of battle--he should only have dealt with slave traders working west of the mountains. He doesn't have enough men to clean the rabble out of the passes as well, the ass."

"So Merius could be . . ." I trailed off, not able to speak over the lump in my throat.

"Killed?" Mordric finished. "Yes, though I doubt it. He and other high-ranking men are more likely to be taken hostage, held for ransom. These brigands and slave traders are thieves, not killers if they can help it--they're more interested in coin than blood."

I swallowed, my voice hoarse when I finally spoke. "But he's too proud to be anyone's hostage, to let anyone under his watch be taken hostage. They might hurt him badly or even, even k-kill him before he would give in."

"You see only his reckless side."

"I bet if Merius were taken hostage," Selwyn said unexpectedly, "I bet he would pretend to go along with it and then find a way to escape. He's one of the best bluffers I know when he has his temper in check."

Mordric chuckled, a grim sound. "Yes, I taught him that much."

I clutched my arms around me, suddenly cold. Merius, a hostage? Merius, dead? He could be either right now, and I would have no idea until weeks or months had passed. I had cried earlier over my lost coin, my hunger, my cold feet--now that I finally had something worth crying about, all my tears were long gone, leaving my eyes dry and burning. It was worse, not being able to cry. All the unspent fear whirled around inside, faster and faster till I thought I was going crazy. I chanted a quick prayer under my breath over and over again *God, let him live.* But there had to be thousands of such prayers throughout the world every minute, and most of them would never be answered. Why should mine be?

We stopped then, and I realized with a start that we were in the Landers courtyard. Selwyn opened the door and hopped out. Then he turned and offered me his hand. My portfolio under my arm, I took his assistance and stepped down. There was a rapid patter of slippered feet over the cobbles, and then Dagmar threw her arms around me.

"Thank God you're all right. Thank God." She pulled away a little, wiping her eyes. "Don't ever run off like that again--I thought you might be dead, you wicked girl."

"I'm sorry. I'm sorry." I hugged her back, realizing then that she was not only older sister but also surrogate mother. "I should have explained . . ."

"Later. Right now you need food, rest." She began to lead me towards the house.

I resisted as I had resisted Mordric earlier, suddenly remembering why I had been so anxious to escape from him in Calcors. "No--I can't go in there again."

"Safire, nonsense. Now, come on."

"No. If I go in there, I'll get sick again."

Dagmar's face was half in shadow, but even in the flickering lantern light, I could still see her brow furrow. "What, because of Whitten? Safire, you won't have to see him again, not for awhile. He's agreed to stay in a whole other wing of the house until we sort this mess out. Now, come on--you'll feel much better after some food and a nice hot bath."

"No, not because of Whitten. I can't explain, but . . . but I'll get sick again if I go in there."

By this point, Selwyn and Mordric were standing beside Dagmar, and the two men looked at me as if I were crazy. I took a deep breath, but before I could speak, Dagmar grabbed my hand and led me around the back of the coach. "I'll talk some sense into her," she threw over her shoulder at the men. "Now, what is it?" she continued in a low voice.

"There's a spirit in that house. An evil spirit. She hates me, and if I go in there again, she'll attack me like she did two months ago, and I may not recover this time." Even as I said the words, I cringed.

"Oh, Safire, not this. Not this again." Dagmar covered her forehead with her hand. "You know it's just your imagination--you have to know that. Please." She lowered her hand, her eyes mutely pleading. I knew she was afraid, afraid of what Mordric and Selwyn would think. A charge of trafficking with spirits was no light matter, an almost certain prelude to the more serious charge of witchcraft. I swallowed. We had only just come under this House's protection, and Mordric was none too fond of me or my connection to his son. If he wanted to get rid of me, this would be the perfect excuse. But I couldn't go back in that house. I just couldn't. I remembered that cold laughter, those invisible, icy hands at my neck, and shuddered.

"I can sleep in the hay loft, a tenant's cottage, the stables, anywhere--I won't run off again, I promise." I grabbed the edge of the coach wheel.

"What are you talking about? Beggar girls sleep in hay lofts. Safire, you're a noblewoman--it's time you started acting like it." Dagmar tugged on my arm. "Now, no more of this nonsense. Mother never acted like this, for all her talents. You'll feel better once you've eaten, visited Father, slept in your own bed. Come on-- this is ridiculous."

"What are you saying? What's ridiculous?" Selwyn demanded, coming up behind Dagmar.

"The whole thing is ridiculous," Mordric said, joining Selwyn. "Your sister is more patient than I am, Safire. You'd best mind her." He pried my fingers from the coach wheel, and Dagmar and Selwyn pulled me away.

"No!" I dug my heels in, struggling. "Let me go! If I go in that house, she'll kill me."

Dagmar paused. "She?"

"Yes . . ."

We were near the front steps, and already I could smell the cloying scent of the roses. It filled the air, my lungs, and I broke into a fit of coughing. I wasn't expecting the ghost here, so soon--I thought she'd at least wait until I was in the House, but evidently she'd been impatient for my return. She stood in the open doorway, her arms out, a shadow against the light. I froze, my muscles rigid with fear, and Selwyn muttered something about childish tantrums. I barely heard him. The ghost spread her arms further and giggled, the golden snakes of her hair growing down the steps. The hair moved fast as flowing water, hissing like silk over stone. There came that horrible girlish giggle again.

"Mind yourself lest you trip, little witch," she said, her voice high and thin as the winter wind whistling down the distant hills.

Her hair curled around my ankles. It felt like I'd suddenly stepped in a frigid stream, and I screamed, trying to kick the stuff off me before it grew up my legs.

"Safire, really . . ."

The hair filled the courtyard now. It surrounded us. I couldn't feel my feet, and I screamed again, kicking blindly. Her giggling swelled into an icy crescendo of laughter that pierced my ears.

"Catch," she said, throwing out her hands. Hundreds of rose petals, all colors, fell through the air. They fluttered past me, slicing into the bare skin of my arms and hands with razor edges. The petals landed with a faint tinkle, ice striking rock. Blood welled up from the cuts, and only then did I feel the sharp, burning pain of them. Nothing hurt quite like a hundred small cuts all at once. "No," I sobbed. "No, please . . ."

"Safire." Dagmar's voice was far away. "Safire . . . she's bleeding!"

"How the hell did that happen?" Selwyn demanded.

"The rose petals," I gasped.

"What?"

"The rose petals." I gulped, unable to speak above a whisper. "The roses . . . can't you smell them? It's so cold . . . she's going to kill me."

Chapter Twenty--Mordric

Safire slipped from Dagmar's and Selwyn's grasp and writhed on the ground. The lantern made the blood look blacker as it ran in rivulets down her arms.

"Damned witch--what did you do to yourself now?" I said.

She rolled over on to her hands and knees and began to crawl towards the edge of the courtyard, coughing and choking as if she were inhaling smoke rather than clean night air. Since Dagmar and Selwyn seemed rooted in place, I stepped forward and grabbed her upper arm. There was so much blood flowing from the cuts on her skin that my palm grew slick, and I had a difficult time keeping hold of her.

"No," she gasped. "No, let me go. Please--she's killing me."

"There's no she here, except you and your sister," I snapped. "We should have taken you to the insane asylum. Now, be still." I lifted her and started towards the house.

"No!" she screamed, flailing her arms and kicking. Blood spattered my shirt and cloak.

"Damn you, be still!" I had to stop in order to keep from dropping her.

"You can't take me in there." Her breath came in hoarse rasps. "Please . . ."

Dagmar finally took a tentative step towards us. "Dagmar," I said curtly.

"Yes, sir?"

"Go and prepare some bandages and hot water."

"No--you can't go in there!" Safire began struggling again.

"She's says she'll hurt you too. No, Dagmar--stop!"

I had to give Dagmar credit. She never hesitated after my order, even when Safire screamed at her to stop. She went straight up the steps and through the doorway. Safire stared after her, her struggles subsiding as Dagmar walked out of sight, apparently fine. "You didn't," she muttered. "Thank God you didn't. You lying cold-blooded battleaxe, you can't hurt her. Just me."

"You're talking to the air, Safire."

She laughed, the high-pitched cackle of someone going mad. "Ah, yes, the air. It's just the air, you insane witch. Odd how the air cuts like a hundred razors." She bared her arms. "Odd how the air reaches icy hands around my throat and chokes me." Already rising on the skin of her neck, I could see the bruise marks of fingers, as if someone had throttled her. Peregrine, maybe? I paused, glanced over her more closely. But Peregrine hadn't cut her. That had just happened, here in the courtyard. But how? I met her gaze again.

"Have you ever smelled anything so sweet it made you gag?" she whispered. "I'll never be able to smell roses again without retching." She hid her face against my shoulder.

Roses--so many roses, it made one sick. Even as the witch said it, I smelled the roses. And swore. I dropped her to the cobbles. Then I was on my knees beside her, shaking her shoulders. "Stop it! Stop it, you damned sorceress! I'll have you burned . . ." I choked, the thick perfume searing my lungs.

Her eyes widened. "You smell it too?"

"Stop it!"

"I can't. It's not from me. It's from her."

"She's dead. She's dead, damn you. She's been dead ten years . . ." Even as I said it, Arilea's brittle laughter echoed through the night.

"Sir? Sir?" Selwyn was touching my shoulder. "Sir, you might want to stop . . ."

I turned on him, the bitch's dulcet tones still ringing in my ears. "Stop what, you interfering dolt?"

He backed away. "Well, sir, she's fainted again."

I glanced down at Safire, who was indeed unconscious. And I was still shaking her. I stopped. She lay limp and disheveled, her face white. I straightened the edges of her cloak before I grasped her in my arms and slowly got to my feet.

Bring her to me, love. The mocking words were the barest whisper in my mind, but I turned my head sharply towards the open doorway which Safire had been staring at so intently a few moments ago. Nothing but the golden spill of candlelight from the front hall chandelier shimmering over the wet stone steps. I shook myself. It was my imagination. The ale from the inn had gone to my head. The witch was insane, babbling nonsense.

I stepped towards the doorway. And immediately stopped. The roses. The damned roses again, smothering the suddenly frigid air with thick, heady scent. I held my breath as long as I could, but there was no escape. The smell made me dizzy. "Damn it," I said with difficulty. Then I gagged.

"Sir?" Selwyn sounded distant.

Bring the witch here, my love. Arilea's voice was caressing. *Just up the steps. It will be close enough.*

Before I could stop myself, I said, "Close enough for what?" Now I was talking to the air.

Her giggle reminded me of a naughty child. *You'll see.*

"Get her yourself."

I can't leave this threshold. I'm bound to the House for eternity.

Safire moaned, stirred in my arms. I glanced from her to the doorway. Now that I was closer, I thought I saw the vague shadow of a woman on the steps, but it was only a trick of the light. It had to be. I squinted, tried to make it out, and her laughter rang through the courtyard again.

"You bitch," I muttered.

"What was that, sir?" Selwyn asked.

I ignored him. "What game are you playing now, Arilea?"

"No games." Her voice was such a silky hiss that it barely registered that I was now hearing her in my ears and not just in my mind.

"Then what do you want with her?" I held out Safire.

"The same thing you do. Believe me, when I'm through with her, she'll never sink her claws in Merius again." Icy venom dripped from her voice, a venom that had heated my blood many a time. A chill ran down my spine, and I closed my eyes. Ten years since I had touched her, buried her in the ground, and she still haunted my nights.

"What's the matter, love?" Her voice lowered, became softer.

"You know what the matter is."

"No, enlighten me. Come hither." She gave a merry peal of laughter. "Do you remember that night, the night I came hither?"

"No," I shot back. "You've mistaken me for my brother."

"You're showing your weak spot, Mordric--it's rather affecting, how jealous you still are of a dead man. I was terrified of you that night, you know, the night you told me to come hither."

"I don't know why. It's not like you were a virgin. Far from it, in fact."

"Oh, you do remember," she mocked before she laughed again. "But you're wrong--I was a virgin. I saved myself all for you, and look how scandalously you lie about it, even to yourself. It's not very nice, this tendency you have to cast me as a whore in all your memories."

"Perhaps because you were a whore."

"So bitter," she purred. "No, but I was terrified of you. So serious and quiet and intense, nothing like your dashing older brother. You were just back from battle, and you carried your sword everywhere, even when you came to see me. You barely spoke four words to me during our courtship. Yet somehow I knew."

"Stop it, you bitch."

"Your endearments always have left something to be desired. I don't think you've ever said you loved me, not once."

"Probably because I never have. Ours was a union of convenience." My arms began to ache, and I shifted Safire's weight.

"Hah--convenience was the furthest thing from your mind. You may have never said it, but we both know it." Her voice dropped to a whisper. "When my handmaids pushed me into the chamber that night, I was so scared I was shaking. You were writing a letter at the desk, and when you heard the door, you looked up, put down your pen, and corked the inkwell, as if I was merely part of your schedule. That comforted me, how methodical you were. You always seemed to know exactly what you were doing. We watched each other for the longest time, me trembling so hard my teeth rattled. Finally you motioned to me and said 'come hither' and I had no choice but to come. Those were the only two words you spoke that night. It was later I realized it was your way of jesting me, that ridiculous 'come hither'--your wit is so dry sometimes it evaporates before one comprehends what you've said."

"Charming story, but you've left off the end."

"What, Gaven?" She laughed. "Gaven wasn't the end--he was a small incident in the middle that you've fixated on for too long. Merius is yours, Mordric."

"No." I shook my head. "No, I don't believe you."

"I never had another man besides you."

"He seduced you . . . you yourself told me."

"Did you ever actually see us in bed together?"

"No, but that doesn't mean a damned thing. You're lying again, you viper. I know your games."

"I only played them to amuse you."

"Bitch." I lunged forward, still clutching Safire. Instantly, the cold enveloped us like a sodden cloak, and Arilea's laughter echoed through the courtyard. Safire began to struggle, whimpering. I fell back, out of the chill.

"Oh, bring her back." Arilea's voice held a petulant note. "The fun was just beginning."

"You baited me with Gaven. All you wanted was for me to lunge and bring her closer. Conniving . . ."

"I'm just trying to protect our son, Mordric."

I glanced down at Safire, pale, gasping for air, a slight weight in my arms. Then I glanced up at the doorway again. There was a shimmer there, a wavy distortion of the light that was gradually materializing into something more solid--the slender figure of a long-haired woman. Arilea. I blinked. For an instant, her hair seemed to twist like snakes, slithering down the steps. Then the snakes dwindled and vanished into the yellow reflection of candlelight from the doorway. The figure faded as well, leaving only the hint of a shadow. But I had seen enough. I took a deep breath, my arms tightening around the witch.

"Merius is a man now, Arilea. Leave him alone."

"What, like you do? You're manipulating him constantly. Now, this witch comes along, a catastrophe for him, and you sit back and twiddle your thumbs. Fool," she hissed. "She'll ruin his career, his life--is that what you want? Don't you want to protect him?"

"That's what I'm doing." I turned around and walked away from the house, away from her. A wail of rage filled the courtyard, so high-pitched the window panes rattled and almost cracked. The sound of it was like ice water down my back, and I shivered. Then, suddenly, it was gone. I shook my head, feeling groggy as if I'd just awoken from a long sleep. My arms ached from holding Safire for so long.

Selwyn and Dagmar were there, gaping at me. Dagmar held a limp scrap of linen in one hand, presumably a bandage. "Sir," Selwyn began, stepping forward.

"Yes?"

"Sir, shouldn't we . . ." he hesitated. "Maybe we should take her into the house."

"No." I walked to the end of the courtyard and stepped on to the gravel drive that led to the gatekeeper's cottage, just past the orchard.

Selwyn hurried behind me, followed by Dagmar. "Sir, she needs bandages . . . maybe . . ."

"Bring the bandages then."

"But where are you taking her?"

"To the gatekeeper."

"But the house is closer," he sputtered.

"She can't go in the house."

"Sir, surely you don't believe . . ."

I stopped him with a stare. "What I believe and don't believe is none of your affair."

He swallowed. "Yes, sir. But . . ."

"Go back to the house, Selwyn."

Selwyn stopped and just stood there, gaping as Dagmar and I continued down the track. Dagmar had had the presence of mind to grab a lantern from the stable. The weak circle of the light wavered on the gravel in front of us. After a few moments of silent walking, Dagmar cleared her throat. "Sir?"

"What?"

"My sister, what she says sometimes, about spirits . . . well, she's a little odd that way. There's really no reason to take her to the gatekeeper's cottage simply because she had a fit. She has them sometimes, and there's no rhyme or reason to them, so she'll be fine in the house, once we get her in there and she realizes there's nothing to be afraid of."

"Dagmar?"

"Yes?"

"Do you see the cuts on her arms, the marks on her neck?"

She spared a glance at Safire. "Yes."

"Where did they come from?"

"I don't know. Maybe someone in Calcors attacked her before you found her. Maybe . . ."

"She had no marks on her when I found her. And who did you think I was talking to in the courtyard a moment ago? Not to you or Selwyn surely."

"Well, to be honest, sir, I thought you were talking to yourself."

"That would make me crazy. You think I'm crazy?"

"N-no."

"Don't be so quick to assume your sister is, then."

The wind blew through the orchard, the flower-laden boughs creaking. We were almost to the cottage when Safire stirred. "Let me down, please?" she said.

I set her on her feet. She staggered forward a few steps. "Be careful," Dagmar exclaimed, grabbing for her arm. "You've lost blood."

"I know." Safire shook off her sister's hand. "Sorry," she continued, sounding cross. "It's just I feel a fool."

"Why?"

"Well, for one thing, you think I have fits for no reason, that I'm slightly off kilter."

"You heard that?"

"I heard everything."

"I'm sorry, Safire, but I just can't believe . . ."

"You don't have to believe it," Safire snapped. "I suppose

you never believed Mother, either."

"Mother never screamed bloody murder and collapsed for no reason."

"That's because Mother never met up with anything like what's in that house." Safire nodded in the direction of Landers Hall. "If it would do any good, I'd tell you never to go in there again, but you won't believe me."

"There's nothing in that house . . ." Dagmar trailed off.

Safire looked at me, her eyes gleaming in the lantern light. "You know. You talked with her, saw her there at the end."

"Come on." I took her wrist.

"Get a priest," she continued as I knocked on the door of the lit cottage. "I don't know if it will do any good, but get a priest. He might be able to exorcise her."

"I don't believe in priests."

"That's an odd statement from a high courtier," Safire retorted. Dagmar cleared her throat and poked Safire in the side, but the witch ignored her warnings, continuing "Do the king and his bishops know you're a skeptic?"

"I do what is proper in chapel, no more, no less."

"So you're a hypocrite?"

At that moment, the door opened. Young Orlin, the gatekeeper, stood there, his wife hovering behind him. He was in his mid-thirties, black-haired and strong, a former fighter under Herrod. His bastard nephew, actually, though the relationship was but a whisper among the servants. "Yes, my lord?" he said.

I thrust Safire forward. "Guard this girl."

Orlin's brow furrowed. "Sir Whitten's wife?"

"That title is in dispute," Safire said.

"You have a spare bed chamber, Orlin?"

"Yes."

"Keep her there. She's of noble birth--treat her as such in the house, but do not let her roam freely without escort. She is not to leave the estate grounds."

"Understood." Orlin opened the door all the way, and I pushed Safire ahead of me into the oak-paneled sitting room. A long settle had been pulled close to the fire crackling on the stone hearth.

Orlin, his wife, and Dagmar trailed me into the room, and with five of us, it was overflowing. Safire whirled around as soon as the door slammed shut behind us, her gaze narrow.

"So I'm to be a prisoner, then," she said.

"No, my lady, prisoners live in dank cells with fleas and rats for companions."

"Prisoners are also kept against their will. What else would you call this?"

"Disputed marriage or not, you're a ward of the Landers, which means you'll do as I say. Would you rather be a ward of the Baras?"

Her eyes glittered, never leaving mine. If I believed in such things, I would have sworn she was casting a curse. "No," she said finally.

"Good. Now, Dagmar, see to her cuts."

"Could you bring a bowl of hot water and a clean rag?" Dagmar asked Orlin's wife, who scurried from the room, a quiet, nervous mouse of a woman.

Safire examined her arms. "The cuts are on the surface, mostly. I don't need bandages."

"Sit down, sister," Dagmar ordered.

Safire rolled her eyes, but she sat and bared her arms. "As if bandages could stop that hell spirit," she muttered.

"Orlin," I said. "Leave us for a moment."

He nodded and ducked through the door after his wife. "Now, listen you," I said, turning to Safire. "You're not to mention what transpired in that courtyard tonight or what happened in my study two months ago."

"But that house is dangerous. She's dangerous . . ."

"Not to anyone but you."

"You don't know that."

"Do you see any cuts on my arms? Throttle marks on my neck?"

Safire shook her head. "She may not be able to hurt you as she hurt me, but she's an angry, powerful spirit. Anyone could suffer from the slow poison of her presence. She could whisper in your ear in a quiet moment, creep into dreams at night . . ."

At that instant, Orlin's wife returned and silently deposited a steaming bowl of water and a cloth on the side table. She disappeared through the doorway as swiftly as she had entered it, leaving us alone again. Dagmar picked up the cloth and dipped it in the soapy water. She wrung it out before she turned to Safire and began to wash the cuts. The witch winced but bore the sting in silence.

"What's this prattle about dreams?" I found myself saying. "You're mad."

"Don't you dream?"

"No. It's a waste of sleep."

One corner of Safire's mouth turned up in a half smile. "Everyone dreams. Some just don't remember."

"I don't dream, either," Dagmar announced. "Now, be still. You're wiggling too much."

"You do dream--I've heard you talk in your sleep," Safire said.

"I told you to be still."

"If I had dreams, I would remember," I said, pacing over to the window. The iron chandelier in the center of room swayed, light bouncing against the dark mullions. I stared at the opaque glass. There was no outside to be seen. Yes, I had dreams of Arilea, though hell would open under my feet before I admitted it to this fool girl. They were but sleeping memories of a dead woman, nothing more than a fleeting aberrant weakness on my part. After all, we had been married fourteen years. I could hardly help but have memories of the bitch, and not all were bitter. She had been a beautiful woman. Nothing supernatural about that. But what of the times I had awakened with her rose water choking the air, her silken shifts in my bed? How could those have been dreams? I could hardly have conjured actual scent, much less real silk, from the recesses of memory only. I shook my head, pressed my palms on the window sill as I leaned my brow against the glass. The solid oak under my hands, the cold glass, seemed suddenly no more real than my memories. Spirits, hell.

I fumbled in my cloak pocket, searching for my flask. Instead I pulled out a crumpled bit of parchment. Safire's drawing, the one I had picked up from the street earlier when she had dropped her portfolio. I smoothed out the wrinkles, my fingers shaking as I swore under my breath. A simple thing really--a sketch of some dock children rolling a hoop on the wharf, being chased by a dog. Well done, detailed without losing the sense of movement or action. If she'd been born male, the witch would have made a good battlefield artist. I and my men had had a few who trailed us here and there like camp whores, artists sent by the king to record the glories of his battles. Poor bastards--most had lost their lives or been taken hostage to rot in foreign prisons. There had been no gold in the royal coffers to waste on lowborn painters' ransoms. Lowborn or not, one still had to admire their ability to capture an entire battle on a scrap of parchment.

I glanced at Safire. She and Dagmar were talking quietly as Dagmar wrapped the bandages around her arms, neither paying me any mind. She didn't look a witch, certainly. Merely a young noblewoman, fairer than most but otherwise no different. I again examined the sketch I held. For a moment, the figures seemed to be actually moving. There was the clack of the hoop over the cobbles, the yells of the children, the dog's pant as it loped across the page. Then I blinked, and all fell motionless, back to the illusion of movement rather than the movement itself. I stared at the picture, hypnotized. It was a spell.

"What are you?" I said then, still staring at the picture.

The two sisters were giggling over some silliness, and Safire was the first to look up. "What was that, sir?" she asked breathlessly, tucking a loose curl behind her ear. It was a natural female gesture, so natural that I doubted myself. But then, out of the corner of my eye, I saw the sketch begin to move again. The parchment felt warm between my fingers, stirring like something alive.

"What are you?" I thrust the drawing at her. "A witch?"

She straightened at the sight of the drawing, the laughter dying on her lips. "Where did you get that?" she demanded sharply.

"You don't deny it . . ."

Her eyes flared. "I'm naught but a woman, sir. I simply see more clearly than most." She snatched the drawing from me.

"Safire, be careful of your bandages," Dagmar exclaimed, reaching for her sister's shoulder.

I retreated to the window, my arms clenched together as I watched Safire. "What woman draws like that?"

"A skilled one," she retorted.

"A devilishly skilled one, to make the figures in that sketch move. I even heard the sound of the hoop on the cobbles."

Her brow furrowed. "Merius said something like that about one of my sketches. He thought it was a trick of the moonlight." She glanced down at the drawing as if seeing it for the first time. "How odd."

"How odd indeed," I said icily. "The magistrate burns witches, my dear."

She gazed at me, not blinking. "I've sold many drawings, sir, and no one besides you and Merius has ever seen anything out of the ordinary about them. I'd say the witchery lies with you, not with me."

"It's not just the drawing." I found myself shaking and cursed as I began to pace. "God damn it, it's everything. My dead wife, the smell of roses, the way you seem to pluck my secret plans from the very air, even how you look at people, as if you were seeing through them . . . God damn witches, God damn Arilea, God damn you all!" I grabbed the back of a chair to steady myself, but the chair began to jerk about violently, drumming against the floorboards.

Instantly, Safire was up and across the chamber. She rested her hand on my arm, her touch cool. "Shh, it's all right."

I snatched my arm from her grasp. "How dare you touch me?"

She grabbed my other arm with both hands. "Damn witch!" I swore and raised my palm to slap her away, but then I froze, my hand in midair. A strange sensation was running up my arm from her hands, a tingling warmth that moved through the veins to my heart and then to the rest of my body. All my muscles loosened, as if I'd just had several shots of the best whiskey, and the shaking stopped. "What the hell?" I muttered. "What in God's good name was that?"

"Shh. It's all right." She looked up at me, her grip on my arm slackening. Her eyes were clear and bright as green glass, her voice low and soothing. I found myself staring down at her as if in a trance. What sort of pact had Merius made with the devil for this creature?

"You've cursed me," I said flatly, though the words seemed to be another's, not mine.

"No, sir. I can no more curse anyone than you can, though I wish I could sometimes."

"What was that, then? That warmth?"

"Certainly not a curse. Do you feel better?"

I nodded slowly. "I'll not send you to the stake just yet."

"Oh, Safire," Dagmar breathed. She staggered backwards against the side table, gripped it with white-knuckled fingers. "Safire, what have you done now? They're going to burn you this time for certain . . ."

Safire ignored her. "It must be well nigh impossible, to be forced to believe in something after believing in nothing for so long."

"Save the platitudes for the priests." I took a step back, crossed my arms. "They mean nothing to me."

She shrugged. "Platitude or not, it would be a shock for anyone, what you heard and saw in the courtyard tonight."

I bent down, picked up the poker, stirred the fire before I threw more kindling on the flames. Sparks shot up the chimney, and I straightened, rested my hands on the mantel. "I joined the king's guard when I was sixteen. I've killed men in every country marked on our maps, seen depravities you couldn't even begin to comprehend. I'm well accustomed to shocks."

"In other words, you think me presumptuous?" She moved to the corner of the hearth and into my field of vision.

"Yes." I glared at her. Her tangled curls burned in the firelight, and her skin had a faint shimmery sheen to it, pale as a pearl. There was something not quite human about her. "Changeling," I spat. "I should by all rights cast you out, let the magistrate burn you."

Safire lifted her chin. "You should, but you won't."

"Safire, for God's sake. Sir, please," Dagmar said. "Sir, she doesn't know what she's saying. And she's never hurt anyone. She's a little odd, but that shouldn't condemn her to . . ."

I raised my palm to silence her. "Be still," I said. "Your

concern for your sister is admirable, but when you speak, you show yourself a fool. I said I should condemn her, not that I would. There's a difference."

Dagmar swallowed. "Yes, sir."

"Now, it's late. I'll think more on this matter tomorrow." I looked at Safire. "You'll stay here until I decide what's to be done with you. And no more of your antics. Do you understand?"

She nodded, cleared her throat. "Sir?"

"What?" I asked warily.

"Maybe you shouldn't go back in that house, at least not before a priest exorcises it. She seems to feed off of you, your anger. It's a form of possession, really."

I gazed at her for a long moment, her pink-cheeked youthful earnestness. "It would take a hell of a priest to chase away Arilea," I said finally. "Good night." I paused. "Little witch."

~ ~ ~ ~ ~

The minute my head hit the pillow, I was asleep. The night passed with no dreams, and when I awoke, the sun had just cleared the hills. I couldn't remember the last time I had slept so soundly without the aid of whiskey. Briefly, the unbidden thought of Safire's hands on my arm the night before crossed my mind--that strange warmth in the blood and the lifting of an invisible weight from my muscles. I snorted. If it had happened to another man and not myself, I would have said that it sounded like he'd gone giddy at the touch of a young woman. But it hadn't been like that. It had reminded me more of the touch of an apothecary stitching up a wound, the way she had put her hands on me. Businesslike yet gentle, with a calm coolness and a sense of purpose. Healing hands.

Absently, I pulled on my clothes, laced up my shirt, buttoned my trousers, not realizing until I had finished that I had fastened the frogs of my jerkin crooked. I swore and began again, this time watching myself in the mirror. Safire's and Whitten's marriage could likely be annulled with little difficulty. After all, there had been a prior, if unofficial, betrothal between her and Merius, and the girl had been out of her mind--there were several witnesses to the fact. Of course, Whitten had taken it upon himself to consummate the union, against strict orders to the contrary. That might complicate matters.

I yanked on the bell pull. Baldwin appeared a moment later, rubbing his eyes. Lazy cur--he was likely dozing on duty again.

"Bring Whitten here immediately."

"But sir, he's still abed . . ."

"I don't care. Drag him if you must. Just get him."

"Yes, sir."

Whitten came more quickly than I had expected. He always knew when he was about to get lambasted and being a coward, generally tried to avoid it as long as possible. Maybe he had finally realized that waiting exacerbated my temper, not that it could be much more exacerbated on this occasion.

"You knock like an old woman," I growled. "Get in here."

He entered, pale and tousled as if he had tossed and turned the entire night. His linen was stained and wrinkled--he must have slept in it. Unshaven, bleary-eyed, he didn't look presentable for a peasant's dog. And this was supposed to be the head of the House of Landers. Thank God I hadn't let him near court since he'd graduated the academy.

He shut the door behind him and leaned against it. "Sir," he said, yawning as he inclined his head in a sorry acknowledgment.

"Straighten up. You're not fit to kennel with the hounds, but you should at least try to stand like a man."

"Sir, I know what this is about, and . . ."

"Silence. If I ask you a question, answer it. Otherwise, silence. Do you understand?"

He nodded, staring at his toes. "Now, do you know what happens to men who rape virgins?" There was a long pause. "Answer me."

"They're," he swallowed, "they're castrated."

"Yes, and they also pay thrice the amount of the traditional dowry to the virgins' fathers. What about men who rape other men's wives?"

"Same thing, except the fine goes to the women's husbands."

"Very good, Whitten," I said, caustic. "So what should your penalty be?"

"But . . ."

"What, you think you've done nothing wrong?"

"Well, sir, she is my wife, and . . ."

"In name only. Remember the day you and I and Dagmar discussed this? I told you myself that you were not to touch her. Are you trying to tell me you don't remember?"

He shook his head. "No, I remember. You said that until she came out of her fit and was herself, that I couldn't touch her until then, that the marriage was to protect her title and lands from peasant fortune-hunters."

"You agreed to that. So why did you touch her?"

"I thought she was lucid."

"Horseshit," I hissed. He flinched.

"Sir, I was drunk, and sh-she was in the hall, and . . ."

"You're telling me you were drunk every time you tumbled her?"

"But there was only the one time, sir."

"One or a hundred, you're still as guilty. And I bet there was more than one time. Also, if you had been drunk and raped a virgin, you would still be castrated. You were drunk. That's no excuse. I slapped my wife a few times, even drew my dagger once, but I would have done the same when I was sober. Being drunk just made me quicker on the draw."

He started and looked up for the first time since entering the chamber. "Sir, I . . ."

"Did I ask you a question?" I barked.

"No, sir." He focused on his feet again.

"Now that we've eliminated ignorance and drunkenness, tell me the real reason you tumbled her against my orders."

"Well, she is a pretty little thing, and . . . well, sir, she didn't stop me."

"Of course she didn't stop you. She was out of her mind, not herself. That's the only way a girl like that would lay with you."

His head drooped lower. "I am sorry, sir. I didn't realize the wrong I did until . . ."

"Save your petty apologies. I'll have no more of them. You have no real realization of what you've done anyway. This isn't one of your serving wenches or barmaids, Whitten. Do you understand that at least?"

"Yes, sir."

"If it were up to me, I would have you lashed within an inch of your life. But there is Safire's reputation to consider. A consummated marriage is nearly impossible to annul. The marriage was never consummated, do you understand? The fact that it was is to remain a secret of these walls, and we can only hope that you didn't get her with child. If I were you, I would be praying on my knees for the next month that she is barren."

He raised his head. "Sir, there is one thing . . ."

"What?"

"Well, sir, I wasn't her, her first, if you take my meaning."

I shook my head. "Whitten, you irredeemable ass. Of course you weren't her first."

He gulped. "She said Merius gave her that gold ring, that it's a betrothal ring."

"Whitten, Whitten . . ." I was still shaking my head. "This harvest I had planned to betroth you to the queen's niece, Cyranea of the Hellas Isles. Then suddenly, I threw over this irreplaceable political alliance of a marriage to marry you off to a mad sparrow noblewoman, and you thought all this time it was only because I wished to save the poor creature's already questionable reputation?"

He puzzled this a moment. "Merius seduced her," he said finally, "but you can't let Merius marry so low, so you sent him off to battle and married Safire to me."

"Yes. Your statesman's savvy grows minute by minute," I said acidly. "I told you not to touch her for several reasons, Whitten, only one of which was her lack of wits at the time. While the marriage remained unconsummated, you were but my dupe in Merius's eyes, an easily forgivable offense. Now that you've left your mark on her, he'll not be so forgiving."

"He's going to kill me," Whitten groaned.

"It'll be no less than you deserve."

"I'm sorry, sir."

"I told you before I don't want your useless apologies. You've fouled up my plans and crossed me in more ways than you're capable of understanding. At some point, I had hoped to annul your marriage to Safire after Merius's ardor for her had cooled. That way I could have arranged more suitable matches for all three of you. Now, your idiot's lust has made that a far more difficult task, if not impossible."

"Sir . . ."

"Get out of my sight. If I were you, I would make myself scarce. And if you even so much as look at Safire or attempt to talk to her, I'll flog you myself."

He nodded as he grabbed for the doorknob. He fled the chamber, leaving the door swinging on its hinges. Cursing, I pulled it closed with a bang that likely woke the whole house. Sniveling ass--I would have hit him if he had stayed any longer. Damn it, Merius had wooed the witch, bought her a ring, gone off to battle so that he would have free claim to her when he returned, and for that drunkard to paw her like she was no better than a loose tavern wench was . . . I froze in the middle of yanking on my boots, balanced on my left foot. I sank down on the bed, still holding one boot as I stared straight ahead at the open wardrobe, the grays, browns, blacks, and blues of my doublets and jerkins, the unadorned linen of my shirts.

I had told Whitten that Merius would be justified in killing him. What about killing me? I had arranged for Merius to leave, deceived him into going. I had arranged the mock marriage, attempted to coerce Safire. At the time I had thought her a fortune-hunting hussy, but even if that were the case, I doubted Merius would see it that way when he returned. And it wasn't the case-- whatever else she was, Safire was not a fortune hunter. She hadn't expressed the slightest interest in Merius's inheritance or titles. A true schemer would have tried to worm her way into my good graces since I was the one who held the purse strings. A true conniver would have shown some skill at manipulation. Safire had managed neither of these. She was honest to the point of rudeness, as incapable of concealing her true nature as a flower was incapable of not blooming.

I covered my eyes with my hand. The early light shining through the windows was too bright. Pain split my temples. My original plot had been that Merius would return after several months of fighting and have forgotten the girl, but I realized now that she was not so easily forgettable. He had staked his entire inheritance on her, something he would never have done for any of his barmaids. If Safire had meant little to him, he would have flaunted her. Instead, as with all things he treasured, he had gone out of his way to keep her a secret, especially from me. As well he might, looking at what had transpired the last few months. I groaned again, shaking my head. And those letters--those letters. There had been so many of them, and they hadn't been the usual vapid love slop that young men wrote to get women into bed. They had been more like letters to an intimate friend, interspersed with passages of the raw longing I unwillingly remembered from my first few years with Arilea. His ardor would not cool any time soon.

But he had to know he couldn't marry her. He had to know that--I had taught him better, damn it. Unless he had meant what he had said about joining the king's guard permanently. I raised my head, staring between my fingers at the wardrobe before my hands slid down and clasped together under my chin. He had meant what he had said. Young he might be, reckless he might be, but once he made up his mind . . . I could jest myself all I wanted, but when it came down to it, Merius had become the man I had reared him to be, no longer the boy I could command. He wasn't Gaven's get. He was mine, and he wouldn't be asking for his seal ring when he returned. I had lost my son, my only heir, through my own stupid plotting. I needed whiskey.

I staggered to the wardrobe. My trembling fingers soon felt the cool silver at the bottom of my inner cloak pocket. I pulled forth my flask, sunlight glancing off its battered sides and blinding me. I uncorked it and took a long swig, liquid lighting a fire down my throat, Arilea's laughter ringing in my ears. Wiping my mouth on my sleeve, I glanced around the chamber, the dark corners, the perpetual shadows clinging in the vaulted ceiling, our bed in the middle of it all. "Laugh away, you dead bitch," I muttered before I returned to my flask. It was half gone--it could be all gone in a few more swigs, and I wouldn't give a damn anymore. It was a breakfast fit for fighting ghosts.

There came a knock at the door. I gulped down my last mouthful. "What the hell is it now?" I sputtered.

"Mordric?"

Was that Eden? No, it couldn't be--I had left her at court under strict orders to watch for developments. "The name is sir," I shouted.

"Mordric, sir?" She added the sir as a deliberate afterthought.

Now I was certain it was her--only she would disrespect me twice in so familiar a fashion. "What the hell are you doing here, you trained viper?"

"I have to talk to you."

"I wouldn't recommend you come in unless you want to get beaten for disobeying orders."

The door opened, and Eden slipped into the chamber, closing it quickly behind her. She was still cloaked--she must have just arrived by the morning coach and not even bothered to stop by her chamber to wash off the road dust. "Listen, Mordric . . ."

"No, you listen." I stepped towards her. "I told you to stay at court, not to leave for anything. You were to send Randel if you had an urgent message, but you were not to leave yourself, not until I returned."

Her yellow eyes glinted under her hood. "This was too urgent to leave to Randel."

"Nothing is too urgent to leave to Randel. He's been my steward since before you were born."

"He's still only a servant." She threw back her hood, her snarled hair tumbling loose over her collar.

"Whose bed did you leave to come here? Uncombed, unwashed--you look like a dock wench. Didn't I train you about appearance, its importance-"

She interrupted me. "Merius has been taken hostage. Prince Segar got the word last night."

Slowly, I took another swallow of whiskey, my gaze never leaving hers. "That son of a bitch Herrod," I said finally, corking the flask and pocketing it before I turned back to the wardrobe. "He knew better than to send them into those mountains. Did the prince know whether it was a Marennese or SerVerin band that took them?"

"He thinks SerVerin only because they wrote in their ransom note that they slit the throats of all lowborn prisoners."

"They always say that--it's a lie to create a panic in our court, nothing more. You can bet your last coin that they sold the lowborn prisoners to the slavers." I knelt before the wardrobe and began to remove boots and boxes from the bottom until I had cleared a spot far in the back.

"The prince said the ransom is high, eight bags of gold, and they'll probably hold out for more." Eden came over and stood behind me, her arms crossed.

"They always do, the greedy, flesh-mongering bastards." I ran my fingers over the wardrobe bottom until I found the knot hole. I slipped my finger through the hole and lifted the loose board. A cloud of dust rose as I dragged out a pouch of coin. Spiders scuttled across the boards, and Eden sneezed as more dust filled the air.

Her eyes widened as I pulled out pouch after pouch of gold. "That's three bags at least," she said after about the twentieth pouch.

"Yes." I straightened and slid the board back into its spot. She helped me put the boots and boxes back, her eyes still skipping to the dusty pile of pouches when she thought I wasn't watching her. "That coin hasn't seen the light of day since I was married," I said.

"Where did you get it?"

I shrugged. "Different places. I was quite the card and dice player when I was in the king's guard."

"Surely it's not all from that."

"No."

Eden considered this for a moment, but she knew better than to question me further about the coin's origins. "Do you want me to take all of this to the prince? If so, I'll require a trunk . . ."

I shook my head. "Take only seven pouches, a bag's worth. It would be too dangerous for you to take more than that, too difficult to conceal. In fact, don't go by the public coach. I'll arrange for Ebner to take you in the carriage, and then he can return for me tonight." I stood, closed the wardrobe, and went over to the writing desk. There was a fresh piece of parchment already laid out. I uncorked the inkwell and tapped the quill of the pen against the desk as I thought for a minute. Then I dipped it in the ink and wrote:

The bag that Eden bears is to be sent to the ransomers immediately. I'll bring the rest tomorrow when I return to court. Mordric

I folded the note, sealed it, and handed it to Eden. "Deliver this to the prince and no one else. I don't trust King Arian not to keep some for the church, dishonest monk that he is. I don't much like the idea of Merius's fate resting on Prince Segar's judgment, but at least he can be blackmailed into behaving, unlike his praying father. Rather suspicious, really, a king with no vices. No wonder the rest of the world distrusts us."

Chapter Twenty-One--Merius

By second full moon after departing Cormalen, there were only fifty-three of us left from the original band of one hundred. Gerard and I were the only remaining men of rank. "It's a hell of a thing," he whispered to me one night when we both couldn't sleep. "It's a hell of thing, commanding these men to certain death in these hellish mountains."

"Yes." I gazed up at the moon. It was an odd bronzy orange, nothing like the moon at home. The stars were different too--I hadn't reckoned on that when we had left. I savagely tore off a bit of jerky with my teeth. Why couldn't the damn sky at least be the same? I didn't want to die under this weird moon and these foreign constellations. "It's a sad way to be promoted."

"What do you mean?"

"We came to command only through the deaths of others, our friends."

Gerard shrugged. "Someone has to do it, Merius."

"I know that. Well, since we're in command now, let's turn around."

"What?"

"You heard me." I swallowed the jerky and took another bite. "What are we doing here? It's a suicide mission. We can't possibly pick off enough SerVerinese to make it worth our deaths, the deaths of these men."

"That's defying orders."

"So what? When Herrod made those orders, he had no idea it would be like this. They gave us a horrid map--God knows where we are now. We were supposed to be back in the foothills two days ago. Let's cut our losses, find our way back. I don't want these men's deaths on my conscience, and you obviously don't either, since you brought it up."

"I'd feel a coward if we turned around now."

"Why? You've killed at least two dozen of these southern dogs, faced death everyday without flinching. Blind obedience is not courage, Gerard."

He reached for his pack. "Not two dozen, Landers. Thirty. At least."

I lightly punched his shoulder. "You should have started with whoever taught you how to count. I'm the only one here who's killed thirty. Three dozen, actually."

He snorted, pulled out his pipe. The moonlight gleamed against the ivory stem as he fumbled for his flint and dagger. "Careful," I said as he struck sparks into the bowl of tobacco, and it began to glow. "You never know who's watching. Or sniffing."

"Oh, Landers, shut up. They can't see or smell this little spark from far away. A fire maybe, but not a pipe."

"They may not be far away." I took a deep breath and crossed my arms as I looked around.

"We'd hear them." He sounded less certain, though, and I noticed he shielded his pipe with his hand.

"Maybe."

Just as I spoke, a pebble fell somewhere close by, a small plunk amplified against the mountain sides into a hundred echoes.

"Damn." Gerard put down his pipe, and we both stumbled to our feet, peering around at the hulking shapes of the rocks. Our companions slept on, huddled piles of cloaks and packs and weapons, the men themselves hardly to be seen in the dark.

There was a sudden yell, and a torch flared red along the edges of the path leading off to the east, the path we would have followed in the morning if we stuck to our orders. Both Gerard and I woke the men, but it was too late. Shadows poured down the side of the mountain, and SerVerinese scimitars flashed in the moonlit bowl of our camp.

Gripping my sword, I put my back against the mountain so

no one could come at me from behind. There were plenty coming at me from the front. I had heard rumors that the SerVerinese could see in the dark as well as cats, and I believed it. We were surrounded.

The first man who came within length of my blade appeared nothing more than a shadow. I slashed at him blindly, and he leapt away. Then he approached again, his sword raised to block my blows. I stabbed under it, but instead of parrying and lunging towards me, he leapt away again. *That's odd.* Usually these SerVerinese were aggressive attackers, willing to sustain deadly injury if they could manage to nick you with their blade. Maybe this was a young one.

Careful to keep my back to the mountain, I moved forward a few yards and lunged towards him. Yet again, he moved away, waving his blade in the dizzying arc they taught all their warriors as an intimidation tactic. It irritated me more than anything else. Why wouldn't he engage? They were attacking us, so why was he backing away? It was almost like he was drawing me out . . .

I froze, my eyes darting around the perimeter of the camp. There was a flat expanse of rock at the far end, torch light bouncing across it. I saw the giant shadow of the bowman, the ten foot high curve of the bow, the spear-sized arrow. Then he released.

My feet, my body, nothing would respond to the frantic stream of thoughts coursing through my mind. *Mother, Father, court, Whitten and Selwyn and Gerard as boys, the academy, my horse Shadowfoot, Safire . . . oh hell, Safire, sweetheart, I'll never see you again.* Then I ducked, but it was too late. I was dead. No, not dead . . .

There was a sudden sting in my lower arm. What the hell? I glanced down. A six-inch shaft of a dart was sticking through my sleeve, blood welling around it. I pulled it out. It was a miniature arrow with a sharp iron tip, fletched with feathers on the other end. I dropped it, rubbed my wound. The sting had become a burning, a burning that slowly spread up my arm and into my torso. I glanced up, suddenly remembering the swordsman who had acted as bait. He was standing there, scimitar lowered, watching me. A rage filled my limbs, and I lurched towards him, my sword extended. My legs felt heavy, though, as if I were walking through water, and everything seemed to slow. I closed my eyes, my heart pounding in my ears.

Then I collapsed to the ground, and everything went dark.

~ ~ ~ ~ ~

It was light when I awoke. I lay on my belly like a snake. I groaned and closed my eyes again, trying to stretch. My arms were bound tightly behind me, though, and I couldn't move them. Someone turned me over roughly and forced brackish water down my throat. I swallowed gratefully. My mouth was so parched it felt cracked, and my throat was sore as hell. Some effect from that poison they'd shot into me, I supposed.

When I opened my eyes again, the sun was higher. I was resting on the ground in the circle of rocks that had been our camp last night. Gerard lay beside me, our packs beside him, but there was no sign of any of our men. Our captors had evidently been shrewd enough to pick us for the noblemen and commanders from among our motley crew, though the only way they could have told us from the peasant recruits were the insignias on our weapons, the finer mesh of our mail. Otherwise, we were equally as filthy, flea-bitten, and ragged as the others. Traders then--only traders and the highest ranking SerVerin knights knew enough to tell a Cormalen nobleman from a Cormalen commoner. And only traders would have wanted us alive rather than dead. We were worth more alive.

I struggled up until I was kneeling. It was only then I noticed the two men standing behind us. The taller quickly came over and helped me stand. Then he barked an order to his companion, who took off running down the path and out of sight.

About a quarter hour passed. Gerard awoke and was dragged to his feet. SerVerinese began to appear a few at a time until there were at least sixty surrounding us. Gerard and I watched the ragtag jumble of traders warily. They were olive-skinned for the most part, with long black beards waxed into elaborate curlicues and points, dirty clothing in all manner of bright colors, and enough jewels winking in their ears and on their fingers to embarrass a mercenary woman. They looked like a flock of tropical birds with soiled plumage, foreign and forlorn against the dark rock of the mountains. Their flamboyant appearance belied their deadly skill at fighting, however; woe to the man who underestimated them. All had long scimitars strapped to their belts and bows made of a sleek, black wood I had never seen. So Gerard and I stood, silent and still. Three months ago, we might have challenged our captors and died brave fools, but we were too exhausted for that now.

The leader of the traders (at least, I assumed he was the leader because of the nearly unintelligible invective that poured from his mouth on to the hapless ears of his underlings) snatched our packs and began to rifle through Gerard's. Since we had run so low on supplies, there was little for him to search, and he soon found Gerard's seal ring on a chain. Gerard had stopped wearing it after a SerVerin warrior had grabbed the chain and tried to strangle him in the midst of battle. The trader examined the ring for a moment before he picked up Gerard's sword and looked at that as well. Then he looked at us with dark eyes and held out the ring and sword.

"What House is this?" he asked in SerVerinese.

"What the hell is he saying?" Gerard whispered to me.

"He wants to know what House you're from."

"I'll not tell him. They'll get no ransom from my father."

"You have to say something, or they'll kill you. Lie, make up a House name--they'll not know it's a real House for several weeks, with how slow these message riders are. We might have a chance to escape . . ." I was cut off when the trader cuffed me, whipping my head around.

"No talking between prisoners!" he yelled.

"He doesn't know your tongue," I said in my poorest SerVerin. "I must translate for him."

"Too many words--you use too many words."

Shrewd son of a bitch. "I would use less if you wouldn't use so many," I retorted, enraged by the feel of the blood running down my cheek from where he'd hit me with his heavily bejeweled hand. Then I cursed myself, for I realized that in my anger, I had spoken with a well-educated courtier's accent. To hell with passing myself off as the son of a simple country squire now.

He straightened, looked at me narrowly. He handed Gerard's things to a stripling boy beside him before he picked up my pack and emptied it. I had Safire's letters and hair tucked in my shirt pocket under my mail, so all he found were my rations, oils and stones for polishing my blades, an arrow fletching and repair kit, and my last pair of dry woolen hosen, a treasure I had been saving for the return journey. After pawing over these articles, he picked up my sword and stared at it, running his fingers over the large flourished L of the insignia and ruining the smooth finish of the blade with his oily hand prints. Then he looked up at me again.

"Landers," he said finally, a greedy gloating in his voice. "You're of the House of Landers."

"No." I shook my head. "The House of Lyrre."

"You lie." He cuffed me again. "There is no House of Lyrre among the first families of the northern barbarians."

"It's a minor House."

"You're not of a minor House," he said. "You're a lying Landers." He smirked. "Seven, eight bags of gold at least for you."

I closed my eyes. Father would never pay that much, not for me, not after I'd given up my seal ring. Damn it.

~ ~ ~ ~ ~

The traders took us on a path that seemed to run almost due west, for the sun was in our eyes every afternoon. They laughed at us and our pale heathen eyes when we squinted. Mostly, though, the insults and mistreatment that generally went with being a prisoner of war were absent. My name had bought us that much.

Gerard and I kept a sullen silence for the most part. If we tried to talk to each other, the leader cuffed us. However, sometimes at night, when the traders stopped to make camp and everyone was busy, we managed a few whispered conversations.

"What's that stench?" Gerard said one night when we were tied back to back and hobbled to the ground like horses.

I sniffed. "Dinner."

"I suppose it'll be like that offal last night. Dog meat--it made me sick to eat it."

"It's an honor they'd even give us meat. Usually they starve their prisoners on hard tack and water."

"Some honor." He began to wiggle around, his movements tightening the ropes around my wrists.

I shoved him back as best I could. "I'd rather not lose my hands, Gerard, if you don't mind."

"Sorry, my shoulder blade itches."

The leader passed, casting us a cursory glance, and we fell silent for several moments. Then Gerard cleared his throat. "Merius?"

"What?"

"They sent a rider west when they caught us, to send word of the ransom, and now they're taking us in the same direction, down to the coast."

"Well, yes--how else will they get their ransom?"

"Do you really think they'll get it?"

"No." I stared at the jagged black horizon, the first stars piercing the darkening sky behind it. "My father won't pay that much. I gave him my seal ring before I left."

"What?"

"My duties lie with the king's guard now, not the House of Landers."

"But, but Merius," he sputtered. "Your inheritance, offices . . ."

"They're not mine anymore." I smiled for the first time in several weeks.

"You sound pleased about it, you crazy son of a bitch."

"I am pleased about it. I'd rather be doing this."

He snorted, and a nearby horse jumped and neighed. Several men looked our way, and we sat still until everyone returned to cooking dinner.

"Anything is better than being under my father's thumb," I said finally.

"He might still pay it. You are his only son."

I shook my head. "We can't make that gamble. What if he doesn't pay it? They'll likely kill us."

"So, escape?"

"Yes."

"But how?"

"At night, after we reach the lowlands. It's too dangerous here."

He grunted. Some of the men came to feed us then, and we got in no more conversation that night. I heard Gerard choking down the meager meal of stew and pack bread behind me, and I grimaced, swallowing fast with as little chewing or tasting as possible. I wished he hadn't said that about dog meat. I had been able to pretend last night that it was something else, stringy beef perhaps, but now I kept picturing the hounds who lived in the Landers stables. They ran out with joyful barks to greet every carriage and wagon that rolled into the courtyard, their tails wagging wildly. My jaw locked shut, and I gulped the last of the stew. It burned all the way down my throat and into my gut. The horrid taste remained, a spicy greasiness that no amount of water seemed to wash away.

I closed my eyes, quickly tried to concentrate on something else before I retched. Safire's letters and lock of hair were still in my pocket, undisturbed. I couldn't touch them because my wrists were bound, but at least I could think about her. I wondered if she had started to worry yet--it had been several weeks since I had sent my last letter. I hoped not. I didn't like to think of her worried. I liked to think of her laughing. She chortled--I had never met another girl who chortled before, but she did, the witch. Especially when I tickled her or kissed her on an odd spot. I had discovered it our first night together. Suddenly, when I kissed her ear lobe, her girlish giggle had deepened into this gurgling chortle. It was erotic as hell.

As my captors extinguished all flames but the main watch fire for the night, I felt the cold, hard rocks under me, digging into the aching muscles of my legs, and imagined my bed at court. Then I imagined Safire in my bed, and everything was sweet for awhile until I nodded off.

~ ~ ~ ~ ~

It took only two weeks or so to reach the foothills. At first this surprised me, since it had taken our band of men a month to traverse the mountains to the point where we had been attacked.

As I thought about it, I realized it wasn't so odd we had back tracked so quickly to the lowlands. The traders knew secret shortcuts, we had run into no skirmishes, and men seemed to travel faster when the going was downhill and there was the hope of good coin at the end.

My only amusement as we trudged along was listening to the traders. The leader Raul was a tyrannical man, and there was much muttering against him. Because of my pale skin, the men apparently forgot that I understood most of what they said. We had different guards everyday because the duty was considered a punishment, and Raul meted out punishment frequently, depending on who displeased him the most on a particular morning. On our last full day in the foothills, a young loudmouth named Ferzan and his brother Senkal guarded Gerard and me.

"That old heathen Raul," Ferzan kept saying as he cast dark looks ahead where Raul and his main cronies rode at the front of the caravan.

"Shut your mouth," Senkal said finally, cuffing Ferzan across the back of the head.

Ferzan muttered some curse I didn't understand, and then he punched Senkal back. "I'll not shut my mouth while that old liar leads us. He's a disgrace, a yellow cur."

"Take your punishment like a man, brother."

"A real man wouldn't let another cheat him out of coin."

"It wasn't your loot to keep. All gets divided equally among the men, no matter who finds it. It's the rule of the traders--you know that."

"Then why does Raul get a quarter of it, if it's divided equally? It seems equal means something different for the leader." Ferzan spat on a rock.

"I'm tired of your whining. You sound like a eunuch, and all you do is get me in trouble."

"You're the eunuch, defending that thief."

"Now, see here, we'll have plenty of coin, once we deliver these two and collect the ransom."

"That's what you think," Ferzan snarled.

"He's right," I said in SerVerin. Gerard glanced at me, his eyes wide.

Both of our guards' heads whipped around, and they stared at me. "You see here," Senkal said finally. "You're not to speak, you barbarian filth. Your tongue defiles the language of the gods."

"What do you mean, I'm right?" Ferzan asked, his gaze narrow.

"Don't talk to him, Ferzan. We're not to talk to the prisoners."

"You just did."

"That's different. He needed to be reminded of his place."

"Others besides you two have forgotten my place and spoken in front of me as if I had no more understanding than a dog."

"That's because you don't. We can always return you alive without your tongue. Think on that, barbarian." Senkal spat in my general direction, but there was no real venom in it. Of the two, Ferzan had the guts.

"Who else has spoken of the ransom in front of you?" Ferzan had taken the bait.

I shrugged, looked defiant. "I really couldn't say. I can't keep all your heathen names straight." Senkal punched me on the side of the head until my ears rang, but it was worth it.

"Could you point them out?"

"I might." I tipped my head towards the front of the line. "Those two, up there with Raul. The tall one with the silver studded vest and the jeweled dagger and the short, sniveling one with the squinty eye."

"Those bastard curs--they're Raul's toady henchmen, they are."

"Ferzan," Senkal hissed. "You'll get us both with daggers in our backs tonight. Shut up."

Ferzan ignored him. "What did they say, barbarian?"

"Why should I tell you?"

He hit me in the back. "Because I asked you. Next time it'll be your kidneys, and you'll piss blood for a week. Now talk."

"Let's just say they'll be getting their own quarter of the ransom."

"I knew it," he muttered. "I knew it. Those toadies--I'll be damned if they'll cheat me or my brother out of our shares."

~ ~ ~ ~ ~

By that evening, the camp was a seething mess of plotting and counter-plotting. Ferzan had told all his cronies what I had said, and now they were whispering amongst themselves and glaring in Raul's direction. Raul appeared not to notice as he feasted with his favorites, telling some ribald story about the emperor's harem and popping dried apricots in his mouth.

"I don't know what you said, but you've stirred a stick in a hornet's nest, Landers," Gerard hissed.

"Just wait."

"Be quiet," Senkal barked. He was still our guard and more on edge than usual since Ferzan had defected from his duties.

We stayed silent after that. Senkal had bound us back to back again but hadn't hobbled us at the ankles yet. I took this as a sign that Ferzan planned to move us sometime later tonight, perhaps when he mutinied against Raul, using us as leverage when things turned nasty.

Ferzan picked up his metal bowl then and walked over to the stew pot at the end of the camp where Raul sat. Raul looked up and saw him. "Ferzan, you lazy cur, you're supposed to be guarding the prisoners," he yelled. "Get back to your post."

Ferzan's back stiffened. All of his friends raised their heads and looked at him expectantly. A few stood up, their hands going instinctively to their scimitar hilts. Ferzan dropped his bowl as he turned to face Raul. It clattered against the rocks. Then all was silent for an instant before Ferzan's face contorted in a wordless roar, and he whipped out his blade and lunged towards the fire.

Raul and his companions leapt up, scimitars already in hand, and charged at Ferzan. Ferzan's fellow plotters responded in kind, racing for the fire with weapons at the ready. Senkal drew his blade just as Raul's and Ferzan's scimitars met with a ear-splitting clang. He jumped over Gerard's legs and ran for the fire, leaving us unguarded.

"Let's see if we can get up like this."

"That's going to take some doing," Gerard grunted. "My arms are already raw."

I managed to cross my ankles. "If I could just kneel . . ." I gritted my teeth and pulled forward on the ropes, tried to bring my lower legs and feet under me. The sores on my wrists rubbed against the rope. "Son of a bitch," I muttered under my breath.

"Damn you, Landers! This rope is cutting my arms off. What the hell are you doing back there?"

"I'm kneeling. By now, I could have said my whole catechism, waiting for you."

After much pulling and swearing, Gerard was kneeling too. Then, carefully mirroring each other's movements, we got to our feet simultaneously. "All right, what do we do now?" Gerard asked.

"Run."

Gerard laughed. "We'll not get far, but what the hell . . ."

He was cut off as one of the traders slammed into us, knocking us back on the ground. The man staggered backwards and then forwards again. I saw then he had a scimitar buried halfway in his belly. He fell back, hit the ground with a sickening thud, and lay still.

"Hell, we have to go through all that again," Gerard said.

I took a deep breath. "You see where that trader landed?"

"Yes?"

"We should try to use that blade stuck in him before its owner shows up."

"I think the owner is dead, Landers. Otherwise he'd still be holding his sword."

"Good point."

After much bruising and swearing, we managed to get to our feet again. The battle was still raging. Dark shapes darted in and out of the fire light, blades gleaming. The groans and curses of dying men filled the night. We dodged a few duels, staying as much in the shadows as possible. It was difficult enough trying to walk sideways in tandem over smooth terrain, and this was far from smooth terrain. We stumbled a number of times before we reached the dead trader.

With precarious balance, we inched downward until we were sitting on the body, the ropes around us pressed against the scimitar blade. "We should both lean forward until the ropes are as taut as we can get them--they'll be easier to cut that way," Gerard said.

"Right." The sweat dripped down my forehead, salty on my tongue. All around was the coppery smell of blood. The body under us was still warm, and I tried to forget what it was as we clumsily jounced up and down, sawing the rope against the blade. Something cracked under me, and I fought retching when I realized the crack was one of the dead man's ribs, breaking under our weight. My wrists and hands were numb when the rope finally snapped. Gerard shot to his feet and then immediately stumbled, not prepared to balance with his arms behind his back. I rubbed the bounds around my wrists against the blade, slicing a long scratch in my right arm before I cut myself free. I shook my hands for several moments, the blood tingling painfully in my numb fingers. Then I stood and pulled the scimitar loose from the body and cut Gerard's bonds.

"We need our swords, some food," he said.

"I know." I slashed the air a few times with the scimitar. "This will do for now, though I'd feel better with my own sword. These curved bastards are unwieldy."

Raul had taken our swords as part of his private loot, so we headed toward the fire and his end of the camp. Bodies lay everywhere, the sick, sweet stench of burning flesh in the air. Some of the men were still alive, crying for their wives, water, anyone to put them out of their misery. However, they weren't all dead or near death. Somewhere, I heard the clanging of swords. We stuck to the shadows and the rocks, keeping a watchful eye as we came to the remains of the fire. There I discovered the source of the burned flesh smell. Raul had fallen there, and his leg was in the fire. I turned away quickly and put my hand over my nose, glad we'd had no supper.

Raul had been the only trader with a horse, a giant bay mountain gelding. We found the poor creature tethered around an outcropping of rock. He had been in the thick of the fight, and he was straining at his rope, rearing and pawing the air. As we came closer, he reared higher, neighing in a shrill, horrible horse scream that sounded like a child being tortured. Gerard grabbed his bridle, and the horse almost lifted him off his feet.

"Strong blackguard," Gerard panted. "Help me, Landers."

I tucked the scimitar in my belt before I took the bridle on the other side and ran my hand gently down the gelding's neck to his withers, whispering to him. His ears flicked back and then forward again, and the whites of his eyes disappeared. I patted him, noticing that our swords in their scabbards were tucked under the saddlebag flaps. "That lazy cur Raul--he didn't even take off the saddlebags."

"They don't seem to brush down their beasts as they should, either. Look at this mud."

"You don't want to brush them too much when they're out,

unstabled like this--their skin makes its own waterproofing," I retorted.

"That's good to know, Landers," Gerard said sarcastically. "My question is, what good is one horse when there's two of us?"

"He's big enough, he could carry both of us for awhile, at least until we're away from here."

"Maybe."

"It's worth a try." I adjusted the stirrups and checked the girth. "There, you mount first."

Gerard climbed up into the saddle, settling forward as he took the reins. I reached to untie the tether when Gerard suddenly started. "Look out!" he yelled.

I spun around, pulling the scimitar out of my belt before I even saw the trader. The man charged over the rocks and straight for me, his blade flashing coldly in the moonlight. I blocked him and then lunged. He parried, and I ducked as he swung his scimitar in a giant arc that almost grazed the horse. The villain had a long arm. I tried to undercut him, but he leapt away nimbly.

Gerard shouted something and drew his sword. He cut the tether, and the horse vaulted forward, galloping in a circle around me. Gerard leaned down in the saddle and slashed at the trader with his sword. The man dropped to the ground and rolled towards me. He jumped up and charged. I held my ground until the tip of his scimitar seemed only a yard from my stomach. Then I dodged to the side and swung my blade. It caught him in the throat. Blood spurted everywhere, and he crumpled.

Gerard drew the reins tight, and the horse came to a halt, snorting. I dropped the scimitar and grabbed Gerard's hand. I clambered up behind him. We rode for the west, and soon the salt of the sea, the scent of Cormalen and home, filled the air.

~ ~ ~ ~ ~

Herrod's base camp was on the sea cliffs near the Marennese port of Toscar. After leaving the maze of the mountains, it took us little time to find our way back to the camp. We had already cleared the SerVerinese from the these plains on our march to the highlands, and the only fellow travelers we encountered were farmers and merchants. I felt a dull relief at the sight of the camp, too exhausted to care much beyond the thought of a comfortable cot to sleep on tonight instead of the hard ground.

A temporary fence made of wooden stakes had been built around the camp. The Cormalen flag, the golden stag on a green background, flew over the largest tent. Francis, Roland's brother, was one of the guards outside the main gate. He had been in our troop but had broken his arm the last night on the ship and had to stay behind.

"Merius! Gerard!" he called when he saw us. "We thought you were captured . . ."

"We were." I dismounted.

"How did you escape?"

"It's a long story." I lowered my voice. "Have you heard of Roland?"

He nodded, the lines of his lean face tightening. "The messenger brought his sword and ring back with the last letters."

"We built a rock cairn, honored him as best we could."

"I'm certain you did. If only I had been there." He glanced down at his arm, still in a splint.

"We avenged him. And the others," Gerard said as he stepped down, still holding the reins.

"That's what I've heard." Francis smiled grimly. "Now, if you'll follow me--we'll talk more later. I'm sure now you want food and drink and a good wash up. Herrod will be glad to see you."

~ ~ ~ ~ ~

After a quick bath and shave and some fresh clothes, we sat down at one of the trestle tables in the main tent. A steward brought us ale, dried fruit, and a freshly roasted chicken stuffed with herbs and bread crumbs. For several minutes, all we could do was eat. The only food we had been able to forage the last few days had been some stale pack bread from Raul's saddlebags and few sour berries from the bushes along the road, so any repast would have been welcome. The chicken was soon a pile of bones.

Gerard leaned back against a tent post and belched loudly. "Now all I lack is a pipe and a woman."

"A pipe I'm sure you can find, but I didn't see any women on the way in."

"Herrod runs too spartan a camp by half," he grumbled.

"Straighten up!" roared a familiar voice from the entrance of the tent. "Miserable whelps, slouching at table." We jumped to our feet, our arms at our sides, and stood to attention.

"Ah, it's good to see you remember the bite of my switch after all these months," Herrod said cheerfully as he strode up to the table. Two men followed him, carrying a large sack which they heaved on the table before they left the same way they'd come. From the musical clinking, I surmised the sack contained a good bit of coin. "Sit back down, you fools." He sank down on the bench himself and pulled out a large white handkerchief with which he mopped his damp brow. "Too hot in this hell country. I'll be glad to get home."

"So the campaign is a success, sir?" I asked.

He shrugged. "It's never enough of a success to suit me, but I think it'll suit the king well enough. I'd stay here till all these southern dogs ran home with their tails between their legs, but although our men are brave, there aren't enough of them for that. So, how many?"

"We lost forty-seven before the capture."

Herrod nodded, his mien sober. "I figured as much from the reports. That was the worst road, the one you took, and I didn't expect you to go so far on it."

"Our map lost us," I said.

His sudden laugh shook the tent posts. "You'll be a courtier yet, Landers. So, what of the remaining men?"

"Sold, we think, though they used some poisoned darts that kept Merius and me out for a good while. We didn't see what happened to the others," Gerard said.

"Likely you're right--sold. These slavers will sell anyone, given the chance. We'll ransom them back. Now, the good numbers: how many SerVerinese?"

"Between us two, at least sixty," I said. "Of course, we were around the longest and had the most opportunities to fight. Well over five hundred kills for the whole troop, counting our skirmishes on the plains."

"Don't forget the traders, Merius," Gerard said. "You engineered that."

"What's that?" Herrod's gaze was sharp with interest.

We told him the story of the argument over our ransom among the traders, the subsequent battle, and our escape. "Good work," was all he said at the end. "Not all fighting is swords or arrows or cannons, loath though I am to admit it. Making the enemy doubt themselves, fight amongst each other, can be half the battle. Oh, that reminds me," he said as he stood up and tugged the clinking sack forward. "This is your father's, Merius."

Curious, I opened the mouth of the sack and pulled out a handful of coins. Gold gleamed in my hand. I looked up at Herrod, puzzled.

"Gold stars--surely you've seen them before. The king stopped minting them after you were born."

"Yes, I've seen them before. It's not that. It's just . . ." I trailed off, suddenly realizing what I held. My ransom. He had paid it. I stared down at the coins. The scoundrel had actually paid it.

"He's sending more," Herrod continued, mistaking my confusion. "This is only the first installment, of course. They wanted ten bags for you, five for Gerard. There are benefits to having the name Casian," he said to Gerard, who chuckled.

"Ten bags," I repeated. Ten bags was a fortune, even for a high-ranking noble family like the Landers. All of our wealth was tied up with the land, the estate. Certainly, we had an income, but nothing to equal ten bags of gold stars. How had he been able to put his hands on that much so quickly? And why had he? I swallowed, clutching the coin hard in my fist as I looked up at Herrod. "I'll see he gets it back, sir."

Chapter Twenty-Two--Safire

I parted the branches of the underbrush and left the path.
Bracken cracked under my feet as I stepped into the woods. Tipping
my head back, I closed my eyes, the green-gold warmth of the sun
through the rustling canopy of leaves far overhead caressing my skin.
The muffled gurgle of water told me there was a stream close by,
perhaps with mossy stones on its banks and bubbling waterfalls with
pools for bathing. I took a deep breath, imagined I was inhaling the
sunlight.

"Safire," Dagmar called behind me.

"We should have brought a picnic," I said.

"Where are you?"

I opened my eyes. "Right here, just off the path."

"What did you go off the path for? You'll be full of burrs,"
she grumbled, poking her head through the bushes.

"There aren't any burrs."

"Well, come back anyway. Lunch is waiting, and we still
haven't found any flowers."

"We'd have a whole bouquet, if you'd let me pick those marsh
marigolds."

She wrinkled her nose. "They smell."

"They smell of spring."

"Spring must be rank then. Father needs suitable flowers."

"You couldn't get much more suitable flowers for him than
marsh marigolds. That's the insignia of our House."

"They're prettier on his seal ring than in reality. Now, come
back."

"No, I think I'm going to look off the path for awhile. I bet there's some nice flowers this way. I hear water." I started towards the gurgle.

"You'll get lost," she said, but she trudged after me. "Safire, this is nasty. My slippers are already damp."

"Why didn't you wear your old ones then?"

"Because I thought we were staying on the path."

"You could have stayed on the path." I jumped over a log.

"That's all right." She sighed, the long-suffering older sister. "Let's find this stream of yours."

It turned out not to be a stream but a small river. "Oh, pretty," I exclaimed, scrambling down the bank. I kicked off my slippers and waded into the shallows. Minnows swirled around my feet and nibbled at my toes. I giggled and splashed, and they all darted away, darting back again when I stood still.

Dagmar stayed on the bank. "If you catch a cold, I'm not nursing you."

"Quit being such a wet blanket."

"Safire, do hurry up. I'm hungry."

"There's watercress growing here. You could always eat that."

"No, thank you." She made a face. "It's probably got snails crawling on it."

I waded back to the shore. A frog that had been hiding behind a rock suddenly squeaked and hopped into the water, startling me. I lost my balance and stumbled into the river. My foot slipped on a slimy stone, and I toppled into the depths. I came to the surface, sputtering. Even though it was June, the water was still cold enough to knock the wind out of me. Dagmar clambered down the bank and held out her hand. I grabbed it and somehow gained footing on the slippery river bottom. Laughing breathlessly, I staggered back up on the shore, clutching Dagmar's hand.

"Oh, Safire, your frock . . ." Dagmar wailed.

I held out the muddy skirt. "It's an old one. It'll be all right."

"Come on, let's get you back and into some dry things."

"Not yet. We came to find Father flowers, and flowers he shall have." I climbed, struggling in my wet petticoats.

"But there aren't any flowers here except more of those nasty marsh marigolds." Dagmar made it up the bank and straightened. "I say we come back tomorrow and look."

"Tomorrow it may rain." I unbuttoned my cuffs and rolled up my sleeves. Rivulets of water trickled down on to my skirt.

Dagmar sucked in air through her teeth at the sight of the scars on my arms, criss-crossed, angry red lines. "If you'd use the apothecary's balsam salve, those would heal faster."

"I've been using the salve," I said shortly. "It's just that the cuts were made by something unnatural, so it's going to take them an unnatural time to heal. Perhaps they never heal completely."

"Safire, that's . . . oh, I wish you wouldn't talk like that!"

"Why not? It's true."

"But it makes you sound like a raving lunatic. Do you talk this way around the gatekeeper and his wife?"

"No. We barely speak." I walked along the river bank, watching my feet. It was hard walking--my wet skirt hobbled me, and I had to hold it out with one hand to keep my legs free.

"Good."

"Good? We don't speak because they're frightened of me." I stopped, plucked a lonely daisy, and picked off the petals, counting under my breath. According to it, I would see Merius again in eighteen days. The petals fluttered out over the river, and I sighed and tossed the stem aside.

"What?"

"I think they think I made those cuts myself, and it frightens them."

"But that's terrible--what if they tell the other servants that?"

I glanced back at her. "The other servants already think I'm a cold-hearted hussy for not visiting my dying father when he's only a few hundred yards away. There are just some things you can't explain away with a pretty story, Dagmar. Let them think what they want."

"I wish we could move him out of the hall so you could see him, but the apothecary said that moving might kill him."

"I know." I dropped my skirt, clenched my right hand into a fist, and clapped it into my left palm. "If only I could find a way around that hell spirit . . ."

"Safire!"

"Let's talk about something else." The bank was blocked ahead by a willow thicket so I turned away from the river into a stand of poplar trees.

"What should we talk about?"

"Your wedding."

Dagmar flushed. "What about it? You know everything already--you were there."

"Was that the first time you and Selwyn kissed?"

"That's none of your affair." Her flush had turned to a blush all the way to the roots of her hair.

I grinned. "You mean to tell me that you've been living in the same house for the past three months, and you never even kissed him until your wedding day?"

"I didn't say that."

"So you did kiss before--how scandalous." I held my skirt and petticoats high and skipped around a tree. "Oh, she's a likely wench," I sang. "Who kissed me on the tavern bench . . ." Birds scattered from the trees.

"Hush!"

I fell in a heap on some violet-spotted moss, my hands behind my head as I caught glimpses of the far off sky between the poplar leaves. "I'm sorry, Dagmar," I said. "I shouldn't tease so."

She sat down beside me, clasping her hands around her knees. "You know you're right. We should have brought a picnic. It's pretty here."

"Better than that damned sickroom."

"That's all right."

"No, it's not. You've just married--you should be with your husband now."

"Selwyn and I would have waited, but we'd already waited so long, and the apothecary says that Father could be like this for months."

"Maybe even longer." I shuddered as a cloud passed over the sun.

"Do your-" she hesitated, "your talents tell you anything?"

I looked over at her. "About Father? Not really. It's all dark. I think soon, though."

"So do I."

I touched her arm, and she met my gaze. "I'll find a way into that room before he passes."

"But what about the spirit?" she stammered.

"I overcame her once, that time I woke up and was myself after those horrid two months. I can overcome her again, I think. I just have to remember how I did it before." I sat up, patted down my hair, and bracing myself on a worn stump, got to my feet. I shook out my wet skirt as best I could.

We headed back to the river. As we started along the bank, I noticed flashes of pink amid the undergrowth ahead. I sped forward. "Look!" I exclaimed. "I knew we'd find something." Tangles of wild roses grew over the bank. I knelt down. The heady scent surrounded me as I used the loose folds of my skirt to grip the thorny stems. Bile rose in my throat, and I gagged. It was that night in the courtyard, and invisible icy fingers were at my neck . . . no, she wasn't here. It was only roses, innocent flowers, not her. Quickly, I forced myself to think of another memory of roses, a pleasant memory. When Dagmar and I had first gone to court, there had been that man in motley who had brought me a rose out of season, the man who had told me to put it in my hair. Two such beautiful things should go together, he had said. I closed my eyes and pressed my face to a rose blossom, inhaling it and thinking of that man. All I smelled was the rich wine of summer captured in a flower, the lure of realized romance in full bloom. Not her. Never her again. The urge to gag had passed. I sank back on my heels, smiling. It was a small victory but a victory nonetheless.

~ ~ ~ ~ ~

Contrary to my expectations, it did not rain the next day. The liquid gold of June sunlight poured through the mullioned windows of the front chamber of the gatekeeper's cottage. By unspoken agreement, this had become my chamber, at least in the mornings. It had the best light, and after I had finished helping the silent gatekeeper's wife with the breakfast dishes (it had taken me two weeks to discover her name was Maud), I cleared off the table and spread out my drawing things. Maud sometimes came in and knitted or embroidered; otherwise the chamber was completely mine until lunch.

This morning I was alone except for my orchid, which nodded in the breeze from the open window. Dagmar, repentant after tattling to Father, had saved the orchid Merius had given me at court and nursed it on her window sill for the two months I was not myself. After I had settled into the gatekeeper's cottage, she had brought the plant to me, and now I kept it with me constantly like a pampered child.

I spread out a large sheet of parchment on the table, weighing down the curling edges with brass candleholders. Then I untied the leather straps wrapped around my pouch and pulled out bits of black and gray charcoal. My hand moved in broad strokes, quickly filling in the background. I smudged here and drew stronger lines there and backed up to examine the effect. Then I moved forward and attacked the parchment again, scribbling furiously until I had a huge storm brewing on the paper. I found my white chalk and added several lightning bolts flashing in the hills as I hummed to myself. There were faces emerging from the clouds. With pen knife in hand, I sharpened my best black pencil until the point was fine enough, and then I outlined these faces as faintly as I could. Ghosts in the clouds
. . .

There was a knock at the front door, and I heard Maud's light footfalls hurrying to answer it. Voices murmured in the hall, and suddenly the chamber door flew open. "Someone to see you, my lady," Maud said.

I put down my pencil and wiped my blackened hands on my smock. Mordric stepped into the chamber.

"Do you want any refreshment, sir?" Maud asked.

He shook his head, and she bobbed out of the room, shutting the door behind her. It took her several tries rattling the door latch before she got it closed properly. It had never given her any trouble before, but the presence of Mordric tended to make even the most calm natures nervous.

I clasped my hands before me and remained standing, waiting for him to begin. It was the first time I had seen him since the night in the courtyard, almost four weeks ago. He looked strangely haggard and careworn, as if twenty years of hard living had caught up with him in one night. Dagmar had said he'd been doing a lot of riding between here and court since the news of Merius. His aura was no longer a uniform opaque gray and dark red, but glimmered here and there in spots. It reminded me of a tarnished, blood-spotted sword that some lazy steward had stopped polishing halfway through the job.

He remained standing as well, and there was a moment or two of silence before he finally spoke. "Those cuts should have healed by now."

I had forgotten my sleeves were rolled up to keep them out of the charcoal. Hastily, I pulled them back down, covering my arms again. "The scars look worse than they really are."

He clasped his hands behind his back and began to pace in front of the window. "Merius was taken hostage."

"I heard."

"I've paid his ransom. He'll likely return in a few weeks."

"I see."

Mordric stopped and turned towards me. "And what do you see, witch?"

I swallowed. "What do you mean, sir?"

"I mean, what's to be done with you?"

"You have more say in that than I do at the moment, so you tell me."

He commenced pacing again, obviously agitated. The resemblance between him and Merius was becoming more pronounced--perhaps the incident in the courtyard had stripped away the callous mask he had cultivated for so many years. "I won't tell you all the plans I had to dispose of you," he said. "God help me, I even thought of assassination . . ."

"Am I that troublesome?" I asked lightly, though I quaked inside.

He looked at me, smiled faintly. "Yes."

"Why didn't you then?"

"Because I've never had anyone assassinated."

I thought for a moment. "That doesn't surprise me," I said

finally.

"It doesn't?"

"No. You're not that kind of man, although you seem to think you are."

"You're full of bold presumption, miss. I could still have you disposed of, arrested . . ."

"But you won't."

His gaze narrowed. "How can you be so certain?"

"Because you would have let Peregrine take me that night, if you had so little honor."

He shook his head. "It wasn't honor. Honor is a mockery for the young to play at. I only rescued you from Peregrine because I didn't want Merius trying to rescue you later and getting himself killed."

I raised my brows. "Who is mocking who now?"

"I won't take cheek from a dingy wisp of a girl. Have you been playing in the cinders?"

I spread out my sooty hands. "It's from my charcoals."

He shook his head, put a hand over his eyes as if my dirty state pained him. "Indeed, you make a charming hearth sweep, my dear. Have you no aristocratic pretensions?"

"None."

"If Merius is to have any sort of career, whether at court or in the king's guard, he needs a wife who can entertain extravagantly, navigate the snake pit of court society with ease, and lie through her pretty teeth. You, although possessing unusual talents, don't appear to have any of these skills, particularly the last."

"I know I'm not what you planned for him, but perhaps he wants a real wife instead of some pretentious prattler or glorified housekeeper."

"It's not a question of what he wants. It's a question of what he needs."

I crossed my arms. "The duties you've set out for him?"

Mordric stepped closer, at least a good foot taller than me. A month ago, I would have moved away, but now I stayed my ground and glared up at him.

"Safire," he said softly. "I can't let him marry you."

"Oh, you can't?" I laughed. "No offense, sir, but Merius is full grown, and he's given up his seal ring. I don't think he needs your permission."

He shook his head. "You're a stubborn girl."

"So assassinate me."

"You know, noble marriages are for political alliances, legal heirs, and coin. Not for pleasure. Affairs are for that."

I raised my chin. "I'll not be a mistress when I can be a wife. How dare you . . ."

"You can't be his wife now. You're married to another."

"That's your doing, Mordric. And you'd best be begging the king to annul it. Soon, at that," I said sweetly, rage coiled inside like a viper. "Do you want bastards for grandchildren?"

He started, his aura shrinking into an intense band of gray so dark it appeared black. I had surprised him, evidently, for he looked at me more closely than before, measured me with his eyes. "Come now, my dear, surely you don't think Merius would dishonor you so. Honorable men know ways to avoid disgracing their mistresses."

"Even the most honorable man can be bewitched." I smiled. "And passion flows more freely than prudence through his veins, despite all your training."

"Wicked creature," he muttered. "All right, I'll get you your annulment." He leaned against the edge of the table, moving aside my sketch before he crossed his arms.

"Good. Perhaps he won't kill you now."

"Like all young girls, you exaggerate," he said smoothly, though his hands clenched around his upper arms so tightly the knuckles stood out.

"Merius is young too and prone to exaggeration in deed as well as word. You'd best not be around when he returns--you've given him little reason to love you."

Mordric kicked the floor with one toe, watching his feet. "Merius is stubborn, reckless," he said, quiet threat in his voice. "In order to rear him properly, I needed his respect, not his love. Don't remark on things of which you know little. It makes you sound a fool."

I squared my shoulders. I was baiting the bear in his den.

"He speaks fondly of Ebner the horse master, of the cook, of his tutors, of Herrod, all of whom he respects highly. Yet he never has a fond word for you. How is it that you, his own father, gained only his respect?"

Mordric raised his head, his gaze sharp. "How is it that you've kept your tongue for so long?"

"He thinks you hate him."

He shrugged. "I suppose."

"Doesn't that concern you?"

"Why should it? I can't help what he thinks."

"But when he returns, sees what you've done . . ."

"And what have I done?"

I thrust my hands, heavy with rings, under his nose. "Married his sweetheart to his kinsman, for one."

He pushed my hands away. "I thought you were a fortune-hunter. I was protecting him."

"I doubt he'll see it that way."

He blinked, sighed, and looked away, out the window. "No. You're right, witch. He won't see it that way."

"What will you do?"

His body slackened, his shoulders dropped. "I don't know." He cleared his throat, offered a bitter smile. "Perhaps I'll ask Arilea."

~ ~ ~ ~ ~

I stood in the courtyard, staring at the hall in the dawn stillness. The gray half light softened the hard edges of the stones, made the jagged roof line indistinct, so that the house seemed to slump in on itself as if it were tired of being inhabited after many long years. It was a somber place, even asleep.

The sun crested the seaward hills then, and the eastern wall blushed a fiery pink, all the windows twinkling. *I could live here if it stayed dawn all the time--the house looks almost cheerful for a change.* I crossed my arms and shivered. What had it been like to grow up here? Merius had said little about it except for merry stories about boyhood exploits with his friends and his mother reading him poetry and how Ebner had taught him all he knew about horses, but I knew now there was more to it than that. There was his father and that cold thing, his . . . *his mother*. I could barely bring myself to think the words, the gap between Merius's loving memories of his mother and that foul spirit was just too great to make the connection. What kind of woman had she been, to haunt this miserable place with such vicious resolve after she was dead and supposed to be free of earthly concerns? Mordric was not an easy man, but had she really hated him so much that she had let it consume her? Or had she loved him too much to leave? Or had it been a bit of both? I suspected the last, that she would stay here to torment him until she saw him dead. And she loved Merius, I was certain of it, though somehow that love had become twisted until she hated all others who tried to love him, including his own father. And me.

The vague glow of a candle flitted from window to window on the second story of the east wing, heading for the main staircase, and I knew then Dagmar had remembered her promise. I closed my eyes and took several deep breaths. Without an actual spirit at the gatekeeper's cottage to fight, practice had been a hollow mockery at best, but I had tried several times over the past few days to prepare myself anyway. I had come to from one of these fits to find Maud staring at me, broom hanging loose in her limp hand. Her slack-jawed expression had almost made me giggle before I remembered myself . . . and I had better remember myself now. I straightened and resumed concentration on my breathing. No more distractions. Pride, fear, impatience: these were the traps of my enemy. I had to steel my mind against her.

The front door creaked open, and Dagmar crept down the steps towards me, leaving her candle burning on the table just inside the entrance. She still wore her dressing gown but had pulled on a pair of leather everyday slippers which rasped across the cobbles.

I stepped forward. "How is he?"

She shook her head. "Still breathing, but neither Elsa nor I think he'll last the day. Oh, Safire . . ." She reached for me, and we embraced.

"Shh, shh, it's all right," I murmured even as sudden tears heated my face. It seemed I cried all too easily these days. "Come on, now, we have to do this, before the servants wake." Even as I spoke, a rooster crowed from the direction of the stable.

She nodded and pulled away a little, still keeping one arm

around my shoulders as she wiped her nose with a handkerchief. We both gazed up at the house for a moment, taking comfort in each other's solid, warm presence in this world of shadows and cold spirits. Then I started toward the steps, silently counting my breaths and focusing intently on each number as it popped into my mind. Dagmar followed quietly. I had told her last night exactly what I planned and that it was very important she not interrupt me unless I fainted or showed some other sign of great distress. It touched me that instead of arguing or forgetting my instructions, she was being careful to obey them exactly. However, it also made me a trifle nervous; as the younger sister, I was not accustomed to giving orders and being obeyed.

My count faltered, and I shook myself. I couldn't think about anything now . . . concentrate. "Twenty, twenty-one, twenty-two . . ." A breath for every step, a breath for every step . . .

I reached the threshold of the doorway, still counting. After a moment's hesitation, I stepped into the front hall, my insides churning. Any minute, she could descend on me. *Fear*, my mind yelled at me. *Stop it!* That was when I heard her laugh, and my mind's reasonable voice went mute, my brain turned to whimpering jelly.

A cold wind whistled through the hallway. The candle on the side table winked out, and the hall instantly became a maze of muted gray and black shapes. The front door banged shut as Dagmar crossed the threshold. She shrieked and cringed in the corner, her hands clutched over her bowed head.

I grabbed the banister at the bottom of the main staircase to steady myself. Still shaking violently, I closed my eyes and once again began to count my breaths. This time I spoke the numbers aloud--it helped drown out the laughter. I squeezed my eyelids tightly closed like a desperate child making a wish. With each breath, I pictured my lungs expanding, heard the numbers more clearly as I regained my inner equilibrium.

Suddenly, I opened my eyes, my voice faltering. The air I inhaled had turned frigid, tiny bits of ice that sliced at my throat. I coughed, choked as I sagged against the banister. No, the air wasn't ice--it was just air. I couldn't let her play with my mind again and make me sense things the way they were in her warped reality, for when I did, they became real to me too. And when I believed something was real, it could hurt me.

I raised my head, saw the stairs rising into the dusty shadows above. The second story landing was only the vague outline of the railing, a black square in the wall behind it indicating the passageway to the east wing and the private family chambers.

I began to climb up the stairs, all the while watching the doorway to the east wing. There was a faint wavering glow in the doorway, as if someone far down the hall had lit a candle. The glow grew steadily stronger, and I realized it wasn't candlelight. Candlelight was yellow. This light was bluish-white, the color of snow under moonlight.

I backed down the steps. The weird glow lit the entire second landing now, the polished railings glimmering coldly. My breath hung like smoke in the chilly air, and I found my teeth chattering, my arms clenched tightly together over my middle.

Suddenly, she was there, a white face peering at me over the railing, her long beautiful fingers pale as a corpse's against the dark wood. All that was distinct about her was her head and her hands and her snake hair--all the rest was a nebulous, vaguely human figure. *She doesn't want to use her strength to materialize completely.* Evidently she needed her strength to deal with me. For the first time, I realized that if she could hurt me, I could likely hurt her as well, not just fight her off but damage her, much as a priest damaged a spirit by exorcism. But how? I wasn't a priest, and I didn't even know one I could trust enough to help me.

Fool witch came her hiss in my mind. *I'll kill you this time.* She started over the railing, her translucent fingers outstretched, claws ready to rip my skin.

"Why?"

She paused, hovering in the stairwell. Then she laughed, a low, contemptuous cackle. She circled the railing before she suddenly swooped up and then dove down straight for me, quick as a hawk in sight of prey. Instinctively, I threw my hands out.

She grabbed my hair. *She's nothing but air--she can't hurt me.* That was what my rational mind said, but my irrational body hurt. A fire spread over my scalp, and tears sprang to my eyes. Her icy nails were at my throat. A drop of hot blood trickled down my neck, my blood. She was real, and she could kill me.

Blindly, I flung my fist upward with all the force I could muster. My punch caught her in the upper arm. She hissed and let go of my throat and hair. I fell back, clutching my sore knuckles. Hitting her had been like slamming my hand into a block of ice. But it had worked. Somehow, it had worked.

She retreated to the second floor railing. I stared up at her-- her eyes were a transparent silvery white with bottomless black wells where the pupils and irises should have been, her face contorted in a snarl of feral rage. *Death has driven her mad.* I crouched down, preparing for her next attack. Of their own accord, my fingers balled up into a fist. She seemingly had no body to hit, but it was the only thing that had worked so far. But how?

Images flooded my mind in answer. We were struggling together in a lake, and I was kicking her, punching her away so I could reach the surface and relieve my aching lungs. The night I woke up . . . I had fought her off in my dreams the night I had woken up from my two month fit. Hurt her, in fact, as she had not tried to attack me again until the next day, the day I had fled the house for Calcors. My veins tingled with the sudden awareness of power, and I leapt to my feet. I could hurt her as she had hurt me. I was more than clairvoyant--not only could I see and hear and smell the other side, I could touch it as well.

She plunged towards me again. I was ready this time. I jumped up to the third step and grabbed her neck as she did a quick turn to catch me. With an ear-piercing yell, she clawed at my hands. I clenched them tighter around her throat, gritting my teeth. My bleeding fingers were already frozen numb from holding her, and I couldn't feel her claws cutting me. I had wondered if holding her would be like trying to hold smoke--impossible--but it was far different. Her skin put me in mind of the alchemist's quicksilver, cold and unsteady but solid underneath. She was still trying to scratch me, but her struggles grew weaker as I choked her. Suddenly, with a shrill gasp, she melted away, and my hands were left clutching air. I glanced around, startled. Dagmar hurried up and grabbed my elbow.

"Come on, you're bleeding," she said, tugging me away from the foot of the stairs.

"No, not yet." I held tight to the banister, searched the shortened shadows. The sky outside lightened with every moment, cutting around the shapes of the furniture and railings more sharply even as I looked.

"Safire, the servants-"

"Shh." I held up my free hand, staring intently at the top of the stairs. Arilea was gradually coming into shadowy form there, slumped against the rail. Her eyes shined like ice, the only clearly defined part of her. The chill of her gaze reached the bottom of the stairs, a terribly human evil distilled into spirit form. Even Dagmar felt it, shivering beside me. There was a tooth left in this serpent yet.

I'll get you in your sleep she whispered in my mind.

"I don't sleep here." The feeling was finally returning to my fingers, and with it, came pain. I winced and put my hands in my pinafore pockets. Small drops of blood began to soak through the thin white fabric. She had hurt me worse than I realized.

You shouldn't have come here, witch.

"I have to see my father."

"Safire, who are you talking to?" Dagmar demanded. "Your hands . . ."

"Her--I'm talking to her."

Arilea laughed, a brittle sound. *Your father's dead, fool. Now leave.*

I swallowed. "Not yet. He's not dead yet, and I'll see him, despite you."

Why should I let you see him? Merius didn't get to see me before I died.

"Is that why you rest so uneasily?"

Her laughter swelled to a glass-shattering crescendo, and I clapped my palms over my ears. *Rest? You call this rest? Do you really want to be with your father, stupid girl? Stay here, and I can make it so.*

"You can't kill me, or you would have managed it already."

Try me again, and see. I've been kind so far. Now get out.

"If you can kill me, then I can kill you."

Her eyes gleamed, two narrow knife glints in the dark. *No one can kill me, not a priest, not you. I'm already dead.*

"Not kill you, exorcise you." She hissed at the word exorcise, hid her face. "You don't want that, do you?" I continued, moving up a step. "Exorcism means death for you. No?"

Don't come any closer.

"If you hurt me again, I'll get a priest."

No frocked fool can pray me away. Her voice rose shrilly, a painful wail splitting the inside of my skull.

I took another step up, holding the railing. "I don't want to force you over, Arilea, if you're not ready."

The wail became a scream, and I recoiled, my head exploding. *I'll be ready when that son of a bitch Mordric is. I'll see him dead before I leave . . .* the scream faded to a distant shriek, and she suddenly vanished.

I collapsed on the stairs, the tautness leaving my body so abruptly that my muscles went limp. Dagmar clambered up and fell on her knees beside me.

"Are you all right?" She reached for my hands. "We need bandages . . ."

"I'm fine," I managed--even finding the breath to speak was difficult. Slowly I sat up, gasping for air.

Blood crusted on my hands and arms, my skin stiff and throbbing. "I'll be all scars if this keeps up."

"You shouldn't have done it."

"What do you mean? How else am I going to see Father?"

"I know, but . . ." she hesitated. "You know, when I touched you before, I think . . . I could have sworn that . . ."

"You heard her?"

Dagmar nodded. "I don't know how--it was the strangest thing. I heard her laughing, and the cold . . . when I let go of you, it went away."

"It's like that night in the courtyard when Mordric picked me up. He could sense her then too."

"It scared me."

"It should."

She swallowed, met my gaze. Her pupils were so huge her eyes seemed black. "I'm sorry I didn't believe you before."

"That's all right."

Somewhere, we heard the muffled thump of a door being slammed. "We better get moving before the servants see us here," Dagmar said. "Come on--we'll get you cleaned up in my chamber. Selwyn's usually up and dressed by now, so he won't mind. Then we'll go to Father."

~ ~ ~ ~ ~

Father died that night. Dagmar and I were the only ones in the chamber. She was reading aloud from a book of prayers, and I had wandered over to the window, where I traced the diamond-shaped panes with one finger while I stared at nothing. The rasp of Father's breathing was a constant, like someone steadily sawing away at a pine log.

"'And you shall not despair, for when the door opens, you will step into an eternal field of golden grass where only the trees weep leaves in the fall,'" Dagmar read.

I turned from the window. "That was pretty. Could you read it again?"

She repeated the verse. "Do you remember when Father planted daffodils all around the house?" I asked.

She nodded. "Mother's favorite flowers."

"That bit about the golden grass made me think about it. It was so cheerful every spring, the daffodils in bloom. The wind ran over them, and they wagged their yellow heads at each other like sly ladies laughing over some wonderful secret. Mother used to say that about them. I'm sad we missed them this year."

"I know." Dagmar closed the book and set it aside, looking at Father. "He loved her, far more than most men love their wives," she said softly.

"And that was how he told her, by planting the daffodils. He was shy when it came to her. Sweet."

"He's always preferred actions to words."

I closed my eyes. "She's here, waiting for him . . ."

Father groaned. My eyes flew open, and I hurried towards the bed as Dagmar reached the other side. We slipped our arms around his shoulders, grasped his cold hands. His back grew tense for a moment as he fought for air. "Shh, papa," I whispered as I kissed his forehead. "Shh." The candle flickered. Father's breath whistled in his throat, and his back relaxed as he flickered with the candle. Then the flame flared high, as if fed by a sudden draft, and he was gone.

~ ~ ~ ~ ~

We buried him beside Mother in the plot near our house. It was the first time in a month I had been off the Landers estate, and it seemed strange to be going home again, if only for an afternoon. I kept expecting to see Father, writing in his ledger, visiting the hounds, teasing the cook for a sweet biscuit. I pinched myself, but the illusion persisted. How could my loud and boisterous father be silent and still in a box in the ground?

After the funeral, the others left Dagmar and me to wander awhile. Everything was oddly quiet. The few servants had been let go long ago or had gone to work for the Landers, and the house had been shuttered up, the furniture draped with canvas against the dust. Only Boltan and his wife remained to watch the grounds, care for the remaining horses, and receive any letters.

Against Dagmar's wishes, I took Strawberry out of the stable and rode her around the fields for a few minutes. I couldn't bear being in the house anymore where we kept stumbling over Father's absence. Strawberry galloped over the uneven ground, jumped fences and streams, as anxious to run through the sweet-smelling grass as I was. The sky was a huge bowl overhead, the edges a deep cerulean fading to a hot blue-white at the apex. Not a cloud in sight-- it put me in mind of that day in March when Merius and I had trysted on the parapet. Only a scant four months before, yet it seemed years. A perfect dream, half-remembered. I twisted his ring on my finger, squeezing the raised peridot and pearl design into my palm until it felt fiery as a brand.   Father would have approved of Merius's and my match eventually, after all his bluster had been spent and he saw that Merius really meant to marry me. He had wanted me and Dagmar happy, his little girls. Now he would never even see his first grandchild, neither he nor Mother. The abrupt thought punched me, and my world wobbled on its axis. The ground shook before us, the grass moving up and down like waves on the sea, and I wondered, suddenly dizzy and sick, how Strawberry kept her footing in a world that had lost its center. No Mother, no Father--Dagmar and I were orphans. Orphans. I was too young for this. How arrogant I had been a few months ago. I knew nothing about life, not really. I would have to muddle my way through, clutching always for a warm, familiar hand that didn't exist anymore. I gagged over the unshed tears in my throat and urged Strawberry forward. Maybe if she galloped fast enough and far enough, we would find the center again. Somehow, though, the more we searched, the more we ended up heading back in the direction of the house, the last place I wanted to be.

Finally, I surrendered, and Strawberry and I returned to the stable. As I dismounted and led Strawberry around the paddock, Dagmar emerged from the house. "Finally back, I see," she said, shielding her eyes.

"You should have taken Charger and come with us."

She came into the paddock, leaned against the side of the stable. "You know the only one who can ride Charger is Father . . . was Father."

I reached out and squeezed her shoulder, and she bit her lip and lowered her head briefly. Then the moment passed, and she was practical Dagmar again. "We should be returning soon. It will be time to dress for dinner in a few hours."

I looked around. "I don't want to leave," I said, surprising myself with the truth. I didn't want to leave. This was the last place I wanted to be, yet I didn't want to leave. What was wrong with me?

She sighed. "I suppose they'll let the house to some tenant. I hope whoever it is leaves Mother's daffodils alone."

"Who's going to let it?"

"Mordric and Selwyn. They would hardly let it sit empty."

"Don't we have any say . . . oh, I should know better than to even ask that." My hand tightened on Strawberry's bridle. "Well, they're not getting my books. Or Strawberry. And they're not getting your embroidered bed curtains that you worked on so hard. What about Father's weapons, his seal ring, Mother's silver? Those are ours, not even part of the dowries. Whose dowry did the house go with anyway?"

"Yours. Mine had the best land, so you got the house."

"They got the house, you mean. Of course, when the

annulment . . ."

"Safire, don't talk about that now."

I plowed on, ignoring her discomfort. "Mordric promised me one, and I should get my dowry back with it."

"You think he'll keep his promise?"

My eyes narrowed. "He better, or I'll send his dead wife after him."

Dagmar smiled in spite of herself. "Put away Strawberry. We have to go soon. Now, what happened to Boltan?"

"There he is, coming around the side of the house. Who's that with him?" A cloaked man on a horse accompanied Boltan.

"Looks like a messenger." While we watched, the man handed Boltan a piece of parchment and then spurred his horse forward, down the drive to the main road. Boltan saw us and waved as he walked across the lawn.

"This is for you, sweet," he said, holding out the parchment. It was a letter with a red seal. "From Marenna," he added with a wink.

I snatched it from him, dropping Strawberry's bridle. The seal was unmarked. My hand shook as I turned it over and saw Merius's strong script flowing across the front. "Oh God," I muttered inanely. "Oh, thank God." It had been so long, and although Mordric had told me Merius had been ransomed and would be fine, his words had done little to relieve the constant dull ache of worry I felt. It had just been so long since the last letter.

With unsteady fingers, I tore the seal and unfolded the parchment.

Dearest Safire,

I can barely write this, sweetheart, my hand trembles so. Thinking about you has been half comfort and half torment in this hellish place, and every day, I've begged God to let me live so I could see you again.

I've relived all our moments together a thousand times in my mind and read your letters to tatters, and it's never enough. The desire of my heart, my love, my want--all is twisted into an endless wick that will never burn out, the wick you lit the night you grabbed my hand and dragged me into the dance. You forward witch. I love you, I need you, I want you so badly right now it hurts. I need to watch you sketch, smell your hair, feel your hands, dance with you, see the artlessly graceful way you slip into (and out of) your clothes, bring you pears, hear your chortle of a laugh, talk with you for hours, and then . . .

My duties here will soon be discharged, and then I'm free to leave. I'm not certain when the first ship out of here is, but I'm on it. I hope to find you well and waiting as anxiously to see me as I am to see you, my love. After the ship docks, I'm obliged to go directly to court. Send a message to my chamber there if you cannot come yourself. If you're still willing, we can marry in Corcin or anywhere you wish.

All my love,
Merius

I sagged against Strawberry, all my muscles weak. I closed my eyes. It was too much. First Father, and now this . . . my grief for Father and my intense joy at Merius's news mingled inside, a dizzying whirlpool that left me light-headed. My hand closed on the letter as I gripped Strawberry's bridle, the only two solid objects within reach. *Merius, my love, dearheart, you're coming back to me.* I clutched the letter to my chest.

"Safire?" Dagmar asked, touching my shoulder.

I threw my arms around her. "He's coming back, oh thank God, he's coming back," I sobbed, soaking her sleeve, his letter, with four months' worth of tears.

Chapter Twenty-Three--Mordric

I emerged from the council chamber, tailed by Sullay the fool. "You know, Mordric, it's not to the nobles' advantage to increase the SerVerinese tariffs. We merchants can barely make ends meet now, and if we can't afford to ship the wheat from your estates, we . . ."

I glanced back at him and lost all semblance of politic pretense. "You mean you can't make the ends of your belt meet. You merchants grow fat off our grain and then whine you're not getting enough."

He puffed up like a ruffled rooster. "Excuse me, but I . . ."

"Fine, you're excused." I waved him away as Peregrine stepped out of the alcove beside the council chamber entrance. Peregrine gave me the barest nod of acknowledgment, ignoring Sullay. Sullay and Peregrine were two of the wealthiest merchants on the council and therefore allies in the same way that Cyril and I were allies: always amiable to each other in public, even if it killed them. For Peregrine to ignore Sullay on his first day back from the SerVerin Empire was a momentous insult indeed.

Sullay went red, the vein standing out in his forehead. "You'll regret this," he muttered darkly before he turned and stalked toward the stairs.

"Your first day back at court, and you're already insulting your staunchest ally?" I asked quietly as we stepped into the alcove, away from prying ears.

Peregrine shrugged, impatient. "He'd insist on joining us if I gave him the slightest encouragement. He'll recover--he needs me more than I need him."

"Indeed," I said, my voice as dry as the SerVerin desert. Peregrine certainly rated his political influence high, too high perhaps. Arrogant dandy. "So, what news from Emperor Tetwar?"

"Our campaign against the slavers spooked him. He lost far more men than he expected in the mountains."

"Really?" I considered this a moment. From all accounts of the campaign so far, it had seemed a blow for our side: the troops that had gone the furthest, like Merius's troop, had lost better than half their men, and of the men who had survived, many had been taken captive, which meant expensive ransoms and hostage exchanges, hardly a victory without dire cost. Prince Segar had faced blistering criticism in the council chamber. Even though I had supported the prince, however, few dared criticize me. After all, my only son had been among those ransomed before he escaped and made himself a hero through his own recklessness. Merius's headstrong nature had its political uses after all. "So the campaign succeeded in its purpose of alarming Tetwar," I said finally.

"Apparently--Tetwar didn't expect our troops to hold out so long in the mountains. He didn't understand why our men kept coming after half their comrades were killed or lost."

"He underestimated our men, the fool."

Peregrine nodded. "He thought their comrades' deaths would frighten them, not make them so angry that--and this is a quote from him--'they fought like barbarian fiends.'"

"Many of his soldiers are the children of slaves, impressive when they march but not to be trusted in actual battle. No wonder he's spooked--he little realized the power of a volunteer force. A man's word and his commitment are far stronger when he and his fathers before him have free will."

Peregrine gave an unexpected chuckle. "He even admitted his best fighters were the slave traders, not his army. Of course, at the time, he'd had a good bit of the whiskey I brought as a gift."

"It's odd--the SerVerinese are weaned on fermented goat's milk, but they can't handle Cormalen whiskey."

"They have no need of whiskey, sir--they have no winters to weather, as we do."

"True enough. So, it sounds like his thirst for battle has been quenched."

"For the present."

"For the present, yes--even though half his army are straw men, he still outnumbers us." I leaned against the wall, my arms crossed as I pondered. How long would it take Tetwar to figure out the weak spot of his army? He was wily, but slavery had been part of the SerVerin Empire long before his birth. It would be as difficult for him to imagine an army without slaves as it would be for me to imagine one with slaves. The sheer numbers of his soldiers dissuaded most would-be opponents from testing the SerVerin Empire openly on the battlefield. With the appearance of overwhelming force, his straw army had so far accomplished its goal of avoiding war while expanding territory.

Besides, even though Tetwar was wily, he was also young, and his reign young with him. He wouldn't want to challenge the bastion of SerVerin military tradition, not until he possessed the political assurance of a man at least a dozen years his senior. And what would he do, when he had that assurance? Start replacing his force with mercenaries? I couldn't imagine that would garner him much public support. So, Cormalen had at least a few years to plan before facing the SerVerin Empire on the battlefield. The campaign had bought us time, if nothing else.

"What did he say of the wheat tariff?" I asked.

Peregrine shrugged. "He grumbled but not much else--I think he was still nonplussed by his troops defeat at our hands. Of course, I mentioned the tariff as a mere possibility--once it's put fully into practice, he may have a stronger reaction."

"Likely so." I straightened, noticing Randal approach. He paused a respectful distance from the alcove--he must have an urgent message, to come find me like this. "Thank you, Peregrine. We'll discuss this again before we present it at council--you've given me a good general picture, but I want more details." I turned to leave.

"Sir, there is a another matter," Peregrine said.

I halfway turned to face him. "Make it quick, then. My steward's waiting."

"Safire." His voice grew quiet, his eyes hawk-like gleams in the alcove shadows.

"What about her?"

"You know I've made offers for her hand . . ."

I cut him off. "She's married to Whitten, has been since before you approached Selwyn the first time with your suit. You can't be betrothed to a married woman. What don't you understand about that?"

"Sir, you won't put me off that easily." His voice rose. "That marriage is a sham, obviously made for some convenience, perhaps to protect her virtue while she was ill--it could be easily annulled. Now I'm prepared to offer . . ."

"Whatever your offer, it won't be high enough. Now there are plenty of eligible maidens with large dowries and powerful fathers. You could do very well for yourself--you have the skills to make a fine, perhaps great, career at court. An orphaned sparrow noblewoman like Safire would only weigh you down, Peregrine. I've always thought you were more savvy than to make a marriage for lust. Affairs are for that."

"Are you suggesting I take her for a mistress?"

"No, I'm suggesting you put her out of your mind before you make a complete ass out of yourself. And how dare you insinuate a lady lately married into the House of Landers would consent to be your mistress?"

"I meant no insinuations, sir," he said, sullen.

"Indeed." I suddenly felt weary. Young fool--would I have to draw my sword on him this time instead of merely threatening it? "Even if Safire lacked virtue and would consent to be someone's mistress, somehow I doubt she'd risk the consequences of an affair for you. She doesn't fancy you--that much is clear. You'd best forget her and find a woman who matches you in lack of virtue."

He paled, the lines of his face taut. "Sir, I'll stand no insult."

"Really? Then why do you pursue Safire? She exhales insults more than air."

"She does have a sharp tongue--I doubt Whitten knows how to handle her."

"Forget a sharp tongue. You'll have a sharp sword at your neck if you don't desist. I know you're used to purchasing whatever you want, but Safire's a Landers now, and she's not for sale. Perhaps

you've been in the SerVerin Empire too long among the slavers--here in Cormalen, we don't buy or sell our women at market, Peregrine."
I stalked from the alcove and down the hall, Randal hurrying after me.

"Why did you come find me?" I asked Randal after we'd gone down a flight of steps and down the hall that led to the parapet, after I was certain Peregrine hadn't followed us.

"It's Merius, sir. He's returned."

The muscles of my midriff clenched, my ribs squeezing my heart until it pounded in my ears, the same tense ache I'd felt when I'd stabbed my first opponent at sixteen. "When?"

"I saw him in the courtyard a few minutes ago."

I crossed to the nearest window and searched the courtyard. "He'd be in his chamber by now, sir," Randel said behind me.

"Yes, of course," I said absently. "I'm supposed to be meeting with Cyril at the next quarter hour in the prince's chambers. Deliver my apologies to him."

Randel nodded. "Anything else, sir?"

"No."

After Randel left, I remained at the window for awhile. The imperfections of the glazed glass panes distorted the bustle of the courtyard until it seemed only a moving blur of colors and shadowed faces. Even if Merius were down there, I couldn't have picked him out from the other vague figures, but still I looked, strained my eyes. It seemed I had been looking for him for a long time when I sighed and turned away from the window.

~ ~ ~ ~ ~

Merius's chamber door was slightly ajar. I knocked and pushed it open. He stood facing the desk, shuffling through the stacks of letters from friends and allies and council notes that had piled up during his absence. Safire's message, which had arrived only yesterday, was somewhere at the bottom of the stack where I had concealed it, not so that he couldn't find it but so that I would have the chance to see him before he did. The witch had informed me a few weeks ago that she would write Merius a letter to explain the situation since I still wouldn't allow her to leave the Landers estate, a letter that would at least let him know where she was and why she

was there. I still feared letting her wander around on her own--she
seemed intelligent, but she was also young and brash with little
apparent sense, and it would take only one foot wrong for her to end
up in Peregrine's or some other miscreant's clutches. A letter,
though--that had seemed harmless enough. Until now, when
Merius's return had become a reality.

He glanced up from the letters as I stepped into the room.
"Good afternoon, Father," he said, as casually as if I were a servant
and he'd merely been out for a morning ride. I noticed though, how
his hand tightened on the parchment he held.

"Good afternoon."

He seemed taller than when he had left, though I soon
decided that was only a trick of the light--he'd become leaner, and
that made him seem taller. His skin had taken on the leathery look
that bespoke long, rough days out in the wilds. He had the stance of
a soldier now, the unconscious tautness of one always on the verge of
a battle--fiercely unyielding yet resilient. He was the only survivor of
the seven children Arilea had borne me, a sturdy, laughing baby who
had somehow thrived amidst the dark damp of Landers Hall and the
poisoned air of a vicious marriage.

"I brought your gold back. The sacks are in your chamber,"
he said.

"Good. I have your seal ring." I held it out.

He glanced at it, then quickly looked down at the letters.
"That's not mine anymore, Father."

"Horseshit."

He raised his head, met my gaze. "Didn't you hear what I
said before I left?"

"I heard you, but oftentimes intentions change, especially
those spoken in haste and anger. I won't hold you to that."

"You don't have to. I'm holding myself to it."

I drew a deep breath before I answered. "What do you want,
Merius?"

"Nothing. You did more than I expected when you paid my
ransom. I brought back every coin of it, so we should be even."

"I don't want it back. It's yours."

"I won't take your coin."

"Proud fool," I spat. "You earned it when you escaped. Now take it, Merius."

He slapped the letters on the desk. "It always comes to this with you, doesn't it? You think you can bribe everybody."

"How can it be a bribe when you earned it?"

His eyes narrowed. "I earned my freedom, not only from those traders but from you as well. I'll not put a price on that. Now leave."

I ignored his command. "You think I paid that ransom to buy your good graces?"

He shrugged, began to pace. "You're not a difficult man to predict, Father. You always have an ulterior motive."

My muscles were tense as bowstrings. "Ulterior motive? Merius, you're my only son."

"I'm also your only heir," he shot back, "and in order to get ahead at court, you need a legitimate heir, don't you? That's what you've always told me."

The heaviness of my hip flask weighed down my pocket. My hand started to reach for it--already I could feel the liquid warmth heating my throat, loosening my muscles, my ribs releasing their clutch on my heart. Then I noticed Merius watching me, and I crossed my arms, every sinew in my body at the breaking point.

"I can sire other heirs," I said hoarsely.

"Then save the coin to buy them back when the time comes. Leave me alone." He returned to the letters, his back to me as he rustled through the pieces of parchment.

"I can sire other heirs," I repeated with difficulty, each word punching the air, "but you will always be my only son, Merius. Please."

His hands grew still, and the chamber fell completely silent before he said evenly, "Please what, Father?"

"Don't do this. I was the second son, with few prospects except the king's guard. I distinguished myself as best I could, made more coin than I'd expected in places I'll never speak of again, and then I returned to Landers Hall when I had enough. I took every copper and invested it a dozen times over in the land, made even more coin, used that to win your mother's hand. Then my hangdog brother, the one my parents put such hopes in, didn't want the responsibilities of court, so I had to leave the guard and assume his offices. When he died, everything came to me. Again, I saved it, I invested it, to make it into an inheritance for you. You're the only man I would trust with it."

"You've an odd way of showing your trust," he said softly, his back still to me as he gripped the carved edges of the desk.

"That depends on how you look at it. Who else knows so many of my plots? Who else would I let draft my private letters? Who else would I leave in complete charge of the estate? Not Selwyn, surely. I never had to return to Landers Hall when you were here except once or twice--in the last three months, I've been there at least eight times."

He glanced sideways at me over his shoulder. "If I take back my seal ring, I'd have some requirements."

"Like what?"

"As you said, I'm a man now. I make my own decisions about my life--who I marry, for instance. You can offer advice, but no more than that, or I'll return to the king's guard without a backwards glance."

"All right. Anything else?"

He bent over the desk, his head bowed. "Never mention my mother to me again, unless I ask you a question about her. Then you speak of her respectfully."

I thought of Arilea, the lies she had told him. That I had hit her when she was with child, for instance. That was a lie. I had never hit her when she was with child. I had only struck her a few times that I could remember, threatened her with my knife once to get her to shut up about Gaven. But somehow she had always contrived to have Merius in the chamber during these incidents, generally when I was too drunk to realize he was there. That bitch-- God I hated her. But he had been so young, and it was too late now to tell him that she, his beloved, long dead, forever beautiful mother, had manipulated him. And I had struck her, though not as he remembered it. He was right--best never to mention it again. Even now, after her death, she was still stealing my son. Bitterness burned my tongue, and I was silent so long that he said sharply, "Father?"

I started. "You're right--I'll not speak of her again."

He nodded, his head still bowed.

"Is that all, Merius?" I continued after several moments.

He cleared his throat and turned to face me. "Yes, that's all."

I fumbled in my pocket and found his ring. "Here." I held it out.

He took it, rolled it around his palm for a minute before he pocketed it. Then he picked up the letters again and leaned against the desk as he began to sort through them. "I'll return to my duties here next week. I have something to attend to in the meantime, and I'd like to stay at the hall for a few days," he said absently.

Oh hell--in the midst of our discussion, Safire's letter had completely slipped my mind. "Take as long as you need," I said without thinking, my body frozen and faraway as I watched him put down half the stack and flip through the remaining messages.

He looked up then. "I'm certain you have pressing business elsewhere."

I shook my head but reached for the door knob. Somehow, though, I couldn't turn it--my fingers wouldn't function. My legs wouldn't cooperate, either, my feet seemingly rooted to the floorboards. What was wrong with me? I didn't want to be here for this, but I couldn't move. He looked at several more letters and quickly set them aside before he paused over one. His fingers tightened on this letter, all the others fluttering to the floor, forgotten. I was forgotten as well as he stared at the letter, turned it over in his trembling hands before he ripped the seal and shook open the folds of crinkling parchment. His eyes scanned over the text, his lips moving slower and slower as he got into the body of the letter. Finally, his lips stopped moving altogether, his set face sickly pale under his tan. "No," he said then, his tone flat. "No."

"Merius . . ." I stepped around the foot of the bed, towards him.

He looked up, held out the letter. "You," he said quietly. "You did this? You did this . . ." His voice trailed off as the realization sank in. "Oh hell. Hell." He crumpled the letter, gripped it as he began to stride around the narrow space between the desk and the bed like a caged tiger. "Safire, sweetheart . . . if that drunken ass touched her, he's dead. I'll kill him. I'll kill you too. How could you do this to her, Father, you son of a bitch . . . God damn it!" He stopped and ripped the letter into little shreds and threw it on the floor before he resumed pacing.

"I thought she was a fortune hunter."

He drew up short, stared at me. "What? What fortune?"

"Yours. Your offices, your coin, inheritance . . ."

"I surrendered all that before I left. She knew that, knew what kind of life we'd have with me in the guard, and she accepted it. All you have to do is take one look at her and know she's not that kind. Fortune hunter? Fortune hunter?!" His voice rose. "What kind of excuse is that?"

"I know all that now, but at the time . . ."

"No, no, there's going to be none of this. None of your lies. What you thought is that you couldn't have your only heir marrying the daughter of a sparrow nobleman. You wanted the king's whiny nag of a niece for me so I could have a 'position' at court. I know how you think--God knows you've lectured me enough about it." He went over to the bed. His saddlebags lay there, empty. He began stuffing random things in them, a shirt, a belt, a spare dagger, loose coin, whatever lay within arm's reach.

"I . . . I thought she was another one of your affairs that had gotten out of hand, thought you were making a disastrous mistake."

He barked a bitter laugh. "Disastrous for whom? For you? For the Landers position? I suppose it never occurred to you to wonder if she was a disaster for me. For me, Father--I'm the one who's marrying her. Not you, not the Landers position, but me. And I love her. To me, she's the best thing that's ever happened, the one reason I risked my life in Marenna, the one reason I fought like hell when others gave up just so I could see her again. I know you can't understand that, but that doesn't give you the right to ruin it." He buckled the bags with jerky motions and slung them over his shoulder.

"I can fix it, Merius."

"Fix it?" He chuckled, moving around the foot of the bed. "This isn't the hobby horse Whitten rode into the window or the bow I broke. You can't fix this one."

"An annulment . . ."

He stopped a few feet in front of me, stood there and stared at me without blinking for several moments. Then he heaved a deep breath. The punch shocked me, even though I saw him draw back his fist, saw it coming. It hadn't seemed real until his knuckles connected with my jaw. I stumbled back, bracing myself on the wardrobe. Pain radiated towards my ear as the inside of my mouth went numb, and I wondered if he had cracked a tooth.

"I'll deal with you later." He turned and strode towards the door.

"Merius . . ." I managed, my tongue too stiff to fit itself around any other words.

He paused, his hand on the door knob, and glanced back at me. "I have to see Safire now. I presume she's at Landers Hall?"

I nodded, and he ducked out into the hall, slamming the door behind him with such force that the map of the seas under glass that he had hung on the wall fell to the floor and shattered. The air was sour and burned my lungs, but somehow I continued to breathe it, not moving until the sound of his footfalls had faded in the distance.

Chapter Twenty-Four--Merius

A royal stable boy in spotless livery napped beside the entrance to the stalls. He jumped at the hurried thump of my boots. "Sir," he gasped, tugging his vest straight.

"I need a horse."

"Yours, sir?" he called over his shoulder as he counted down the stalls.

"No, mine's not here."

"You're Sir Merius?" He paused and looked at me.

I bit my tongue, prayed for patience. "Yes. I'm in a hurry, if you don't mind, so . . ."

"Your horse is here. Big black stallion, Shadowfoot, right?"

My brow furrowed. "Yes, but . . ." I had left Shadowfoot at Landers Hall for the duration of the campaign.

"Your father brought him here. Few days ago."

"He did?" I only realized my hands clutched into fists when the sharp pain of my fingernails digging into my palms made me look down. I took a deep breath, tried to relax my fingers, but it was almost impossible. The rage would be long in relinquishing its hold on me. I had a fierce need to get on Shadowfoot and gallop until both of us were dropping with exhaustion--maybe then some of the tension would expend itself. If I didn't do something soon to escape this place and see Safire, it would take an act of God to keep me from finding Father and running him through with the blade he had given me when I was fourteen. I shook my head and stuffed my hands in my pockets, not able to stop the image of his blood on my sword from flooding my mind. He had best watch himself.

The stable boy trotted ahead of me until we reached Shadowfoot's stall. I stretched my arm over the barrier and rubbed the horse's nose, glad at the sight of him. He, at least, could never betray me. "Hello there, you big lummox. Did you miss me?"

He neighed in response, and I reached into the box of carrots that had been nailed to the tall wooden post that stood between the stalls. The boy had disappeared in the direction of the tack room. He emerged several minutes later with a loud clinking of bit and saddle stirrups. When he neared me, he dropped the saddle, and a cloud of straw dust rose in the sunlit air. For a moment, the entire place glowed golden and truly deserved to be called a king's stable. Then we both sneezed, and the dust scattered.

"Sorry, sir," the boy gasped. "The leather's been fresh greased, and it's . . ."

"That's all right. Let's just get it on him." Grunting, I slipped the bridle over Shadowfoot's head. Then I lifted the rope that held the stall door in place. Shadowfoot snorted and pranced out of the narrow space, obviously ready for a good run.

"Steady, boy," I said to him, gripping the bridle as the stable hand lifted the saddle on him. I tightened the girth. Then I busied myself buckling on the saddlebags.

The boy peered at me over Shadowfoot's back. "What was it like, Marenna?" he asked suddenly.

"Not like here. It's very dry, and the mountains have hardly any trees on them."

"Did you . . ." he hesitated. "Did you kill a lot?"

"Over thirty."

His eyes widened. "With your sword?"

"Some. And some with my bow." I moved to mount then.

"Was it hard?"

I took a moment to answer. "Yes. I only killed those who had taken slaves, who tried to kill me or my comrades first, and it was hard."

"I want to be in the king's guard. My brother says I can't since I haven't any noble blood, but Celanus Stitt is a guard, and he's no more noble than I am."

I mounted, took the reins. "Can you fight, handle a sword

and bow?"

He nodded proudly. "I hit the most bulls-eyes for my age in the last parish contest."

"Then you can be a king's guard." I tossed him a coin for his trouble and then spurred Shadowfoot forward. He needed little encouragement, lunging toward the courtyard so fast that I barely had time to tug on the reins to slow him before we crashed into the stable gate. He had caught my eagerness to flee this place.

~ ~ ~ ~ ~

When it grew too dark to see the road, I reluctantly stopped at an inn for the night. Shadowfoot, after several months of only stable yard exercise, needed a good brushdown and a few hours' rest. I removed his saddle and used the brush on him myself, finally leaving him when I had filled the oat box and water pail in his stall. Then I climbed the stairs to my chamber, lay down on the scratchy straw filled mattress, and spent the entire night with my hands behind my head as I stared at the beams of the ceiling. Safire was only seven or eight leagues away, and I was too jittery to sleep.

As soon as I saw the first gray light over the horizon, I rose and splashed some water on my face. I grabbed some bread and cheese in the common room before I headed out to the stable. Shadowfoot waited for me, and soon we were back on the road.

It was late morning when we reached the outskirts of the Landers estate. I drew rein, and Shadowfoot slowed to a walk. Everything, so drab and muddy when I had left, was suddenly green and rustling. Midsummer now, and I had last seen her in March. Would she still be wearing my ring? Would she even still speak to me, after what my father had done? I hadn't reached the end of her letter yesterday--it had seemed ardent at the start, but after absorbing the shock it had contained, I couldn't seem to remember much else about it. And what lies had Father told her? God knew. My hands tightened on the reins.

Instead of taking the main drive to the house, I swung Shadowfoot up the narrow path that ran beside the river. It was a secret trail few used--when Selwyn, Whitten, and I had wanted to sneak away from the estate, we had always gone by the river.

Shadowfoot, familiar with the path, deftly stepped over all the gnarled tree roots and stones that crossed the hardened dirt. I settled back in the saddle and let him have free rein while I inhaled the damp mossy air of the river bank and caught glimpses of the sky through the canopy of leaves overhead. Despite all my attempts, however, I couldn't chase away the half-sick feeling of nervous anticipation that clenched my middle. This was worse than going into battle.

I tugged the reins sharply, and Shadowfoot stopped with a whicker. I could have sworn I heard something over the roar of the water. I glanced all around. There it was again, clearer this time. Laughter. Women's laughter, too, by the pitch of it.

The foliage broke in front of me, and Safire staggered across the path, barefoot and holding a straw hat. Her own hat dangled halfway down her back on loose drawstrings, her hair tied with a fraying green ribbon. I made some strangled sound in my throat, the first syllable of her name, and she whirled around, the laughter dying on her lips. Her eyes grew enormous, and slowly, she lifted her hand to her mouth, her breath coming in shuddering gasps that shook her whole body. We couldn't stop staring at each other, and my eyes, long parched for the sight of her, drank in every detail. Her fey, elfin-featured face, the wild curls of hair that always escaped around her forehead and ears, the perfect hollow of her collarbone, the ripe curves she couldn't hide under demure lace, her long arms . . . I paused on her arms. There were scars there, slashes that formed a crooked red ladder on her soft skin. Quickly, I glanced at her hands. Scars there, too. What the hell? Then I saw my ring still on her finger and forgot everything else for the moment.

"Safire, stop! You left your shoes and took my hat . . ." Dagmar charged on to the path. She halted when she noticed her sister standing so still. She followed the direction of Safire's stare, starting at the sight of me. "Oh dear God," she muttered.

Gripping the pommel, I swung my leg over and dismounted, each small action magnified and slowed so that it seemed minutes before I stood on the ground beside Shadowfoot. Safire suddenly dropped Dagmar's hat and raced toward me, crying. I stepped forward and caught her as she tumbled over a root and then she was in my arms and I was in hers . . . I crushed her to me, showering kisses on her hair and face until her lips locked with mine. The world fell away, and I groaned at the sweet, eager feel of her, the familiar warmth of her body in my arms, the smoky cedar essence of her hair and skin. We were starved for the taste of each other, and it was torture when she finally broke away, sobbing for breath.

"Breathe, sweetheart." I laughed unsteadily, both arms still clutched around her as her arms were clutched around me. "God, I've missed you."

"I, I m-m-missed you too," she managed through sobs.

I kissed her eyelids and cheeks until most of the tears were gone. "Shh, don't cry. Shh."

"I can't help it." She fumbled in her skirt pocket and dragged out a rumpled handkerchief. Turning away a little, she delicately blew her nose. "I'll collect my wits soon enough. It just seems forever, Merius. I had a dream last night, you know, a dream of Shadowfoot galloping on the road, and I knew then you were coming home for certain."

"Let me look at you." I backed away, keeping my hands on her elbows. "You're so lovely--you look fresh sprung from a daffodil."

"It's the frock." She cast her eyes down, suddenly shy, and held out the golden folds of the skirt, busied herself straightening the green sash. Then she smiled and glanced at me from under lowered lashes. "So, have you tanned all over?"

I raised my brows. "No, parts of me are still pale. Like a skewbald horse, brown patches and white patches."

She tucked her fingers in my belt, pulled me closer. Then she leaned up on her tiptoes and whispered, her lips brushing my ear, "I want to see you all skewbald."

I chuckled. "Witch. That may happen sooner than you think."

She blushed, and I stole a quick kiss. Then Dagmar snapped a twig. Safire and I both jumped.

"I'm sorry," I said. Keeping my left arm tight around Safire's shoulders, I took Dagmar's hand in mine and quickly touched her knuckles with my lips. "I've been remiss."

"That's quite all right," she said briskly, meeting my eyes briefly before she glanced away. The last time I had seen her had been in the court library, and she had not liked me then. Evidently, her enmity was still strong. "We should go back to the house. It's almost time for tea," she said as she bent down, picked up her hat, and jammed it on her head. "Here are your shoes, Safire." She pulled a pair of leather slippers from her pinafore pocket and handed them to Safire. "Put them on before you get a thorn in your foot." Then she turned on her heel and started off down the path.

I glanced at Safire, who shrugged. "Never mind her," she murmured. "She's in a mood."

"Aren't you going to put those on?" I nodded to the slippers in her hand.

"No." She shot me a sideways look. "I'll not let you go yet, just to put on some shoes." We began to follow Dagmar down the path. Shadowfoot trailed beside us.

"What were you two doing out here, anyway?"

"We were taking a walk, and I had a notion to wade in the river." She nuzzled my hand on her shoulder. "I didn't expect you for several more days."

I cupped the back of her neck in my palm. "I didn't expect myself for several more days. Herrod sent Gerard and me home earlier than we thought he would."

"I heard how you protected your friends, how you escaped," she said softly. "It sounded all so dashing, like reading one of Lhigat's war poems. You're a hero to everyone at the house, especially me."

I felt my face grow hot. "It wasn't all like that," I said awkwardly. "But thank you, sweetheart."

She caught my hand in hers. "I know it was very hard for you--your aura's changed," she stammered. "It's sharper somehow, like a blade that's been honed, so I know it was horrible in parts, that you saw your boyhood friends die and almost died yourself, but that makes you even more a hero to me. I'm so proud of you."

I swallowed hard and squeezed her hand. "I just wanted to return to you. I . . . I had hoped we would marry now, but . . ."

She bit her lip. "You got my letter then?"

"Yes. I know what my father and that drunken son of a bitch Whitten did to you. I was a fool--I should have married you before I left," I finished bitterly.

"It wouldn't have worked anyway. He would have found a way around it, and we'd be worse off than we are now. You were right. This way I can get an annulment from Whitten, and then . . ."

I shook my head. "He'll not do it. He said he would, but he likes nothing better than lying. I know my father."

She flashed an odd little smile. "Oh, he'll do it. I worked my witchery on him."

"On Father?"

She kept smiling that secretive smile that made tingles in my toes. "It's been a long four months, my love."

"Obviously, if you swayed my cold statue of a father." I hesitated, but was too overcome by curiosity not to ask. "What did he do, anyway, to marry you off to that ass? Did he blackmail you somehow? Threaten you?"

"He . . ." she paused. "He threatened to break Dagmar's betrothal and reinstate my father's debts, but I don't think he really would have done it."

"Don't believe it. He's ruined a lot of people, Safire, including my mother." She stiffened. "What is it?" I asked.

"Nothing."

It was a long moment before I asked, "Did . . . did Whitten touch you at all?"

She pretended to be fascinated by a clump of violets. "I don't remember. I don't think so."

I stopped and forced her to look at me. "What do you mean, you don't remember? Don't be afraid to tell me."

She met my gaze, her pupils so large her eyes appeared black. "I told you, I don't remember, Merius. There were a couple of months when I wasn't quite myself."

"Mad, you mean? Safire, what the hell did they do to you?" I gripped her shoulders, Shadowfoot's reins slipping from my hand. "Tell me."

"You may not believe me if I tell you." She paused, and then, taking a deep breath, raised her arms. "Do you see these scars?"

"Yes, I was going to ask you about them."

"They're from ghosts, spirits," she said quickly. "There are ghosts in Landers Hall, and they attacked me."

"Ghosts?"

She shook her head. "You don't believe me, do you?"

"No, no, I just wasn't expecting that."

She turned, began to walk again. "It's all right," she said. "It's all right. It's a ridiculous story, I know, and . . ."

I gripped her shoulder and forced her to slow down. "Safire, stop it. I believe you. You can heal with your hands, you can see ghosts. It's fine. Now, quit being such a little fool and tell me what happened."

"I'm sorry, I'm used to people not believing me. Dagmar . . ."

"I'm not Dagmar." I took her hand. "Remember what I told you our first night together?"

She smiled in spite of herself. "You said a lot of things that night."

"There's nothing wrong with you, Safire. You're too beautiful to burn. I love you. Do you remember that?"

Her fingers tightened around mine. "There's just so much-- so many things have happened, it's hard to know what to say first."

"The ghosts attacked you. Then what?"

She stared ahead, lost for a moment in another place. "It was about a week after you left. My father and I came to Landers Hall to meet with your father about our betrothal, and they argued with me, bullied me a bit, but I didn't give in. Even when your father threatened me. I had noticed when we came in his study that it was cold, but I thought it was just the house. Drafty, you know. My father left the chamber at one point--now that I think about it, that was the last time I saw him before he collapsed . . ." She trailed off.

"Your father--I forgot when I saw you. I'm so sorry. I wanted to meet him . . ."

"Thank you, love. He would have respected you, approved our match if he had met you, but we'll talk about that later. There's just so much . . ." She sighed. "Anyway, he left the chamber, and your father and I sparred for a bit. It kept getting colder, but I ignored it. Until I felt the icy fingers creeping around my neck." She shivered. "There was whispering, horrible, cruel words--I thought I was going crazy. I'd seen spirits before, but they had always been caught up in their own invisible hells and hadn't bothered with me. It just got so cold . . . oh Merius, it was awful. The fingers ripped at my hair, strangled me, and I couldn't stop them. Your father thought I'd suddenly gone delirious. I was frantic to escape but the door was stuck and I couldn't get away, and then I fainted. I woke up two months later in an unfamiliar bed with no idea where I was or what had happened."

"You don't remember anything? I mean from those two months . . ."

She shook her head. "Little bits and pieces, but they all seem like part of a vivid dream that just kept going on and on. And then there were these long periods where it felt like I was floating at the bottom of a deep lake, very peaceful and suspended in the water. It was strange. I can't describe it, really."

"So what brought you out of it?" We had reached the end of the path and now were in the knee high grass of the long pasture. Dagmar was at the top of the slope near the house, a distant, dogged figure. Shadowfoot had wandered ahead and was grazing a few yards away along the edge of woods. The wind blew across the shimmering green expanse in murmuring waves, a warm summer sweetness in the air. Safire stopped and gazed at the far peaks and gables of the east wing of the house. I wanted to drag her down in the grass with me, out of sight of the house, out of sight of everything except the sky and each other.

"Your ring brought me out of it," she said finally. "I felt it on my finger one night, touched the peridot, and remembered you and that day on the parapet." She threw her arms around me. "Let's get out of here, Merius," she said, her voice muffled against my shirt. "If only for tonight."

I rested my chin on her hair, ran my hands gently over her back. "Where do you want to go, sweetheart?"

"I don't know. An inn. Anywhere, as long as you're there."

"Some place where no one knows us and no one will think to look for us."

She grinned, her impish eyes glinting. "Some place with private chambers and good locks. And nice beds."

"If we make it to a bed." I tickled her middle, and she

screeched laughter, trying to escape.

"Merius, no, stop, Merius . . ."

"Stop what? This?" I covered her mouth with mine, and we kissed clumsily, both still breathless and laughing.

Chapter Twenty-Five--Safire

Dagmar had already gone into the house by the time Merius and I reached the courtyard. Shadowfoot made a beeline for the stable, whickering at the sight of Ebner emerging from the paddock.

"Sir Merius," the horse master exclaimed. "We didn't expect you for another week . . ."

Merius let go of me briefly to shake hands with him. "How are you, Ebner?"

"We've had some fine foals since you left. Red Clover has a newborn chestnut filly, and there are several others."

"You have to see Clover's, Merius--she has a five-pointed white star between her eyes, and she's such a lovely pale chestnut," I said. "I want to call her Moon's Envy."

Ebner grinned at me. "I suppose you think you get a vote for the name, since you were at the foaling."

Merius shot me a look. "Ebner let you near his mares?"

"I was at the Rivers when Clover started," Ebner said, "and this minx here happened to be near the stall and knew what she was about. She has a lady's touch, better than any of those fool stable boys. I've rarely seen a smoother foaling."

"I didn't know you were a horse woman, Safire," Merius said.

I winked at him. "There are many secrets you've yet to discover about me."

"Good." His eyes crinkled slightly at the corners, a smile just for me. He let his fingers trail over the nape of my neck as he put his arm around my shoulders, and I shivered. We would drive each other mad with teasing long before nightfall if this persisted. His voice rumbled in my ear as he asked, "So, has Silver quickened yet?"

Ebner shrugged, rubbing Shadowfoot's neck. He seemed too preoccupied with thoughts of his horses to notice Merius's close proximity to me, our exchanged looks. "Too early to tell. We bred her with the Casian's prize stallion after you left--cost a pretty copper, that one did."

"It'll be well worth it, if the king takes the foal."

"You think like your father," Ebner said.

Merius's arm stiffened against my shoulder blades. "In some things."

"Will he be returning soon?"

"He didn't say," Merius said. "Now, we're leaving in little over an hour, so Shadowfoot should have some oats soon."

"All right." Ebner took the bridle.

"Thank you."

He waved at us, already engrossed with examining Shadowfoot's hooves before he led him to the stable.

"An hour?" I said.

"Yes--will that give you enough time to pack and such?"

"Well, yes, more than enough, but I thought you would want to see Selwyn, perhaps the Rivers."

He chuckled, ran his fingers up my neck and into my hair. "Sweetheart, the only one I want to see at the moment is you. I certainly wasn't dreaming of the Rivers every night for the last four months."

He loosened the ribbon holding my curls back. His fingertips brushed my ear lobe as he cupped my jaw in his palm. Our eyes locked, and my breath caught as a tingly heat rose inside. He looked older than when he had left me, the lines deeper in his face, a new scar cutting a white mark through one eyebrow. I imagined there were other scars healing on his body, masking the deep wounds still bleeding his spirit.

He seemed to read my mind, for he said then, his voice low, "You're so lovely, balm for eyes that have seen too much ugliness in the last few months. I can hardly bear to stop looking at you, much less stop touching you. I have no idea how I left you in the first place."

"I have no idea how I let you go." I rubbed my thumb over the stubble on his cheek, then ran my hand down the length of his arm, over his wrist and palm until our fingers entwined. "Come," I said, tugging him toward the road to Orlin's cottage. "Since we can't stop looking at each other, you'll have to watch me pack."

He half smiled. "All right, but why are we going this way?"

"Because I stay with Orlin and his wife."

"Oh." The unspoken question lingered in the air.

"I don't go in the main house at all if I can help it. I figured out how to fight off the ghosts, but they stir more at night, and I'll not risk another attack."

"Ahh." He paused. "I thought perhaps it was because of Whitten."

"Your father forbade Whitten to see me again, until this mess is sorted out," I said quickly as his hand tightened around mine. His free hand dropped to his sword hilt, the knuckles already white. "Merius?"

"What?"

"Why are you holding your sword?"

"You said you don't remember exactly what happened to you, Safire, which means Whitten could have done anything to you. And even if he didn't, he still acted as my father's cat's paw. I should find him right now, talk to him."

I began to shake. "No. No, I don't think he's here."

"How do you know? You're not supposed to be seeing him."

"He's just not here, all right? It shouldn't require you drawing your sword just to talk to him anyway."

"Why are you protecting him?"

I turned on Merius, clenching his hand. "How dare you accuse me of that? I'll be damned before I protect that drunken fool."

"Then why don't you want me to find him, confront him? It needs to be done, Safire."

"Because the mood you're in now, you'll get in a fight, you'll kill him, and then you'll hang, you ass. "

"I never said anything about pulling my sword on him."

"Ha--you just reached for it at the mention of his name.

Don't tell me you wouldn't."

"He hurt you."

"As you said, he was only your father's cat's paw." Perhaps if I mentioned Mordric, it would re-direct Merius's anger from Whitten to a more distant target for the moment.

"Oh believe me, I haven't forgotten Father," Merius spat. "He's going to get his." The quiet venom in his voice, so like Mordric's, sent a chill down my spine.

"Merius, love, please . . ." Everything I said was only making it worse. My body was trembling so hard now that I had to stop, lean against Orlin's fence. I closed my eyes--all I could see on the back of my eyelids was the shadow of the gallows. Merius enfolded me in his arms, and I clung to his shirt. Our auras intertwined, his swirling like a silvery storm cloud. I braced my hands against his back and drew away what tension I could from his heart and muscles, hoping that it would be enough to quell his rage, enough to get us away from here for tonight. His rage ran deep, a boiling sap in his veins, and it burned me inside to absorb it.

"Don't, Merius, please don't," I said finally, my voice muffled against his shirt. The tension I had just taken from him welled up and mingled with my own hot tears as I began to cry. "Just take me away from here, and we'll get the annulment. Then confront them peacefully if you must, but please don't put yourself in harm's way again, not if you care for me. I'm fine, now that you're here, but if something happens to you . . . I don't think I can take much more. We've already lost so much."

"Shh, nothing's going to happen to me."

"How can you promise me that, when you're planning to fight a duel with your own father?"

"Safire, I'm not stupid--there are many forms of vengeance, and not all involve the sword or the hangman's noose."

"I don't need vengeance." My movements jerky, I wiped my face on my sleeve.

"I do."

"But why?" I demanded, my hands fisted against his chest.

"Because I should have been here to protect you, and I wasn't-"

"But . . ." I was cut off by the appearance of Orlin at the gate.

He and Merius shook hands and greeted each other warmly. I chose that moment to sneak up the stairs of the cottage and gather my favorite frocks, my sketch board and drawing things, grooming articles and small clothes, and stuff them all into a large leather pouch. At the bottom, I slipped in a sheer shift of light golden green silk for tonight. I had rescued the silk from the chamber where the Landers women spun and made it into a bride gown Merius would appreciate.

My hands still quivered from the argument with Merius, and I dropped my hairbrush twice before I managed to pack it. I had expected he would want vengeance, honor-bound as he was, had even told Mordric so, but it was still a shock to hear him speak the words himself and see him reach for his sword. I couldn't get the image of him swinging at the end of a rope or bleeding to death from a stab wound out of my mind. I had worried so long about him dying or being injured in Marenna, and when he had returned, I had thought my worries would somehow all disappear. How stupid of me. I wrapped my kohl pot in a scrap of cloth and jammed it in the pouch.

A scuffle at the door made me look up. I had expected Merius but instead there was Dagmar, her arms crossed.

"When you didn't come into the house, I watched from a window and saw you leave the courtyard to come here. You're going off with him, aren't you?"

"My place is with him."

"You're not married to him, Safire."

"According to the ancients' law, we're married. I gave him my virginity."

"The ancients were a bunch of heathens, and it's a scandal, what you're doing. You're married to Whitten."

"Not by my will. I never consented to that mockery, and it makes me ill to think of it." I flung the pouch over my shoulder and glared at her.

"Consent or not, you have an obligation until the annulment's final . . ."

"I have an obligation to Merius." I brushed past her and started down the steps.

"What about our parents' memory? What about me? Don't you have an obligation to us?" She hurried after me. "You disgrace the family name with adultery . . ."

I turned, and she backed up a step. "You expect me to stay true to a drunkard who took me in a stupor so you won't be disgraced? How dare you use Father and Mother to shame me?"

She swallowed, her face gray in the shadowed stairwell. "I'm sorry. I just don't want you to make a mistake. You've always been so impetuous, my little sister, and I've had to watch out for you. We're the only two left since Father passed, and . . . and you're safe here." Her eyes gleamed, a tear swelling and running down her cheek. "Don't leave, Safire."

I caught her in a one-armed hug. "We'll be back. And whatever happens, Merius could never be a mistake."

"Safire, he seems . . ."

"Seems what?" I offered her a spare handkerchief from my bag as she choked back tears.

"He seems," she blew her nose. "He seems wild. Carrying swords and daggers everywhere."

"Selwyn carries his sword."

"Not in the house. Besides, there's something different about how Merius carries his."

Like he might actually use it? Somehow, I couldn't imagine Selwyn whipping out his blade, but I kept my evil tongue to myself. "He's in the king's guard, Dagmar. He has to carry weapons at all times."

"Likely excuse," she sniffed. "He strikes me as just plain dangerous."

I grinned. "That's how I like him."

"Like his father, not someone you'd want to cross."

"Good thing he's on my side then," I said airily. "Good bye, Dagmar."

"Wait . . ." She pounded down the steps after me as I ducked into the sitting room and retrieved my orchid from the window sill. I nodded to Maud, who was knitting in the corner. She stared at me, having likely heard the entire conversation on the stairs. Then, slowly, she inclined her head in return.

"Thank you for your hospitality," I said. "Farewell."

She cleared her throat. "Farewell, my lady."

I laughed like a child and raced from the room and down the front steps into Merius's arms. He drew me close, still talking to Orlin. Dagmar followed, stopping on the threshold when she saw Merius.

"Are you ready, sweet?" Merius asked me then.

I grinned at Merius, at Dagmar, at Orlin, who watched us with narrow eyes and then nodded, as if he just made some satisfactory connection in his mind.

"I'm ready."

"Perfect. Orlin, good day to you."

"Good day, sir."

Merius took my bag, smiling when he noticed the orchid. Hand in hand, we began to walk down the road, back to the stable. "Take care of her," Dagmar called, still standing on Orlin's threshold.

Merius half turned for an instant. "I will. Always."

"We'll take care of each other. Good bye, sister," I yelled.

"Good bye. Come back soon."

~ ~ ~ ~ ~

When we reached the shore road, Merius steered Shadowfoot to the right, away from Calcors. "There's an inn this way, near Syrene," he said. Syrene was a village about three leagues down the coast. "Is that all right with you?"

"I told you my main requirement--as long as you're there, I don't care about anything else." I leaned my head back, and we kissed. He had his right arm around me, his body warm and solid against my back. Butterflies rose inside, tickling my rib cage with madly fluttering wings as he coaxed my lips apart.

Shadowfoot stopped and began grazing along the side of the road before Merius noticed his left hand had slackened on the reins. "We'll never get there at this rate," he muttered, his mouth still inches from mine as he urged Shadowfoot forward. The horse took off at a brisk canter.

I giggled, ran my fingers through his hair and drew him down for another kiss. "We have months to make up for, love."

"I'll not argue with that."

Miles of sea cliffs and ocean drifted past, barely registered by either of us. If we passed another traveler, I couldn't have said. If the sun sank to the horizon, I didn't notice. Shadowfoot trotted patiently onward, the motion of his back rocking us closer to each other. I couldn't hold a thought beyond the warm circle of Merius's arms, the tingling scratch of his stubble against my cheek, the fresh scent of soap he'd washed with earlier and the stronger male smell of sweat and leather and pipe smoke under that, his kisses and whispers. The poet in him wooed me until I forgot all else except the night before us.

When we turned to the right, down a road away from the shore and toward the twinkling lights of a large house, I came out of my rose-colored haze long enough to say with lazy surprise, "It's dusk."

He rested his chin on the crown of my head. "Yes, my love?"

"Are we here? Is this the inn you mentioned?"

"I don't know, but it's an inn."

"Good."

He dismounted and helped me down from Shadowfoot, the strong grip of his hands on my sides taking my breath away. Every time he touched me was a seduction, and I waited impatiently while he unbuckled our bags from the saddle and gave the inn stable hand some instructions and a coin for his trouble.

We left the stable and approached the front doorway. Merius braced his hand on my back, a protective gesture as we entered the inn and the rollicking common room. Blue smoke wafted everywhere. A gap-toothed, hiccupping sailor bellowed shanties in the corner while his mates shouted and banged their mugs, while in another corner, there was a tense crowd gathered around a dice game as bar maids wove their way around tables and benches with trays balanced on their heads.

I laughed and leaned against Merius, so overjoyed that my body could hardly contain it. "What is it?" he asked.

"I'm just so happy."

"Me too."

A tall grizzled man in a red tunic approached us through the smoke. "I'm the innkeeper," he said. "Warren's the name. Chamber?"

Merius nodded, reaching into his pocket. "How much for your best?"

"Two silvers. Do you want any supper?" Warren asked as he took the coin.

Merius and I exchanged a look, and he grinned before he glanced back at the innkeeper. "Maybe later. How late is the common room open?"

"Till ten, sir." Warren gestured to a barmaid. "I'm showing them to their chamber," he told her.

"Yes, sir."

We followed him up a steep staircase, well-lit with mirrored wall sconces. He took a candle from one before he entered a long passageway. We'd almost reached the end when he stopped beside the last door to the right. Keys clinking, he unlocked the door and flung it open. "Here you are," he said. "Do you need a fire?"

"No," Merius said.

Warren touched the flame of his candle to the taper on the bedside table. The chamber slowly came into focus--tidy, with planking painted a light green on the walls and a large oak bed with wine-colored curtains. I tested the bed, sinking into the full feather tick.

"Comfortable," I remarked, glancing at Merius. "And quiet." Only the barest echo of the revelry in the common room could be heard.

The innkeeper shrugged. "That's what you paid for. Let me know if you need anything." He left then, pulling the door closed behind him.

Merius dropped our bags to the floor, watching me without blinking. Since we had entered the chamber, his eyes had not left my face, even when the innkeeper had spoken. His steady gaze had become a physical presence between us, a heat that bathed my skin with a tingling glow as I flushed and looked at my trembling fingers. Suddenly, he crossed to the bed and picked up my hands, his fingers gentle as if he were touching an angel wing. He surrounded my hands with his, his fingertips grazing my wrists.

"You're cold, sweet," he said quietly.

I raised my eyes, looked at his face for a moment before I spoke. "I'm not shivering because I'm cold."

"I should have told him we needed the fire."

"We don't need the fire."

He smiled and leaned down. Our lips brushed each other. Releasing his hands, I opened my mouth and deepened the kiss, pulling him farther down. He angled his head, his tongue flitting across mine, his lips lightly, easily drawing me out as if I were a nervous foal he wanted to gentle. I leaned back on the pillows, and he followed, his mouth never leaving mine as he knelt over me, his hand cupped around my side just under my left breast. He was a starving man with a feast laid before him, yet he had enough control merely to sip and taste. For now.

My blood felt hot enough to boil, tickling the insides of my veins with tiny bubbles which rose and burst, a sweet torment. I sighed and arched against his hand, and he let his thumb stray upwards, his lips less soft as he pressed down on my mouth with greater urgency. His wandering thumb found the knot of my bodice laces and the rest of his hand followed as he began to tug at them.

Suddenly I remembered the green shift. "Wait, love," I murmured as I pulled back.

He reluctantly loosened his hold on me. "What is it?"

"I need a moment alone." I trailed my fingers up and down his jaw. "I've a surprise for you."

His eyes glinted, dark sparks in the flickering candlelight. "Wicked tease. You waited deliberately-"

I grinned. "Anticipation is good for you."

He chuckled. "It better be a good surprise, witch." He touched my neck, combed his fingers through my hair. "I love you, Safire," he said softly. "If it kills me, I'll make certain you want for nothing."

"All I want for is in this chamber." I flirted with the laces of his shirt collar, twisting one around my finger over and over again.

He squeezed my shoulder before he drew away and got to his feet. His eyes ran over me. "I'd wait forever for you, but don't make me wait too long tonight, sweet. You'll kill me."

"What doesn't kill us makes us stronger." I laughed and knelt on the edge of the bed so I could bait him with a quick kiss. "Now go, because I can't wait much longer for you either."

As soon as the door closed behind him, I hurried over to the washstand, where I shed my clothes. After performing some necessary grooming, such brushing my hair and dabbing scent on my wrists, I dug through my bag until I felt the silk at the bottom. I pulled the shift out and dragged it over my head. It was a tight fit in spots so it took me a minute or two of teeth gritting to get it right without ripping it. It had taken me forever to sew, since I couldn't enlist Dagmar's aid to pin the seams and darts. She would have been scandalized--only naughty women wore colored silk small clothes. I twirled before the washstand mirror, tugging the material down until the hem hung halfway between my hips and knees. I practiced a coy simper in the mirror but couldn't manage it through my fits of nervous giggles. Then I tried a sultry pout with the same results. Hell of a sophisticated mistress I would make.

I bit my lip and fluffed out my hair. The silk felt wonderful against my skin, all cool and whispery, but what would he think? There came a knock at the door then, and I spun around, my hands gripping the edge of the washstand behind me. "Come in," I said, clearing my throat.

Merius entered, carrying a bottle of wine in one hand. He moved with the strong, quiet grace of a hunter, part of the aura of danger that made my loins burn. I swallowed, wondering if my unladylike lust, my need for him, showed on the outside--my skin felt on fire. Did other women feel this way? They never talked about it, if they did--all I had ever heard on the subject were complaints about men's crude demands.

All thoughts of other women and men flew out of my head when I saw the way Merius looked at me. His stare traveled slowly down from my face all the way to my feet and then back up again. His expression betrayed nothing beyond stolid concentration, yet I noticed how he fumbled behind him to check the latch on the door, how his knuckles went white where he gripped the wine bottle.

I stepped forward, my hands letting go of the washstand. I

realized then my legs were shaking so hard that I probably should have stayed where I was. Before I could find something else to hang on to, Merius had tossed the bottle on the bed and grabbed me. Our mouths came together, and a surge of blood rushed through me, my heart pounding in my ears as he gripped my body against his. His lips were taut as bowstrings against mine, our kisses rough and urgent. I nipped him with my teeth, feeling his pulse quicken where I grasped his neck. He pressed me against the washstand, and the basin and pitcher rattled. His hands roamed over me, hot through the shift. I arched my neck as his mouth moved down my jaw, a low moan escaping my lips when he reached my throat. He kneaded my back until his hands slipped under my bottom. My legs curled around his waist as he carried me to the bed, our lips locked together.

He lowered me on to the pillows and then reached behind him to tug off his boots. With quivering hands, I loosened his collar, his belt buckle. His sword and dagger clattered to the floor as I jerked his belt free.

He leaned over me, and we resumed our kissing, his hand running up my thigh and under my shift. "Your skin feels softer than this silk," he said, catching a handful of the shift in his fingers as he inched the hem up to my waist.

I shivered at his touch; my chattering teeth nibbled his ear. "You're still trembling. Are you cold?" he muttered, his mouth moving over my collarbone, his thumbs circling my nipples as he pushed the shift all the way up my torso.

"This'll heat me up." I pulled him down on top of me, and our arms went around each other. He held me as close as he could without snapping my ribs; the warmth of his silver aura enveloped us. I discovered then I wasn't the only one shaking uncontrollably.

We rolled around the bed, wrestling off each other's remaining clothes in a mad flurry of kisses and impatient caresses. He was even leaner than I remembered, and he moved over me with the playful strength and stealth of a wild cat. I never knew where or how he was going to touch me next. My fingers found new scars, and I kissed every one, the searing liquor of his aura on my lips.

When he was finally inside me and we were moving together, tears stung my eyes. He kissed my eyelids. "You taste of the sea," he whispered, breathless. "Shh, my love."

My hands tightened on his shoulder blades. "Merius . . . oh, dearest. Don't stop. Never stop."

"I wish." His chuckle was cut short by a groan as I wrapped my legs around him. "Good God, Safire . . ."

The candle had sputtered out by the time we collapsed together on the pillows. My breath came in short gasps, and I stared into the darkness, half in a trance as red stars exploded and slowly faded overhead. Merius's arm was tight around me, his hand stroking my hip. For several minutes, we lay there in silence, catching our breath as we floated back down to earth. When I finally felt enough myself to move again, I turned over and nestled my face in his shoulder, my arm loosely across his middle. His hand shifted to the small of my back.

"Did that candle burn out on its own?" he asked lazily.

"I don't know--it must have, I haven't felt any drafts."

"Sweetheart, we could have been in the middle of a blizzard, and we wouldn't have felt any drafts."

I grinned, my face hot against his skin. "Probably not."

"You're blushing."

"How do you know?"

"I can hear it in your voice."

"Oh." I propped myself on one elbow, and our mouths met in the dark. Unlike our other kisses, it was slow and patient, a kiss for its own sake, since we were too spent at the moment for it to lead to anything more.

"Sweet," he muttered when we paused. "You know, if that candle burnt all the way down, that means we've been here for hours."

"Minutes, hours, days, I couldn't say."

"Me either. You've witched the time away."

I gave a low, throaty laugh, and suddenly found myself on my back, Merius over me as we kissed again with more heat and less patience. "Again so soon?" I murmured. "Goodness, my love . . ."

"It's your laugh, that damned chortle. How do you do that?"

"What, this?" And I laughed again, loving the sudden impatience of his hands as he rekindled my body.

This time I cried out so loudly I had to bite the pillow as we finished. "Do you think anyone heard?" I panted when we lay tangled in the damp sheets.

"I don't know. Are you all right?"

"That was a smug question."

"It's just you seem a trifle," he paused, "overwhelmed."

"That sounded even smugger."

"Is that a word? Smugger?"

I smacked him with a pillow, and he laughed. "Witch. I love you, Safire."

"I love you too."

After several more kisses, rolling around, and giggling on my part, he extricated himself from the sheets and me. "What are you doing?" I asked, hearing the creak of the floorboards as he felt his way around the chamber.

"I'm trying to find the tinder box, another candle." There was the raspy clatter of metal against stone in the direction of the fireplace.

"I am starting to feel a bit like a toadstool, kept in the dark," I conceded.

"We can't have that." The feather tick shifted as he sat on the edge of the bed. I found him and rested my chin on his head, my arms draped over his shoulders as he fiddled with the tinder box.

"How do you open this damned thing?" The metal lid squealed in protest, and we both winced. The flint and steel rattled as he swore under his breath.

"Is there anything I can do?"

"You're doing a fine job as a back rest."

I grinned, realizing my breasts were cushioning his shoulders. "Do you want me to move?"

"Hell no."

"I don't want to distract you."

There was a spark, and the candle flared. "There," he said with great satisfaction, looking at me. "Half the fun of making love to a beautiful woman is being able to see her."

I brushed his ear with my lips, my hands wandering over his chest and midriff. "Merius," I whispered. "Love, you're a man any queen would fancy. I'm blessed to wear your ring. And nothing else."

He caught my hands in his. "Forward wench. Where did you find that wicked scrap of silk?"

"I made it."

"We'll have to find you some others like that. It's most becoming." We heard a distant thump then. "Must be from the common room," Merius said after a long moment. "That reminds me--are you hungry?"

"A little."

He bent down and retrieved his trousers and shirt from the floor. "Anything special you want to go with the wine?"

I shrugged. "Bread, cheese, whatever they have that can be eaten in bed."

After he left, I stood up and stretched before I slithered back into the green shift. Humming to myself, I straightened the bedclothes and plumped the pillows. As I pulled the quilt up, something clattered to the floor. Exclaiming, I knelt and ran my hands over the floor boards, feeling around for the object. It was a cold bit of metal, a ring. I held it up to the candle. The flourished L glinted in the light. A Landers seal ring, too large to fit me. It had to be Merius's--I had left mine on the table in the bedchamber at Orlin's cottage, along with Whitten's troth ring. I sank on the bed, gazing at the seal.

By the time Merius returned, I had curled up under the quilt, cold without him there. I had put the ring on the bedside table, every once in a while looking at it, puzzling over it. What did it mean? Had Mordric given it back to him? Why? The only reason I could think of was that Merius had taken back his court duties, but I couldn't imagine him doing that, considering our current predicament.

Merius entered carrying a loaf of crusty brown bread and several cloth-wrapped packages that I couldn't identify. "Cheese," he announced, naming each package as he set it down. "Butter, blackberry jam, and smoked trout. What would you like to start with?"

"The bread and butter please. And give me the heel piece if

you don't want it." I sat up, the blanket pulled around my shoulders. "But I should do that . . ."

"You stay right there. If you like, you can pour the wine in these. The cork should already be loose." He produced two goblets from his cloak pockets and set them on the bedside table before he resumed cutting the bread. His dagger was fine for affairs of honor, but its smooth edge stuck to the bread and had already made a growing pile of crumbs on the floor beside his feet. The mice would have their own feast tonight.

"Merius?" I said, setting the wine bottle down after I'd tugged the cork free.

"Yes?"

"Did you get this back from your father?" I held up the ring.

He turned around at the mention of Mordric. "What?" he said, taking a step towards me as he squinted at the ring. "Oh, that. Yes, he returned it to me." He reached out, and I gave him the ring. "Where did you find it?"

"In the bedclothes. It must have fallen out of your pocket."

He gazed at the ring for a moment, his face impassive, his aura swirling like silvery smoke that suddenly flared into icy flame. His fingers clenched into a fist around the ring, and with a sudden oath, he hurled it at the fireplace grate. I flinched as it bounced against the rocks.

"Merius? Dear heart?"

He looked at me, then came over to the bed and gathered me in his arms. I could feel him shaking. So I rubbed his back and waited, the shudder of his breath in my ears. He clutched me, his muscles tight as rigging on a ship in a storm.

"He never should have gone after you," he said finally, his voice hoarse. "Never. It was a fight between him and me, and he should have kept it that way. I should have realized he let me leave too easily, that it was another of his manipulations, but . . . but I never thought he'd be so dishonorable . . . God damn it, he's my father. How could he do this? There are times I've thought he hated me because of what he did to Mother when he drank. He hit her, you know, slapped her around. Even threatened her with his dagger once. But despite all that, he hardly laid a hand on me, went out of his way not to hit me even when I provoked him. And he slaved over my training, taught me himself at the sword, brought me to court a year early because he didn't trust the servants to watch me. God, I resented that, but I understand it now. I was difficult at that age, always performing daredevil stunts and getting out of my lessons. Even his impossibly high expectations--I even understand those, though I've often thought they would drive me mad. The truth is, he's never expected any more from me than he expects from himself. When I saw him at council, I was proud to be his son. Everyone at court is terrified of him . . . Safire, I respected him, even while I hated him for what he did to my mother, resented his attempts to control me. I respected him, that son of a bitch."

I knelt so that our faces were level, my right hand smoothing his hair while the left one rubbed the tense ache from his shoulder. "You feel so good," he whispered, his arms tightening around me again. "The way you touch me, feel in my arms--you don't even have to speak."

I drew his cheek to my shoulder, resisted the urge to take away his anger and pain with my witch hands. It hurt to see him so upset, but if he could bear it then so could I. I had taken away Mordric's rage the night he had brought me to Orlin's cottage but that was because I was afraid he would do immediate harm to himself and Orlin's furniture. This was different. Merius had frightened me earlier with his wild threats against Whitten and Mordric, but I understood better now.

"He's done a great wrong to you," I said after we'd held each other for several minutes.

"A great wrong to us, sweet."

"Yes." I sighed. "He's wronged me, wronged us. Worst of all, he's betrayed you."

"No, he hasn't." Merius's voice was flat. "You can't betray what you don't love."

"It's easier to believe that, isn't it?"

"Believe what?"

"That he doesn't love you."

"He doesn't love anyone. He values them, values me. Hell, he paid my ransom, even swallowed his pride enough to offer me that ring back, all because he was afraid of losing his only heir, his most useful possession. That's how he defines love--how useful you are to him."

I thought for a minute before I spoke. "You know, he could have easily had me assassinated, found a way to make me disappear so that you'd be none the wiser when you returned. Yet he let me live, protected me from Bara, even protected me from Whitten after he realized what I meant to you. He told me himself that I was a catastrophe to your career, all his plans for you, yet he let me live. He let me live, Merius. If he only considered you his most valuable chess piece at court, do you think he would have done that?"

Merius began to shake his head, his hands clutching the folds of my shift. "It's a lie. Everything he does, it's a lie."

"Words are lies, not actions."

"I don't give a damn, Safire. I still want to kill him."

"I understand, dear heart. He's hurt you terribly, betrayed you."

Merius abruptly got to his feet and went over to the side table where he'd started slicing the bread. He buttered several slices with his dagger and placed them on napkins along with squares of cheese. Then he cut a large hunk off the fish, which he neatly divided in two between the napkins. I ached to run to him and kiss away his hurt as he would have kissed away mine. He didn't want me to see him like this, though, and I could respect that. We were in love, but we weren't accustomed enough to each other yet to let down the masks of our sexes. So I stayed on the bed.

"You know," he said then, returning to me with the food, "he let me take back that damned ring, my duties, unofficially swear fealty to him and the Landers, all the while knowing what he'd done, knowing that I would want to avenge you when I found out. It was pointless--why did he do that?"

"Perhaps he wanted one moment when he could pretend that none of it had happened."

"Conniving blackguard," Merius muttered.

I passed him a glass of wine. "Why did you take the ring back?"

He took a bite of bread, chewed for a moment before he

answered. "I don't know exactly. Several reasons, I suppose. I thought about you, about our children, how much more I could offer you if I had my inheritance back-"

"Oh no Merius . . ."

"It's a legitimate concern, Safire. We're going to marry--I have to be practical. What if I get you with child? We need coin for that. Besides, Father seemed different, willing to respect me as my own man." He shook his head, swallowing hard as if his bread had just turned to sawdust. "God damn him, I'll kill him for this," he said quietly.

I glanced down at my cheese, suddenly not hungry. With child, he had said. My insides seethed--my womb felt full of writhing snakes, a dark secret I had carried now for several days. For the second new moon since my fit, I had missed my bleeding. Of course, that could be anything--I had missed bleedings before. Even two times in a row. And nothing had come of it. Nothing . . .

In a daze, I set my wine glass and food on the table and sank to the pillows. The air in the chamber was heavy, thick as cold syrup in my lungs, and I barely felt Merius grip my arm. "Safire? Safire?" he said slowly from a great distance.

"I'm fine," I managed. "Just a little faint."

"You're cold as ice. Here." He lay on his side behind me, cupped my body with his as he wrapped his arms around me like a shawl. "I should have told him to light the fire."

"You're warmer than any fire." It was true--already the feeling was returning to my limbs.

"Was it something I said?"

"No, dearest. I just . . . it's just all of this suddenly hit me. It feels sometimes like I've been awake every night for the last several months, what with Father and this mess with Whitten and missing you . . ."

"I couldn't sleep for missing you either. And we were on alert all the time in the mountains . . . here, maybe you should eat some more. You've hardly touched your food."

Obediently, I ate the rest of the cheese and bread with long sips of wine. I insisted he eat my fish, however--although I usually loved smoked fish, my stomach rebelled at the oily smell of it. My stomach had been rebelling a lot lately.

When we had finished eating, he brought me some water and made me get under the bedclothes as if I were a sick child. As he covered the remaining food and corked the wine bottle, I wondered at his tenderness. Certainly, he hadn't learned it from Mordric. My own father had usually disappeared at the first sign of female illness, sending a servant to make the necessary ministrations until all was better again. But Merius was different, as good a nurse as Dagmar, even if he was somewhat less concerned with being tidy. Maybe it was because his mother had had so many miscarriages and stillbirths--she must have been sick frequently. Poor little boy.

He shed his clothes on the floor before he crawled into bed beside me. As he leaned over to snuff the candle, I reached for him. Our arms entwined and then our bodies as we held each other in the dark.

"Make love to me, Merius," I whispered after the silent minutes had drawn out into at least a quarter hour and neither of us was asleep.

He cleared his throat. "Are you certain you're-"

"I feel fine now." I gave him a long kiss as a demonstration of my fitness.

"You are fine indeed." He chuckled, his eager hands already seeking out the secret places of my body.

Perhaps if we made love enough times, if he spent enough of his seed in me, the baby would somehow become his. This was a child's thinking, but I was little more than a frightened child at that point, an innocent girl desperate to erase a violation she couldn't remember, a woman who still believed in fairy tales.

Chapter Twenty-Six - Merius

After her bath at the inn one morning, Safire sat on a stool by the window while I brushed her hair. "How many days have we been here?" she asked.

"A week, I think." My hand followed the brush as I ran it from the crown of her head all the way to the ends of her hair.

She arched her neck, her eyes closed. "Really?"

"I heard the church bells this morning, so it must be holy day."

"You're right--I heard them too. It doesn't seem that long."

I set aside the brush and began to massage her scalp with my fingertips, her sun-warmed hair slipping over my hands. In the mid-morning light, the strands glowed brilliant as molten copper flowing between my fingers. "We'll soon have to figure out what to do next."

She sighed. "I suppose."

"Herrod's ship should have docked by now, and he'll be back in Corcin. He told me to report to him when he returned."

"You still want to take rooms in the city?"

"It's not a question of want. We'll have to, at least for the next several months. It's all we can afford."

Her fingers fiddled with the tassels on the edges of blanket she'd wrapped around her shoulders. "There is another possibility, Merius."

My hands stilled in her hair. "What?"

She glanced back at me. "My dowry."

"Oh, love, Father will have sold that by now."

"He hasn't sold it, Merius. It's not his to sell."

"What is your dowry, anyway?"

"The house of Long Marsh and everything in it and the land around it. We could live there. Your father can't turn us out because it's my dowry, and I never signed that godforsaken betrothal contract officially giving the Landers the rights to it. I don't think he would try to turn us out anyway." Her voice rose as she became more excited. "It would be perfect--Boltan and his wife are still there, and Strawberry . . . we could sell the other horses that are left for coin, and . . . oh, I've missed Strawberry, Merius."

I leaned down and kissed her upraised face. Our mouths met awkwardly, my lower lip against her upper one and vice versa, an upside down kiss that made her giggle. The charred cedar scent of her skin and hair was on me. Her mouth was soft and gave under mine easily. Sometimes when I kissed her, there was the faint salt of the sea on her lips, the mysterious sadness of an ancient woman inside the merry witch-girl, the woman I had as yet barely touched or seen.

I broke away finally. "Have you been crying?"

"No," she said.

"You taste of it." I straightened and gazed into her eyes. "Have I done something wrong?"

"Of course not, Merius--it's nothing to do with you. It's just that I'm still grieving Father."

"Naturally, with how little time has passed. I just wish . . ." I trailed off.

"What?"

"I wish you wouldn't go off alone to grieve. I wish you would let me comfort you."

She swallowed and glanced down at her hands, twisting in the folds of the blanket. "I don't want to burden you," she said. "We're so happy here--I wish we didn't have to leave."

"Me too, sweet." Sometimes I wondered about the men I had fought with, my comrades who had died and the men I had killed. Had they sweethearts? Certainly some of them had sweethearts, maybe even wives. How blessed was I, to return home to my love--the privations of battle made me cherish her as I never could have before. She unfurled as softly as a flower in my arms, the glory of her blossoming mine alone to bring about, mine alone to savor. God, she was lovely, my night witch. Even if those other men had sweethearts, they could never have Safire. She had chosen to be mine. I closed my eyes, inhaling her as I buried my face in the fiery curtain of her hair. The essence of her made me lightheaded.

"I've set aside coin for your wedding ring," I said huskily. "You can have anything you like on it--I'll not dishonor you with another Landers ring."

"It's no dishonor, Merius. That's your House, and I'll wear its seal gladly if you put it on my finger." She clasped my hand.

I knelt behind her and kissed her shoulder where it peeped over the blanket. "You have a spattering of freckles across your back here-" I kissed under the nape of her neck, "and here, like a speckled egg."

"Don't kiss them--no, stop." She pulled the blanket up over her shoulders.

"Why not?" I tugged the blanket back down.

"They'll never go away now. Merius . . ."

I paused. "They'll never go away?"

"'Bathe in buttermilk, freckles go away,'" she quipped, "'Bathe in kisses, freckles stay.'"

I grinned and kissed another freckle. "Silly--you made that up."

"Why would I make up such a thing?" she demanded indignantly. "And stop it--I've worked hard to get rid of those freckles."

"Well, I like them, and I'm going to kiss every single last one so they never go away." I moved down her back, not heeding her stifled shrieks of laughter. "In the old stories, the changelings were always freckled."

"No, they weren't. You're thinking of moles, not freckles," she snorted. "Ass."

"You're still a changeling." I stood and planted my last kiss on the crown of her head. "Now, while I'm still clothed, I should go see to Shadowfoot."

"Wait--I'll go down with you," Safire said, letting the blanket fall as she rose from the stool.

I leaned against the door and watched her as she whisked around the chamber. In the space of a few minutes, she dressed, picked the clothes off the floor, made the bed, straightened the growing collection of combs, her mirror, brushes, my razor, and bottles on the washstand, and covered the food from breakfast. Like a bird building a nest, she darted about so quickly I hardly had time to comprehend what she was doing before she was on to the next task.

As she went to stow my inkwell in the bedside table drawer, I remembered something I had planned to do upon waking this morning. "Wait, sweet, I need that for a moment."

She handed me the inkwell, and I pulled a piece of parchment and my pen out of the drawer. I dipped the quill in the well and wrote *Selwyn--If you can, meet me at the crossroads tavern tomorrow at four in the afternoon. Thanks, Merius* The table wobbled, and I swore at it, an ink blot swallowing half of my signature. "Damn--well, at least it's mostly readable." I shook the page and rewrote my name and the date.

"What's that?" Safire asked.

"A message to Selwyn."

"Oh--can I write something to Dagmar at the bottom?"

"Here." I gave her the pen, and she started writing. There were many pauses between words when she looked up, her lips pursed. Then she commenced scribbling again--for someone who could draw an apple that looked real enough to eat, her handwriting left much to be desired. At times it was difficult to catch the words between the blots. 'Something' became several sentences and ten minutes, and then two paragraphs and a quarter hour before she finally corked the inkwell and sprinkled a little sand on the parchment. Then she looked up. "Oh, I forgot to mention my trunk--I wanted her to check the latch. There was something wrong with it . . ." She chewed her lip, gazing at me as if somehow I had the answer.

I had long since leaned against the door, my arms crossed. "There looks room for a postscript, if you write small."

Still chewing her lip, she glanced back down at the letter before she shook off the sand and uncorked the ink well. I closed my eyes, hearing the scratch of the pen as she composed a postscript. When she was done, I reached for the letter. I folded and addressed it, only hesitating when it came to the seal. After a moment's deliberation, I pulled my seal ring out of my pocket and used that.

"Thank you. I didn't realize I'd taken so long."

"We're in no hurry, love, and I know how ladies are about their letters."

She flushed. "I didn't mean it to be a letter, but there just suddenly seemed so many things to tell her." She paused. "Do I look all right?"

My gaze ran over her, stopping on her eyes, eyes that reminded me of sunlight through new leaves. I cleared my throat. "You look lovely, as always."

Her flush deepened, and she smiled. "I mean, to go downstairs--am I presentable?"

I took her hand, pulled her towards the door. "You're so presentable I'd introduce you to the entire court and the king right this moment, if I could. Now come on."

~ ~ ~ ~ ~

The crossroads tavern had changed little since the night Selwyn, Whitten, Peregrine, and I had gone after the horse thieves. There were only a few dim figures scattered in the common room as I made my way to our customary corner table. Imogene quickly came over, bangles clinking.

"Haven't seen you in a month of Sundays," she purred, touching my shoulder.

I started, then remembered that I had been interested in her briefly before I met Safire. The thought surprised me--it was of a past so vague it seemed to belong to someone else, not me. I had liked her bangles, her dark eyes, resented the way she flirted with all the sailors. I could hardly imagine it all now. I glanced at her and smiled as I would at a fond memory. And shrugged off her hand. "I've been away, at battle."

"That's what they said." She drew back and crossed her arms, hiding her hands. She returned my smile, but the luster had left her eyes--it was a look of hurt puzzlement. She wasn't accustomed to men turning down her favors. "What can I get you?"

"Ale will be fine."

Selwyn pulled out the bench across the table from me just as Imogene brought my second mug. He barked his order, and she spun around in a swirl of skirts, her heels smacking against the splintery floorboards as she stomped towards the back room.

"What's wrong with her?" he said. "All I did was order . . . If she spits in my ale . . ."

"She's more likely to spit in mine," I said. "How are you, Selwyn?"

"Fine, fine," he mumbled, still staring at the back room doorway. Then he let out a gusty sigh and turned towards the table. "I'm fine. Where have you been?"

"At an inn."

"Dagmar's worried sick, you know. Been driving me up the wall this last week with her fretting over Safire. You shouldn't have done it, Merius. Your father-" he broke off.

"What about my father? Has he gotten the annulment yet?"

Selwyn nodded. "Thank God," I muttered. The tension that had gripped my middle since entering the tavern suddenly disappeared, and I sank back against the wall. I drained the last of the ale. I could picture Safire's face when I told her, the pearly glow that lit her skin when she was overjoyed. "Thank God."

Selwyn's brows knotted together, and he cleared his throat. "So you really mean to marry her?"

My hand tightened again on the mug handle. "Yes--what the hell else do you think this is about?"

We both started as Imogene slammed down Selwyn's mug and departed, her face stony.

Selwyn waited a moment before he answered. "I thought . . . I thought maybe you'd lost your head," he said carefully.

"What?"

He stared into his mug, running his fingers up and down the sides. "Merius, we all have moments of weakness when it comes to women. Now, she's a fine-looking girl, and I can see how this happened, but-"

"But what?"

"Never mind."

"No, I want to hear what you have to say. It will give me some idea of whether I merely punch you or if I need to challenge you to a duel."

"You always do this. You always take things too far. Like your inheritance--what was the point of throwing that away, you fool?"

I stood, my hand on my sword hilt. "You've insulted my betrothed and insulted my honor by suggesting I shouldn't marry her. A duel is more than appropriate, cousin."

"I'm sorry. I just . . . Merius, she sees spirits, for God's sake."

"I know--she told me."

He rose, leaned forward across the table. "Did she tell you she had a fit for two months where she wouldn't speak and didn't even recognize her own sister? Did she tell you she ran off to Calcors? Your father and I looked for her for hours--God knows where she was. Or maybe I should say Satan knows where she was. When we finally found her and brought her back to the house, she had a screaming fit on the front doorstep and these cuts just appeared on her arms, out of nowhere. There's something not right with her, Merius. She's a witch. You've cast aside everything for a witch." His voice rose.

I grabbed him by the collar, dragged him around the table, and shoved him against the wall. "You listen here," I said evenly. "Never speak of her that way again. She is your sister-in-law, soon to be my wife. If I find out you had any part in what happened to her when I was gone, I'll kill you when I kill Father and that drunken bastard Whitten. She is not a witch. She sees things others can't see, but that doesn't make her a witch. That makes her beautiful. I'll not hear you say anymore against her just because you're too stupid to see her for what she is. Do you understand?"

"You're crazy," he croaked, sweat beading his red face. "She's bewitched you . . ."

I shook him. "I asked you if you understand."

He nodded, and I released him. He staggered back to the bench. "Damn you, Merius." He choked and rubbed his throat, glaring at me with bloodshot eyes.

I sat down. Imogene sauntered over with a pitcher of ale and filled my mug. "I haven't seen you two fight since we were children," she said. "Don't make me have to call Jasper."

"Don't nose in your patrons' affairs, and you won't have to call Jasper." Selwyn hunkered down on the bench, his mouth set in a sour scowl.

"I apologize for him, Imogene," I said swiftly. "He seems to have left his manners at the Hall. Here." I squeezed a silver into her palm. "Keep the change."

"Thank you," she said, her voice clipped as she shot Selwyn a flinty look. She set the pitcher on the table and wiped her hands on her apron. "Here, keep this so I won't inconvenience you again with my presence, Sir Selwyn."

"There was no call for you to be rude to her." I said as soon as she had moved on to the next table. "She may not have been born a fine lady, but she deserves common decency nonetheless."

"Forgive me, but you had just finished trying to strangle me. Manners to a nosy, common wench were the last thing on my mind."

"Manners are manners--they should be ingrained by now, with all the teaching we had. And you deserved worse than what you got. I meant what I said, Selwyn."

"I know." He shook his head, took a sip of ale.

"I don't care much for Dagmar, but you don't hear me insulting her to your face, do you?"

"No. Dagmar's a good, sensible woman, and . . . I reckon I just didn't realize how serious your intentions were towards Safire."

"You know now."

"Dagmar will be happy to hear it. She's been nagging me something terrible the last week." He gave a forced chuckle. "She doesn't let me forget I'm married, that's for certain."

I refrained from comment. "So, where is Father? At court?"

"No." Selwyn gulped the last of his ale and poured another glass, splashing it everywhere. "He returned about five days ago and locked himself in his study. All that goes in are bottles of whiskey and messages from our slut cousin Eden, and all that comes out are messages to our slut cousin Eden."

"Haven't you seen him?"

"No, just the night he returned. The only one he'll see is the steward."

"Randel returned with him?" My father's steward Randel had never stayed at Landers Hall--Father had never spent enough time there to warrant his steward's presence except when Mother had been alive, and then she had brought his meals and such. "He must be staying a month at least."

"No one knows. We've had several call for him--tenants, Devons' head warehouse clerk, even Sir Cyril, the head of the king's council. He'll see none of them."

I shrugged. "Probably best, if he's drunk."

Selwyn leaned forward over his glass. "I bet," he said quietly. "I bet he would see you."

"He'll see me next at the end of my sword." My rage lay at the base of my spine, a quiet whip ready to pick up and lash out at a moment's notice. Only when I was with Safire did I forget. I swallowed, my fingernails white where I gripped my mug.

"Merius, you have to see him."

"Why, save to kill him?"

"He's your father, damn it. You're the only one who can talk to him. He has to go back to court. Whitten and I, we can run the estate, but court . . . I wouldn't even know where to start."

"Ask Eden."

He sputtered. "If I wanted the particulars of the prince's bedchamber, maybe."

"I'm serious. He trained her, same as he trained me. Hell, she probably knows more than I do--she always had more of an interest than any of us, and it's easier for her to pry things out of him."

"I'm not talking to that hussy--she's dragged the Landers name through filth."

"Suit yourself."

"Merius, she's a disgrace."

"I didn't say she isn't. I just said she seems to have a way with Father, if you want someone to talk to him."

Selwyn shook his head. "It amazes me he's never taken her to task, with how much he's disciplined you, me, and Whitten for tumbling wenches. No honorable man will marry her now--I just don't understand it."

"He uses her at court."

"What for? Infecting our rivals with the pox?"

I looked at him over the rim of my mug. He was right--he really had no idea about court, how to maneuver there. The subtleties, the spying, the manipulations that went on. He would never be able to fathom it, with his simple talents for figuring a column of numbers and keeping the ledgers straight. Court required morbid imagination, shrewd calculation, and constant observation. I had never thought of Father as having an imagination until now, but that was only because it didn't run in the same vein mine did. "Never mind," I said finally.

~ ~ ~ ~ ~

The inn bed floated on a green sea. Waves crashed over the side, salt spray staining the curtains. I called for Safire, searched the bedclothes, but she was nowhere to be found. The more I searched, the more of them there seemed to be until I lay tangled in sheets, unable to move. A wave rose up, a hideous monster of water, foaming and frothing at the edges as if it were rabid. It rolled towards me with a growing rumble. I yelled but there was no sound over the roar of the water as it hit the bed.

I awoke in a cold sweat, grasping for my sword. Still half asleep, I continued to search for the sword until I remembered it was in the corner by the door. I had kept it by the bed until a few nights ago, when I had awakened from a jumbled nightmare about Father and the slave traders with my hand on the hilt, ready to swing.

We had closed the bed curtains earlier, and all was formless dark around me, the air stuffy as if the whole bed had been shut up in a trunk. I flailed around for Safire, but her side was empty.

There came a muffled choke from the chamber outside the curtains and then a long, low wail and after that another choke. "Safire?" I asked, pushing aside the curtain.

Moonlight silvered my feet as I swung them down on the floor. I padded around the bed, feeling my way through the shadows. Safire sat huddled on the window seat, her face hidden in her arms. Her back heaved with sobs.

I touched her shoulder. "Sweetheart?"

I sat down and put my arms around her. Her hands, damp with tears, crept around my neck, and she buried her face in my shoulder. "What is it? You thinking about your father again?"

She shook her head. My hand ran over her hair all the way down to the small of her back, over and over. Her sobs grew quieter.

"Are you sick?"

"No."

"What is it then?"

"I can't tell you."

"Why not?"

"It's too horrible . . ." Her words trailed off.

My stomach knotted. "You have to tell me."

She choked, caught her breath. "I know," she said finally.

"What is it, Safire?"

"Just give me a moment." She shivered, and I wrapped my arms around her.

"All right." She took a deep, shuddering breath. "I think," she started. There was a long silence, then it all came out in a torrent. "I think I'm with Whitten's child . . . Oh God, Merius . . . Merius . . ."

"Shh, shh. Shh, sweet. It's all right," I said. Obviously, it was not going to be all right, but I could think of nothing else to say. I wasn't thinking at all. My mind had frozen around those words. Whitten's child. A numbness descended on me, a buzzing that grew louder and louder in my ears. "Shh, shh," I heard myself say again, almost as much to quiet my head as to quiet her. "Shh, you'll make yourself sick with crying."

"I already feel sick." She put her hand to her throat.

With no clear purpose in mind other than taking some action, any action, I rose and went over to the washstand, where I found a candle. With trembling hands, I lit it from the still warm embers in the fireplace where we had toasted bread earlier. I set it on the washstand before I dropped it. Then I filled the basin with some water, picked up the towel, and carried both over to the window seat. Water splashed out on the cushion as I put it down. I soaked the towel and wrung it out before I slid my hand under her chin and lifted her face. I bathed her hot skin with the cool water, then folded the towel several times and placed it over her eyes and forehead.

"Here, hold it there."

"Oh, that feels nice," she murmured, leaning back against the window. "How do you know to do that?"

"It's what I do for too much drink--thought it might work for this too."

"I don't feel so sick." She lowered the towel so she could look at me.

"If you do again, you can retch in the basin." I glanced at the basin, then quickly glanced away--I wanted to retch myself. I cleared my throat and perched on the window seat, watching her. "Are you certain Whitten is . . . I mean, I thought you didn't remember him touching you," I stammered.

"I don't. Remember, I mean."

"Well, then, could it be mine?"

She bit her lip, then shook her head. "I don't see how, dear heart."

"Maybe from before I left?"

"I would have had the quickening by now. Besides, I remember bleeding right after you left."

"If you haven't quickened, then how do you know you're with child? I thought that was how women knew for certain."

She wiped her eyes with the towel, sniffling. "It is, but there are other signs before the quickening. I've missed two bleedings now, I've been sick in the morning, I've . . . Merius, I just know I am. There's no explaining it."

"All right, all right." I could think of no more questions to stave off the truth. I got to my feet, my arms crossed, and began to pace. The ice of shock began to melt, replaced by a flame of rage that fed off itself as it grew to a blaze inside. I found my arms shaking as my pace quickened, and my legs carried me in ever tightening circles around the hearth, then around the bed, then around the hearth again. That sot. That sniveling bastard. *I'll drown him in his own ale cask, then run him through for good measure as I dispatch him to hell.* How dare he put his drunken hands on her? How dare any man besides me touch her?

"Merius?" Safire said, her voice ringing in my ears.

I turned to her in mid pace, so fast that I almost stumbled.

"How long have you known about this?"

"The baby? Little more than a week."

"You've known the whole time we've been here together, and you didn't say anything?"

She cringed. "I didn't know how to tell you. I don't want it to be true. It's been like a fairy tale since you came back, and I couldn't bring myself to ruin that for either of us. We've been so happy here. It was foolish of me, but I thought if we stayed here long enough together, without anyone to bother us . . I thought it would go away."

"You should have told me, Safire. You should have told me that sniveling bastard touched you. You lied to me about him touching you. Why did you lie to me?"

"Lie?" Her voice rose. "Lie? Of course I lied. If I had told the truth, you'd have run off and killed him, and then you'd have been arrested and probably hung. You think I want to lose you because some sot put his hands on me?"

"You should have told me. You should have trusted me."

"Of course I trust you--why do you think I'm telling you now? But Merius, I love you. I can't," she stammered, "can't bear for you to see me like this."

"See you like this? What do you mean?"

"You're the only man who's ever supposed to touch me, the only man I've ever wanted, the only man I would willingly give myself to. I feel so used now, so unclean--I keep taking baths, but it doesn't help. It doesn't help, Merius. The only time I forget is when you're with me, and even then I get flashes of him sometimes. I don't remember but for a few flashes, just enough to know what he did. I don't know how you stand to look at me, now that you know . . . I can hardly stand to see myself in the mirror." She choked then, her face hidden in her hands.

The rage crested inside, a fiery wave, the rabid wave in my dream. I strode over to the corner where my sword waited. It was too fine a blade to sit in the corner. I had sharpened it just the other day, and it would slice through that drunkard's throat as easily as slicing a sheet of parchment. I went to fasten the scabbard to my belt, only to realize I wore no belt. All I wore was a shirt. My hands shook as I found my pants, my belt, my boots, the rage rippling in ever growing waves throughout my entire being now. He would die tonight. And then . . . nothing. Just his death. That had become the sum of all my years of training, of honing my body, of going to battle: Whitten's death. I could see nothing beyond.

I felt Safire's eyes on me, watching as I dressed, as I buckled my sword and dagger to my belt, but I dared not look at her. She would bewitch me if I met her gaze, perhaps weaken my resolve. "There's coin in my bag, if you need it," I said, if only to hear the sound of something besides the blood pounding in the veins of my ears.

"Merius, what are you doing?"

"I'm going to kill Whitten."

"No . . ."

"I don't want to hear it, Safire. You should have told me before, as soon as you knew. You lied to me."

"I'm sorry. Here . . ." Out of the corner of my vision, I saw her rise and start towards me.

I whirled on her, and she stumbled back. "Don't you dare touch me. You'll use your witch hands again to calm me, and I'll have none of it."

"Don't you dare leave," she yelled. "Merius, no, they'll hang you for this."

"Not if I do it right." I reached for the door latch.

I finally met her eyes, red-rimmed from tears and wild. "Will you be back?" she asked simply, though it was far from a simple question.

I heaved a sigh, using my lungs like a bellows to feed the rage within. I had to resist her--she'd tempt me right out of my good intentions. "I don't know."

She stepped towards me. "What do you mean?"

"What I said. I don't know. Now leave me be, witch." I quickly sidestepped through the door, pulling it shut behind me with a bang. I heard her run towards it, struggle with the latch on the other side as I held it firm. I grabbed the key from my pocket and locked the door.

She immediately started pounding on it, and I tried not to

think of the barely healed scars on her arms, the heavy iron hinges and latch cutting at her hands. Another man had claimed her, sired a child in my stead, and I had no idea what to do with her until I killed him.

"Damn you," she screamed. "How dare you lock me in here? Merius, please . . ."

Her cries faded quickly as I pounded down the steps. The innkeeper would let her out soon after someone heard her, but not soon enough for her to follow me. I had to get away.

~ ~ ~ ~ ~

Shadowfoot carried me through the night. All was silver moonlight and black shadow, the edges of the road and trees as stark as my thoughts. The night felt cool and soft as the touch of Safire's hands. I heaved a deep breath. That witch. She had me under a spell. The last week had been ecstasy, happiness beyond anything I had ever allowed in my dreams or hopes. My whole life since my mother had died seemed endless frustration, pursuing one prize after another: graduating first in my class, practicing at the sword till I dropped, watching Landers Hall like a trained hawk, sitting forever at those deadly dull council meetings, pretending that I gave a damn about court, concentrating on stupid, meaningless details that made my head swim. All this, only to have Father say that I wasn't trying hard enough, that I had failed him. That I wasn't earning my place as his son. It had driven me mad. He had driven me mad.

Then I had met Safire, and he suddenly didn't matter anymore. All I had to do was take her in my arms to make her happy with me. I recited my poems, the poems I had written in shameful secrecy, and she loved me. I kissed her freckles, and she laughed-- and loved me. I handed her my handkerchief, and she cried--and loved me. I pleased her just by being in the same chamber with her. To her, I was Merius. Not Merius of Landers, not Merius, Mordric of Landers's son. Just Merius. It had been so simple.

Until tonight. How could she be with another man's child? My hangdog cousin's child, no less. I gripped the reins. She had lied to me, not only in word, but in deed. She had told me she loved me, she had let me touch her, she had lain beside me at night, wife in all ways but name, when all the while she knew she carried another man's child. I had even asked her outright if he had touched her, and she had said no, knowing it wasn't true. Why had she done that? If she loved me, she should have been honest. Instead she had put me under her spell, quelled my rage with her witch touch, led me through the gates of a false heaven. I gritted my teeth and touched the hilt of my sword, as if to assure myself it was still there. I pictured the edge of my blade at Whitten's throat, the beads of blood welling up, crimson against his pasty skin. He would plead for his life--I knew him too well to think he would take his death like a man, deserved though it was--but I would silence him. Then perhaps the world would make sense again.

I urged Shadowfoot forward. Candlelight from windows warmed the shadows of the night. The crossroads tavern, the same tavern where I had met Selwyn earlier today. I raced Shadowfoot through the courtyard and into the stable, stirring up the sweet dust of last year's hay crop till I sneezed. I dismounted Shadowfoot and clapped his flank, our signal for him to trot into one of the stalls. He found some treasure in the trough and fell to, blissfully unaware that he would carry a fugitive on his back before dawn. I turned from him, toward the stable door and the tavern beyond. Whitten would be here, I was certain of it. He came every night he could, particularly when Father was at Landers Hall so he could escape Father's scrutiny, the same scrutiny that had dogged my steps since I had first toddled from my mother's side.

The common room was blurry when I entered it, so smoky that it obscured all the sharp edges. It reminded me of opening my eyes under water where there were no straight lines and bent light. Vague figures sat at several tables, the skirted shape of Imogene floating through the smoke. I strode toward the back corner. A lone someone hunkered over a tankard at our old table, the same table where we had played cards hundreds of times and shared countless stories and drinks.

The cloaked man started as I slid on to the bench across from him, then he tossed back his hood. "I didn't know you had returned, Merius," Peregrine said and took a sip of his ale.

I started myself--I had honestly thought he was Whitten, but now that I sat across from him, I had no idea why I had thought that.

Peregrine and Whitten looked nothing alike, even when concealed by a cloak--Peregrine had broad shoulders and bulging muscles, a born wrestler. I had never feared facing him at the sword or on the archery range, but he had bested me more than enough at hand-to-hand combat for me to recognize his build even under a cloak.

"Why are you here?" he asked after a moment's silence.

"Where's Whitten?" I demanded.

"He's your cousin--you tell me." Peregrine drained his tankard and slammed it down on the table. Imogene instantly approached and poured him more ale. Without a word or glance exchanged between Imogene and me, a tankard of my favorite ale appeared at my elbow.

"Peregrine, have you seen Whitten at all? I need to find him."

"You're not the only one."

"Are you looking for him too?"

"I've been waiting for him all night. We were supposed to meet here."

"What for?"

"None of your affair." He chuckled bitterly and drained his tankard a second time, afterwards reaching for mine. He quaffed that as well. I gaped at him, too shocked to stop him. The man who had never lowered himself to drink ale around his comrades was now doing so in vast quantities. Whatever I had pictured happening when I came in here, it was not seeing Peregrine of Bara stinking drunk.

"You damned Landers, all of you--you can't have everything, you know," he said finally, staring in the bottom of his empty tankard.

"Really? And what do we have, Peregrine?"

"Your father is a sneak and a liar." He looked at me, as if he hoped I would punch him so he could punch me back and start a brawl.

"So, what else is new?"

"If some man slurred my father like that, you can bet I'd punch him."

"It's not a slur when it's true."

"Oh, you're so clever," he mocked. "You're just gutless--

you're afraid to punch me because you know I'll punch back."

"I have bigger fish to fry tonight than some drunk merchant." I started to stand.

"Sit down--I'll tell you where Whitten is."

I remained standing. "Where?"

"Tupping the most beautiful woman I've ever seen. The sot doesn't even know what to do with her--that marriage is goddamned travesty, and your father's responsible for it."

He was talking about Safire. Without thinking, I reached across the table and grabbed him by his cloak collar. "So I don't have the guts to punch you?" I hissed at his startled face. "What's this?" I slammed my fist into his jaw.

He hit back, his aim wild with drink but his knuckles as hard as ever. He clipped my ear, my head ringing like the bells on holy day. I swore and shoved him back in the corner.

"You two better stop it right now," Jasper the innkeeper roared from the bar. "I'll throw you out on your arses like I did when you were fourteen. Your father don't want you brawling like a common drunk, Sir Merius."

We both sank down on our benches, glowering at each other across the table. "I'm surprised you defend your father, Merius," Peregrine said after a long moment, luckily misinterpreting the reason for my anger. "Even you have to see what a waste it is, Safire married to Whitten. She could have been mine, damn it. I offered to pay her father's debts to the Landers, everything, and your father wouldn't hear of it. He likely has some secret plot--he always does. In the mean time, the finest field in this province is being plowed and seeded by a feckless drunkard."

I blinked, ran my tongue over the inside of my teeth, forced myself to ignore his vulgarity, though if he used one more insulting term to refer to Safire . . . "I didn't realize you'd made an offer for her."

"Several. The last one in particular was very generous, considering her poor dowry. Your father wouldn't accept any of them. Instead he married her to Whitten when she was out of her mind. I don't understand it."

"If her dowry's so poor, what do you want her for?" I asked.

"Peregrine, you've never been the sort to marry just because you wanted a good tumble. You could take a mistress for that."

He barked a laugh. "Safire--be a mistress? You obviously don't know her. She's too proud and impractical for that kind of arrangement. No, the only way to pluck her is to marry her."

"But there's plenty of willing women, beautiful women you could take for mistresses or wives. Why her?"

"Merius, you dolt," he slurred, too drunk now to care what he said, "haven't you ever wanted a particular woman to the point of distraction? There's no rhyme or reason to it--you just want her. You'd do anything to claim her for yours. Now, take that lust and multiply it ten times, and you'll have the barest inkling of what I feel when I see Safire. Her skin is paler, smoother to the touch than the finest SerVerin ivory. She smells sweet like cedar on fire, and she holds herself so high, the unearthly wench, though her father was but a sparrow nobleman with debts piled to the roof. You know, these sparrow noblemen--they bring their daughters to me like fruit on a platter, their last treasure to sell before the creditors call. In all these years, this endless parade of daughters, Safire is the only one I've ever wanted to buy. She'll wish she'd let me buy her by that time that drunken fool finishes with her."

"You're mad," I said, feeling slightly unreal as I did every time I wore my court mask. "I'll grant you that Safire's beautiful, but the few times I've seen her at Landers Hall since my return, she's blistered me with her tongue. She's far from an ideal wife for a man like you."

Peregrine shrugged. "She just needs a strong hand. You know yourself--the best horses are often the ones with the most spirit before they're broken."

My whole body felt unreal now, a marionette with strings to be pulled by the real me. If I allowed myself to be here and fully present, I'd draw my sword on him, which I dimly knew would be disastrous. So I kept myself far away as the marionette Merius said, "And just how would you break her, Peregrine? Beat her?"

He shrugged again, obviously growing impatient with the conversation. "I'd beat her if I thought it would work--most wives need a beating at one point or another. Honestly, though, I don't think Safire would take well to that kind of treatment. She's too high strung and stubborn, too pretty to mark up anyway. No, there are more interesting ways of handling disobedience than beating."

"More interesting ways? Like what?"

He grinned. "Merius, you really are an ignorant ass. When you marry a woman, you own her. It's your responsibility to train her, and you'll have no one but yourself to fault if she remains unruly. You know how I'd train Safire? I'd lock her away for awhile. I'd be the only one with the key, the only one she ever saw. I'd bring her meals, her amusements, her baths even. And if she used that wicked tongue, as I'm sure she would, I'd simply forget to bring her the book or extra blanket she asked for, even forget to bring her a few meals if she really disobeyed. I'd make her dependent on my whim for all her needs, and despite her stubborn pride, she'd soon realize how generous I could be if she made the effort to please me. Imogene," he yelled suddenly, banging his tankard on the table. "Imogene, you're slow as shank's pony."

I took the opportunity to breathe. My lungs burned--my whole body felt frostbitten, inside and out, the tingling pain settling in my gut. Light-headed, my already over-active imagination hummed along, showing me picture after sickening picture of Peregrine with Safire. These images were worse, far worse than anything Whitten had done to her. Whitten was a weak fool who had likely taken Safire in her fit because she wasn't able to fight back. If she had never had that fit, Whitten never would have had the guts to touch her. Peregrine, though . . . I shook my head, my hand over my eyes to block the light so I wouldn't see anything but darkness, anything to block the unthinkable images parading my mind. Her bearing Whitten's child now seemed a small concern compared to what Peregrine might do. Thank God the annulment between her and Whitten hadn't been formally announced yet. Once Peregrine knew about the annulment, I wagered he would be as swift to snatch her up as a merciless hawk with his prey. And what recourse would she have, alone with no coin and a cuckoo child growing inside her?

I had left her tonight hell bent to kill her ravisher and then flee as a fugitive from justice. Fleeing had seemed easier than handling the reality of another man's child in her womb. However, if

I left her now and a man like Peregrine took her, I could never live with myself. I had left her once already to go on the campaign, and she had been hurt and bruised by my callous family in my absence. My witch, my lovely, sweet, spirited witch, with her healing hands and spooky sketches and fiery temper. She was not quite of this world, and she needed someone more practical than her to help her navigate through it. I was far from practical at times, but at least I had inherited a touch of my father's cunning. We would need it, with hawks like Peregrine already circling.

"What's the matter, Landers?" Peregrine scoffed. "Did my punch addle you so much that it struck you dumb? You're an odd one sometimes, you know--there's been gossip after council about your trances. You'd best watch your mind wandering if you expect to keep your position."

"I'm not the one in my cups and obsessing over another man's wife and her SerVerin ivory skin. Why don't you take one of your smuggled ivory statues to bed? That's as close as you'll ever get to touching her," I finished with more of a snarl than I had intended.

Peregrine lunged at me, and I punched him in the face with glorious abandon, for once not constrained by the worry of Father lambasting me on the morrow. Tankards flew as we knocked the table aside. His fist landed on my jaw, so hard that I wondered dimly if he'd cracked it. I swore and hit him square in the eye, then dodged aside as he dove for me. He ran into a bench and stumbled. I kicked him to the floor, and he hollered something unintelligible and grabbed my leg. I fell on the hard boards, the wind knocked out of my chest, and then he was on me, his fist drawn back to hit me. In a moment of exquisite painful clarity, likely caused by my inability to draw breath, I felt another surge of rage, rage at Peregrine, rage at Whitten, rage at Father, rage that gave me the strength to grab Peregrine's descending fist and roll him on to the floor. Even though he was drunk, he got in several good hits, but I didn't feel the pain anymore. He was a stronger fighter at hand-to-hand combat than I, but he lacked my advantage tonight. I pummeled him, blocking his hand when he reached for his dagger.

"You goddamned dishonorable cheat," I yelled. Though I wore both my sword and dagger, I would never have dreamed of reaching for them in a fistfight like this.

He twisted his arm out of my grasp and went for his dagger a second time, even though I had as yet to reach for mine. "Oh, you've asked for it, you son of a bitch," I growled. I grabbed his dagger before he could and cast it aside.

He caught the edge of my left cheekbone in a punch that made red stars explode in my head. I shook myself, disoriented for an instant, and he hit me again in the same place. I bellowed with pain, reaching for him. He tried to roll away from me. I lunged forward and gripped his shoulders. With as much strength as I could muster, I threw him against the overturned table. He hit the back of his head on the table edge, tried to get back up, and then fell back again with a groan. "Damn it," he muttered.

Rough hands grabbed me and dragged me to my feet. "Your father's going to hear about this," Jasper said, he and his grim-faced son pushing me toward the door.

I felt the wild urge to laugh. "Go ahead, tell him."

"He'll make you a lot sorrier than I can--now get out. If I see you here again, I'll call the magistrate, whether you be Landers or no. You're banned from these grounds for the next year for brawling."

I slowly walked to the stable, guided by the lantern light. That pain emerged as I walked, my whole face throbbing. He had gotten in more hard hits than I had realized--my fingers felt the long slash he'd left along my jaw with his seal ring, my nose oozed blood, and my left cheekbone hurt enough to be broken. Already, I could feel the soreness in my muscles, a soreness that came after a really good fistfight--I wagered tomorrow I'd have bruises all over. Well, at least he'd gotten his, the nasty merchant bastard. If he ever so much as glanced at Safire, I'd pummel him and knock him out again for good measure.

Shadowfoot neighed in greeting. I mounted him, exhausted suddenly. "Let's go, boy, and see if Safire'll fix me up."

~ ~ ~ ~ ~

Though it was well after two in the morning when I unlocked the door to our chamber, Safire was still awake. She had several candles lit and the fire burning, despite it being a mild night. We looked at each other as I entered and shut the door behind me with a quiet click. She wore a plain white shift, the cloth thin from many washings, so thin I could almost see through it. Her knees were drawn up under the hem, her slim arms clutched around them as she rocked back and forth on the bed. With her hair pulled back from her face, her eyes seemed enormous, with deep shadows under them from too little sleep and too many tears.

"Merius, your face," she exclaimed then, unfolding and rising from the bed. "Oh, dear heart, what . . ."

"I got in a fight."

She came over, stopping abruptly a few feet away. She held out her arms, hesitant, as if she didn't quite know how I would respond. I grabbed her to me in a bear hug, inhaling the cedar sweetness of her hair. She began to sob against my shoulder, her tears soaking my shirt. "Shh, shh. It's all right."

"I didn't know if you were coming back, and then when you came through the door, I couldn't read your expression or your aura, and then I saw all the blood . . ."

"Shh, never mind that now. Is there really a lot of blood?" I glanced over her head at the mirror. There was a lot of blood, more than I had expected, mostly dried now. "Do you think you can mend it? My cheekbone feels pretty tender."

She drew away, just far enough so I could see her face. Her eyes gleamed sharp through a haze of tears. "Heal it, you mean? I don't know. Are you staying?"

"Of course I'm staying, sweet."

"With the way you stormed out of here so sudden, yelling that you didn't want me to touch you with my witch hands, I had to ask."

"Safire, you can't blame me for being upset."

"You're upset? I've sat here locked in for hours, not knowing where you went, what you were doing, if you'd be back. My talents told me you were still alive, but that's about it. For all I knew, you'd killed Whitten and fled on the first ship, never to return."

"Then you should--" I broke off, realizing that I was about to say *Then you should have told me about the baby as soon as you knew.* All that would do is land us in another argument, an exhausting proposition at this moment. I took a deep breath. "So we're both upset--what do we do now? I'm too tired for arguing. Can we put it off till tomorrow?"

She sighed. "Sit down then."

I perched on the edge of the bed and watched as she brought over the basin, water lurching over the sides and splashing on the floor. She then soaked a washrag before she gingerly scrubbed my face with it. The water was cool and soothing, and I closed my eyes, already feeling the tingle of her healing touch through the rag.

"So, you got in a fight, but not with Whitten. Someone else, someone you've hated a long time and wanted to fight," she said.

"How do you know that?"

"I just do, Merius. That's what happens when you're a witch--you just know things sometimes."

"I told you, I'm not going to argue tonight."

"I wasn't arguing, just stating a fact of my life." She wrung the rag out in the basin, and the water turned pinkish.

I decided it was probably best to ignore her tone--we were both tired, and her touch was gentle enough even if her words held an edge. "I fought Peregrine, if you must know."

"Peregrine?" The rag stopped for a moment as she absorbed this.

"Did you know that he made several offers for you to Father while I was away?"

"I knew he made at least one--I didn't realize it was several. He's been making offers for me for years, so many I've lost count. Truly, there was so much going on that he was but a minor annoyance in the midst of it, the swine."

"If he talks to you, even so much as looks at you ever again, I want you to tell me immediately."

"Why, what did he say?"

"Never mind that. You're not the only one who lies and keeps secrets to protect someone, evidently."

"Damn it, Merius." She threw the rag in the basin and put her hands to her face. "I told you as soon as I could. There's a difference between knowing something and being able to tell it, especially when you know it's going to hurt the listener to hear it. I love you so," she choked, "and you've been hurt so much already.

That made it even harder."

"Sweetheart, please." I stepped towards her. Her shoulders shook, the muscles in her arms so tense that her frail bones looked on the verge of snapping.

"Dear God," she said. "What are we going to do?"

"We're going to marry tomorrow, as we planned."

"But . . ." She raised her head, staring at me. "But . . ."

"But what?"

"But that's why I told you tonight before you married me, a ruined woman with a cuckoo's child. When you left tonight, I didn't know if you still wanted me for your wife or even your mistress . . ."

"Mistress? Safire, what kind of man do you think I am?"

"Merius, I didn't mean it like that. I just . . . well, things have changed, and--"

"Just listen for a moment. I want to be very clear about this. We need to marry tomorrow, as soon as possible, and then leave Cormalen for awhile, until well after you've had the baby."

"But you don't have to . . ."

"If anyone besides you and me knows the truth about this baby, it could invalidate the annulment. The king would never have granted it if he'd known Whitten sired a child on you, especially if it's a son."

She began to shake her head, her hand going to her mouth. "To everyone," I continued, reaching for her hand, "there has to be no doubt this baby is mine. Otherwise, they'll take you back to Whitten, to that house."

Tears streamed down her face, and she choked, her fingers tight around mine. "Merius, this is too much of a sacrifice for you . . ."

I put my finger to her mouth. "Shh--I'll be the judge of that." I traced the outline of her lips. "My lovely night witch," I whispered. "Sweet and wild as a wood rose in May. When I think of that sot daring to touch you . . ."

"Don't think of it, Merius," she said shakily. "Don't think. Please. We're fine here, together--we'll be fine."

"I can't help but think of it. My boyhood friend, my cousin-- he took advantage of you, you couldn't say no or even know what was happening to you. That son of a bitch."

Abruptly, she let go of me, putting her hand over her mouth. She vomited in the basin, gagging. I stood up and held her shoulders as she finished. A sourness filled the air, and I felt the bile rise in my own stomach. I swallowed, my eyes watering as I emptied the basin in the slop jar and clapped the lid down on its contents. The smell still lingered. I cracked the window, and it quickly dissipated. I wished that my family was so easily disposed of.

Safire leaned against the wash stand, wiping her face with a damp towel. She dried her mouth, then lifted the pitcher and started to pour a glass of water.

"Here." I took the pitcher and finished pouring the water for her.

"I'm sorry, Merius."

"Why? It makes me feel sick myself--it's no wonder you retched, what with the baby and all."

"If I hadn't cried myself silly, you mean." She sniffed. "Now, let me finish healing your wounds."

"You can finish in the morning--you should lie down, and I'm pretty exhausted myself."

"We can't leave your cheek till morning, Merius. I think the bone's cracked."

"That bastard Peregrine can't hit that hard." I winced even as I spoke--my cheek did hurt badly, worse than I'd realized.

Her eyes were narrow. "I'm sure you won the fight and that Peregrine looks a lot worse than you. But he still got in some nasty punches. Now get on the bed."

"All right, but I didn't know you could heal a cracked bone."

"There are a lot of things I can do." She grinned and pushed me towards the bed.

"Really? Like what?"

"You'll see. Shh--just sit down here, on the edge."

Cool hands encircled my head as Safire knelt on the bed behind me. "Be still now, my love," she whispered, her breath warm against my ear and neck. Her fingers were light as she gently massaged my temples, then my forehead, then my face, her deft touch tingling. It felt as if she were making new skin for me with her fingertips.

"Witch," I muttered, closing my eyes. "You'll make a fine warrior's wife--you can patch me up after every battle."

"Shh--I told you to be still."

I drew a sharp breath when her fingers reached my cheek. She barely touched the bone, and I bit back a yelp. How could I not have noticed the pain before? It was the kind of pain that went straight to my gut and made me queasy.

"Picture the pain as a helmet that's too tight," she whispered, her fingers unbearable as she rubbed my cheek. I wanted to howl, pound the floor with my feet, but instead I gritted my teeth and pretended my father was in the chamber.

"Merius, forget your father, what he would think. Forget everything, everything except the helmet. It's so tight--you can think of nothing else but how tight it feels, how much it hurts, how much you long to take it off . . ." She repeated this over and over, her fingers rubbing heat into my cheek, a tingling heat. Whenever she took away my headaches, her fingers were cool, blessedly cool, but now they were hot. The heat itched, and I longed to scratch. It reminded me of the itch I'd felt when my arm had started to mend after I broke it against the parapet wall, an itch that I couldn't reach to scratch because it was under the cast, under my skin, in my very bones as they knit back together.

"Merius," Safire's voice broke into my thoughts. "You're starting to drift again. Helmet--remember the helmet, dear heart. It's so tight it hurts, hurts . . ." I concentrated, remembered the confining weight of my helmet, how much I hated wearing it, how it would hurt if it were too small.

In less than a minute, Safire cracked the helmet with her magic hands, the pieces falling to my feet as the pain vanished. A liquid light filled my veins, and I felt then that everything was going to be fine.

Chapter Twenty-Seven--Safire

I awoke to the grayish light of a stormy dawn. We had forgotten to close the bed curtains last night, and I could see the silvery streaks of the rain on the diamond-shaped panes and hear the plinking of the drops on the slate roof overhead like a thousand tiny bells ringing at once. It was the perfect morning to snuggle under the blankets next to Merius and go back to sleep, but I found myself unable to close my eyes. Merius stirred then and murmured something unintelligible. I held my breath, waiting for him to wake. He turned over, pulling the covers with him, still talking and still very much asleep. I smiled. He was as restless asleep as he was awake, fighting with his pillow one moment and kissing me the next. I listened to his breathing settle back into an even, quiet rhythm.

"Thank you," I whispered to the air. The air was a presence today, heavy and dark with the rain. "Thank you that he came back, that he's alive and safe and beside me now."

The air grew still for a moment, as if listening to me, and I felt the brush of invisible fingers on my forehead, smoothing my hair. My mother. I instinctively reached up to grasp her hand, but she was gone, so fleeting that I wondered if I'd imagined her.

I sighed and turned over, my hand drifting to my belly. Already I could feel swelling, a ripe tautness under the skin that hadn't been there before. I prayed that Mother would return, tell me what to do, but the air had fallen still, and I knew I would sense her no more today. She had crossed over, and until I died and crossed over myself, I could only talk to her in dreams and sense her in fleeting flashes like that one that had just happened. So Merius and I were left to sort this mess out ourselves--we didn't dare tell anyone living, even Dagmar, lest it ruin our chances to marry, and the dead with wisdom to impart were beyond our reach.

I glanced over at Merius's long shape under the covers, his hair sticking out in all directions, his arm clutched around his pillow as if he thought someone would snatch it from him. When he had left to kill Whitten last night, perhaps never to return, I had lit every candle in the chamber and then sat on the bed, my arms around my knees as I stared at the light flickering over the wall. I had sat like that for over two hours, terrified to move, even to cry. I had to be still--if I moved, my cracked heart would break into a hundred pieces, never to be whole again. I understood now the ancient stories of shock turning people into statues. It had happened to me last night. Then Merius had returned with his quicksilver aura, the very air around him sparkling, and I had found myself able to move and speak again. My heart was still cracked, but I knew even if I jarred it and the pieces fell apart, he would be there to help me put it back together.

My brash, brilliant, sweet-tempered, not-quite husband. I sighed again and combed my fingers through his hair. The dawn of our wedding day, and Merius was estranged from his family and position because I carried his drunkard cousin's get in my womb. This was supposed to be a grand day, filled with feasts and dances and merriment, not a day for us to sneak off and find the first priest who didn't ask too many questions. Dagmar wouldn't even be there to stand behind me at the alter as I said my vows. I had been at her wedding and shared her joy--what had Merius and I done so wrong to warrant fate cheating us out of a public celebration of our union? The all-too-familiar prickle of tears stung my eyes, and I savagely swallowed them back, wiping away stray drops with the corner of the sheet. If Merius woke and found me crying yet again, he really would leave me, and I wouldn't blame him.

What kind of bride was I, anyway? How could he still want me after all that had happened? He should marry a chaste, demure beauty from one of the first Houses, not some unruly witch with another man's seed growing in her belly. Of course, Merius was unruly himself and likely would have found the chaste beauty dull after five minutes, so it seemed we deserved each other. But we didn't deserve to start our life together with another man's child in my womb.

It was so unfair, first to have Whitten take advantage of my witch fit, and then have his seed take root . . . I found myself curling up in a ball, my hand knotted in the folds of the shift over my belly, as if I could somehow will myself to miscarry. My whole body shook as I concentrated on my womb. Perhaps I could make my monthly blood come, and it would be like Whitten had never touched me. Never touched me . . . a sudden weight pushed me deep into the feather tick, and all went dark and airless. I choked, something pressing hard against my throat, so hard I could barely get breath. He had held his arm against my throat to keep me limp while he . . . the memory mercifully ended as soon as it began, one of those flashes that had been coming more often since Merius's return. I uttered a low, guttural whimper like an animal in pain in an effort to keep from sobbing. No more tears, not yet--my eyes already felt raw as peeled onions from tears, and I was sick of crying.

"Safire?" Merius muttered, letting go of his pillow and reaching for me. He suddenly surrounded me, his arms tight against my back, my cheek against the rough warmth of his bare chest. "Wake up, sweet--I think you're having a nightmare."

"I'm awake." I took a deep breath, the searing liquor of his quicksilver air in my lungs.

"What is it?"

"It's just not fair, Merius. Your seed should have taken root, not his."

He sighed and turned over on his back, pulling me with him so that my head still rested on his chest. I could hear his heart beat, my head rising and falling with each breath he inhaled. He stared up at the bed canopy for a long while before he said, his voice hoarse, "'And so the nightmares gallop along/Their black hooves pounding, pounding in our sleep. . .'"

"Did you write that?" I moved my head so I could see his expression.

He nodded, his face pale in the gray light, his eyes dark and sad. "Nightmares shouldn't come when we're awake--it's bad enough we have them when we're asleep."

I nodded, squeezing my eyes shut. "Maybe if I miscarried, it would be like this never happened." He fell silent again, his fingers moving lightly up and down my back. He was quiet for so long, his heartbeat louder and faster in my ears, that I finally said, "Merius?"

"How would you do that?" he asked, his voice neutral.

"What? Miscarry?" When he nodded, I continued, "I don't know exactly--I know some women do it deliberately, but no one's ever said how. I thought maybe I could use my talents somehow--I tried last night, but it didn't work. I've never been able to heal myself, and I think this is the same kind of thing."

"You tried last night?"

"Before you woke and found me crying, I tried."

"Safire . . ." His hand tightened against my back.

"I couldn't bear to tell you, I was so ashamed and scared you'd go off in a rage if you knew, but I knew that I could never in good conscience marry you without telling you. I thought if I could make myself miscarry, you'd never have to know what Whitten did."

"Safire, if you ever conceal anything like that from me again . . . damn it, I can't stand being lied to or deceived. It reminds me of Father's dealings, and I won't tolerate that kind of behavior from my wife."

"Why do you think I told you when I did? If deceiving you was my motive, I would have waited until well after the ceremony to tell you."

"I know that--I just hate the thought of you hurt and bearing this alone. You should have turned to me first instead of pretending happiness this past week."

"Pretending happiness? Merius, I'm not that good an actress. Being here with you, away from everything--how could I help but be happy? All you have to do is take me in your arms to make me forget. Perhaps only forget for a little while, sometimes longer, but it's enough. More than enough--it's sustained me."

He leaned over and kissed the crown of my head, then my lips. It was a gentle kiss, our mouths barely open to each other--we hadn't kissed since before I'd told him about Whitten, and the truth now lay between us, an invisible barrier that only time and desire could breach. Knowing myself, much less Merius, I doubted it would take us long to breach it. Not just breach it, but bound over it. I smiled to myself, feeling him already warming to me with growing eagerness, his lips taut against mine.

I pulled away at an opportune moment. "We're not married yet, you know."

He chuckled. "If you insist, my lady, then I suppose we should get ourselves to a chapel."

"That's right. I'll do things in the wrong order every other day, but not our wedding day." I settled back on his chest, and we were silent again for a long moment, listening to the rain and each other's breathing. "Do you know . . ." I trailed off, hesitant.

"Know what, sweet?" His hand moved in my hair.

"Anything about miscarriages?"

There was another long moment of silence, and then he shifted under me, as if choosing his words carefully. "My father, some of the men at court--they've said some things."

"Like what?"

"There's something called bloodweed--courtesans take it a lot."

"Would you know where to get some?"

"No."

"Could you find out?" I craned my neck and looked at him.

"No." He met my gaze, his eyes unblinking.

"Merius, I don't believe you. Surely you could find out where to get some."

"I probably could. That doesn't mean I'm going to do it."

"Why not? You want me to bear some other man's child . . ." He sat up, grabbing my shoulders and pulling me towards him so that our faces were within inches of each other. His eyes suddenly held a wild light, the same light I'd seen in them last night when he'd went off to kill Whitten. I swallowed. "Merius . . ."

"Listen, Safire. Believe me, I don't want to see you bear this child, but I'd rather see you bear it than see you die."

"Die? But the bloodweed sounds safe enough."

His mouth worked as if he couldn't find the words for he wanted to say. Finally, he said, his voice low, "Everyone except

Father says it's safe, but I don't believe them."

"What does that mean? Why doesn't your father think it's safe?"

"He's never said, but I heard the servant women's whispers after Mother died. They said . . . said she took bloodweed, and that's what caused her to die in childbed. I glimpsed the sheets afterwards, soaked with blood." He broke off abruptly and sank back against the headboard, his face turned away.

"Oh, dear heart." I ran my fingers through his hair, down his neck.

"I'll not procure bloodweed for you. In fact, I forbid you to take it." He glanced back at me, his eyes narrow.

"Forbid? That's a strong word for a not-quite husband," I said, and we glared at each other. Merius's aura swirled around him, so strong it reminded me of a bracing wind from the sea, filling sails and blowing away anything insubstantial.

Merius's glare softened, and he grinned. "Bold witch. Shall we dance or duel, sweet?"

I smiled, traced his lips with my finger. "That depends. Which ends with a kiss?"

"Both." He caught my finger in his mouth and nipped my knuckle. "And such a kiss--it's forbidden even between husbands and wives."

"Indeed. Forbidden--such a strong word. It makes me feel defiant."

"I like you," he paused. "Defiant."

I lifted myself off his chest and propped my elbow on the pillow beside his head, my chin against the palm of my hand. We stared at each other for an eternal minute, the rain a lulling rhythm in the background.

"You're so lovely," he said quietly. He ran his fingers down the side of my face. I caught his hand in mine and kissed the perpetual ink spot on the side, my fingertips brushing the ropes of his veins and muscles under their coat of coarse hair. "I should never have left you to go on campaign," he continued. "This would never have happened if I'd been here."

"But you had to go, Merius. You can't take responsibility for something someone else did while you were across the sea, fighting and getting taken hostage and God knows what else. You had no way of predicting what happened, no more than I did, and I have witch talents."

"I should have been here to protect you. I'll never leave you like that again."

"What if Herrod orders you to go on campaign?"

"I'll not go." He gripped my back, holding me tight against him. "I'll not leave you alone for so long again," he repeated, the force of his words rumbling through both of us.

"It's backwards arrogance to hold yourself responsible for everything. What if a bolt of lightning came through the window and struck me dead this instant? Would you blame yourself for that?"

"No, but this isn't a bolt of lightning. This is Whitten, who never would have thought to touch you if I'd married you when I should have."

"All the ifs in the world won't take away what happened." I paused, hesitant to say what I said next. "Killing him won't take away what happened, dear heart."

His gaze was steady, unrelenting. "A miscarriage won't take it away either, Safire."

I sighed and laid my head on his shoulder. "Nothing will take it away," I murmured, closing my eyes. "We don't deserve this."

"No, we don't." He clasped me in his arms, his warmth all around me. "My friend Roland didn't deserve a SerVerinese arrow in the neck, either. Yet that's what he got. Now he'll never hold a woman the way I'm holding you."

"So you feel fortunate, despite what's happened?"

His arms tightened. "I still have you, and that makes me the most fortunate man I know."

"After today you'll always have me, and I'll have you. Always, Merius." I glanced up at him. "Always--I can't comprehend it. Always is a long time."

"Not long enough. What are you thinking, sweetheart?"

"I'm not thinking, I'm feeling."

"What are you feeling?"

"I love you."

I could hear the smile in his voice. "I love you too." We fell silent then, holding each other. The rain lashed against the window, a cozy sound when I was safe and warm in bed with Merius, so cozy that I began to feel drowsy. He yawned and clutched me to him like he had clutched his pillow earlier, as if he were afraid someone would snatch me away. I nestled against him with a grin, my thoughts drifting lazily over the few frocks and gowns I had brought with me. Which would be suitable to wear when we married? Dagmar would have said none of them, but she could be so fussy sometimes. I already knew which article of clothing Merius preferred to see me wear, and it wasn't anything that was suitable for church. So that left me to make up my own mind. I finally settled on one of my simplest frocks, a cream-colored gauze and silk concoction with a green ribbon sash as its only adornment. Only adornment . . . it would be perfect . . . perfect. Sleep was almost upon me when I felt a flame flare to life deep inside at the very root of my being. My mind, on the edge of dreamland, concentrated on that flame, mesmerized by its minute flickers. The flame was so tiny and frail that I would never have noticed it amidst the distractions of the waking world. But it was there. It was no dream, even if I couldn't see it yet with my eyes. And it would grow. My son.

Chapter Twenty-Eight--Mordric

"Eden here to see you, sir." Randel's voice sounded oddly muffled, as if he spoke through wool.

I opened my eyes and realized I was stretched out on the settle, my cloak pulled over my head. I couldn't remember how it got there. I sat up, the cloak sliding to the floor. Blinding light pierced my eyeballs, and I swore, blocking the day with my arm. "Close the drapes, damn it. What time is it?"

"Ten o'clock, sir."

All my bones ached--the settle was hard wood with no cushions and God knew how long I had been laying there. "Hell flames," I said, my throat on fire. "Is there any water?"

Randel moved around the chamber. "Here."

I drained the tumbler. "You said Eden?"

"Yes."

"Give me a quarter hour, and I'll see her."

"Do you want anything to eat?"

"No, later." I set the tumbler down with a loud clink that reverberated painfully in my ears.

"Sir, you haven't eaten since noon yesterday . . ."

"If I wanted nagging, I would marry again. Leave me."

When the door clicked shut behind him, I stayed on the settle for several minutes. Then I rose and made my way over to the side table where Randel had put a large pitcher and basin. Only a few candles lit the chamber, and I bumped into the corner of my desk and a chair. I kicked the chair, and it clattered over on its side. I bent down, my head swimming, and picked it up, but when I went to set it right, one of the legs cracked right down the middle. I threw it against the desk. The leg fell off.

"Merchant-made bastard chair," I muttered, sucking on my finger where a splinter had broken the skin.

I gripped the edge of the table when I reached it to steady myself before I filled the basin. Even so, water splashed everywhere. I plunged my entire face in the basin over and over again. The water was cold and cleared my head almost as well as a good slap. Arilea used to slap me when I got this bad.

Finally I straightened, ran my hands down my dripping jaw. It was covered with straggly beard. I glanced around for a razor but saw none. I could use my dagger but with the way my hands were shaking, I didn't dare.

The door opened as I finished drinking a second tumbler of water. "I told you to leave me, damn it," I growled as Randel entered.

He bowed, seeming not to hear me. "The lady Eden," he announced. "And Sir Cyril will be here momentarily."

"Oh hell." I had already forgotten I had said Eden could see me. And Cyril? My hand went for my sword hilt, only to clutch at air. I glanced around the chamber. I had to have my sword--I felt naked without it. "Before I sack you for being a lying son of a bitch, where did you hide my blade?"

"It's in the corner, sir. Where you left it."

I buckled on the sword as Randel lit a few more candles and tidied the chamber. Without a word, he hid the broken chair behind the drapes, letting in a flash of painful light. Before I could curse, the flash was gone, and Randel was over at the door, inviting in Eden and Cyril. I stood behind the main table where I saw tenants and went over ledgers, my hands braced on the edge. There was a sudden fleeting coldness at my neck, a mocking whisper in my ear *Not long now, my love.* I turned my head sharply, but she was already gone.

Eden slid into the chair directly across the table, her eyes regarding me with a narrow glance. Cyril cleared his throat and claimed the armchair, his back not touching the upholstery. I nodded to both, the barest politeness I could muster. "Randel, bring some refreshment," I said.

Cyril shook his head. "I'm fine, thank you."

"Fruit and coffee for me," Eden said. Then she paused, glancing at me again. "And a glass of water and powders for Sir Mordric."

Impudent hussy. I glared at her but said nothing in front of Cyril. Later she would catch it--she had become far too assured of her place.

"Last I called, you were ill," Cyril said stiffly. "I take it you're improved."

"Save the court pleasantries. Why are you here?"

"All right." He leaned back in his chair, his hands folded together. "I'll be blunt. When are you returning to council?"

"That's none of your affair."

"I'm the noble head of the council. I can replace you. It's certainly my affair, Mordric."

"Fine. Replace me."

Both he and Eden started, a flicker of shock that ran through the chamber with lightning intensity. "So I take it you're not returning at all?" he said finally.

"That's right."

"That's ridiculous," he exploded. "To quit like that . . . you have a sworn duty to this province, damn it."

"It's not your place to comment on my judgment or my duty. I'll stand no insult, Cyril."

He rose. "Mordric, I demand an explanation."

I rose myself, reaching for my sword. "I told you I would stand no insult."

He stepped back, held his hands up, palms out. "All right, all right. I'll not duel with you again, not over this. But I do think I warrant an explanation."

"Why?"

"Despite the fact I'm none too fond of you, we are allies, kinsmen through Merius, and your defection from the council is a grievous loss to our cause. Losing Merius during the campaign was bad enough, but now we're two votes short until he returns."

"He's not returning either, is he?" Eden asked quietly, her

damned sharp eyes missing nothing.

Cyril turned towards her. "What?"

"He's joined the king's guard permanently, I do believe."

"How do you know that?" I said.

"Something Selwyn let slip earlier."

Randel entered at that moment, carrying a small tray. He set it on the table. I reached for the water and powders and gulped it all down, not even taking the time to grimace at the bitter taste. "Eden, you've spoken out of turn, and I shall not let it pass. There was no call for you to speculate publicly in front of our guest about a private family matter, a matter of which you know nothing."

"I thought Sir Cyril deserved to know the truth." Her unblinking gaze never left mine. She would never have been so free with her information unless she had an ulterior motive--Eden planned her carelessness carefully. What the hell was she plotting now, the viper? Bringing Cyril here, telling him private family business in front of me, deliberately baiting me . . . I had trained her too well for it not to mean something.

"Leave us now, Eden. Wait in the hall--I'll talk to you when Cyril and I are finished here. Randel, escort her out." He nodded, understanding that I meant for him to guard her until I could deal with this latest affront.

"Is this true?" Cyril demanded. "Has Merius forsaken his duties?"

I took a deep breath. "Yes, Merius has joined the king's guard."

"And when did you intend to inform the council of this?"

"After I spoke with him."

"So this may not be a permanent defection?"

"I'll be free, Cyril. There's not much hope of him returning. He's forsaken his inheritance as well." I glanced around, searched for the gleam of a bottle, but Randel had taken them all but the decanter of wine, damn him.

There was a long silence. Cyril said finally, his voice quiet, "This is a hard blow. After my son joined the king's guard, I looked to my nephew Darin to fill my council seat, which he will. He's a good, steady sort, Darin, and I'll be glad to leave it to him. But he's not a leader. Merius is a leader. We elders need him, need his new blood, for when we turn dotard and retire. He's the only young noble who could take the reins."

"I know."

"What the hell is he thinking?" Cyril brought his fist down on the table. "His inheritance too--he must be mad. Perhaps the thin air of Marennese mountains addled him."

"He has good reason."

"What reason?"

I stared at my hands, clasped together over my lap. "You spoke more truly than I realized several months past when you said that no man of honor could last long as my son."

"As I said, I'm none too fond of you," he said finally, "but I shouldn't have questioned your honor. You have methods of handling opposition which I don't approve. However, we would have no footing on the council without you or your methods."

"Perhaps not. My methods, as you call them, seem to work well with men like Peregrine. But Merius is not like Peregrine. I interfered where I shouldn't have, and it's cost me my son."

Cyril leaned forward. "Mordric, he's young, proud, hot-tempered, but he's far from a fool. He'll cool down and return soon enough."

"Your son hasn't returned to council."

"My son still has his inheritance. You were wise to bind up your offices and lands in one package, so to speak."

"It was a foolhardy risk, with Merius's stubborn pride."

"Nonsense." Cyril waved his hand dismissively. "You still hold the purse strings--he'll be around in a few months or so, when what coin he has runs out."

"You speak like the hopeful cynic I know you're not. Thank you, but I need no false hopes. He won't be back, Cyril. He'll starve with the dogs in the street before he'll take another coin of mine." I rested my elbows on the table and pressed my palms over my eyes.

"I should have left the cynicism to you." He sighed, and there was a quiet moment. "Perhaps there is some way of mending it you haven't considered?"

I lowered my hands and looked at him. "I've done what I

could to mend it, but it's a difficult situation."

Cyril clapped his palms down on the armrests as if preparing to rise and do battle. "All right then. By your account, Merius's return to the council and his duties is out of our hands. Your return, however . . ."

"No."

He plowed on. "Your return, however, is the reason I came today."

"I no longer have an heir. What's the point?"

"We need your vote, Mordric."

"I don't give a damn about my vote."

"Ah, but the king and I do."

"Fine. As I said, replace me."

"No. It's not that simple. You swore an oath when you joined the council. Your appointment ends with incapacity or death."

"I would consider myself incapacitated at this point."

"On your worst days, you're twice as capable as anyone I could replace you with. If you leave now, like this, the merchant riffraff will win. Is that what you want?"

"Cyril, I told you. I don't give a damn."

He shrugged. "You don't give a damn if that ass Sullay ends up head of council in a year? You don't give a damn if Prince Segar becomes king and taxes us nobles out of existence to pay for his frivolities? You don't give a damn if the SerVerin Empire sees how weak we are with Prince Segar on the throne and the merchants run amuck? You want your grandchildren to speak SerVerinese?"

"You exaggerate. You always use too blunt a blade when you argue, Cyril."

He ignored my insult, carried off by the force of his words. He loved to make speeches. "Whether or not Merius is in the king's guard, I doubt you want to leave him and his children with such a legacy--dishonest merchants like Sullay running the council and the name of Landers but an empty memory of honor and nobility. You've worked for years to build the House of Landers's reputation at court, and now you wreck all of it because you and Merius had an argument? God knows, you two have argued before--what's so different now?"

Blunt edge or not, some of his words were beginning to sound sensible. Or perhaps the effects of too much whiskey had begun to wear off. Whichever it was, I no longer felt so hopeless about Merius. It had only been a few weeks since he had punched me and stormed out of his chamber at court to find Safire, hardly enough time for him to realize the value of his position as a wealthy, influential Landers now that he was married. If he was on his own, a bachelor in the king's guard, it would have been hopeless. Merius was stubborn enough to deprive himself for years to make a point, but I wagered the first time he couldn't afford Safire a new frock or bauble would be a rude shock for him. He wouldn't want to deprive her. His love for that witch was now his biggest weak spot. I smiled to myself, Cyril still blathering on about honor and upholding the family name.

A cold hand brushed the back of my neck, and I swatted at the air, irritated. She had irked me during the last couple weeks with her icy touch and nasty whispers. More than once, I had drained the whiskey bottle to escape her, but that only seemed to embolden her. *Go away, Arilea.*

That fool Cyril doesn't know anything. Merius will never return, not after what you've done. Her voice was soft, cajoling. *You might as well stay here with me.*

I bit back bitter laughter, lest Cyril notice. *With you? You're dead.*

There are ways, love. What do you have at court, now that Merius is gone? You might as well be here with me.

Merius gone? You talk like he's dead too. Hush, Arilea--I've had enough of you.

You'll listen, whether you want to or not. Her voice hardened, her words like water freezing in my ears.

"Get out of here," I muttered, forcing myself to ignore her cursing, her cold breath on my neck. When I ignored her, she lost her power.

"What was that, Mordric?" Cyril asked, pausing in his speech.

"Nothing."

"What do you think about what I've said?"

"You may have a point about Merius. I don't know."

"Will you at least consider returning to council?" he asked.

I smiled. "If I return to council next week, will you shut up now and leave?"

"I'll take your ill manners and scorn as a good sign. I won't leave, though, till you swear on the Landers name to return to council."

"I'll not swear to anything, you ass. I just said I'd return. That should be good enough for you. Here, have some wine--we'll toast to it." I grabbed the decanter and poured us both a measure.

He lifted his glass without further comment until he quaffed it. "Good wine," he said, wiping his mouth before he held out his glass for more.

~ ~ ~ ~ ~

I made Eden wait for an hour after Cyril left. I had to eat, and it seemed best to let the hussy stew for a while. When Randel ushered her into the chamber, she took her seat, her narrow eyes scanning all the exits. The pointed nails of her right hand lightly drummed the armrest, her left hand clutched in the folds of her skirt as she gazed at me.

I took out my pipe and proceeded to fill it leisurely. Not one stray leaf fell to the table in the thick silence. I snapped my fingers for Randel, and Eden jumped. Not much, but enough so that I noticed. Randel brought over a candle, and I lit the pipe, puffing it until there was a large cloud of smoke around my head. "Anything else, sir?" he asked.

"No, you're free to go. Now, Eden," I said, sinking back in my chair. "Was it your idea to bring Cyril in here without informing me first?"

"Yes, sir."

"Why?"

"I knew you wouldn't see him otherwise."

"True enough. He's far from a friend. I already refused to see him once, and you knew that. It was flagrant presumption on your part to bring him here. What do you have to say for yourself?"

She licked her lips and rubbed them together. Then she straightened. "He's the only man who has had the mettle in the last ten years to challenge you to a duel. I figured he was the only one who would last long enough in this chamber to convince you to return to court."

I took a long draw on my pipe. "Bold hussy. Is that what you told him?"

"No, he approached me, worried about your absence from council. I said I would find a way for him to see you, and that's all I said."

"At least you're discreet in your defiance."

"You've taught me well." Her mouth curved into the hint of a smile, the same knowing full-lipped dip she used to lure her marks at court.

"Don't simper--it's irritating." I banged my pipe on the table edge.

"Yes, sir." But she continued smiling. I ignored her.

"So, how should I punish you?"

"Punish me, sir?" Her yellow eyes glowed, amber as a cat's.

"I think confinement here for the summer would be appropriate."

"Here?" The vixen tease vanished. She straightened, her lip curling down in distaste. "Here?"

"The country air will do you good. You can assist Dagmar and Talia with their missions of mercy among the peasants, act like a real lady for a change."

"I'm not ministering to any peasants. They have fleas."

"With how catty you are, a few fleas shouldn't bother you, my dear."

"But you need me at court . . ."

"Eden, I don't need anyone but myself at court. I would like to have you at court--you can be useful. But I don't need you. You'd best remember that and behave yourself in the future."

"Yes, sir," she said. I had to give her credit--at least she wasn't pouting. Eden was not a pouter.

Randel entered the chamber then without knocking, his face pale. "Merius is here."

I stood up so swiftly that my chair toppled back. "Where is Whitten?"

"I don't know." Randel swallowed.

"Selwyn said Whitten was on business in Calcors," Eden said, "which really means he's at the crossroads tavern."

"As long as he's not here, the sotted fool." I tossed my pipe on the table. "Did Merius say anything?"

"He asked if you were still here."

"Is that all? Where is he now?"

"In his chamber with Lady Dagmar--I think they're packing his and Lady Safire's belongings to take . . ."

I was around the table before Randel could finish, heading towards the door. He lifted a hand to my arm. "Sir, he has his sword . . ."

"He always has his sword. That's how I trained him." I brushed past Randel and opened the door.

Chapter Twenty-Nine--Merius

I tossed a pile of my shirts in Safire's trunk and slammed the lid down. Dagmar dropped the book she was dusting and hurried over. She opened the trunk and began pulling out the shirts. "You can't do that, throw them in there like that. The linen will wrinkle."

"I'll worry with that later," I said, grasping the shirts. A seam ripped. "There's not much time . . ."

She wouldn't let go. "It won't take but a minute to pack them properly."

"It's a minute I haven't got. We're due at the Corcin dock three days hence, and . . ."

"Three days?" She sank back on her heels, her grip loosening on the shirts. Her eyes, paler than Safire's, had the greenish glitter of thin ice.

"Herrod's offered me a place in Lord Rankin's escort," I said, with some pride. Posts with ambassadors were difficult for younger guardsmen to get, as they involved being able to navigate the morass of a strange court. My experience on council and knowledge of foreign languages and customs had given me an advantage. The only thing Herrod had been doubtful about was Safire accompanying me, but after he met her, he had winked and said he understood why I didn't want to leave her alone, the pert minx. He really didn't have any ground to stand on, since other ambassadors' escorts had taken their wives in the past, but I had refrained from that argument, seeing it as likely just to aggravate him rather than convince him.

"Who's Lord Rankin?" Dagmar demanded.

"The ambassador to Sarneth."

"You're taking my sister to Sarneth? For how long?"

"A year."

"A year!" Dagmar leapt to her feet. "A year--you can't do that."

"It's not my decision--it's simply the length of the assignment."

"Can't you leave her here?"

"Here? With my scoundrel father and that drunken fool Whitten waiting to paw her--you must be mad." I grabbed the shirts and threw them back in the trunk, the lid falling shut with a crash.

"None of that would have happened but for you seducing her. You're lucky my father's not alive . . ."

"I agree," I said evenly. "I shouldn't have touched her--I love her and had full intention to marry her at the time, but it was still wrong of me to taste the fruit before I plucked it and tempt her to do the same. But we're married now, and that is between us and us alone."

Dagmar's arms were crossed, her bony frame tensed for battle. "How do I know you married her? I haven't seen her since you took her away."

"She sent you a letter about it, two days ago. I don't know why it's not here yet." Some loose coins clinked against the bottom of my wardrobe as I pulled out my old pair of riding boots. Gold, no less. I quickly stuffed them in my pockets.

"Why isn't she here today?"

"Because I didn't tell her I was coming here today."

"What?"

I straightened, looked at her. "She shouldn't be within ten leagues of this House, Dagmar. Those scars on her arms . . . she could have bled to death. And then there's that bastard Whitten-- what if he'd been here? It's bad enough my father's here. I have to see him before I leave, but I sure as hell don't want her anywhere near him."

Dagmar seemed to shrink, her squared shoulders sagging. She sat on the trunk heavily. "You're right, I suppose, but I just want to see her, see she's all right. You can understand that, surely."

I bit back the caustic retort I'd had ready. "She wants to see you, too," I said. "Why don't you come with me when I leave here? Selwyn could spare you a few days, couldn't he?"

She pressed her palms over her skirt, tugging out the wrinkles. "I suppose he could," she said quietly.

There was a sudden racket out in the hall, the clamp of boots and the mutter of low voices. I turned sharply. "What?"

We had left the door cracked since the chamber smelled musty. Now it swung open. Father stepped over the threshold, Eden and Randel hovering behind him. "Merius-" he began.

"What the hell do you want?" I moved around the trunk toward the door, every muscle tensed.

He held up his hands. "There's no need to draw your blade."

I glanced down, realized my fingers were already clenched around my sword. I released it but kept my hand close, at the ready as he himself had taught me. "I'll decide that, Father."

"Sir . . ." Randel put his hand on Father's arm.

Father shook him off. "Leave me." I noticed with no small shock that he had a beard, a straggled, untidy affair. His shirt and doublet were rumpled, obviously slept in. His usual military precision had vanished--he looked haggard, ill from too much drink. Buffeted by a hurricane, the neat, tight rigging of his life had frayed, and now he was adrift. And for a man like my father to be adrift was dangerous. In desperation, he was capable of anything. My hand flitted over my sword hilt, the tiny muscles of my fingers twitching.

"What's this?" he asked, gesturing to the trunks, the piles of books and clothes yet to be packed.

"The rest of Safire's and my belongings." Pretending it was the most natural thing in the world, I bent down and began to stack the books in my trunk. I continued to watch him, though, poised for action.

"You must have a place to live then."

"Yes. I need to talk with you about that."

"What about it?"

I stood, brushed the dust from my hands. "Safire's dowry-- her family house, the stables, the horses, the grounds around it. That's where we're living, where she wants to stay when we return from Sarneth. If you attempt to make a claim on it from her marriage to Whitten, I'll fight you."

He shrugged. "I have no interest in it. Even if I did, neither I nor Whitten could claim it. Since there was no consummation or heirs, that marriage never existed as far as the crown is concerned. I'll warn you, though--without the income from the Long Marsh lands in Dagmar's dowry, it's going to be difficult to keep the house."

"I'll worry about that." I took a deep breath, tried to still the quiver of rage inside. Why did he have to mention consummation and heirs? Did he suspect? I blinked, my knuckles white where I clutched the next book to go on the stack in the trunk. I had to stay calm for Safire's sake. If I sought vengeance now of any kind, even something as minor as punching Whitten, people would wonder, perhaps talk. We couldn't afford any talk, any public speculation about the true nature of that mockery of a marriage and the growing life inside her. It was bad enough her own sister knew about Whitten's violation. That drunken blackguard.

I noticed Father watching me and quickly put the book in the trunk, my fingers shaking. "What's this about Sarneth?" he asked.

"Herrod's granted me a position with Lord Rankin."

"Damn it, Merius." The sudden expletive after all our careful formality jolted Dagmar and Eden, reminding me that we weren't alone.

"You served in an ambassador's escort between battles."

"I was seventeen and didn't have half your training at the time."

"It's a good position, Father. They're not easy to get."

"For most of the guards. But you're ready for a commander's post."

"Herrod would have offered me that, but . . ." *Safire and I have to leave the country for at least a year so we can lie about when the baby is born--that's why I need a post with an ambassador, damn you.*

"But what?" Father's eyes bore into me, that legendary gimlet gaze that had undone so many lesser men at court.

"I'm through discussing this with you. It's none of your affair." I turned my back to him and began shoving books in the trunk.

"I apologize, Merius," he said swiftly, too swiftly. "You're right--it's a fine post. Safire must be proud."

I bit my tongue. Hard. "I said it's none of your affair."

"You know, if you're ever in any trouble, if you need coin . .
."

I barked a bitter chuckle. "I wouldn't take your coin if I was starving."

"What if Safire was starving?" he asked softly. "Would you take it then?"

"That's it." I spun around, my sword drawn. Dagmar screamed, a harsh, short shrillness that cut the silence after the hiss of my blade.

Randel moved between me and Father, his palms out. "Out of my way, Randel," I said.

"No, sir." He swallowed. "I follow your father's orders, not yours."

"He didn't order you to be a fool."

"A fool, sir? A fool wouldn't trust you not to strike an unarmed man. I know you better than that."

"Move, Randel," Father said then. "I don't pay you enough for you to be a bodyguard."

"But, sir . . ."

"Move."

Randel stepped aside, just enough so that Father and I were facing each other. I kept my sword drawn but lowered, my gaze on his every breath, his only movement. For a moment, all was quiet, and I almost grew hypnotized, watching the faint rise and fall, rise and fall of his shirt.

"Merius," he said abruptly, breaking the spell. "Merius, I meant no threat or dishonor to Safire. Quite the contrary. I merely .
. ."

"How dare you even say her name, after what you've done?" I wiped my forehead where the sweat had started to bead in the heavy air.

"I know no other way to speak of her, besides her name."

"Maybe you shouldn't speak of her at all then."

"Forgive me, I know you're upset . . ."

"Upset?" I scoffed. "You've almost made a murderer out of

me, Father. You could say I'm upset."

"Just listen for a moment, Merius. That's all I ask."

"All right." I sheathed my sword with trembling hands, ashamed I had drawn it in front of Dagmar and Eden. "Let the lies begin."

"I just want to tell you that the coin is there. I know you're too proud to take any for yourself, but for her, for your children . . . and not just coin, either. I have connections in every court in this hemisphere . . ."

"Father," I said, surprised at the weariness in my own voice. "I've had enough of your connections."

"I understand that, but it won't be like before. I'm through with all that."

"You admit then that you've used your 'connections'" here I glanced at Randel, "to spy on me?"

"Yes."

"I knew it." I paced over to the main window, my hand fisted over my mouth. "I knew it. That's how you knew about Safire." I unclenched my fingers, ran my hand over my jaw and the back of my neck. My throat felt strangely constricted, as if I couldn't get enough air in my lungs. Every girl I had taken for a sweetheart, no matter how brief, every time I had lost at cards, every time I had been in a fight, every time . . . he had known, more likely than not.

"Merius, I was trying to establish your career at court, keep certain things concealed from our fool of a king. You're always into something--that crazy glider, punching the wrong people, writing seditious verse, romancing barmaids, drinking and gambling . . ."

"It wasn't seditious--you've never said that before. You just don't like poetry."

"Of course it was seditious--what about that one about the king's funeral, for God's sake? What would our august sovereign call that but seditious? The point is, you concealed all of this from me, grew angry when I questioned you . . ."

"And you wonder why?"

"I didn't know what else to do--I used spies for everything else."

"What about Herrod? Was that the first time you'd done

something like that?" I leaned my forehead against the glass and gazed out at the courtyard.

"What about Herrod?"

"He said that you granted permission for him to ask me to go on that campaign, even as you threatened to disinherit me for going."

Father sighed. "I knew if I gave you my approval too easily, you would be suspicious and might not go."

"And the only reason you wanted me to go is so you could go after Safire?"

"I thought she was a fortune hunter, Merius. I know better now."

"That's a relief," I said bitterly. "You-" I broke off, staring into the courtyard. Strawberry galloped through the gates, Safire on her back. The little mare came to an abrupt halt and flicked her tail. Safire dismounted, not waiting for the help of the stablehand who rushed out to her. "Damned witch," I muttered. "You could have fallen on your head." I turned on my heel and strode for the door and the hall, pushing past Father and the others.

Chapter Thirty--Safire

Boltan was sitting on a chair outside the stable in the sunlight polishing harness when I returned from Calcors. He glanced up as I came through the open gate, leading Strawberry by her halter with my left hand, my right arm curled around a messy bouquet of daisies and buttercups. He glanced back down at the girth buckle in his hand, continuing to rub it with his rag even though it could already blind an army with its shine. I let go of Strawberry so she could get a bite of hay from the trough in the paddock before I went over to stand next to Boltan. I watched his polishing for a minute, both of us silent. Then I took one of the daisies and dangled it over the balding spot on the top of his head, the petals just brushing him. He dropped the girth and swatted at the flower. "Little minx. Stop it," he said.

I laughed and put the daisy back with its mates, burying my face in them. "What are you doing that for?" he demanded. "They don't smell like anything."

"They smell warm and yellow, like sunshine," I protested.

Shaking his head, he picked the girth back up. "I would have thought that ring on your finger would give you some sense finally, but I guess not."

"Merius didn't marry me for my sense."

"Good thing, because you don't have any."

I whipped him with a daisy, petals fluttering all over his shirt and trousers. He ignored them, seemingly intent on the girth. "Where is Merius, anyway? Shadowfoot's not in the paddock." I tucked a buttercup behind my ear.

"I don't know. After you left, Merius hitched him up to that old cart and drove out of here in a hurry."

"He hitched Shadowfoot to the cart?" A vague twinge of uneasiness rose in my stomach, but I fought it down. I hadn't retched once today, and I intended to keep it that way. Boltan's wife Greit had already been giving me expectant looks when she brought our breakfast. "That seems odd."

"I thought so."

"I wonder where he went." I leaned against the wall. A cloud passed over the sun, and I shivered. My arms crossed, I closed my eyes. At first all was dark behind my eyelids, but then, hazy at first and then slowly coming into focus . . . stairs rose before me, around me the silent stone and oak front hall, the walls warmed only by elaborate tapestries, the lines of the few chairs and tables scattered about grimly austere with age. I reached out for the stairs, still in disbelief, and felt the edges of the ship carved on the balustrade, worn almost smooth after centuries of hands trailing over it. All around, a dusty chill that penetrated to the bones and crept around the throat, a cold that couldn't be explained only by dampness. Landers Hall. He had gone to Landers Hall. What if Whitten was there? Mordric?

"Oh no," I said. "No, Merius." The daisies and buttercups fell to the ground as I ran for Strawberry.

"My lady?" Boltan called, the harness clattering as he stood, but I was already on Strawberry and racing towards the main road.

~ ~ ~ ~ ~

By the time Landers Hall loomed across the fields, poor Strawberry's sides heaved as she panted for breath. I patted her damp neck. I hadn't meant to push her so fast, but apprehension gripped me at every turn. I found myself digging my knees in and flicking the reins to urge her on, my midriff knotted with tension.

I drew rein briefly at the pain in my middle and touched my belly. Everything seemed all right besides a bit of soreness from too much riding, but I said a quick prayer anyway. Merius hadn't wanted me to ride at all--we'd had an argument about it this morning. I had finally smoothed him down with a few caresses and a soft plea that I wouldn't have a chance to ride Strawberry again for a year and that I would take it ever so slow and that other women in delicate conditions rode. Of course, they didn't gallop.

I glanced down. What did a miscarriage feel like? I had no idea, though I'd heard other women whisper about a sudden cramp in their wombs and a rush of blood warm on their thighs being the first signs. Surely I would notice if I bled. I smoothed my skirt over my belly and rode on, more gentle with the reins now.

What are you so worried about? It's not Merius's seed you carry. Some evil voice not my own whispered inside. I swallowed, tried to shut my ears against the voice. But it was in my head, inescapable. *Really, Safire, your talents tell you it's male. How can you ask that of him, to raise some other man's son as his firstborn?*

"I didn't ask it of him. He offered," I said.

He offered because he's an honorable man. But you know he broods about it late at night as you do, tosses and turns after he thinks you're asleep. A miscarriage would be a blessing.

"Shut up," I said savagely, one hand clutched over my belly as if I thought the voice could somehow hurt the babe. Already, I could feel my son's aura shaping, a wavering candle flame flickering deep inside. Already, I loved him.

You're mad, witch, you and your cuckoo's child. Merius will never accept this interloper son, this drunkard's spawn, no matter what he says now-- why should he? He could have any woman he wanted . . .

"Yes he could have any woman, but he loves me. I know he does--you can never make me doubt that, no matter what you say." Quickly, before the voice could spew all my wretched doubts and fears again, I remembered Merius's arms around me, his lips against my ear. Whenever I woke from a nightmare of the violation I still only remembered in tiny flashes, Merius was there, his whispers in the dark like sweet kisses to my trembling soul.

I knew Merius had fears about the babe, about his ability to be its father under the circumstances--how could he not? I knew he also struggled to keep his rage at Whitten contained lest it upset me. A couple nights ago, Merius had snuck up behind me and reached around to undo my laces--at the sight of his hands, I yelled and spun around, my fists ready to hit before I realized it was him. Then I dissolved into tears, frightened by the way my body had reacted without conscious will on my part. Merius stepped away for a moment, his hands out as if to show me he meant no harm, his eyes distant. In that moment, I knew he slaughtered Whitten in some enraged vision, as if somehow killing Whitten would erase my memories of his violation and make the babe in my womb Merius's get. If Whitten were snuffed from existence, he would be snuffed from my memory, his seed snuffed from my body, and all would go back to the way it should be--that was how Merius felt about it. But he couldn't act on those feelings, lest the world discover our secret and ruin what chance at happiness we had. So instead, he had quieted me in his arms and then coaxed me to bed, where we briefly forgot all but the near comfort and ecstasy of each other. There had been other moments like that, sudden jabs in consciousness that reminded me that we were both walking on an invisible edge.

Suddenly, the Landers courtyard gate was before me, starting me out of my reverie. I realized then I had brought Strawberry to a gallop again without noticing it. Exclaiming, I jerked on the reins. My stomach lurched. For an instant, it seemed I would go between her ears and tumbling over her head. Then I fell back in the saddle, gasping for breath. My hand firmly on the pommel, I flung my leg over and dismounted as a stable hand rushed up.

"My Lady Safire," he said, bowing clumsily. He was one of the young ones, not more than fourteen, his face flushed under an untidy shock of blond-white hair.

"Thank you." Still a bit disoriented from my mad ride, I patted Strawberry and gazed up at the house. I had intended to charge right in the front door, but now I was here, I remembered Arilea. She would likely come after me again the instant I broached the entryway. And I had no idea where in the house Merius might be. Mordric's study?

The front door jerked open then and Merius strode out, his face set in a tight, white-lined expression I had seen before--it meant he was either very frightened or very angry or a combination of both. "If I ever see you ride a horse like that again, I'll tie you up," he announced, reaching for my arm.

I shrugged. "All right, but I won't be much use around the house."

He ignored my nervous jest. "Perry, take the lady's horse and give it water but no feed," Merius said, his voice curt. "We'll be leaving shortly."

The boy nodded and turned for the stables, Strawberry in tow. "How dare you?" Merius spat as soon as Perry was out of earshot. "You could have been thrown . . ."

I turned to face him. "It was an accident."

"You mean you lost control of Strawberry? I find that hard to believe, Safire."

"No, not that. I just didn't realize how fast I was going until I tried to stop. I was worried about you--what are you doing here?"

"Getting our things and warning Father about your dowry."

"We could have sent Boltan for that."

"I needed to see Father myself--I wouldn't have trusted merely sending a message."

"Oh."

"You shouldn't have come here, sweet." Merius gripped my wrist.

"You shouldn't have either. What if-"

Dagmar came racing out of the door then and down the steps. Merius started and pushed me behind him before he realized it was her. She brushed past him, her arms outstretched. We embraced, both of us beginning to cry.

"Let me look at you," she choked finally, pulling away. "Your color's so much better than it was--you were so pale before, and now . . ."

"Marriage must agree with me." I held out my left hand, the golden Landers seal band winking above Merius's betrothal ring.

Dagmar gazed at it. "Why, yours is different from mine. What's this forked tree behind the L?"

"Merius had it redone--it's how you show the family's in two Houses."

She sighed. "Well, the work is exquisite, as nice as mine, though it seems a shame . . ."

"What seems a shame?" I glanced over as two menservants came down the steps, carrying my trunk.

"Oh, never mind me," she added hastily. "Merius said you're going to Sarneth with him."

I nodded. "In three days."

"Oh, Safire . . ."

I squeezed her hand and bit back more tears. "I know, but it can't be helped. I'll write you often."

"You'd better. Merius," Dagmar looked towards where he and Ebner were securing the trunk on the pony cart, "said that I should come see you."

"In Sarneth?"

"No, silly. Here at home, before you leave."

"That would be wonderful!" I clapped my hands together. "But can Selwyn spare you?"

"I don't see why not. It's only a few days."

I hugged her again before I sprinted over to Merius and threw my arms around him.

"What is it?" he demanded, knotting a rope around the trunk.

I kissed his back through his shirt. "Dagmar just said you invited her for the next few days."

"I thought maybe she could help you." He glanced sideways over his shoulder at me. "And keep an eye on you while I'm making arrangements."

"Keep an eye on me?" I swatted him. "She'd do better to keep an eye on you--I wouldn't get in trouble but for you."

Merius turned around, his palms coming to rest on my hips. "Is that so?"

Ebner snorted, then pretended to test the rope holding the trunk when Merius shot him a look. "I think it's secure, Sir Merius," Ebner said. "What I'm worried about is this cart--no amount of rope is going to hold it together. You'd best not drive it too fast."

At that moment, the two menservants came down the steps, carrying Merius's trunk. We scrambled out of their way as they lumbered towards the cart. Gasping for breath, the veins popping out in their foreheads, they heaved the trunk up beside mine. The left hinge of the cart gate suddenly gave way, and the gate dropped with a crash. Shadowfoot gave a disgruntled neigh and flicked his tail at the sound.

"What do you have in there, dear heart?" I exclaimed. "Rocks?"

"No--books. And coin," Merius added when he noticed my grin.

"Books? Did you pack the whole Landers library, sir?" Ebner grunted as he tried to secure the trunk. "This cart won't hold together five minutes--I'd wager my life on it."

"Then you'll have a short life," Merius said. "Damn it, Ebner, what are you lifting it for? Here." He reached for the trunk.

"I'm trying to tie it."

"Not that way--tie it around the sides."

"And secure it to what, exactly? This cart isn't fit for kindling." Ebner straightened and ran the back of his hand over his sweaty forehead.

Dagmar glanced over the cart critically, her arms crossed. "Why don't you get the carriage, Ebner? I don't think anyone's using it this afternoon."

"That's a fine idea, my lady," Ebner said. "I could drive the carriage, and you could ride Shadowfoot alongside, sir."

"I'll not use the carriage." Merius's tone was harsh, the already taut lines of his aura tightening like silver wires on the verge of snapping. "I'll use this cart or nothing."

Ebner and Dagmar gaped at him. "Merius," Dagmar said finally, "I'm not riding back with you in this rickety thing, and I don't think my sister should either. I don't think it's safe."

"It's fine--I came here in it," Merius said, and I touched his shoulder to draw away some of the tension, sensing that pewter cast in the air around him that usually meant trouble. "I'll not be beholden to the Landers for the use of their carriage."

"Sir Merius, do you know you look more like your father every time I see you--it's uncanny," Ebner remarked, a furtive grin pulling at the corners of his mouth as he slipped his hands in his pockets.

Merius gave Ebner a long look. "I should sack you for saying that."

"Sir, I'm not your retainer. Only your father can sack me."

"Ebner, just secure the trunk. We should have left here ten minutes ago." Merius paced around the cart, checking the wheels and Shadowfoot's harness, giving the stallion a pat as he passed him.

I silently thanked Ebner for knowing just what to say to distract Merius from his anger.

"Safire, he really does have a wicked temper," Dagmar whispered to me. "He drew his sword earlier on Mordric for no reason . . ."

"No reason?" I hissed. "He has plenty of reason to draw his sword on Mordric. I'm glad for his temper--he uses it to defend me. I'll never have to fear another drunkard or any other man laying his hands on me again, with Merius as my husband. You should be happy for me."

"All right, all right." She patted my shoulder. "I don't want to quarrel."

"Good, because as much as I love you, I'll not have you criticizing my husband."

"He loves you just as you are, despite your headstrong nature," she conceded, "and that does make up for his faults. It's rare to find a man with such a loyal heart, sister--temper or not, he worships the very stones you tread."

I nodded, swallowing as I watched Merius. Ebner held up the gate on the back of the cart as Merius knelt on the cobbles, trying to fix the broken hinge. My heart seemed too large for my ribs to contain it, its beat rocking my body. *Merius, I love you.* I thought, again and again, the words matching the rhythm of my heart, the rhythm of the earth turning under my feet, my imperfect love somehow reflecting the perfection of the eternal, if only for a precious instant.

Merius glanced up sharply, his eyes meeting mine as if he heard me somehow in his mind. He gave me his crinkle-eyed smile before he looked back at the hinge. I smiled, then cast my gaze down at the cobbles, shy suddenly. We'd just shared an intimate moment in the midst of a bustling courtyard, and I wondered if anyone else had noticed.

The air grew heavy on my shoulders, and I looked back up. Mordric stepped into the open doorway of the house. His aura hung around him like a thunderhead, lightning crackling in its depths.

"Merius," he said.

Merius stiffened. "What?"

"Are you coming back in here?"

"I've said what I needed to say." Merius straightened and slammed the gate at the back of the cart, and I winced.

"All right. Farewell, then."

"Farewell. Father."

Mordric remained expressionless, but the shadows across his face darkened. He looked older with every breath. Slowly, he turned to go back in the house. I almost shouted, for I thought I glimpsed a flash of blue-white light against the dim interior, a mocking face, clear as ice, and a high laugh, distant as frosty sleigh bells in the winter hills, reached my ears. Then it was gone.

Dagmar touched me. I jumped and gave a little scream. "Are you all right?" she demanded.

I shook myself, still staring as Mordric disappeared through the doorway. "I'm fine. Just remembering that morning."

She didn't need to ask which morning. "Should I go pack my things?"

"Probably--I think Merius wants to leave so-o-n . . ." My mouth dropped open, my words stifled in my suddenly tight throat.

Whitten came around the side of the house nearest the river, his hands in his pockets, whistling an old sea shanty. His eyes on the ground as he kicked at loose cobbles, he didn't notice any of us. My mind raced, my thoughts swirling ever faster as the rest of me went cold and then numb. He had been polite afterwards, I recalled, almost solicitous, tucking the quilt over me. And before, there had been the prickle of his arm hair under my chin as he held me down. It had been almost impossible to breathe, with his arm against my neck and the overpowering haze of whiskey and sweat, and I had gone limp, sometimes unconscious. The mute me, the me who couldn't remember, had endured it, not knowing what he was doing, even as my voice screamed inside and I struggled against him in the prison of my mind. I had been locked in my head while he had his way with my body, a powerless witness to my own violation.

A cry escaped me as my knees suddenly buckled. Dagmar dropped beside me, her arm going around my shoulders. Whitten's head shot up, the whistle dying on his lips. He froze, his gaze skipping to Merius. The only sound was the metallic whisper of Merius's sword as he drew it from its scabbard.

"You sotted son of a bitch," Merius said, with no inflection. He sprang forward, light as a cat.

Whitten took a few faltering steps back towards the corner of the house. Then he realized Merius would head him off that way, and he changed direction, running for the front steps. Merius swore and twisted around in mid-stride.

"Merius, no!" I screamed as he chased Whitten up the steps, almost on him. "No!" But he was beyond hearing my voice.

As soon as Whitten crossed the threshold, a gleam of silver came down across the doorway, blocking the path. Merius's blade, which he held before him, glanced off this silver line with a clear ring, and he halted so fast that he almost toppled back down the steps. Mordric stepped into the light, pulling the silver line back in the shadows, and I realized then it was his sword.

"God damn it, Father--let me by."

"No, Merius." Mordric was calm, so calm that I wondered if he had rehearsed for this moment. "Go dunk your head in the rainwater barrel--it'll douse your temper."

"I'm not thirteen and this isn't a fist fight over some girl. If you don't move, I'll . . ." Merius paused, took a deep breath, "I'll fight you."

I blinked then, my clutch tightening on Dagmar. We were both shaking so hard the whole courtyard seemed to tremble. Praying silently, I looked skyward. As I tilted my head up, I saw the distinct outline of Arilea's white face in the arch of the doorway, snakes of hair dangling over Mordric's head as she reached for him with long, pale fingers.

Chapter Thirty-One--Mordric

Merius shifted into a slight crouch, his feet shoulder width apart, his sword at the ready. All the subtle moves I had drummed into him until they were instinctive. His face, not many years past boyhood, was pale but hard, the bones stretching the skin into a look of taut alertness. Nothing would miss him, and he would not back down. The warrior I had trained him to be. *Is this what you wanted, bitch?* She laughed somewhere overhead, her cold fingers resting on my shoulder. I barely felt the chill anymore.

"I'll not fight you--you're my son," I said, bringing my sword forward into the doorway, the flat of the blade towards Merius in case he decided to charge again. "But I'll not let you pass, either. You'll have to slay me."

He blinked, then pointed his sword towards the inside hall, where Whitten had fled. "You don't understand what he's done. He deserves to die."

I spared a glance at Safire, huddled with her sister on the cobbles. Her gaze met mine, bold but haunted. "I know what he's done. I'll handle it."

Merius gave a single laugh, a sound of bitter disbelief. "You're the one who let him do it, the one who gave her to him. Yet now you want to mete out punishment--you must think I'm mad, to trust you."

"It's my place to punish him, Merius. He disobeyed my order. I never meant for him to touch her--I just wanted them married in case she was with your child."

"Is that what this was all about?" he asked, mocking.

"Covering up my mistakes again? Father, out of my way." He lurched forward.

I crossed my sword with his, stepping sideways to cover the entrance completely. "I'll not see you hang over a fool drunkard. Your honor, even Safire's honor, is not worth your death."

He raised his sword, his eyes narrow. "What if I hang over you? Is it worth it then?"

"You speak in anger," I said.

"God damn right I do. Now out of my way."

"Fine. Kill me." I sheathed my blade.

He gritted his teeth and started to bring his sword to my throat. I watched him and waited, not blinking. He had the sword halfway raised when it stopped in midair, the blade trembling. He began to shake his head, biting his lips together, his eyes clouded like an old man's. Then, as if someone had cut an invisible string, his hand suddenly dropped, the tip of his sword hitting the step. "Oh no," he whispered. "No, Father."

Safire bolted from her spot on the cobbles and came running up the steps. She reached for Merius. He grabbed her to him and buried his face in her hair, his back heaving.

Look what you've brought him to, the torment you've caused him Arilea hissed. *He's barely a man and already he's old.*

You're the one who's made him old. But there was little fight left in my words.

Perhaps--I had to leave him too soon. It's not all your doing, for certain. She sighed, touched my hair. *You seem tired, my love.*

A small crowd was gathering, Selwyn, Eden, a couple servants, all gaping at us. Damn it--at least they hadn't been there to hear what I'd said about Whitten. *Good--the more witnesses, the better.* Arilea's voice had grown clearer--I almost could hear it in my ears, almost sense her lips brushing my neck.

"Witnesses for what?"

Can you feel my hand? Icy fingers crept over my shoulder and started down my arm, a light tickling sensation that made all the hairs on my head raise. My muscles loosened the way they had after Safire had touched me at Orlin's cottage, except this was cold, not warm. Like the tingling calm that came before freezing to death. I shook myself, tried to shrug her away, but they were the half-hearted efforts of a man in a trance. This was little but a dream anyway. She wasn't really here--I was imagining her, like all the other times.

"Stop it. Just stop it," I muttered.

I'll take that as a yes. She laughed softly. *None of your mistresses have ever touched you like this.* Her hand closed over mine, her fingers flowing between mine. Though I could feel her, I couldn't get a grip on her--touching her put me in mind of trying to catch spring water in my palm. It felt so real I looked down. My hand had an odd shimmer to it, a haze of icy light.

"That's because none of my mistresses are dead," I said with great effort.

Somewhere Merius's witch screamed. "Merius, let me go, let me go--she's on him--" Her voice was suddenly cut off.

Arilea laughed again. *We'll have no silly witches here* she purred. She brought my hand down, closed my fingers over my dagger hilt. I hesitated, stiffening. *Come, Mordric--you know you want it.* She began to nibble my neck--when she reached my ear, I groaned. She felt more solid now, less cold. When I looked down, I could see her fingers over mine, transparent but clearly visible, like frosted glass. My hand gripped the dagger.

Now, draw it out. Her voice was a husky whisper, the way she had spoken in our bed so long ago. Without a thought, I pulled the dagger out, the blade glinting--I had just polished it the other day.

I stared down at it. *No, Arilea--it's the coward's way out.*

It's the honorable way out she retorted. *Merius will hang if he kills you. Is that what you want?*

I shook my head. *No. God, I'm so tired. I can't see any of them now, even Merius.*

Don't worry with them. Here, let me help you. She guided the dagger up to my chest. *Now, you know better than I where it needs to go.*

I found the bottom of my breastbone with my fingertips, touched the ribs to the left. There was a small space between the ribs where my heart was exposed, a space I had learned about in the king's guard. I positioned the dagger over this spot. A drop of blood blossomed red on my shirt. This wasn't so difficult.

Arilea swirled all around me, her golden hair twining around my neck, the smell of roses thick and intoxicating as it had been between our sheets. Her lips were warm as she kissed my mouth. I kissed her back, and she no longer flowed like water between my fingers but was solid, flesh against my flesh. I could see her clearly now, the sparks of a familiar fire leaping between us.

Chapter Thirty-Two--Safire

"Oh God, Father . . . Father, no. No . . ." Merius whispered, his voice broken. His grip loosened on my shoulders, and I tore away from him. I fell to my knees beside Mordric. He lay crumpled on his side across the threshold. My muscles straining, I rolled him over until he was face up, the dagger buried halfway to the hilt in his chest. He should have been dead already. Yet there came the whistle of shallow breaths, faint movement behind his closed eyelids--he was fighting this. Fighting her.

Get away from him! Arilea's high, thin scream pierced my ears. I ignored her and put my hand to the hilt of the dagger. It vibrated against my fingertips, a rhythmic trembling as his chest rose and fell. I puzzled over this for a precious instant before the bile gnawed at my stomach with sudden, sickening realization. The dagger was beating with his heart. I gagged in my hand at the rusty smell of blood, then turned back to him with a savage determination. I had to do something. I didn't know what, but it would come. Nothing could hurt him now anyway--I might as well try. I grasped the hilt and closed my eyes, concentrating on the blade.

"Don't pull it out," Merius said, kneeling behind me. "Not yet. If it's missed his heart and lungs, there still might," he swallowed, "might be a chance."

"It hasn't pierced his heart," I whispered, "but it's very close."

"How do you know?"

"I can see it, hear it." As long as I touched the dagger hilt, Mordric's heart beat in my mind. I could picture where the tip of the blade had breached his ribcage, a hairsbreadth from his heart, so close that one wrong movement would instantly kill him. I inhaled another deep breath. My own heart pounded in my ears. Mordric's heartbeat grew fainter, each breath shallower than the last, the breathing of someone dying. I didn't know what to do. Whenever I healed, I matched my breathing and heartbeat to the breathing and heartbeat of whoever I was healing. I had to follow them, find them, in order to lead them back to being well again. I couldn't follow Mordric, though, or I might die with him.

"How dare you die like this," I hissed, so angry suddenly that I wanted to shake him. "You won't let anyone help you, even now."

Icy fingers suddenly wrapped around my throat, searing my skin with their chill. *Witch. This time you die, you and your unborn.*

I choked, clawing at her hands. Dimly, I heard Merius yell my name. Everything went red before my eyes. I reached back blindly, feeling for her. My hands closed around her neck, and with my last remaining strength, I squeezed. She gasped, her ghost skin seeping around my numb fingers. The baby . . . I had to protect the baby from her.

You protect that drunkard's seed? she screamed. *Merius should be rid of you and your ill-begotten. He deserves a woman who'd slay herself before she'd bear another man's child.*

Her words echoed my own cruel doubts, and I hesitated. She laughed, her fingers closing around my windpipe. Tears sprang to my eyes as I struggled for breath. My hesitation would kill me. Me and my baby. We would die here, and Merius and the others watching would never know why. They couldn't sense her. To them, it would look like I had mysteriously choked to death on the steps. She laughed again as if she sensed my thoughts. *They can't help you, witch.* As the darkness began to eclipse my sight, the tiny flame of the baby's aura in my womb flickered as my consciousness flickered. Soon there would be more flickers, flicker upon flicker, until all was dark. I screamed, but no sound emerged from my throat.

"Safire, please," Merius said. "Sweetheart, what's wrong? For God's sake, breathe. Please . . ." I could no longer see him--all was dark--but I could still hear him, feel his fingers frantically moving over my throat, loosening my laces. His touch was so warm it chased away some of Arilea's chill, but it wouldn't be enough. I needed an inferno to get rid of her. An inferno . . .

I'll make you cross over, Arilea. A white hot force rose inside, something I had never felt before. It flowed through my veins, a molten light that left me reeling. The heat centered around my middle, my womb a furnace. Ripe with new life and fighting to save it, I harnessed a witch power beyond me. Heat to melt her ice--it was so simple. Why hadn't I thought of it before?

Arilea's hands let go of my throat. She hissed, as though burned, and there was a charred smell in the air. I kept my grip on her, the fire in my body traveling through my fingers and into her. I had no control over it. I drew the heat from myself, from the babe growing inside, from Merius, from all the living things around us, and I couldn't stop it. Instinct to protect myself and my baby had taken over me. Arilea began to melt, a silvery-white shape that shrank in my hands. She screamed, an unbearably high pitch--all around, I heard windows crack and then smash on the courtyard cobbles. As though from a great distance, I saw Merius and Dagmar on the steps, their hands over their ears. My own ear drums popped.

"Cross over, damn you." I shook her and then discovered I was shaking air. The scream died in a whimper. She was gone.

Before the heat left me, I grabbed the dagger still in Mordric's chest. As if the metal had been set in the smith's fire, an orange glow spread from my fingers down the length of the blade. I narrowed my gaze, concentrating my body, my breath, my thoughts, all of me into the hilt.

"Safire?" Merius put his hand on my back, then swore, snatching his hand away. "Good God, you're burning with fever. Here . . ."

"Don't touch me." The orange blade turned red, then white. Sparks hissed black against the linen of Mordric's shirt. He stirred and muttered something, fumbling for the dagger. I began to shiver, my focus going blurry.

"It's no good. He's dying," Merius said dully. "Now stop it--you'll hurt yourself . . ."

I pulled the blade from the wound, then collapsed on the top step. The dagger clattered to the cobbles, still red hot. It landed in a puddle with a sizzle, steam rising in clouds.

"Sweetheart?" Merius knelt over me. "Can you hear me?"

I swallowed, nodded, my eyes slipping closed. "Listen, I'll get you some water. Safire . . ." His voice faded as I fell back, back into the blissfully cool darkness.

Chapter Thirty-Three--Merius

I slid my arms under Safire's back and lifted her to me.
"What is it?" Dagmar asked, leaning over us.

"She's fainted, I think." I cradled her in my arms. She still
felt feverish, her face flushed, but nothing like before--blisters were
already rising on my hand where I'd touched her earlier. I pressed
my lips to her forehead, silently praying. It had been a long time,
though, and I kept stumbling over the words in my mind, so instead I
found myself begging, over and over again *God, help her. Just help her,
please.* I glanced up at Dagmar. "Could you get some water, maybe a
little brandy?"

She nodded and stepped towards the doorway before she
halted, her mouth dropping open. "What?" she muttered, gaping in
the direction of Father's body.

I glanced over at him. Father was moving, his hand reaching
for the charred hole in his shirt where the wound was. There was
hardly any blood, which shocked me almost as much as the fact he
was still alive. Then I glimpsed the wound. No, no, it wasn't
possible . . . I lunged out and grasped his shirt, ripped the burned
linen until his chest was exposed. There was a pale, raised line over
his heart, like a wound many months old.

"She couldn't have, she couldn't . . . How did she do that?" I
whispered.

Dagmar bent down, touched the wound. "It's cauterized,
partly healed." We looked at each other, then looked down at Safire.

"The dagger--when she was holding it, it was like she'd had it
in a smithy's fire, white hot. But how did she do that? And how did

she not burn herself to death?"

Dagmar shrugged, resigned. "She's a witch, Merius," she said softly so no one but me heard. And without another word, she straightened and went into the house.

I rocked Safire a little. She moaned, which I took as a good sign, and stirred, which I took as an even better sign. Perhaps God had heard me after all.

Father opened his eyes then and glowered at me. "Burns like hell, all the way to my heart--what did she do to me?" he asked hoarsely, coughing and clutching for his chest.

"She saved your life," I said under my breath.

He shook himself and glanced around as if he were searching for something. "Your mother was . . . Arilea . . ."

"What about my mother?"

His gaze narrowed, returned to its customary gray coolness, opaque as agate. "Nothing. Never mind, Merius." He coughed again as Ebner and Randel rushed up the steps. Evidently Eden had gone to find them, though I wasn't sure of anything beyond the small world of this threshold anymore.

Dagmar returned with the water. I propped Safire against me as Dagmar attempted to pour a glass full into her mouth. In the end, more seemed to get on her frock than into her, but at least it was something. "I'd better get her back to the house," I said, glancing at the darkening sky. The gargoyles at the corners of the eaves leered down at us, the fanciful addition of some long dead ancestor. My grasp tightened on Safire as I remembered the spirits, the shattering window panes, that unearthly scream. I shuddered--it had sounded like someone dying. "This place isn't good for her."

"I'll come with you, at least for tonight." Dagmar stood, her hands on her hips.

"You can ride Strawberry."

I gingerly got to my feet, carrying Safire. I spared one last look at Father. With Randel's and Ebner's help, he had managed to sit, his shoulder braced against the door jamb. As if he sensed me looking at him, he turned his head then and met my eyes. He nodded once, his expression thoughtful. If he had been another man, he might have looked sad, perhaps even lost, but Father had never been lost in his life. I returned the nod, a brief, final acknowledgement of all he had given me and all he had taken away. Then I started down the steps. I didn't expect I would ever see him again.

People lingered in the courtyard, Eden, Selwyn, servants, some picking up the broken panes and others whispering and staring. I ignored them, my boots crunching on the glass. Dagmar ran over to Selwyn and started talking to him in a low voice. He nodded impatiently, still gaping after me and Safire, and she ran back up the steps and into the house, likely to pack her things.

Against his better judgment, Ebner had left Shadowfoot hitched to the pony cart. I had to smile a little at that--the poor horse, a huge, fine stallion, hitched to a little rickety cart. He turned his head and knickered at me.

"I know, boy--we'll get you away from that contraption soon enough, and it'll all be just a bad memory."

He wrinkled his lips, showing his teeth, and pawed the ground, impatient to be gone.

"Merius," Safire murmured then.

"Shh, don't talk just yet."

"Where are we going?"

"Home, sweetheart. We're going home." I carefully laid her across the cart seat.

She blinked once, smiled a little. "Good."

Chapter Thirty-Four--Safire

"There'll be talk," Dagmar remarked at breakfast that last day, spooning strawberry jam on her toast with jerky motions.

"Talk about what?" I asked.

"About you and Merius leaving so soon after what happened," she hissed, glancing around as if the walls could listen.

"You don't have to whisper, not here." I tossed my napkin on the table before I raced to the doorway and shouted, "I'm a witch! Do you hear me? A witch!!!!" My voice echoed throughout the halls, all the way to the attic rafters, the eaves outside where robins built their nests.

"Safire!" Dagmar half rose, ready to do battle. "Sit down right now--you're acting like a child."

I giggled and plucked a peach from the earthenware bowl on the table. Then I went over to the window and looked out at the yard, still shimmering with dewy spider webs, the oaks around the house old friends I had climbed as a child. When I had donned the long skirts of a young lady, I could no longer climb trees (at least not within sight of the house), so I had sat under the oaks instead, my back against the rough bark of their solid trunks as I daydreamed the odd fancies of a fledgling witch. They were the grandparents I had never known, cradling me in their gnarled branches and roots, bathing me in cool green light through sunlit leaves during long summer afternoons, their wisdom so ancient it could not be spoken but only felt. My heart gave an odd dip suddenly as I realized I wouldn't be looking at, touching these trees again for a whole year, perhaps longer. I couldn't remember a time I had been so long away from them. Quickly I bit into the soft golden sweetness of the peach.

"I'll miss these trees," I said.

"The trees around Landers Hall are older and better kept. Boltan should prune these--it's been years since they were properly tended."

"How would you like to be pruned?" I demanded. "Perhaps you'd look better without a finger or two."

"Safire, really." She sniffed into her porridge. "You can't let things grow all wild. You'll not be able to find the house when you come back--it'll be lost in a thicket."

"If Boltan goes near these trees with the pruning shears, I'll sack him."

"Ha--that'll be the day. That'd be like sacking Father."

"Who's getting sacked?" Merius asked as he strode through the doorway, wearing his high black riding boots and long cloak. He grabbed a peach and two pears and started juggling them, his eyes on me.

"You," Dagmar said.

He spared a grin in her direction. "Good morn, sister."

"What are you? A street jester?" Dagmar might have scoffed, but I noticed she couldn't help but watch his deft movements, so quick that he indeed rivaled one of the jesters in the market square. All that training at the sword . . .

"He looks like a highwayman to me." I took a bite of my peach, returned Merius's stare as I savored honeyed softness on my tongue. He stopped juggling and returned the fruit to the bowl. Then he came over to me, our eyes still fixed on each other.

"My lady, since you have no baubles for me to steal, then I demand a kiss."

Dagmar snorted, and I giggled as he leaned down and kissed the corner of my mouth, then my lips. He smelled of dew in the first warmth of the morning sunshine. "You've been outside," I murmured.

"I've been to Calcors." He straightened, his hand tingling as it came to rest on my shoulder blade.

"Already? You must've rose before dawn," Dagmar

remarked. "What took you to Calcors so early?"

"I secured our passage on the *Valiant*."

"I would have thought you did that days ago--aren't you sailing with the tide this evening?"

"I paid part a week ago to secure our cabin, and the rest this morning," Merius said lightly, though his fingers tightened over my shoulder blade, stretching the thin cloth of my bodice against my skin.

"You didn't pay it all at once?" Dagmar raised one brow, obviously doubtful, and I wanted to smack her.

"No--I had to plunder several carriages between here and Calcors, make off with the queen's jewels, before I could afford the second half," Merius continued in the same light jesting tone, but his hand cupped my shoulder now as if he were afraid to let go of me.

"I told you I married a highwayman, sister," I said, savagely taking the last bite of my peach. "Didn't you believe me?"

"Safire, I'm only looking out for you," Dagmar said. "Neither Father nor Mother are here, and it falls to me to see after your welfare. I want to hear from Merius himself that he has the means to support you in Sarneth now that he's forsaken his inheritance."

"How dare you . . ." I started, Merius's grip tightening on my shoulder.

"It's all right, sweet," he cut me off. "Dagmar, I wouldn't be taking her to Sarneth if there was any question that we'd suffer want there. The king's guard pays enough for us to live comfortably. Perhaps not extravagantly, but comfortably."

"Are you satisfied?" I demanded, glaring at her.

"You know," she continued with maddening older sister imperturbability, "I still don't understand why you're rushing off like this."

"Because Merius is in the king's guard, and Herrod assigned him to a guard post in Sarneth."

"But why do you have to go so quickly? Why can't you stay here a few months, let Merius save up his wages, and then join him when he's settled?"

"Did you miss the part where we got married? I'll not be

parted from him, not when there's no need for it."

"Safire, I just know there's going to be talk, with you leaving so quickly after what happened . . ."

"There's going to be talk anyway," Merius said. "There already is talk. Better for us to get out of here and out of people's minds as quickly as possible."

"So you taking her away like this, from me, from the only home she's ever known, is to protect her?"

"You know, Dagmar, I respect your devotion to Safire, but you need to accept that she's a married woman now. Her place is with me. She made a vow to me, just as I made a vow to her. I'll not let any harm come to her, not as long as I draw breath. All right?"

Dagmar nodded, her face suddenly in her hands. "It just scares me sometimes," she said finally, her voice muffled.

"What scares you?" I went to her and rubbed her shaking shoulders.

"What you can do--it scares me."

"Why? I would never hurt anyone . . ."

"No, no--I know that. It's not that." She looked up, kohl in dark, teary streaks under her eyes. "You know, it used to scare me when we were children and we heard about the witch burnings--I always worried they would come and take you and Mother away. Please, Safire, keep it hidden, like Mother hid her talents. She taught you how . . ."

"I don't know if I can hide it like Mother did," I said gently.

"Why not?"

"Because I'm not Mother. That spirit in the House of Landers," I said, careful not to say whose spirit in Merius's presence, "that spirit almost killed me because I didn't know how to use my talents. I never want to hide my talents so much that I never learn how to use them. I'm vulnerable no matter what I do--we're all vulnerable no matter what we do. Don't you think I worry about you, that perhaps you inherited Mother's weak lungs? But I would never let my worry for you eclipse my hopes for you. I love you, and I'll miss you, sister."

Dagmar nodded. "I love you too."

"We'll be back before you know it," I continued, hugging her with all my strength. It was a long moment before we relinquished each other.

Merius touched my shoulder, and I glanced back at him. "I hate to rush you, sweet, but we should leave for Calcors by noon," he said. "Are you all packed?"

"Mostly." I smiled at him and put my hand in his, our fingers intertwining.

"Will you come to the docks to see us off, Dagmar?" Merius asked. "Boltan will be happy to escort you."

She shook her head. "It would be easier for me to part with you here. If I see you board the ship, I won't be able to imagine that you're still here when I get lonesome."

"I'll write you as soon as we reach Sarneth."

"You better," she said. "I'll be counting the days till you're safe at home again."

Dagmar had just called this place my home, and she was right. The trees in my ancestors' forests had become the timbers of this house, the stones under their feet its foundation. My childhood still rustled in the leaves of the oaks, my girlish storm of tears still fed the creek at the edge of the lower field, my prayers over my parents' graves still whispered in the windswept grass. I shut my eyes for an instant, overwhelmed suddenly at the reality of leaving. Dagmar had baked a gingerbread this morning for us to take on the voyage, and the warm scent of it lingered, a ghost of Mother. I took a deep breath.

Merius's fingers tightened around mine, insistent. I opened my eyes and looked at him, already knowing he would be looking at me. The morning sunlight lit the auburn in his dark hair, coppered the stubble along his jaw, the flint gray of his eyes sparking devilish merriment. He was happy to be off on an adventure, happy to be on the move, happy to take me away with him. He didn't have to say it, not to me. I could sense it. His silvery aura danced, blinding in the sunlight, a shimmering net he used to catch the world around him. He had me caught forever. He had told me once that I was an impossible knot he wanted to untie. Somewhere in all his untying, he had loosened me from girlhood and bound me to becoming a woman. His woman. I was his now, as he was mine. This fledgling man, my Merius, my home.

I smiled at him, raised one brow. "Are you ready to go?"

About the Author

As a child, Karen suffered frequent bouts of insomnia. The only way she could settle into sleep many nights was to imagine stories that played out like movies on the dark ceiling over her bed. Since her mean parents refused to replace the TV after the cat blew it up by peeing on the cord, all Karen had left to entertain herself in the lone wilds of the Minnesota wilderness were books and her own stories. As Karen grew, the stories grew with her. One day when she was fourteen, she told her mother one of these stories for probably the hundredth time. Her mother, who knew Karen very well, turned to her and said, "You know, Karen, you keep talking about these stories, but you never write them down. You keep saying you're going to write a novel, but I don't believe that you will." This comment infuriated Karen so much that she started writing her stories down and hasn't stopped since.

Other Works

Karen is currently revising *Tapestry Lion* and writing the first draft of *Phoenix Ashes*, the next two novels concerning the House of Landers.

You can learn more about Karen's current projects at her website www.karennilsen.com.

Acknowledgements

I am lucky to have many talented writers as friends.

My special thanks to Doug's critique group, specifically Doug, Cheryl, Margaret, Cynthia, and Jim, who all read the first draft of *The Witch Awakening* the way a novel is meant to be read, beginning to end instead of piecemeal, and offered invaluable feedback on the story as a whole.

Special thanks to Robert's critique group. They introduced me to the joys of being part of a writers' group and their examples and advice continue to help me hone my craft.

Special thanks to the many friends and mentors who have encouraged me through the years with my writing, too numerous to name here. Just know that without each and every one of you in my life, I never could have written this book.